Question Quest

Question Quest

A XANTH NOVEL

Piers Anthony

OPEN ROAD

INTEGRATED MEDIA

NEW YORK

ISBN: 978-1-5040-8947-0

This edition published in 2024 by Open Road Integrated Media, Inc.
180 Maiden Lane
New York, NY 10038
www.openroadmedia.com

Question Quest

Chapter 1

LACUNA

Lacuna was slogging through a blue funk. It clung to her body, making her seem prematurely middle-aged. It infused her clothing, making it dowdy. It smirched her face, making wrinkles start to think of appearing. It washed through her hair, rinsing it dishwater dull. In fact, it permeated her whole life, making her thirty-four years old.

She had been young once; she was sure of it. She and her twin brother, Hiatus, had been genuine mischief as children. She remembered fondly how they had messed up the wedding of Good Magician Humfrey and the Gorgon, when they were only three years old. At that time their parents, the Zombie Master and Millie the ghost, had been sharing the Good Magician's castle, because it dated from the time eight hundred years before when their parents had first lived. It had seemed only natural that the cute twins should carry the end of the bride's long train. But they had done more than that. Hiatus had made eyes, ears, and noses sprout from things, that being his talent, and Lacuna had changed the print in the manual so that instead of saying things like "until death do you part," it had said "the few measly years before you croak." For some reason Lacuna's mother had not found that very funny. Well, Lacuna was older now, and could see her mother's point. But it only reminded her how she herself had never married. She would have settled for the worst of weddings, for the sake of a good marriage. Or for a mediocre marriage, instead of mediocre old maidenhood.

Later they had moved to New Castle Zombie in southern Xanth, which had been fine. She and Hiatus had had separate rooms, and had teased the poor zombies mercilessly. Somehow it seemed that the best of her life had been used up in childhood. Once she grew up and joined the Adult Conspiracy, her life had become a time of tedium followed by a period of monotony trailed by an age of boredom working into years of sheer unmitigated blah. Finally the funk had set in, and now she was fed up to her tired eyeballs with it. So she was doing something about it: she was visiting the Good Magician with a Question.

Now she came to the region of the Good Magician's Castle. It was not as she remembered it, because it kept changing. She understood that, and was not put off. She knew that she would have to brave three challenges before she could get in and see the Good Magician. At least they should be interesting.

A low jungle surrounded the castle. The magic path she was on led right up to it, then petered out in a thicket of hands and feet. She recognized the type: palmettos. The palms were on stems, their fingers splayed, while the toes grew along the ground, covering it up.

Well, such plants were generally harmless. The palms could get a bit fresh when buxom young women brushed by them, but they would probably just ignore Lacuna. Still, it was best to find a path through them, because dangerous creatures could hide among them and attack the feet of someone who plowed blithely through. So she walked to the side, finding a space between plants.

In a moment her way was blocked again by thickly growing palmettos whose fingers clutched at her plain cloth skirt and whose toes tried to catch her dull shoed feet. She avoided these by turning to the side again. But this wasn't getting her into the castle; she was actually going away from it now.

She reversed her course and explored on the other side. But seemingly promising avenues curled their way into dead ends, preventing her from getting any closer to the castle. How strange! How could the magic path have been overgrown like this? It was supposed to be enchanted to—

Then she realized that this was the first challenge! She had to find her way through this thicket of hands and feet, without getting into trouble. It could have been worse; she would really have hated walking over a potato patch and having all those eyes peer up under her skirt and wink at the dull color of her panties. Men never quite appreciated why women always cut the eyes out of potatoes, first thing. Or maybe they did, because when men got hold of potatoes they planted those eyes in the ground, where they would grow into plants with more potatoes and more eyes.

Fair enough. There was always a solution to the challenges, if the person had the wit to find it. It had been that way in Magician Humfrey's day, and remained so in Magician Grey Murphy's day. Murphy had tried to run the castle without the challenges at first, but had been overwhelmed by folk with Questions, and so had adopted Humfrey's policy. He also now required a significant service for his Answer, which could be anything up to a year of mopping floors in the castle. That tended to discourage frivolous Questions.

Well, she was prepared to mop. It wouldn't be any duller than her prior life. But she doubted she would have to, because she had something she believed Grey Murphy wanted very much: the key to his freedom from Com-Pewter. Com-Pewter was an evil machine made of pewter and glass and crockery and wires and things, who sought to rule Xanth. Com-Pewter had two and a half great assets in this quest. First, the evil machine could change reality in its vicinity, merely by printing new situations on its screen. Second, Grey Murphy was bound to serve Com-Pewter the moment he finished his service to Good Magician Humfrey, who was absent for the time being. Second and a half, Com-Pewter had inanimate patience. So it could wait a lifetime if need be, and the moment Humfrey returned, Pewter would have the service of a full Magician and could more actively set about taking over Xanth. Lacuna could do something about that, and she thought Grey Murphy would be interested. Certainly his fiancée, the Princess Ivy, should be, because she didn't quite dare marry Grey until that little business was settled. If not—well, then, Lacuna would mop.

Provided she could just get into the castle! The more she tried to make progress toward it, the more she seemed to make regress away from it. The palmettos did not seem to move, yet somehow they were always in her way. Where was the path through?

Or was she supposed to get rid of them somehow? To cut a path through? She didn't have a suitable knife, and her talent of printing wouldn't do for this. So there had to be some other way.

She paused and pondered. She was fairly well educated, because there wasn't much point in changing print if a person didn't know what it meant to begin with. She ought to be able to think of something.

Then it came to her. She was standing at yet another dead-end pathlet, having just about lost herself amidst the palmettos. "I think I'll get out of this stupid patch of hands and feet," she said loudly. "I'm tired of these pointing fingers and scuffled toes and pointless paths." Then she marched resolutely back the way she had come.

But almost immediately she encountered more palms and toes, blocking her way out. She had to turn aside, trying to move directly away from the castle and not succeeding. She made a snort of impatience and moved on, looking for the outward path. "I know it's here somewhere," she muttered. "I came in on it, after all!"

But somehow the way continued to elude her. She moved faster, as if trying to find her way out before the palms could change their positions and block her off, but this didn't work either. She only found herself driven back farther into the thicket. The more she struggled to get through, the farther back she was driven by the uncooperative paths.

Finally she found the entire circle of palmetto between her and the magic path away from the Good Magician's castle. She had only succeeded in passing through the thicket the wrong way.

"Well, if that's the way you want it," she said with irritation-bordering on mirth. She turned to face the castle, having navigated the first challenge.

Behind her the palms rustled and the toes scuffled in the dirt. They were chagrined. They had been outsmarted. They had labored successfully to foil the route she said she wanted, not being clever enough to see through her trick. Had they had brains as well as palms and toes, it might have been a different matter. But of course that Was the nature of these challenges: to find the weaknesses of them and successfully exploit those weaknesses to win through.

Now she stood by the moat. There was a boy of about ten swimming in it. He looked ordinary, except that his hair was blue. That suggested that there was no moat monster or other threat in the water. The drawbridge was down, too, so if this wasn't an illusion or trick, she could cross without challenge. That was just as well; she didn't fancy getting wet.

She put a foot cautiously on the end of the drawbridge. It was solid. However, a section of it might be illusion or have a trapdoor or something, so she would proceed with excruciating care. The worst challenges were the ones a person didn't expect.

Something flew by just in front of her. It appeared to be a ball of water. It landed and splatted on the bank. It *was* water.

She looked in the direction from which it had come. There was the boy, scooping up another handful of water and forming it into a ball.

"Are you going to throw that at me?" she asked.

"Sure, if you try to cross the moat. I'm supposed to stop you, you know."

"Oh, so this is a challenge?"

"Sure. Nothing personal. You look like a nice lady."

It had been so long since anyone had said anything like that to Lacuna that she almost blushed with pleasure. But this was business. "A little ball of water wouldn't stop me."

"Then how about a big ball?" He scooped up a double armful, and formed a ball of water as big as a beach ball.

"You couldn't throw that," she said.

For answer, he heaved the ball over the drawbridge. It just seemed to float up without much effort on his part. Such a mass could indeed knock her off the bridge.

"Well, then, I'll just have to wade or swim across," she said.

The boy swept his hand across the surface of the moat. Suddenly there were waves on the water, cruising outward and lapping the bank. He made another pass, and the waves got larger. They were formidable enough to make her hesitate.

"Your talent is water magic," she said. "That is impressive. What's your name?"

"Ryver." He scuffled a toe in the water. He seemed shy, now that she was getting personal.

"So you must be serving a year, for an Answer."

"Yes."

"If I may ask—why did you come to the Good Magician?"

"Oh, sure, you can ask! I asked him how I could find a good family to adopt me, 'cause I want to be a real boy, and I need a real family for that."

"You're not real?" she asked, surprised.

"I'm not a real boy. Not a flesh one, I mean. I'm made of water."

"Made of water?" Now she was really curious. "You can work with water, and control it, but that doesn't mean you're not human."

"I can work with water because I *am* water," he said. "See." Then he dissolved. His feet flowed away, and his legs, and the rest of his body, up to the head. "I look like a boy, but it's all water. I'd rather really be a boy, and have water control as my talent. And I will be, if a family adopts me. The Good Magician says."

She nodded. "So after your term of service is done, you will set out on a search for a good family that wants a boy your age."

"Sure! Do you think I'll find one?"

He seemed so eager that she didn't want to dash his hope. But it did seem doubtful. Most families preferred to raise their own ten-year-old boys. "Did the Good Magician say you would find one?"

"He said his Book of Answers said that I would, if I did my job well and was polite to my elders. So I'm doing those things."

He certainly was! He was effectively stopping her from crossing the moat, but he was being courteous about it, warning her rather than hitting her with water, and answering her questions. He seemed like a nice boy.

"Well, I hope that's right. But meanwhile, you know I have to find a way across despite your efforts."

"Yes. I wish you luck, but I have to stop you if I can. If you try to swim and my waves make you start to drown, I'll save you. I wouldn't want to hurt anybody."

"I appreciate that." There was no irony in her statement; it was clear that this was a challenge, not a duel to the death, and Ryver was just doing what he had to do.

She considered for a while, and pondered for a bit, and thought for a moment, while Ryver dissolved his head into water, then reformed into a whole boy, including clothing. He looked completely real, and she was sure he *was* real; he just wasn't made of flesh. If adoption into a human family enabled him to be transformed into flesh, that would nice for him. She understood that ordinary people were mostly water anyway; Ryver just took it farther.

She got a glimmer of a notion. "Ryver, can you read?"

"Oh, sure. The Sorceress Ivy taught me to read. She showed me how to start, and then Enhanced me into being competent. That's her talent, you know. But you know, most of the books they have at the castle are sort of dry, pardon the term, and not much fun, if you're not into arcana."

Lacuna had suspected as much. "It happens that my talent is changing print. I can also make print appear where there was none, and I can control what it says. Let me show you something interesting to read."

"Oh, no!" he exclaimed. "I won't make a deal to let you get through! That's not right."

"Dear boy," she said, "I am not trying to bribe you. I'm trying to trick you, which is fair enough. I am going to show you some print, and' if you don't find it interesting, don't read it."

"It won't work," he said.

She glanced at the now calm surface of the moat. Abruptly words appeared on its surface, sliding across from right to left, forming a moving band of words. They disappeared as they reached the left margin, so that the whole moat wouldn't get covered with print.

ONCE UPON A TIME THERE WAS A WATER BOY NAMED RYVER WHO WANTED TO BE A FLESH BOY, the rolling print said.

"Hey, that's about me!" Ryver exclaimed.

"Well, actually it's a standard story; I just filled in your name to make it more interesting."

"That's okay." He continued reading, because otherwise he would lose some of the moving words. He was, as she had suspected, fascinated by references to his own name. Many folk were, especially if the references were complimentary. It could work even better if the references were insulting, but she lacked the gumption to write trash.

She poured it on. NOW ONE DAY RYVER WAS SITTING BY THE BANK OF THE MOAT, WATCHING THE FISH, WHEN A STRANGE CREATURE CAME BY. IT WAS A DRAGON LOOKING FOR A TASTY FLESH MORSEL TO FRY. "HA!" SAID THE DRAGON. "I SEE YOU ARE JUST THE KIND OF PERSON I NEED. COME WITH ME AND I WILL GIVE YOU AN EXPERIENCE LIKE NONE OTHER."

"Nuh-uh!" The live (or water-formed) Ryver grunted. "You won't fry *me*, you vicious animal!"

He was evidently getting into it. Lacuna heated up the script. "OH, IS THAT SO?" THE DRAGON SNORTED, HIS BREATH SCORCHING THE PLANTS BY THE BANK. "I'LL HUFF AND I'LL PUFF AND I'LL FRY YOUR HEAD OFF!"

"Yeah, fire-brain? I'd like to see you try it!" the real Ryver said.

SO THE DRAGON HUFFED AND IT PUFFED AND IT BLASTED OUT SUCH A BLAST OF FLAME THAT THE GROUND TURNED BLACK AND SPARKS FLEW FROM THE STONES AND STEAM ROSE FROM THE MOAT. BUT IT COULDN'T FRY RYVER, BECAUSE HE WAS MADE OF WATER. THEN RYVER MADE THE WATER RISE UP AND SMACK THE DRAGON RIGHT IN THE FACE.

"I guess that doused your furnace, soggy-snoot!" the boy cried happily.

WELL, THAT MADE THE DRAGON ANGRY. SO IT OPENED ITS JAWS AND CHARGED. IT CHOMPED RYVER RIGHT THROUGH THE CENTER, BUT ITS TEETH HAD NO EFFECT, BECAUSE THEY COULDN'T CHEW WATER. AND RYVER SQUIRTED JETS OF WATER IN ITS EYES AND EARS. THE DRAGON HATED THAT, BECAUSE NOBODY LIKES TO HAVE HIS EARS WASHED.

The text continued, and the boy kept reading avidly. He didn't even notice that Lacuna had crossed over the drawbridge. That was all right; she had left enough text in the queue to hold him for half an hour. She hadn't known how long it would take for him to be completely distracted, so had put in plenty. Anyway, she was pleased that someone really liked her writing. She had learned to tell stories to children when she was babysitting, and rather enjoyed it. Ryver was a perfect audience.

Now she was across the moat but still outside the castle wall. There was a door right before her. She walked up and turned the handle. But it didn't work; the door was locked, and she didn't have the key. Obviously she had to find the key; this was the third challenge.

She looked around. There was a fairly narrow path that circled the castle just inside the moat. It was lined by bushes that resembled shelves; their stems were vertical and their branches horizontal, with the leaves filling in to complete the pattern. They had squared-off large berries that looked rather like books on the shelves.

A boy was sitting on the bank, picking the berries and eating them. He looked a lot like Ryver.

"Who are you?" she inquired, not really expecting an answer.

"I am Torrent, Ryver's twin brother."

Could she believe that? Well, maybe for now.

"What sort of plants are these?" she asked.

"They are library bushes," he responded. "They have endless information, which I get by eating the fruit."

This was almost too good to be true, so she knew it probably wasn't true. But she would find out. "Then you must know where the key to that door is."

"Sure. Here it is." He handed her a large wooden key.

She tried the key in the lock. It wouldn't fit. It was the wrong one.

She returned to the boy. "It's not the right key. Where is the right one?"

"On the other side of the castle."

She doubted it, but proceeded on around. There was a small metal key lying on the path. She picked it up and walked back around to the door. It didn't fit.

She looked at the boy, who was still eating berries. Twice he had directed her to the wrong key. He was obviously not telling the truth. How could she make him tell the truth?

She decided to experiment. "Torrent, are you part of this challenge for me?"

"Yes."

"So you are supposed to misdirect me, and prevent me from finding the key."

"No."

"And you do that by lying to me."

He hesitated, and she knew why. If he lied, she would know it, which would make the lie worthless, but if he told the truth he wouldn't be misdirecting her. "No."

Which meant that he did. "So you lied about your identity, too. You are Ryver."

"No."

"Then where is Ryver? He's not out there reading the print on the moat."

He looked back there, and winced. He must have had to tear himself away from it with the story unfinished. He didn't answer, which was answer enough.

"And you're not supposed to be part of this challenge," she said, remembering that he had answered yes to that question before, so it was a lie.

"I can be if I want to be!" he said defensively.

"And now you're telling the truth."

He hung his head. "You trapped me into it. Anyway, it doesn't matter, because it's only about the challenge that I really had to lie."

"Why not just refuse to tell me anything about the keys?"

"Because—" He stopped. "I can't tell you."

"Because lying has something to do with the solution!" she said, catching on.

"No."

"Which means yes. And the berries—do they have anything to do with it too?"

"No."

"So they do. Exactly what kind of berries are they?"

"Poison."

"Hardly. You've been eating them." Then a light flickered. "You were a truthful boy. Now you're an untruthful one. You've been eating the berries. You said they are libraries, but I think they are lie berries. They make you lie!"

"No!"

"And if I ate one, it would make me lie."

"No."

"But it's hard to lie, if you don't know the truth. So maybe the berries do have a lot of information, so they know how to lie about it. So the person who eats them knows the truth, which he won't tell."

"No."

She picked a berry and popped it into her mouth. It was sickly sweet. Then she spoke: "The key is—" Information coursed through her mind. "Over there." She pointed to what she knew was the wrong key, under a bush.

But now she knew where the right key was. It was under the water at the edge of the moat, hidden by mud. She went there, reached down, and fished it out. It was made of delicate stone. Then she took it to the door. It fit, and in a moment the door was unlocked.

She looked back at Ryver, who was staring sadly after her. Information sifted through her mind as she continued to feel the effect of the berry. Now she knew why he had come to join this challenge, changing places with the gnome who was supposed to be eating the berries and doing the lying. He was lonely. He really did want to be part of a family, and she, as a passing human being, was a step closer to the illusion of that than being alone was. He was taking the opportunity to be closer to her, to interact with her, even though it had to be negative. She felt sorry for him.

She didn't say anything, because she would be forced to lie until the effect of the berry wore off. She turned and opened the door. She had made it through the challenges, and it had been interesting, but she was not completely pleased. She saw now that she was not the only one whose life was blah.

Chapter 2

HANDBASKET

Ivy was just inside the doorway, waiting for her. "I knew you would make it through, Lacuna!" she exclaimed, stepping in for a hug. In the old days she had been one of the children Lacuna had baby-sat, and they had always gotten along well. Ivy was now an attractive young woman of twenty-one, and evidently happy in her relationship with Grey Murphy.

"Well, I'm not glad to see you," Lacuna said, then paused, dismayed. "Oops, that lie berry I didn't eat—"

"Oh, that's all right; the effect wears off quickly if you don't eat many."

"I ate bushels."

"Which means you ate only one, because if you *had* eaten bushels, you would say the opposite. Come on, I think Grey is ready for you. He doesn't look satisfied; you must have an awkward Question."

Lacuna shrugged, so that no lie would come from her mouth. She followed Ivy to the central chamber of the castle where the Good Magician awaited them.

Grey was now a nondescript young man of twenty-two. He was the son of Evil Magician Murphy, who dated from eight or nine centuries before, but like the Zombie Master and Millie the Ghost, he had come to the present period of Xanth's history. The senior Murphy was no longer evil, of course; he had renounced that as a condition of being allowed to settle in this time. He seldom used his power of cursing things so that they would go wrong in any way they could, and only did it for beneficial effect. That might seem contradictory, but it wasn't; if he cursed something evil, than that evil person or thing went wrong and couldn't accomplish its malign purpose. Grey had never been evil, of course. But he had the liability of having to serve Com-Pewter, because of the deal his parents had made long ago, thinking it would never take effect. His father couldn't curse the evil machine directly, because he had made his deal with it to get out of Xanth in the old days, but had been able to curse the evil plot. That had helped save Grey—until Good Magician Humfrey returned.

Grey stepped forward to shake Lacuna's hand. That was one of the quaint Mundane ways he retained. It meant that he was greeting her in a friendly but not assuming way, and expected the same attitude from her. "I don't suppose I can talk you out of asking your Question?" he inquired plaintively.

"Magician, my life is blah. All I want to know is where in my dreary life I went wrong."

"You mean that's it?" Ivy asked.

"Yes. Then maybe I'll know what to do about it."

Ivy turned to Grey. "That seems simple enough."

"It isn't," he said. He glanced again at Lacuna. "I would really rather you didn't ask it."

"Well, I don't want to cause you distress, but it seems little enough for me to ask, considering that I made my way through your challenges and am prepared to offer a significant service."

Grey frowned. "I am not yet completely proficient in the magic of information. The Good Magician Humfrey would know how to handle this much better than I do. But there have been rumblings, and they suggest that your Question is a lot more complicated for us both than it seems. In fact, they indicated that if I Answer it, the situation of Xanth may change significantly. I don't want to take the chance. So, with no malice toward you, I must decline to Answer."

"Grey!" Ivy said, appalled. "I've known Lacuna all my life! She's a good person. She has such a simple Question. How can you do this?"

"I know just enough of Humfrey's magic now to know that this is best," he said unhappily. "Now if she cares to ask some other Question—"

"No, only this one," Lacuna said firmly.

"Then I'm sorry, but—"

She fixed him with an Adult Stare. He was not yet so long beyond childhood as to be immune to its effect. He scuffled his feet. "I did not come here to take No for an Answer," she said. She might be dull, but she knew her rights. "I insist: tell me Where Did I Go Wrong?"

Grey obviously felt properly miserable, but still he clung somehow to his position. "I won't—"

It was time for the carrot. She had learned how to wield stick and carrot; it was a necessary secondary talent of all baby-sitters. "I have in mind a rather special service, to repay you for your trouble."

"Well, if I were to use your service, I'm sure you could confuse other applicants by putting misleading printed messages on the walls. But—"

"Magician, I can free you from your obligation to the evil machine. Even after Magician Humfrey returns."

Both Grey and Ivy jumped. "You can do that?" Ivy breathed with sheer faint hope.

"I can go to Com-Pewter and change the print on its screen to say that Grey Murphy's obligation is no longer in force. Since what's on that screen changes reality to conform, that will be true. There will be no further obligation."

Ivy turned to the Good Magician, her eyes shining. "Can she do that, Grey?"

Grey dived for a huge tome sitting on a table. He leafed rapidly through it, staring into the depths of its musty pages. He paused, then looked up. "Yes, it is here. She can do it. If she prints the right words on Pewter's screen. If she has the nerve to broach the evil machine in its evil den. There is one key word that must be used at the end or it won't be effective."

"Key word?" Lacuna asked.

"'Compile.'"

"You mean to assemble something?"

"Compile. It has a special meaning for Com-Pewter. It locks in whatever has just been printed on its evil screen. Com-Pewter can change anything except itself, and this changes Pewter itself. I understand about this, because of my experience with similar machines in Mundania."

"Then—" Ivy started.

Grey raised his hands in surrender. "That is the one service I cannot refuse. I will have to Answer Lacuna's Question."

Lacuna smiled, vastly relieved. The truth was she wanted to free Grey anyway, because she knew how happy that would make Ivy. But it was best to do it this way.

"Very well," Grey said grimly, turning the pages of the Book of Answers again. "I shall have to Answer, and hope the consequences are not as bad as they could be." He found his place, read the entry, and looked up, perplexed. "This is really of no practical use to you. Are you sure—?"

"I am sure."

He sighed. "It says that you should have proposed to him."

"That's no answer!" Ivy protested. "It doesn't say whom or when! I mean, of course it's all right for the girl to propose; I asked Grey to marry me, and he accepted. But—"

"It is enough," Lacuna reassured her. "I know what it means. If only I had thought of it!"

"Who—?"

"It was twelve years ago, when I was Grey's age now. He was Vernon, and his talent was making others experience vertigo. Certainly he made *me* feel that way, but that was because I was infatuated with him. He was a handsome man and a decent one. I would have married him, but he never quite asked me. I think he was too shy. I mean, in those days I wasn't as dull as I am now. Later he married a mean woman, who told him he had better, if he knew what was good for him, but she certainly wasn't good for him. She made his life miserable. I think that was *her* talent. The stork never brought them any children, probably because it knew they would have been miserable in that house." Lacuna shook her head sadly. "I can see it so clearly now, now that I have the Answer: that was indeed where I went wrong. He was humble, thinking his talent to be of no value. I know he would have accepted, had I only thought to ask him. But I didn't."

"But what good does it do you to know that now, when it's twelve years too late?" Ivy asked.

"None, except the private satisfaction of knowing my mistake. The next time I meet a man I should marry, I'll ask him. Of course he probably won't accept, since I'm middle-aged now and not worth anyone's notice, let alone marriage. But at least—"

Ivy was troubled. "Grey, I know that's all she asked, but it just doesn't seem enough, considering the service she is going to do for us. She will free you from the bane of your life. Isn't there some way to free her from hers? Maybe to send her back, so she can do it right?"

"I really don't think—" he said.

"Look in the Book," she insisted, with That Tone, which only members of the Female Conspiracy could mistress.

He shrugged and turned the pages again. He found his place and stared. "It—seems to be possible. But—"

"Possible?" Lacuna exclaimed. "For me to change that bad decision?"

"Yes. But the details are so technical I can't understand them at all. This book gets into programming language, and it will take me years to figure out even part of it. Only Humfrey, who had a century to learn the nuances, could fathom this Answer."

"Then I must go ask Humfrey!" Lacuna said. "Right after I do my service for you."

"But Humfrey is at an impossible address in the gourd," Grey protested. "And he doesn't want to be disturbed. He must be doing something extremely important."

"He will talk to me," Lacuna said confidently. "I was at his wedding."

"Actually, he's in the anteroom to Hell, the awfulest region of the dream realm. You would hardly care to go there."

"Oh yes I would! If there's a way to change where I went wrong and make it right—why that would do for my life what I will do for yours! Magician, tell me how to reach Humfrey!"

"I really don't think—" But he didn't finish, because Ivy was fixing him with the Stare, another aspect of female magic.

"You don't need to," Lacuna said. "I must do it. If I have to give another service for that Answer, then I'll gladly do it. Let me just go to Com-Pewter and take care of that; then I'll return here and—"

Grey sighed. "No, if you feel that strongly about it, I will help you visit Humfrey without further charge. I will do it now. Your service to me can wait."

"Well, if you're sure—"

"I'm *not* sure. But it seems it was mused."

"Fated," Ivy murmured.

"I'm getting as bad as what's her name," he said, flustered.

"Metria," Ivy said.

"The Demoness Metria," he agreed. "Getting the wrong word." He looked at Lacuna. "Anyway, I'll send you to see Humfrey now. But I warn you, it's not a pleasant trip."

"My *life* is not a pleasant trip! I could use some excitement."

"Well, then, you can go to Hell."

Lacuna was taken aback. "But—"

"In a handbasket," he said. "That's where Humfrey is, and it's the only way to go there, if you don't belong."

"Oh." For a moment she had been on the verge of mistaking his meaning. Folk from Mundania could have some crude Mundanian manners clinging to them.

"But you can do that tomorrow," Ivy said. "You will want to rest here tonight."

"No, I don't think I do. I'd rather go straight on and get the second Answer from Magician Humfrey."

"As you wish," Grey said. He went to a locked cupboard, unlocked it, opened it, and brought out a sealed jar. He unscrewed the lid and took out a tiny basket, like a thimble made of wickerwork, on a thread. He flipped the thread up toward the ceiling and let go of the basket. It hung there, suspended from nothing.

"This is the basket," Ivy said. "It's one of the magic devices we found in Humfrey's collection. He evidently used it and sent it back. You will ride in it to Hell."

"But I can't fit in that little thing!" Lacuna protested.

Grey smiled. "Your body will rest in a coffin, just as Humfrey's does. Only your soul goes to Hell. Don't worry, your body will be quite safe here, until you return to it."

Ivy walked to a low solid bench. She lifted its top—and it came up, manifesting as the lid to a plushly lined coffin. "Lie down in here," Ivy said.

Lacuna was beginning to have, if not exactly second thoughts, first-and-a-half thoughts. Sleep in a coffin? But if it was the way to go, then she had to do it.

She got into the coffin and lay on her back. Somehow this action made her feel even older and duller than she hoped she was. Grey put his finger behind the hanging tiny basket and pushed it toward her. "Get into this."

Lacuna wanted to protest, but found herself floating up toward the basket, which was rapidly expanding. She caught its edge with her hands and climbed in. It was now quite ample in size; she could stand upright within it and peer over the edge and down.

She saw her huge body lying there in the coffin. It looked every bit as blah as she had feared.

She turned to face the other way. As she did so, the basket began to move. It was swinging along at the end of its rope, which was firmly knotted to the stout handle. The room, indeed the entire Good Magician's castle, seemed to have disappeared. She was on her way.

The basket tilted and moved down. Lacuna clutched the edge with both hands. She was passing through a region of shadows and clouds. Behind the clouds were vague flashes, as of lightning, making the outlines show momentarily. Some of the clouds resembled monstrous ugly faces, as if Cumulo Fracto Nimbus, the meanest of clouds, had posed for his portrait.

One of the clouds opened its big mouth, and the basket swung right into it. The scenery changed; now there were things floating, ranging from tiny acorns to huge acorn trees. This was evidently the "dream realm, normally accessed through the peephole of a gourd. It seemed there were other ways to visit it. To Hell in a handbasket! Who would have expected it! At least it was interesting.

But some of the scenes through which she was passing were more than interesting. They were grotesque. There were human forms in various states of distress, and animals who seemed lost, and assorted objects that looked broken. The stuff of troubled dreams, spare props, perhaps hanging here in limbo, waiting to be fashioned into truly unpleasant episodes for those sleepers who deserved them. Lacuna had seldom suffered from bad dreams; that was part of the boredom of her being. How could a person rate bad dreams if a person never did anything of doubtful validity?

Then a vague face formed, neither interesting nor dull of itself. From its mouth poured numbers in scattered order. These numbers grew larger as they moved, becoming individual pictures. They were odd indeed! One was of a man walking along with two left feet, making him pretty awkward. Another was a blue or purple horse; actually she couldn't quite tell what color it was, because it seemed to keep changing, never being fixed. A third was of a man whose head was a pile of animal manure.

Suddenly Lacuna caught on. "Figures of speech!" she exclaimed. "In the realm of dreams they are literal! A man with two left feet, a horse of another color, a dunghead!" These folk were worse off than she was, which made her feel both better and guilty. How awful it must be to be literal.

Then, abruptly, the basket swung into a small chamber. It bumped against the floor, almost overturning, and she had to scramble out. She had arrived.

As she caught her balance, she saw the basket swinging up and away. "Oh!" she cried, grabbing for it, but she was too late. She had lost her transport back.

But Grey and Ivy knew where she was. Surely they would send the handbasket back when they realized that it was empty. She had to believe that!

She looked around—and there sat old Good Magician Humfrey in a hard wooden chair! She recognized him instantly; there was no mistaking the gnomelike features and great age of the little man. He seemed to be snoozing.

That was all. The rest of the chamber was bare, except for another chair.

She sat in that chair. There did not seem to be much else to do. She smoothed out her dingy dress, noting that she wore the same clothing as usual despite being in spirit form now. That was just as well; she would not have liked to go naked to this infernal region, though probably it was not the best place to keep secrets. This surely was not Hell itself, because there was no fire. It must be Hell's waiting room.

But why was Humfrey still waiting here? In fact, what was he doing here anyway? Where was his family? It had been ten years since the man had disappeared from his castle along with his wife and son, leaving Xanth in the lurch. Chex Centaur had discovered his absence, with her companions Esk Ogre and Volney Vole; the challenges seemed to have been in the process of being set up for the three, when the occupants of the castle had suddenly departed. It was the great current mystery of Xanth: what had happened?

Well, perhaps that wasn't her business, though she was as curious as the next person. She had just one Question which was her business with the Magician. She would just have to stifle her interest in the rest of his life.

She did not want to wake him from his snooze. But she wasn't sure how long she could safely remain here. If this was Hell's waiting room, at any time a door could open and a demon could appear, saying "Next!" in that bone-chilling tone. Then either Humfrey would be taken, or she herself would. Either way, her chance for her Answer would be gone.

"Ahem," she said politely.

One of Humfrey's eyelids flickered. Then both did. His eyes popped open, fixing on her. "Lacuna! What are you doing here?"

"You recognize me?" she asked, startled.

"Of course I recognize you! You baby-sat me when I had been youthened by overdosing on the water from the Fountain of Youth. You were a rather sweet sixteen at the time, quite unlike your present blah state."

She had forgotten how sharp he was on information. Of course, he was the Magician of Information. Even in his youthened state he had been very quick to learn things. So after most of eighteen years without seeing her, he had identified her present nature with dismaying facility.

"I came to ask you a Question," she said.

"I'm not answering Questions now. Go to the castle. Murphy's boy is supposed to be minding it."

"He is. He sent me here. He said that only you could give me my Answer."

"Why? Doesn't he have the Book of Answers there?"

"Yes, but he can't decipher the technical parts, and my Answer is there."

He nodded. "It does take most of a century to master the programming language. I happen to know. I did it faster because I had special training. But he'll get there in due course."

"I can't wait a century!" she protested. "I've already gone from sweet sixteen to blah thirty-four. I'll sink into dismal anonymity before another decade is out."

He glanced at her appraisingly. "More like six years."

"Six years?"

"A person is only allowed three great mistakes. Your first was in not marrying that young man. Your second was in turning thirty. Your third will be in turning forty, and that will finish you as a potentially worthwhile female human being."

He certainly understood her situation! "Magician Grey Murphy told me of the first mistake. If I can change that, I'll be left with only two strikes against me, and my life may become worthwhile. The rules aren't the same for married women. That's why I came to you."

Humfrey considered. "I suppose I might as well do something while I'm waiting here. Suppose I give you the coding so that you can show Grey Murphy how to get your Answer from the Book?"

"That would be fine!" she said.

"And what service will you do me in return?"

"What do you need?"

"I need to have the Demon X(A/N)th take notice of me!" he said. "I've been cooling my heels in this waiting room for ten years, waiting for him to ask me what I want."

"You mean you're not going to Hell?"

"Not exactly. I'm here to take someone *from* Hell. Then I can return with her to Xanth."

"With her? Who is she?"

"My wife."

"The Gorgon is in Hell?"

"No. She's waiting for me to get my business done here. It's Rose I'm after."

"Rose is your wife? But what about the Gorgon?"

"What about her?"

"How can you have a wife in Hell when the Gorgon is your wife?"

"I married Rose before."

"But then—"

"It's a long story," he said shortly.

Lacuna realized that Humfrey must have done more than twiddle his thumbs in the century or so he had lived before meeting the Gorgon. Rose must have been a wife who died. "But no matter how long it is, if you bring Rose back, you'll have two wives, and that's not allowed in Xanth."

"Who says it isn't?"

"Queen Irene. When Prince Dolph got betrothed to two girls, she said he could marry only one."

Humfrey sighed. "That does complicate things. But the Queen's word is law on matters of social protocol, however inconvenient it may be. Her son must have been most upset."

"He was," she agreed. "But he finally worked it out."

"He was young. I am too old to adjust to such nonsense. What am I going to do? I can't leave Rose in Hell."

"You are asking me? But you're the Magician of Information."

"True. I shall have to think about this. I shall review my life, and gain the perspective to make the right decision. Herein lies your service: use your print to record my biography."

"But I have nothing to print on," she protested, surprised.

"Print on the wall."

"Yes, I could do that," she agreed. "But what is the point of printing it? Why can't you just review your life in your head?"

"Because my head isn't that big!" he snapped. "Also, I'm trying to attract the attention of the Demon X(A/N)th, and maybe the story of my life written on the wall will do it."

"Why do you want to see the Demon X(A/N)th? I thought you were here to rescue your former wife."

"I am. But only the Demon can authorize it."

Lacuna nodded. It was beginning to make partial sense. "And you have waited here all this time, heating your heels, being ignored by the Demon? Why don't you take a break where it's more interesting?"

"Because the Demon doesn't want to deal with me."

"But then the Demon may never take note of you!"

"No. It is in the Big Book of Universal Rules: the Demon has to meet with his appointments before doing anything else. So I shall wait here until he appears."

"But all this time—surely you can afford some time off. He's probably asleep and it won't make any difference."

Humfrey fixed her with a steely gaze. "You don't understand the psychology of the Demon X(A/N)th. He will appear here the very instant I step out. Because the rules also say that if the Demon appears, and there is no person in the waiting room, because the person didn't have the interest to remain, then the appointment is vacated. Then he won't have to see me at all."

Lacuna was appalled. "You mean the Demon knows you are here and is deliberately ignoring you, hoping to catch you out? And it has been this way for a decade?"

"Exactly. So I don't dare step out. I was lucky the Demon didn't realize when Grey Murphy and Ivy tried to wake me in the dream coffin four years ago. But I know *I* won't be able to get away with that again. The Demon may have been inattentive once, but he never makes the same mistake twice."

Now she knew why the Good Magician had disappeared and never even left word. He had been unable to, without risking the loss of his mission. So he had remained here in this absolutely dull waiting room, doing nothing. Waiting for the Demon.

"Your recent life has been a worse blah than mine!" she exclaimed, suffering a revelation.

"What else is new?" he inquired sourly.

"But still—suppose the Demon came this moment and said it was all right to take Rose out of Hell and back to Xanth. What about the Gorgon?" For Lacuna had known and liked the Gorgon, whose terror was all in her face, not in her nature.

"It's bad enough trying to figure out what to do about Grey Murphy when I return," the Magician grumped. "It isn't right to send him back to Mundania to avoid Com-Pewter."

"Oh, that's no problem," she said quickly. "I will free Grey by changing the print on the evil machine's screen."

He stared at her. "No wonder I overlooked that Answer! It's obvious! Simply a matter of overwriting Pewter's directive and using the key command 'Save and Compile.' I could have given him that Answer before."

She shrugged, not wanting to annoy him further.

"Well, if you are so good at seeing the obvious, what's your solution to my problem of two wives?"

She spread her hands. "Maybe they could take turns?"

"That's ridiculous!" he exploded. "It just might work, if the Queen doesn't interfere."

"Well, if one wife is technically dead, while the other is alive, maybe Queen Irene couldn't object."

He sighed. "It may not come to that. The Demon X(A/N)th isn't going to grant my appeal anyway."

"But—but then why—"

"Because it would be unthinkable not to make the effort. I was less experienced before, and didn't consider such an approach, but now it must be tried."

Lacuna wondered what kind of a woman Rose was to warrant such devotion from such a normally truculent man. To sit in Hell's waiting room for a decade, expecting a negative response!

She knew better, but she couldn't help arguing a little more. "Why won't the Demon grant your appeal?"

"For the same reason he doesn't want to meet me: it's more complicated to deal with this matter than to ignore it. The Demon cares nothing for my convenience, only for his own."

"Wouldn't it be easy for him just to hear your appeal and turn it down and be done with it?"

"He can't do that. The rules say that he has to be fair. If he is fair, he may have to grant my appeal. So he is avoiding me, hoping I will give up and go without his hearing me."

The two were really in a contest of wills, she saw. Humfrey wanted something that the Demon X(A/N)th didn't want to give, so they were locked in this endurance contest instead. It was sad. But it was also somewhat like Humfrey's own treatment of those who pestered him with Questions at his castle. He was being served as he served others. Probably he would not appreciate having that pointed out, so she stifled whatever remark she might have been tempted to make.

"How will he avoid granting your appeal, if he has to play fair?" she asked.

"He will cheat."

"But—"

"Fairness is as the Demon says it is. He will give me a chance to gain my objective, if I put my own soul on the line. If I win, I take Rose; if I lose I will be confined here with her. Then he will see that I lose."

"But how can he—"

"Very simply. He will ask me a Question that I as the Magician of Information should be able to answer. It will be about some future event. Then he will see that whatever my Answer, it will happen otherwise. Thus I will lose."

"Then you really have no hope," she said, disturbed.

"I have hope. I have no chance."

"You are throwing your life away for nothing! And even if you should win, you'll still have the problem of two wives. They won't take turns if they are both alive in Xanth."

"Tell me something that isn't obvious."

She shook her head. "This just doesn't make sense."

"So it would seem."

Then she knew that he had a plan. She couldn't imagine what it was, but she had confidence in his information. He would find a way through the rigged contest—if he could only get the Demon's attention. He couldn't tell her his plan, because the Demon might be listening and then would know how to foil it.

Still, she had one more question. "If the Demon X(A/N)th knows you are here, and is ignoring you, why should printing your life story make any difference? Won't he just ignore that too?"

"Only up to a point. My life story is true, though much of it is unknown to all others except the Demon. It must be true; I dare not falsify any part of it. Therefore, it will be difficult for me to relate, in places. Complete honesty is always painful and seldom advisable. But at the point it catches up to the present and starts into the future, its truth will be undefined. I will be able to tell it as I hope it will be."

"But then you could say that you are going to rescue Rose from Hell by yourself and return to Xanth!"

"Precisely. I will be able to define my own future. Therefore the Demon must at that point come to meet me and deal with my appeal, lest he lose it by default."

That was a most sophisticated strategy! It was obvious that the Good Magician was much smarter than she was. Still she had a niggling confusion. "Why didn't you tell your story before, instead of waiting all this time?"

"The spoken word lacks the authority of the written word. Until you came, I was unable to transcribe my autobiography to print."

"But why didn't the Demon stop me from coming here, then?"

"I suspect you were too insignificant a detail for him to bother to keep track of. Had you been beautiful or smart or highly talented, as my wives are, he would have seen you coming. Now it is too late; you are here."

"How fortunate that I am so ordinary," she said, with a hint of a mixed feeling.

"You are not ordinary, Lacuna, you are dull. You are almost completely uninteresting. How you got to be a leading character in this story is almost beyond my significant resources to ascertain."

Surely it was true. That was why she had come here.

"Well, we had better get on with it," she said with a certain boring resignation. She focused on the far wall, and the print began to appear:

THE STORY OF THE LIFE HISTORY OF THE GOOD MAGICIAN HUMFREY, THE MAGICIAN OF INFORMATION. *CHAPTER ONE.*

"Oh, don't be so cumbersome!" Humfrey snapped. "Just title it *Question Quest.* And start with Chapter 3; you've already wasted two chapters with your own dreary business, may the Muse of History forgive you."

"Yes, of course," she agreed, properly chastened. "What should the title of Chapter 3 be?"

"Oh, anything," he said impatiently. He began to dictate.

Chapter 3

ANYTHING

I was born of wholesome parents in the year 933. This calendar dates from Xanth's First Wave of human colonization. Some few human folk had settled in Xanth before then, perhaps around the year 2200, but then Xanth became an island; there were not enough of them to maintain the population, and they faded out by—1900. It was probably good riddance. The main evidences of their presence are the crossbreeds they generated: harpies, cowboys, werewolves, mermaids, and similar ilk. Later the isthmus was restored and more humans crossed over, generating the centaurs. But only with the First Wave did human history become continuous, so that was the Year Zero.

Successive Waves of human colonization from Mundania brought shame to Xanth, until after the Fourth Wave, in 228, when Magician Roogna assumed power, built Castle Roogna, and ushered in Xanth's Golden Age. Castle Roogna was deserted when King Gromden died in 677 and King Yang took over. The human influence in the peninsula slowly declined, ushering in what was called Xanth's Dark Age, had anyone noticed or cared before it was too late.

But this summation becomes tedious. The tabular history of Xanth will be provided in an appendix for those few who are morbidly curious about the dead past.

However, one good thing had happened recently: the year before my birth, Magician-King Ebnez adapted the Deathstone into the Shieldstone, protecting Xanth from further Waves. Magician Roogna had had the power to adapt living magic to his ends, while Magician Ebnez adapted inanimate magic; both were to have significant effect on human events. This was to usher in a period of historical calm. The Twelfth Wave became known as the LastWave, because there were no more Waves until 1042 when King Trent's Mundane army settled peacefully in Xanth.

Thus it was my fortune to live in the most peaceful part of Xanth's Dark Age. Actually, it was rather dull. There is a blessing: "May you live in boring times." I would rather have suffered the curse of interesting times.

I was the youngest of three children. My older brother inherited the farm, and my older sister was incurably bossy. It therefore behooved me to set out alone for far adventures. Unfortunately the only trade I knew was what I had learned at home: tic farming. We grew tics, which constantly twitched, and harvested and bundled them for the clocks of other folk. Once in the clock, the properly ripened tics measured the time. Without them, the clocks had nothing but tocks and were useless, but with them they proceeded in a steady line of tick-tocks and kept good time. There were few clocks in Xanth, because there were few people in Xanth, and my family's farm provided all the tics that were needed. It would have been pointless to start up another such farm. My training was useless in the outside realm.

I had one other liability: I had unmitigated curiosity. That was all. I had no magic talent that I knew of. In those days there was no requirement in that respect; it was the later Storm King who idiotically decreed that every citizen of Xanth had to have a magic talent, however minor. The only real rule at this time was that only a Magician could be king. That dates from the Fourth Wave and has generally worked well, because only a Magician has power to enforce his edicts. So I, as a talentless young man, without athletic ability, small of stature and unhandsome, became one of the nonentities of Xanth. Others neither knew nor cared what I was doing, as long as I did not bother them.

So I walked from village to village, exploring and looking around, learning all I could about everything I could, unobtrusively. Since villages were far apart, most of my time was spent on the paths between them. These paths were unkempt and often dangerous; this was between the times of enchanted paths, other than those set up for special purposes by tangle trees and the like. During the Golden Age paths abounded, and in the contemporary age they do too; that's the advantage of a strong kingship.

I was fifteen years old, and looked twelve. Sometimes folk took me for a gnome. It had always been thus, and I was used to it. In fact it was an advantage at times, because they didn't consider gnomes to be people, and would speak as freely around them as around animals. I perked my ears and closed my mouth and learned their secrets. As a rule these were not worth knowing: who was making a tryst with whose wife, who was stealing from whom, and who had most recently been eaten by the local dragon. But I remembered their names and faces and secrets, because of my insatiable desire to know everything knowable.

I had, as it turned out, an excellent memory, which I buttressed by notes I made in my one possession of any value: a notebook. Thus I would mark "Kelvin—slew golden dragon," or "Stile—Blue Adept" or "Zane—Thanatos" or "Darius—Cyng of Hlahtar," and the entire curious history of each person would be recalled when I read each note. Of course these were all inconsequential folk who never made any mark in Xanth and were forgotten by all others. But to me they were interesting. Who might guess what adventures they might have had or what success they might have achieved, if only they could have been delivered into more advantageous situations? For that matter, what might I myself have accomplished had I lived in a culture where curiosity was valued?

So it was that I found myself on the path leading from the Gap Village, where I had lived so far, to the land of the dragons, only I did not know that at the time. I was merely following the path of least resistance. That was foolish, as I was soon to learn, because if the path of least resistance does not lead to the nearest tangle tree, it leads to some equivalent disaster.

I heard a noise ahead. It sounded like a dragon going after prey: a sort of screaming and hissing, followed by a dull thunk. I ducked off the path, knowing better than to be on the scene when a dragon was feeding. But then I saw a shadow and a figure just above the trees. It was a flying dragon, dripping blood. It was evidently done, here.

I resumed my trek. The best direction to travel was opposite that of a dragon, and that was the way I was going anyway. I rounded a turn, entering a glade.

Here I encountered two objects on the ground. One was a unicorn, writhing from a bad injury, thrashing its horn about in pain. The other was a girl.

I wasn't sure what to do about either unicorns, like all equines except the centaurs, were rare in Xanth, and I had seen one only twice before, and only fleetingly. Girls were not as scarce, but I had had little more contact with them outside my family, and indeed my experience with my older sister had rather turned me off them. It was hardly ideal, traveling alone, but it was better than being constantly bossed around.

The girl spied me. "Help Horntense!" she cried, gesturing to the animal.

There she was, bossing me already.

Conditioned by a decade and a half of conditioning, I had no choice but to obey. I approached the unicorn. It was a mare who appeared to have broken *a foreleg*. There was also blood on her horn. I hesitated, because a wounded animal can be as dangerous as a whole one. But I saw that it was pain, not threat, which made her thrash for my attention; she was hoping I could do something for her.

As it happened, I could. I had noticed some boneset herbs growing beside the path a short distance back. "I shall return," I said, and hurried away.

I broke into a run, zooming along until I reached the herbs. I had a spare bag in my knapsack, which I drew forth. I found a good plant, took a stick, and dug carefully around it. I lifted it from the ground with its root and the earth around it, in much the manner I would transplant a tic plant. At least my experience as a farm boy was coming in handy. I set it in the bag carefully.

I carried the bagged herb back down the path. Now I could not run, lest I shake up the plant. Other plants might not care, but a shaken boneset was not good.

I reached the glade. The unicorn was now quiet. The girl had dragged herself over and was cradling the animal's head. She spied me. "Oh! I was afraid you were gone!"

"I was just getting this plant," I explained, somewhat lamely, though in truth the two of them were the lame ones. The unicorn had a foreleg broken, and the girl seemed to have turned an otherwise serviceable ankle; it was beginning to swell.

"Do you know anything about healing?" she asked.

"Not much. But I thought maybe this herb might help." Actually I was quite sure it would help, but something about being near to the unicorn, or maybe the girl, made me less assertive.

"A stupid plant?" she demanded. "Horntense could make two bites of that!"

"Don't eat it!" I protested, alarmed. "This is boneset."

"What's that?"

"A magic herb that sets bones. Let me plant it here, so it can operate." I felt more confidence, having discovered that I knew something she didn't.

I used my stick to dig a hole by the animal's broken foreleg. Then I slid the herb into it, and packed the earth around firmly.

"Now if I can touch the leg—" I said, reaching for the unicorn's injured extremity. She did not shy away, so I put my two hands on it and drew it slowly toward the plant. I set it right beside the herb, touching it.

Immediately the boneset's leaves quivered. Its stems reached out and curled over the broken leg. Vines tightened around it. Suddenly they clenched, and there was a muffled crack. The unicorn emitted a squeal of agony and jerked her leg away.

"What happened?" the girl cried.

"It set the bone," I explained. "That's the herb's magic."

She looked at the unicorn's leg, which was now unbroken. "It did!" she breathed, barely believing. "The leg is better!"

"No, it's just reset. It will take a few days to heal, if I find the right herbs. The animal shouldn't put much stress on it, meanwhile."

"She's not an animal!" the girl said crossly. "She's a unicorn."

It was no use arguing with a girl, so I didn't try. "A unicorn," I agreed.

"That plant—do you think it would work on my ankle?"

I shrugged. "It should, if it's broken at all."

She turned herself around and put her leg out. I caught it and guided it to the boneset plant. The stems took hold, circling her foot and ankle, tightening. I saw that though her ankle was bruised and swelling, her bare leg was rather nicely shaped, under the dirt.

"Is it going to hurt?" she asked belatedly. Her arms and face were dirty too; she had really sprawled in the dirt.

"For a moment," I said.

"Hold me, then."

I had no experience holding girls, and was awkward. I sort of kneeled beside her and put my arms around her shoulders. She turned into me as she sat and put her head against my shoulder and her arms around my middle. There was something quite soft about her chest.

The plant tightened. There was a pop. "Oh!" she gasped, her arms clenching around me.

"It's done," I said. "There must have been a small break, but now it's set. But you shouldn't walk much on that foot until it heals."

"It feels less worse already," she said, lifting her head from my shoulder and squeezing the dampness out of her eyes with the bends of her wrists. "But I shall have to walk; I need to fetch food."

"I can fetch food," I said, for no good reason. "I know how to find good things to eat."

"Oh, *would* you?" she asked eagerly. That made me feel good, for even less reason.

I went out and cast about for things a girl would find edible. I could get by on stewed slugs, having verified that they were easy to catch and nutritious, but I suspected she would not. I was in luck: there was a pie tree nearby and some milkweeds. I brought an armful of pies and pods back.

The unicorn had climbed to its feet and was grazing. She had the sense to keep weight off her hurt leg, and seemed to be managing well enough on three hoofs. The girl was now sitting with her back to an ironwood tree, trying to brush herself off. She had ratty brown hair and eyes to match, but a slender waist and quite full hips. She wore shorts under her skirt; even so her legs were impressive. She was probably a couple of years older than I, and looked five years older.

Not that it mattered. I was only just recently noticing such features in girls, and wasn't sure that the new perspective quite compensated for their bossiness. Anyway, girls only laughed at me, if they noticed me at all. So I might as well ignore them back.

I brought my armful and set it down before her. "Oooo, wonderful!" she exclaimed, delighted. "This is just perfect!"

Foolishly numbed by this unexpected praise, I said nothing.

"Sit down," she urged. "We must eat this before it spoils."

Why was I so glad to comply?

She started in. The girl had the ability of her kind to eat and talk simultaneously. "We've never been introduced," she said somehow while

chewing a chunk of cherry pie. "My name is MareAnn. My talent is summoning equines and making them mind. What's your name and talent?"

"I'm Humfrey. I—I don't seem to have a talent."

"You mean you haven't discovered it yet?"

"That must be what I mean." No one *had* to have a magic talent, but
the great majority of folk did, and I felt somewhat out of sorts.

"Well, it will surely turn up. I'm fifteen. How old are you?"

I gaped. "You're that young?"

"Of course I am! What about you?"

"I'm—I'm fifteen too."

She glanced hard at me. "You're that old?"

"Of course I am," I echoed weakly in the face of her disbelief.

"Oh, you're a gnome," she said.

"No, I'm human. Just gnomelike."

"Oh. I'm sorry." But she didn't seem sorry, she seemed doubtful. She
didn't want to question my word, so she was stuck in an awkward mode. I
understood exactly how it was.

After a bit, she looked around. "Is there any water near here? I mean
a lake or river, so we can clean up? You have dirt on you, and I must be a
total sight."

"I passed a river a way back. But you wouldn't want to clean up with
me there."

"Of course I would!" she said in her emphatic female way. "Or have I
delayed your schedule too much already?"

"Schedule?"

"You are going somewhere, aren't you? And you'd be just about there
now, if it wasn't for me and Horntense?"

"Oh. No. I was just going away from the Gap Village, nowhere in particular."

"The what village?"

"The Gap. You know, the chasm."

"No, I *don't* know! What chasm?"

Then I remembered: there was a Forget Spell on the Gap Chasm. I
lived right beside it, so was immune, or so I then believed, but she was
from elsewhere, so hadn't heard of it or had forgotten it if she had. That
was the nature of the ancient spell. It was pointless to tell her much about

it, because she would only forget it again. "Just a big crevice. It doesn't matter. My village doesn't matter either. It's just sort of there. I want to go somewhere more interesting."

"Well, where I came from is just as dull! Our village in on the bank of the Sane Jaunts River, and the only interesting things there are the dragons, and they're dangerous. Don't I know! That flying dragon almost got us. I thought we were beyond their territory, and relaxed, but evidently not."

"Nowhere in Xanth is beyond their territory," I said. "I thought maybe there would be fewer of them the way I was going."

"Are you kidding? It's Dragons Galore country!"

I was dismayed. "I guess I'm going the wrong way, then."

"Well, then, turn about and go with me. I'm not going anywhere either, just away from home."

"You want to travel with me?" I asked incredulously.

"Well, you did help me, and you seem harmless. I have found that traveling alone isn't much fun, and it's sometimes dangerous. If Horntense hadn't managed to spear that dragon with her horn before it got us, we could both be dead now. And you seem to know so much. I mean, you got the boneset plant and the pies and all. You're a real blessing to a girl in distress!"

I couldn't help it: I was getting to like MareAnn. I couldn't believe she was only my age, but why should she lie? It was true she was bossy, but less so than I was used to, and it really wasn't bothering me much now. "Well, if you want to," I agreed, trying to make it sound somewhat more reluctant than it was. In those inexperienced days I cared what others thought of me.

"I will summon you a unicorn," she said brightly. She put her fingers into her mouth and made a piercing whistle.

"But—"

In a long moment, there was the sound of galloping hoofs. Then a unicorn stallion appeared.

"Help me stand," MareAnn said.

I put my hands on her shoulders awkwardly and tried to lift her, but it didn't work. Then she reached up with her arms and I took her hands and pulled, and she came up smoothly. She winced as her bad ankle took weight, and leaned on me. She was taller than I, and fuller in the chest and hips, but not actually heavier because her waist was smaller.

The unicorn slowed to a walk as he burst into the glade. He approached our party cautiously. I watched him with similar caution; if a unicorn horn could spear a dragon, it could do the same to me. "Uland, this is Humfrey," MareAnn said. "Humfrey, this is Uland Unicorn. He will be your steed for now."

"But I don't know how to ride a unicorn—or anything else!" I protested.

"Oh, you don't need to know how. Unicorns are magic. Uland will teach you."

I remained dubious. "The—the river isn't far. Why don't we just walk?" But as I spoke I realized that that wouldn't do for her. "Or maybe you should ride Uland, and Horntense and I will walk."

"Yes, I suppose that is better," MareAnn agreed. "Help me up, then; he's too tall for me to mount readily."

Again I was somewhat at a loss. How was I supposed to put her up on the steed? Heave up on her hips?

"Like this, silly," she said. She bent her left leg at the knee. "Lift on this."

Feeling hopeless, I took hold of her leg, avoiding the injured ankle. I lifted—and she heaved and suddenly swung up on the unicorn's back. She had somehow braced against me and done it, and I hadn't quite seen it happen.

She looked down at me and laughed. "You don't have much experience, for sure!"

"Well, I never claimed to," I said, nettled.

She was immediately contrite. "I'm sorry, Humfrey. You just looked so startled it was comical. Please, I don't want to offend you. You are helping me a lot. I like you."

This time I felt myself blushing. She had apologized to me, complimented me, and said she liked me. That was a bigger dose of positive expression than I had ever had from a girl before.

She must have noticed, but she didn't comment. That was a relief. My sister would have baited me unmercifully, trying to make me blush worse, and probably succeeding.

I set off down the path toward the river I had passed. Horntense limped along behind me.

"I wish I knew where there was a healing spring," I said. "You and Horntense could certainly use it."

"A what?" MareAnn asked.

"A healing spring. Our village elder has a vial of healing elixir which he traded for last year, and when someone is injured, we use a drop of that. But those who know where such springs are keep it secret."

"Why?"

"So they can make gouging trade deals with others."

"That's disgusting!"

I turned to face her. "That's the way it is. But if I knew where one is, I could get some elixir and make you and Horntense better."

"Say, I'll bet the unicorns know!" MareAnn exclaimed. "They can't tell us, *of* course, but maybe Uland would take you there."

"But—" I said, and at the same time the unicorn stallion snorted.

"Now stop that, both of you!" MareAnn said severely. She had the typically femalish talent for spot severity. "You don't want to ride, Humfrey, and Uland doesn't want to show you where the spring is. But we can work this out."

"He knows where it is?"

"Yes. Didn't you see Uland twitch his ear yes when I mentioned it? But unicorns don't share secrets with our kind, for which I can't blame them."

I hadn't seen. I would have to learn the equine signals! "Maybe we could give Uland a bottle, and—" But I saw that it wouldn't work. The unicorn had no way to hold the bottle.

"Look, Uland," MareAnn said. "It would really be a big help to Horntense and me if we could get some of that healing elixir. We're both in pain, even if we don't make a big thing of it. Suppose Humfrey swears never to reveal to anyone else where the spring is; would you take him then?"

Uland flicked his tail.

"He wants to know whether you are to be trusted," she translated.

"Well, I don't know," I said. "I mean, yes, I keep my word, but I don't know how he would know that."

"He can tell. But it's dangerous."

"Dangerous?"

"When a unicorn tests someone, it's pass or fail. You either pass, or you're dead."

I was dismayed. "I don't want to die! Suppose he makes a mistake?"

"Unicorns don't make that kind of mistake. So if you agree to be tested—"

I gulped. "Well, all right. But I hope he knows what he's doing!"

MareAnn slid down off the unicorn's back. She hopped to Horntense and braced against her. "Okay, Uland."

The stallion advanced on me. I stood my ground, not at all bravely. He lowered his horn so that it bore directly on my chest. With one shake of his head he could stab me through the heart!

"Now make your statement," MareAnn said.

"My what?"

"Your agreement not to reveal the location of the spring to any other person."

Oh. "I will not tell or show any other person where the healing spring you take me to is," I said, somewhat awkwardly.

Uland thrust his head forward. The horn plunged through my heart.

Then it was out—and I stood there, feeling nothing. Except a burgeoning dose of panic. But it was too late for that. I was done for so fast I had never felt it.

"Uh—" I said, even more awkwardly than before. I made ready to collapse with whatever dignity I could muster.

"You're not hurt," MareAnn said.

I stared down at myself. There was no wound, no blood. "But—"

"You spoke the truth," MareAnn said. "If you had lied, that horn would have felt solid to you. Only truth blunts it."

Now I understood. Weak-kneed, I resolved never to depart from the truth in anything.

"Get on Uland," MareAnn said. "He says it isn't far. We'll wait here."

"But I don't know how!" There was another truth.

She hobbled over. "Bend your leg at the knee."

I stood beside the unicorn and bent my left leg, as she had. She took hold of it. "Now throw your right leg over as I heave."

She heaved, and I lifted my right leg up and over the back of the unicorn. Suddenly I was up there, precariously perched. Her hold had been like a ladder, lifting me up. Now I understood how she had mounted with my help. It wasn't magic, but it was so neat a trick that it might as well have been. "Uh, thanks," I said.

"You're welcome," she said, and smiled up at me.

I felt dizzy. She was so lovely when she did that!

Then Uland was moving. Hastily I grabbed a handful of his mane and hung on. That seemed to be what was required.

I was riding, to my amazement. The unicorn was running like the wind, and this was no cliché; his feet seemed to be striking on air, and he was going right through the forest as the wind does; I saw leaves flutter with our passage. Yet it was perfectly smooth on his back; I might as well have been on a boat on a fairly calm lake.

My fear of riding was quickly becoming pleasure. But I suspected that it would not be like this on a less magical animal. "This is fun, thank you," I said.

Uland wiggled an ear. That meant yes. I wasn't guessing; I found that I really did understand his signals, now that I was riding him. That was surely magic. I had not realized before just how wonderful unicorns were.

Soon we came to a small pond in another glade. It did not look special, but the foliage near it was quite healthy.

Uland stopped, and I dismounted by putting my right leg back over and sliding off on my stomach. MareAnn had done it more elegantly on her backside. Well, I was a beginner, and she had a better backside than I did.

I fished two bottles from my pack, the only ones available. I was sorry they weren't larger; this water would be invaluable. But I would not use it to trade anyway; all I needed was enough for MareAnn and Horntense.

I knelt to dip the first. The bank under my knee gave way, and I tumbled face-first into the pond. The bottles flew from my hand. Realizing what this would mean, I made a desperate grab in air and caught one before I submerged.

The spring was deep. I sank down, down, taking in a mouthful inadvertently. Then I remembered to try to swim, and paddled my way back up.

My head broke the surface, and I choked and gasped. But I had the bottle, and it was full. I pulled myself out, dripping, then fished for the stopper.

My eye fell on Uland. He was shaking with equine laughter. I had to laugh too. I must have looked pretty foolish. I still did, really, for my clothing was dripping and my hair was matted across my face. How clumsy could a gnome like me get?

I put the sealed bottle into my wet knapsack. Then I approached the unicorn. He was still too tall for me to mount from the ground, and MareAnn wasn't here to boost me with her nice little hands. "Maybe if you moved next to a rock," I suggested.

He hooked his nose in the signal for jump.

I shrugged. Anything was worth a try. I jumped—and to my amazement sailed right up and onto his back.

How had that happened? I had never before been able to jump like that! My small gnarled legs were only good enough for modest performance. Yet this time they had responded like those of an athlete, and my coordination had been perfect.

Uland was racing like the wind again. By the time I stopped being bemused, we were back at the path where MareAnn and Horntense waited.

I slid down, this time doing it expertly. "I have it!" I said.

"You're all wet!" she exclaimed.

"I fell in," I said, abashed.

"You fell into the healing spring? You must be supremely healthy now!"

And that was it! I had been completely doused in the elixir, even swallowing a mouthful. I was healthy all over. My muscles were working at their full potential. I realized now that I could also see far more acutely than before and hear much better. My whole body bristled with sheer fitness. So leaps which had been impossible were now easy. Uland had known.

I brought out the bottle. "No, save it," MareAnn said. "Just give me your shirt."

I got out of my knapsack and shirt. She took the shirt and wrung it out over her extended leg. A few drops fell on the ankle. "Oh, it's working!" she exclaimed. Then, standing firmly on both feet, she turned to Horntense. She wrung out some more elixir on the unicorn's leg. Immediately Horntense put down the leg, standing without pain.

MareAnn returned the shirt to me. "Thank you so much, Humfrey," she said. "We really appreciate it." Then she kissed me.

I was too stunned even to blush. I felt as if I were floating. An entire new view of girls was dawning on my limited outlook.

"Now let's go on to the river," she said. "I'll ride Horntense; you ride Uland."

Numbly, I held her leg so she could mount. Then I went and jumped onto the stallion. Then we were at the river. I was still trying to realize how I felt from that kiss.

MareAnn jumped down and started stripping off her clothes. "But—" I started. My senses were in perfect health, but my mind was boggling.

She turned to face me, her shirt off. "We have come to know each other well enough in a short time. And we are not going to do anything lascivious. We never have, and we won't now. So it's all right; we can wash together."

"We—not—?" I said, finding no straw to grasp.

"Because the unicorns would go."

Unicorns. Something fell into place. The reason most people could not approach unicorns was that only childlike innocence was acceptable. I was old enough to have the first hint of a notion of what the Adult Conspiracy was concealing, but I had never had occasion to explore the matter. Until I did, I would be able to approach unicorns. That was the way of their kind and ours.

I dismounted and removed my clothing. MareAnn and I swam together in the cool clear river, as naked and innocent as a faun and nymph. But my ungrateful background mind wished it could have been otherwise. MareAnn had been shapely but dirty because of her fall; now she was shapely and clean, and to my eye lovely.

"Why are you staring at me?" she asked naively.

"I never saw anyone so beautiful," I said before I thought.

It was her turn to blush. "No one ever said that to me before. Thank you, Humfrey."

I realized with a pleasant shock that she was indeed my age. Her body was that of a grown woman, while mine was that of a grown gnome, but her experience in life was parallel to mine. It was hard to imagine her being ridiculed for her proportions, but evidently neither had she been praised. She appreciated a sincere compliment just as much as I did. That was a great comfort to know.

Yet I also realized that it was a special type of interest I was finding in her, and that it could in time lead to a good deal more than innocent compliments. But I had the wit to keep that to myself. This wasn't deceit, it was courtesy. And caution.

So we swam, and washed, and then ran around naked while we dried, playing tag and finding fruit and nuts to eat, and it was about as nice an hour as I could remember experiencing. If this was the beginning of the rest of my life, I was well satisfied.

Chapter 4

SURVEY

Now it was near evening. "We had better find a place to sleep," MareAnn said.

I had planned to clamber into a suitable tree for the night. I realized that more was required now. She would never be mistaken for a gnome, and a tree was hardly her style. Somehow this inconvenience did not bother me. "I saw a house a little farther back. Maybe the person who lives there will let us sleep on the floor."

"We can get some pillows and a blanket," she agreed.

We rode the unicorns, and in a moment the distance which had taken me hours was covered, and the house was before us in its small clearing among the weeds. It was such a perfectly ordinary cabin that now I was uncertain. "Sometimes things aren't what they seem," I said.

"But what else can this be but a house?" she demanded. "Do you think it's going to eat us?"

Shamed by her unconcern, I dismounted, approached the house, and knocked on the door. It opened on its own, revealing a fairly nice interior with a table, a chair, and a bed. There was a pile of blankets on the bed and several pillows. That was all. I still did not quite trust it; that self-opening door was magic, and too convenient. Tangle trees made their approaches inviting and seemed harmless—until the unwary creature was lured within their grasp. This obviously was not such a tree, but its manner was similar.

"Where is who lives here?" MareAnn asked, coming up behind me. I liked having her do that, acting like a friend, and her friendship was becoming important to me. In fact, my relationship with her was as devious and intriguing as my concern with this house, for different reasons.

"It seems to be empty," I said. "There's no smell of occupancy." For my nose was now healthy, too, and could detect far more than ever before.

"Then it must be just waiting for someone to live in it," she said brightly. "We'll be here only a night, but it's perfect for that." She pushed on past me and went inside.

I was not sanguine about this, but couldn't let her chance it alone, so went in with her. Nothing happened. Apparently this was indeed a house waiting for an occupant. If it belonged to someone, that person should not mind us using it briefly, if we did no damage. But suppose it did not belong to someone? What then was its purpose? I feared that we could not be sure that its purpose coincided with ours.

MareAnn told the unicorns that we wouldn't need them until morning, and they departed. It had to be nice, having such a magic talent. If only I had something similar!

I looked at the bed. "I'll put some pillows on the floor for me," I said.

"Oh, don't be silly! We'll share the bed, of course."

I certainly had no objection. I was gaining a whole nother perspective on girls. I was getting to like being bossed. I was discovering that it depended very much on which girl was doing the bossing and how I felt about her. MareAnn was bossy in a pleasant and trusting manner.

So she changed into her nightie, which she had in her purse, which like all such items was magical in its own way. A purse always held more than was possible. I knew enough to avert my gaze so as to avoid seeing her panties, as I had when we washed together in the river. It was all right to see a girl bare, if she didn't mind, but panties were something else. At least, so the Adult Conspiracy indicated. I used my undershorts, because nothing else had dried yet, and we squeezed onto the bed under the blankets.

Then MareAnn had a second thought. "You don't know how to summon the stork, do you?"

"No," I admitted.

"Good. Because that's the prime thing unicorns don't like. I'm in no hurry to learn." She settled back.

I, unfortunately, had my burden of curiosity. I did want to know about the stork, and about everything else in Xanth. But it was very nice lying so close and warm with MareAnn, and if not learning the stork-summoning ritual was the price of that, then I too was in no hurry. For now.

"Tell me about yourself," she said.

I was surprised. "But don't you want to sleep? Aren't you tired?"

"Yes, of course. But I like to know something about the person I sleep with."

That seemed reasonable. So I told her what little there was to know about my dull life, and how I hoped to learn everything there was to know about Xanth, someday, maybe, if I was lucky.

The odd thing was, she actually seemed interested. "I think that's very commendable, Humfrey. I'm sure you will learn more about everything than anybody else does." She snuggled against me, relaxing. She was marvelously soft and warm and nice to be next to.

"And—is it all right to learn something about you?" I asked hesitantly.

She laughed. "Why, of course, Humfrey, if you're interested. It's not much. I ran away from home."

"But you seem like such a nice girl!"

"I *am* a nice girl! That's my problem. My father said I was getting pretty grown up for my age, and it was time for me to get married and learn about the stork. He was going to marry me to the village bell maker. But I didn't like the man, because his bells make people stupid."

"Make them stupid?" I asked, feeling that way myself.

"Yes, real dumbbells. Maybe they just make folk unable to speak; I forget. Either way, I wasn't interested. And if I had learned about the stork from him, I would have lost my friends the unicorns. Of course I can summon other equines too, but the unicorns are my favorites. So I ran away."

I was glad she had, now.

"Thank you, Humfrey," she said.

"But I didn't say anything!" I protested.

"Yes, you did. You distinctly twitched your ear. I felt it against my cheek."

I had not realized that I was now using the language of the equines. It must have come from my association with the unicorns and my improved health after my dunking in the healing spring. That could have given me better control of my ears.

"Yes, I'm sure that's it," she said, kissing the side of my head in the manner she might kiss a unicorn.

Magic could be wonderful.

But as the darkness became complete, something alarming happened. The house abruptly tilted.

"*Eeeeek!*" MareAnn cried in perfectly feminine fashion, grabbing onto me.

My first impulse was to leap out of bed and run outside. But I couldn't, because MareAnn was clutching me closely. So I got hold of the edge of the bed instead, in that manner anchoring us both. My first instinct had been wrong, anyway; how could I have deserted the girl beside me?

The floor tilted back, but that was not the end of it. The whole house was rising! I saw the downward movement of trees in the moonlight beyond the window. It was as if a giant were picking up the whole house.

Then things steadied. "I'd better check," I whispered, drawing myself free of her clutch. I loved the close contact, but a deep suspicion was growing in me.

"You're so brave!" she whispered back.

Brave? Not that I knew of! I just was doing what I had to do. I scrambled away from bed and blankets and crossed the floor to the window. As I did, the house began to rock again, almost throwing me off my feet. I lunged to the window and caught hold of the sill, while MareAnn screamed from the bed.

I peered out. Sure enough, the house was in the air. But it was not floating or being carried by a giant. In the dusky deep shadows below I made out an enormous muscular thigh growing out of the side of the house. I didn't need to see more; I knew that this was the upper part of a great powerful leg and that it was a monstrous bird's leg with giant claws on the foot. I had heard of this type of thing but never expected to see it, let alone be *in* it.

The house paused momentarily. I took advantage of the moment to hurl myself back across the room to the bed. The bed, table, and chair were all firmly anchored to the floor; now I understood why.

"What did you see?" MareAnn asked, eagerly grabbing onto me again.

"Chicken legs," I said.

"What?"

"The house has grown chicken legs and is running around. It's a werehouse, It changes its nature at night."

"You mean like a werewolf?"

"Yes, except that it doesn't eat people. It just runs around. It won't hurt us, as long as we hang on."

"But why? I mean, what does it *do*?"

"It just runs around, and in the morning it will settle down in a new place. Maybe it gets its kicks from giving rides to folk like us." I hoped; I wasn't sure that it was quite as innocent as that, but since I didn't know otherwise it was pointless to alarm her.

The house began moving again. Now we could feel the pulse as the powerful legs walked. The whole house shook as each foot struck the ground. We were lucky that our knapsacks were firmly jammed under the bed, so that they didn't slide around.

"I'm getting motion sick," MareAnn said bleakly.

"Um, I wouldn't recommend that," I said. "I'm not sure the house would like having, uh, you know on its floor."

"I'll stifle it," she agreed hastily.

We clung to each other and the bed. There was nothing else to do, as the werehouse charged on through the night. Sometimes it paused to scratch at the ground; sometimes it leaped and landed jarringly. Mostly it just kept going.

"If this were anywhere else, I'd really enjoy spending a night like this with you in my arms," I said at one point.

"I wonder if stork-summoning can be worse than this?" she mused.

"I hope not!" Then we laughed, somewhat sickly.

I don't know how much sleep either of us got, but we did succeed in not getting sick. In the morning the house settled down, and we made haste to get out of it, not even dressing. At least it had not harmed us; I had been right to avoid alarming MareAnn with my fell suspicion. We carried our knapsacks and clothes bundled in our arms.

We found ourselves in the middle of an unfamiliar village. The folk were just getting up and out. They stared at us. Evidently they hadn't seen the house settle into place, but they saw us clearly enough, in underpants and nightie and generally disheveled. The unicorns were not present; they probably had no idea where the house had gone. Neither did we.

"Uh, where is this?" I inquired in my typically bright fashion.

"This is the South Village," the nearest man said. "How did you get your house built so quickly? It wasn't here last night. And aren't you two rather young to be indulging in that sort of sport? Are you sure you belong to the Adult Conspiracy?"

I exchanged most of a glance with MareAnn. Then we turned as one and went back into the house. It would remain fixed in the day; we had been foolish to run out unprepared. I had resolved always to tell the truth, but I was discovering that there were occasions where the truth was nobody else's business. It was a realization I would remember later in life when folk would pester me for information.

Inside, we dressed. I turned my back so as not to see her don her panties. MareAnn brought out a comb and sorted out her hair, and then mine. Actually, I thought she looked intriguing in her wild style, but this was good too, and I liked the way she fussed over me. That was another truth best left unsaid, since it behooved me not to prejudice her valuable innocence.

"Do you know anything about the South Village?" she asked me.

As it happened, I did. "That's where King Ebnez lives."

"The King?"

"He assumed the throne in the year 909. He has been King for almost forty years. His talent is adapting magic things. He adapted the Death-stone to the Shieldstone, to stop the Waves, so we don't get invaded anymore."

"I knew that! I mean, this is the capital city?"

"There are no cities in Xanth. This is the capital village."

"What are we doing here?"

"It's where the werehouse brought us. Well south of the Gap."

"South of the what?"

"The—well, I don't exactly remember." This was my first experience with the action of the Forget Spell, because I had now been far and long enough away from the Gap to lose my immunity. "Anyway, it's in southern Xanth, and I fear it will be a long, hard trek to return to the north. Can your unicorns find you here?"

"Not the same ones. But maybe it doesn't matter. We wanted to travel, to get away from our situations. Well, we traveled farther and faster than we expected. Let's make something of it."

"Something of it?" I asked blankly.

"Let's go visit the King. Maybe he will have something for us to do."

"But I don't know how to do anything!"

"Yes, you do. You're very good at finding useful things."

"But that's hardly a profession!"

"And I will keep house for you and help keep you warm at night."

Suddenly I found myself persuaded.

So we went to visit King Ebnez. As it happened, he was at home and not busy, so he welcomed the company. He was a portly man in his sixties, with impressive sideburns under his crown. He treated us to a very nice breakfast of greenberries from the greenberry fields and marshmallows fresh from the mallow marshes.

"And what is your business here?" he inquired after we had pretty well stuffed ourselves.

"Humfrey would like employment," MareAnn said immediately.

"Oh? And what is your talent?"

"Curiosity," she said.

The King turned a bland eye on her. "And what is yours, pretty miss?"

"Summoning equines," I said.

Ebnez nodded. "So you would be able to travel readily."

"Yes," MareAnn agreed. "And I will travel with him, to keep his socks dry." I realized that she did not want to remain in a strange village alone for fear that some man might get the notion she was marriageable.

"To be sure," the King agreed. His gentle gaze returned to me. "As it happens, I have need of a surveyor."

"You mean, to find out things about people?" I asked, hardly believing my luck.

"Yes. That is why I asked the werehouse to bring in good prospects. Your talent of curiosity is a good recommendation, and your wife's talent complements it nicely."

"Oh, she's not my wife!" I said, surprised.

"Not yet," MareAnn said quickly. She was not about to let a good job slip away on a technicality or to let strangers think she was unattached. I might have objected, but found I had nothing to which to object. The thought of spending more time with her appealed, even if it did seem likely to compromise her innocence.

In this manner I became the Royal Surveyor. It was to be a more significant position than I realized at first.

It was an excellent job. MareAnn summoned winged horses for us to ride, and that was a marvelous experience in itself. We flew up high above the South Village, and the villagers gaped, thinking I must be a Magician to compel the service of a woman who had such power. MareAnn, for her own reason, did not discourage this impression; she wanted folk to believe that I had powerful magic. I didn't like this seeming misrepresentation, for honesty still seemed to me to be the best policy, but she pointed out that I was not being dishonest, I was merely being polite by failing to disabuse others of their errors. So we compromised: if anyone asked, I replied that I was no Magician. If anyone didn't ask, I didn't volunteer the information. It was much the same with respect to our mutual status as nonmembers of the Adult Conspiracy.

I spent some private time pondering the shades-of-gray ethics involved, and concluded that it was not properly my business what others thought. If there was a foible, such as in the manner a village girl made herself seem beautiful by applying charcoal to her eyebrows and redberry juice to her lips, it was not my place to expose it unless I was specifically asked. It was best to leave folk with their illusions, of whatever nature, especially if I wanted to get along with them. This developing attitude of mine stood me in excellent stead in the course of my work, because *I* needed the cooperation of all whom I encountered.

My job was to survey all the human folk of Xanth and to compile a list of their magic talents. The King was especially interested in the more powerful talents; in fact he hoped to turn up some Magician-caliber talents in young folk who might be potential kings, since only a Magician could be king. At present none was known, and Ebnez was getting old. He was sixty-six and not in perfect health. I offered him some of the healing elixir I had, but he declined; he did not trust drugs. I disagreed, believing that anything beneficial should be used, but it was not my place to argue with a King. So I concentrated on doing my job, and kept my opinion to myself. That, too, was an excellent discipline.

I started with the southern tip of Xanth and worked my way north. There were not a great many people in the peninsula, but they were scattered across it and were hidden in glades and crannies, so it was slow work. I knew that if I missed even one, that one might turn out to be the Magician Ebnez was looking for, and so I would have failed the major purpose of my survey. So I didn't expect it to be easy, but it turned out to be more difficult in several ways than I had anticipated. Let me describe the first example of many.

We flew down past the dread region of madness, and I shivered to think that I would have to survey that too, in due course. We passed Lake Ogre-Chobee, as wide and shallow as an ogre's mind, and Mount Rushmost where the winged monsters gathered. Then on past Mount Parnassus where the fabulous Tree of Seeds grew. There I had my second qualm: would I have to interview the Maenads, the wild women who roved its slopes? I feared I would, for it was not safe to assume that they had no magic other than blood lust. Then we were over the Ever-Glades; which stretched on forever, as it was their intent to lose anyone who ventured into them. It was wise never to underestimate the perversity of the inanimate. Finally we came to the coast, and flew beyond it to Centaur Isle.

We landed in the central square of the main centaur city. An elder of the centaurs trotted out to meet us. He was a powerful figure of man and horse. "Partbreeds are not welcome here," he said gruffly.

"But I'm doing a survey," I said.

"We don't care what you're doing. Two of you are human and two of you are winged horses. You are all partbreeds, and we prefer to keep our isle pure. Please depart at your earliest convenience."

I was baffled by this attitude. The centaurs I had encountered on the mainland were reasonably sociable creatures if treated with respect. "I'm doing it for the King of Xanth," I said. "He wants to know the magic talent of every person in the peninsula."

"Centaurs have no magic," the centaur said coldly. I saw that I had inadvertently added insult to ignorance.

Fortunately MareAnn had quicker wits than I. "We know that, sir. But we thought that there may be among you some inferior humans, and if we can survey them quickly, we can soon begone, and the King will be satisfied and no one will bother you again."

The elder turned an appraising eye on her. MareAnn smiled at him.

I mentioned illusion: when she smiled, she seemed to become twice as pretty as she was. It is an effect I have since noticed in others, too: incidental magic, independent of their particular talents. Seated on the winged horse as she was, in that moment she rather resembled a fetching lady centaur. Had I been the object of that smile, I would have melted halfway into the ground. The elder was too haughty to go to that extreme, but he couldn't help softening somewhat at the edges. After all, he was part equine, and she had power over equines, making them want to do her will. "There are a few servants among us," he conceded. "Very well: I shall assign Chrissy to guide you during your brief stay here."

Chrissy Centaur trotted up at the elder's signal. She was a lovely creature of about our own age, with hair that trailed back from her head and merged seamlessly with her mane. Her full bare breasts were impressive in the human manner, and her brown hide was nice in the equine manner. I could see that the winged horses were admiring her flanks in much the same manner I was admiring her forepart. Centaurs wore no unfunctional clothing, and they considered modesty unfunctional. "Hello," she said shyly.

"Hello," MareAnn and I said together.

"Show them our humans," the elder said, and trotted off.

"Oh, how nice to have someone visit our humans!" Chrissy said. "I'm sure they get lonely sometimes here."

Thus my survey commenced. The few men and women on the isle were indeed servants, and their talents were minimal: what are called the spot-on-a-wall variety. Some magic is truly potent, such as the ability to shatter a big rock into a thousand parts. Some is next to nothing, such as making a faint discoloration appear on a wall. Most human beings have magic, but few have strong magic, and the folk here were evidently the ones who had nothing better to do than serve centaurs. They cleaned out stalls and swept off roofs and did the other things that were beneath the dignity of centaurs, and seemed as satisfied as might be expected.

But in the way of servants, they knew secret things, and one thing they said gave me a peculiar doubt. "You know, the centaurs say they have no magic," a scullery maid confided when Chrissy Centaur was off rounding up another human. "But I think they do; they just won't admit it. They think that the possession of a magic talent is obscene."

That was one of the ironies of the centaur persuasion. Centaurs performed natural functions of all types freely in public, having no sense of modesty about them. But magic was something they girt about with social restrictions. They tolerated it in what they considered to be inferior creatures, and did use magic objects, but that was the limit. Any person who wanted to remain on an amicable footing with centaurs learned, as I did, to honor this foible scrupulously.

If the centaurs had magic talents, then I should be listing those too! But if they refused to admit it, how could I? Was my survey impossible to complete properly?

This ushered in another notion. I had been thinking only of full human beings—but what of the crossbreeds? Centaurs weren't the only ones. What about the harpies and merfolk and fauns? In fact, what about the elves and ogres and goblins? They were all human in their distant fashions, and might have magic talents.

Just how big was this survey likely to become?

Well, in a few days we flew back to the South Village and I made my first report to King Ebnez. "So do you want to try to question all the part humans too?" I inquired.

The King pondered. "I doubt that the human population would accept a part-human king at this time. So perhaps you should query only the full humans specifically, but make incidental note of the others as you come across them. It could be advantageous to know more thoroughly what other creatures inhabit Xanth and of what magic they might be capable."

That seemed like an excellent compromise to me, and my respect for King Ebnez's judgment grew. His four decades of kingship had evidently taught him something.

Still, it was a busy enough time. I discovered that asking questions of people was only the easy part of it. First I had to find them, and to protect myself from problems along the way. I learned caution when we entered the Ever-Glades, thinking that I had memorized the pattern of geography there, and promptly got lost. Only the fact that we could fly up out of them saved us, and even that was chancy because an evil cloud moved in and made a storm, forcing us to remain for several cold wet hours on the swampy ground with encroaching allegories and hypotenuses and other dangerous creatures. I really didn't mind hugging MareAnn for warmth, but the horses were annoyed because their wing feathers got soaked.

Then there was Mount Parnassus. I concluded that the Maenads were human beings, so should be surveyed, but I knew it was dangerous to approach them, because it was their notion to eat stray men. How could I safely handle this?

"Maybe if you stay on the horse," MareAnn suggested, "and take off the moment they charge?"

"Too risky. I understand they can move very quickly when they're hungry, and they're always hungry."

She nodded agreement. We would have to think of something else.

Meanwhile we checked a human settlement near the base of the mountain. It turned out to be the supply depot for the temple of the oracle, near a cave or vent from which magic vapors issued. Young woman called Pythia sniffed these vapors and uttered sheer gibberish, which the priests then interpreted to answer the questions of visitors. Sometimes the great python" forgot himself so far as to eat one of the Pythia, and then a replacement was needed, and so another girl would come from the village. They really weren't eager for such employment, but it was, as they put it, the only game in town, and their families needed the favor of the folk of Mount Parnassus. The average family of Xanth at this time was peasantly poor, as befitted the latter stage of the Dark Age. Any way to gain sustenance was grudgingly welcome, especially when the local fruit and berry patches were picked out and pie trees were between pies.

That gave MareAnn an idea. "Why don't we go ask the oracle?" she asked. "If the answers are always accurate, when duly interpreted, we can find out how to survey the Maenads."

I wasn't sure about this approach, but she smiled at me and as usual I went along with her. She was learning to use her innocence effectively. So we flew to the palace of the oracle. It was nice enough looking, though in disrepair, with a number of stones fallen. It was actually at the base of Mount Parnassus, but neither the Maenads nor the python seemed to be around at the moment, to our relief.

We talked with the head priest. "Certainly we can answer your Question," he said confidently. "What will you proffer in payment?"

"Payment?" For a moment I was blank.

"Surely you did not expect to achieve this valuable information for nothing?"

I had indeed had some such notion, but hesitated to admit it. "What do you normally charge?"

"What do you have?"

I didn't like the direction this was going. "I don't really have anything. I'm just trying to do a survey for the King."

"What manner of survey?"

"I am cataloging all the human talents of Xanth."

"Now that is interesting," he said, stroking his beard. "You will surely pick up much incidental information."

"Yes, quite a bit. But—"

"Suppose we do it on commission?"

"On what?"

"We shall give you your Answer. In return, you will give us half of what you profit from it."

"Half of my information?"

"Exactly. More specifically, you will share what you learn with us. That can be interpreted as all your benefit, but also as nothing, because you retain what you share. It seems fair to call it an equal measure."

I looked at MareAnn. "Does this make sense to you?"

"It seems like a big price for one Answer," she said. "But if you keep all you share, then it's not a painful price. Still, I distrust it. Let's put a time limit on it."

"A time limit!" the priest said, shocked.

Somehow that made me feel better. "One year," I said.

"Ten years," he responded instantly.

So he would bargain. I knew how to do that. We pulled back and forth, and wound up where we both knew we would: five years. It still seemed expensive, but at least it wasn't forever. I really appreciated MareAnn's caution.

So the Pythia, a girl very like the ones we had interviewed in the village, took her perch over the fuming crack in the mountain, and I stepped up and asked my Question: "How can I interview dangerous folk without danger?" For it occurred to me that there might be awkward interviews elsewhere than Parnassus. I figured I might as well get as much for my Answer as I could.

The maiden took *a deep* breath of fume and kicked her legs so that her skirt lifted in a manner that made me that much more eager to get into the Adult Conspiracy. She let out a stream of indecipherable whatever, punctuated by expressions I didn't catch. Maybe I would have understood it better if my attention hadn't been partly distracted by those legs. The priests then made notes and conferred privately. After a bit they emerged to give me my interpreted Answer: "Demon conquest."

I had somehow expected something else. "What do demons have to do with this?"

"We don't know," the priest said. "We merely know that this is the Answer you sought. Do not forget to pay for it."

For this I had yielded a share of all my information for the next five years? "I don't even know whether I'm supposed to beat a demon, or the demon is supposed to beat me," I complained.

"That is a matter of indifference to us," the priest said. "Now please clear out; there may be another client on the way."

We mounted our horses and took off. MareAnn was no better pleased than I. Perhaps she had noticed me looking at the Pythia's legs. MareAnn's own legs were just as good, of course, but in her innocence she made no secret of them, so they were less exciting.

We returned to the village for the night. "How was it?" the villagers asked.

"They told me 'demon conquest,'" I said angrily. "For this I have to give them all my information for five years."

Heads nodded. "That is the kind of bargain they drive."

"Why didn't you warn me that their Answer would be no good?"

"But it *is* good! It is only your understanding that is bad. Once you understand it, it will help you a lot."

"Well, right now we need a place for the night," I said sourly.

"I have a spare bed for you and your wife," a matron said. "And feed for your horses, if you will have them give my children *a* ride."

I looked at MareAnn. She nodded. "Done."

The children squealed with delight as the horses took them up over the trees and around. But I saw tears in MareAnn's eyes.

When we were alone in the bed I asked her about that, for she was normally cheerful. "I would like to have children like that," she said. "I never realized how appealing they are when they're having fun."

"But you can have children," I said. "All you have to do is—"

"Summon the stork," she finished bleakly. "And lose my unicorns."

We weren't using the unicorns now, but I appreciated her point. She faced a most expensive trade-off. I knew how painful that could be, now.

I put my free arm around her. "I'm sorry, MareAnn."

She wept into my shoulder, and I felt very protective. The price of innocence was becoming apparent.

Chapter 5

DANA

A shape loomed. "Excuse me, please."

"I think you have the wrong room," I said, annoyed by the interruption. "This bed is occupied." I had never really liked cold nights before, but now I delighted in them, for they brought MareAnn innocently close for warmth. A third person in the bed would have been too much warmth, however.

"You are the one who went to the oracle today?" It was a girl; I could tell by the dulcet voice. My irritation, surprisingly, began to fade. Perhaps more warmth would be satisfactory.

Still, I kept my voice reasonably sharp. "Yes. But right now we prefer not to converse with others."

"And they told you something about demons?"

MareAnn tuned in to the proceedings. "Who are you?"

"I am Dana. I may be able to help you interpret that Answer."

Suddenly both of us were interested. We sat up in the bed, making room for another. "How so?" I asked.

She sat beside me. It was mostly dark, but I could tell by the way she shifted her weight and the touch of her thigh against mine and her musky perfume that she was an attractive woman. If only I had a better notion what a grown man might do with such a creature! "I know something about demons."

"You know what 'demon conquest' means?" MareAnn asked eagerly.

"No, but I can inquire if you wish."

"How can you do that?"

"I know the demons. They will tell me if they plan to conquer anything soon."

"You know demons?" I asked. "Aren't they mean folk?"

"They can be," Dana agreed. "But they can't hurt me."

"Why not?" I asked, becoming quite curious about this strange woman.

"Because I am a demoness myself."

MareAnn and I jumped. "You?" I asked, now trying to edge away from her. A demon or demoness could assume any form, including that of a person, but that did not mean that there was any other resemblance to a person. Demons were completely callous to the welfare of living folk. "We don't seek any quarrel with you!"

"Nor I with you," Dana said. "You see, I have a problem, and I thought we might be able to help each other."

"How can a demoness have a problem?" I asked, marveling at how much like a living person she seemed. Her body was warm, not cold, and solid rather than vaporous. This was my first direct contact with this species, and it was surprising me in unexpected ways. "You can assume any shape you desire, and you don't have to eat or sleep unless you want to."

"My problem is that I have a conscience."

"But demons don't have souls, so they can't have consciences," I protested. "I mean, they are made of soul material, so maybe it's bodies they lack, but the effect—" I broke off, because it was pointless to babble about the nature of demons to a demoness. She would quickly discover how little I knew about her kind.

"I have a soul."

"But—"

"I don't know how it happened. Maybe a soul got loose from a mortal, and I got caught in it or it got caught in me. I was a normal carefree female demon, and then suddenly I wasn't, because I was concerned about right and wrong. I could no longer play the demon games, because many of them aren't nice. So I went to the oracle to ask how to get rid of the soul, and the priest made me bring a basket of precious stones from the earth in payment, and then they told me that I would have to marry the King of Xanth."

"Marry the King!" I exclaimed. "Ebnez would never marry a demoness! Demons have been banned from association with kings ever since one messed up King Gromden in the seventh century."

"Yes, the Answer does not seem to be of much use to me," Dana said sadly. "I thought if I helped you, you might tell the King I'm not such a bad sort, and maybe he would change the rule and—"

I shook my head. "King Ebnez is a very righteous man. I could tell him, but there's really no hope of—"

"That is all I can ask of you: to tell him," she said. "In return I will do anything you want, provided it does not violate my conscience."

"How do we know you really have a soul?" MareAnn demanded. "I mean, demons can't be trusted about anything."

"Maybe a unicorn could tell if she's innocent," I said.

Dana laughed. "I'm not innocent! I was a normal demoness for centuries before I got souled. I couldn't get near a unicorn."

"Well, we can't afford to trust you without proof," MareAnn said.

"There's a soul sniffer in the North Village," Dana said. "I will fly there with you, if you wish."

"Exactly how can you help us?" I asked. The North Village was a long way away, and this might just be a demon ruse to make us waste our time with a long trip or to lure us into some trap. "It will have to be more than just asking the demons whether they plan to attack."

"I understand you are doing a survey."

"Yes."

"And that you expect trouble trying to talk with the Maenads."

"Yes. That's why we went to the oracle."

"I could assume your likeness and question the Maenads, or anyone else you wish. They can not hurt me."

Suddenly she was making sense! "Let's go to that magic sniffer, tomorrow," MareAnn said. "If Dana proves out, she can be a big help."

So it was decided. The demoness faded out, and we slept, warmly. Next morning we mounted the horses and flew swiftly north, and Dana paced us in the form of an extinct reptilian bird, needing no steed. She resumed human form when we landed, so that no one would know her for what she was.

There was indeed a soul sniffer at the North Village, which was in other respects a thoroughly unremarkable hamlet. But it wasn't a person or animal, as I had expected; it was a place. "Go down the path to the west to the Key Stone Copse," the village elder told us. "There is a key there which only a person with a soul can use to open the door."

"That's all?" I asked. "Just a door?"

"Just a door," the man agreed.

"What's beyond it?"

"We're not sure."

"You're not sure?" I found this hard to believe. "Haven't you gone there to see?"

"There used to be a nice valley with wonderful orangeberry patches; our women and children went often to pick them. But the last three who went, two months ago, did not return. We fear that the door has become one-way, so we are now staying clear of it."

"But maybe those folk are in trouble!" I said. "Someone should go and see!"

He merely shrugged and turned away. So much for community spirit.

"Sometimes I wonder whether souls are as positive as they are supposed to be," MareAnn muttered. "Maybe his has gotten old and worn."

We rode the horses along the path to the west. Soon we came to a dense thicket whose trees and thorny branches were so tangled that we could not see through, and certainly could not pass. The only possible way through was a stone door set in it. On a hook on the door hung a large wooden key.

I lifted the key from its hook, and paused. "Suppose they only *think* this is limited to folk with souls? Maybe anyone can use it, and it's no real test."

"Oh, it's valid," Dana said. "All the demons know of it."

"But you're a demon, and you could be lying—no offense," I said.

"No offense," she agreed. "I could bring a friend to test it—another demoness."

I wasn't sure about this, but had nothing better to offer. I replaced the key. "Do it."

She disappeared. In a moment she reappeared. Beside her was another demoness, who was just as shapely in her human form. Male demons, I understood, delighted in horrendous fearsome forms, while female demons preferred voluptuous partly clothed forms. My experience was confirming the latter case. "This is my friend Metria," Dana said.

"I'm not your friend!" Metria protested. "Demons don't have friends!"

"Demons without souls don't have friends," Dana said. "Perhaps I should say that I am your friend, because I will not betray you, but you are not my friend, because you will betray me in the normal demon fashion."

"That's right," Metria agreed. "How can you look at your cat in the mirror, talking like that?"

"Look at my what?"

"Your feline, tiger, tom, kitty—"

"My puss?"

"Whatever. You aren't talking like a demon at all!"

"Yes. But I'm trying to get rid of my soul by helping these good human folk. I appreciate your coming here to—"

"I came only because there's a chance to make fools of you and these mortal idiots. I love a good laugh at someone else's expense."

Dana turned to me. "I chose D. Metria because she always tells the truth, as you can see."

"But how can she be truthful, when she has no soul?" I asked.

"A soul does not necessarily make one truthful," Dana said. "Many human folk are liars. It merely gives them a conscience, so that they suffer when they do wrong."

"Yes, I find that the truth is the sharpest knife with which to cut people," Metria said. "Nothing shakes folks' values like the truth!"

I looked at MareAnn. She spread her hands. It was evident that our values were being shaken.

"Well, let's get on with it," I said. I reached for the key again.

"Wait, we should have the demons try it first," MareAnn said. "It's Dana who is being tested, not us."

Dana reached for the key. "No, Metria should try it first," I said.

"Fine with me," Metria said. She reached for the key. Her fingers closed on it, but passed right through it. "I can't seem to get a tentacle on this thing," she said, disconcerted.

"A what?" I asked.

"Appendage, extremity, limb, mitt, paw—"

"Oh, a hand," I said.

"Whatever. This key is an illusion; I can't touch it at all."

"That's the way it works," Dana said. "I thought you understood."

Metria glared at her. "You may be an old bag of a century or two, but I appeared only a decade or two ago. I never heard of a phantom key."

Dana glanced at us. "She tells the truth about everything except her age. That's not considered lying, in females."

"Of course it isn't!" Metria agreed. "Women have a right to be any age they want."

"That's true," MareAnn said.

I kept my mouth shut, not wanting to admit to having been ignorant about this female privilege.

"Well, *you* try it," Metria said, glaring at Dana.

Dana reached for the key. Her fingers closed oh it. She lifted it from the hook. She brought it down to the lock.

"Wait," I said. "Let me make sure that really is the key." I held out my hand.

Dana gave it to me. I brought it to the lock, inserted it, and turned it. It resisted, seeming to want to come back out of the lock without completing its action, as if there were a spring behind it. I pushed it in farther, and maintained pressure, so as to complete the turn.

The door moved without moving. That is, it fogged out, and I stumbled through, because I had been pushing against the key. In a moment I was through, yet the door remained in place.

I caught my balance and turned back. There was the door. I put my hand against it, and found it solid. The key was gone from my hand.

But there it was, hung up on the hook on this side of the door. It had magically returned after being used.

But if it was now on this side, then what was on the other side? Could only one person be on this side at a time?

I reached for the key—and had to jump back, because Dana Demoness suddenly popped through, colliding with me. It was a painless collision, because she was marvelously well padded in front.

"Oops," she said, and turned to smoke. I smelled her pleasant essence as it brushed by my nose. Then she reformed a bit away. "It changed so fast!"

I knew the feeling. But I had another question. "The key—how could you use it, when it was on this side?"

"It was back on its hook on the other side," she said. "There must be two keys."

"MareAnn's alone with Demetria," I said, starting to be alarmed.

"Metria doesn't hurt folk physically. She does it all verbally or with illusion. She's probably tired of this game now." Dana looked around. "Odd that we can't get through that thicket wall. Normally, solid things are no barrier to demons. There must be special magic here, making it a demon-proof glade."

Then MareAnn stumbled through. I caught her before she fell. "It was so—" she started.

"I know," I finished.

Then the three of us turned to look at where we were. The thicket arched up high overhead, forming a dome that blocked the direct rays of the sun without cutting off the light; brilliance wafted down to touch the ground. On the ground orangeberry bushes grew, covered with fat berries.

"What a lovely place!" MareAnn exclaimed. "Let's eat some berries before we depart."

We walked to the bushes and started picking and eating. Dana did too. "I never realized what fun eating could be," she said. "Of course the food does me no good, so I shouldn't waste it."

"What happens to what you eat?" I asked, my curiosity manifesting again.

"I just hold it inside me as long as I'm solid. When I turn vaporous—" She fogged. "It drops out." Sure enough, a pile of chewed berries plopped to the ground.

We picked and ate with a will. The berries were delicious. Then MareAnn screamed.

"What?" I asked, hurrying over to join her.

She pointed. There, lying half hidden under the bushes, was a collection of bones.

Dana came across. "Oops," she said. "Those are human bones. Now we know what happened to those last three villagers: they died here."

"Are the berries poisonous?" I asked, abruptly horrified for more than one reason.

"Not that I know of," Dana said. "We demons are pretty good with poisons, and I didn't taste any."

"Then what made them die?" MareAnn asked, shuddering.

"Maybe there's an ogre in here," I said, looking around much more nervously than before.

"Let's get out of here," MareAnn said.

We started back toward the door. But there, between it and ourselves, was a pack of ferocious animals. They had the heads of wolves and the bodies of spiders, and were about half man height.

"Wolf spiders!" Dana exclaimed. "They can't hurt me, but they are surely dangerous to you."

"Now we know how the villagers died," I said grimly, feeling for my knife. But it seemed quite inadequate to the defense.

Five spiders advanced in the line. One remained behind to guard the stone door. Evidently they were experienced in trapping prey. Their technique and the bones indicated that.

MareAnn clung to me. "Oh, Humfrey, what can we do? I can't summon the horses here; they can't get in!"

I drew my knife. It seemed even less adequate than before. For one thing, I was no fighter, and for another, the blade was only as long as one of the enemy fangs. Even if I got in a lethal strike, that would stop only one spider.

Could we flee? No, the glade was entirely enclosed. This was an ideal hunting ground for the wolf spiders. We would just have to fight and die, as the villagers had before us. "Stay behind me," I said. "Maybe I'll be able to occupy them long enough for you to sneak to the door." It was an almost futile hope, but the best that offered.

"Oh, Humfrey, I love you," she said.

"You two are acting as if I'm not here," Dana said. "Both of you get behind me."

Numbly, we did so. She assumed the form of a fierce fire-breathing dragon. She swung her head toward the nearest spider and fired out a jet of flame.

But the spider merely leaped aside, and the flame missed. Meanwhile the others closed in from the sides. It was obvious that not even a dragon could stop them all. A dragon could not guard all sides at once.

"A basilisk!" I whispered. "Can you do that?"

"Shield your eyes," the dragon whispered back. Then it became a tiny lizard with wings.

MareAnn and I clapped our hands to our eyes. It was death to meet the gaze of a bask!

But could the demoness actually kill with her glance? Fire was essentially nonmagical, and she could generate that by forming the innards of a dragon, but the death glance was magical, and demons didn't possess that type of magic. If the spiders caught on—

The basilisk hissed and swung its little head toward the spiders. The spiders did several double takes, then scrambled out of the way. The bluff was working!

Then one spider, perhaps a smidgen smarter than the rest, balked. He had seen the demoness, and then the dragon, and then the bask. He was catching on that it might be illusion. If he called the bluff, we would be in trouble again.

Dana-bask glared at him. He met her gaze. He did not die. He opened his wolf mouth to sound the charge.

I took the gamble of my life. I hurled my knife at the creature. I had never been good at throwing, either, but what else was there?

The knife whistled straight and true. It plunged right into the opened wolf mouth and stuck in the throat beyond. I was amazed. How could I have performed such a feat? I was neither a knife fighter nor a thrower. I had made my effort from unwitting desperation. Then I remembered my dunking in the healing spring. I was super healthy now; my body worked perfectly, as it never had before. It did exactly what I wanted it to—and I had wanted it to throw that knife hard and fast into the wolf mouth, striking with the point. I had underestimated my physical capacity.

The spider gave a whine of agony and collapsed.

The others turned to look. They saw their packmate dropping dead.

The basilisk's tiny grim head swung toward the spiders.

They spooked. They almost scrambled over each other in their eagerness to flee. They ran for the thicket wall and jammed into a niche in it.

We followed. There was a twisted passage amidst the thicket, partly between tree trunks and partly between stray stones, that led through to the other side. This was how the wolf spiders had gotten in, bypassing the thorns and the magic door. Once inside, they had made of the protected refuge a hunting ground.

We gathered stray branches and pulled thorny vines into the aperture. We made it tight again, so that no creature could get through. Of course it would be possible for the wolf spiders to clear it out again, but I doubted that they would, because they believed that this was now the hunting ground of a basilisk. The pack would surely hunt elsewhere in the future.

I went to the fallen spider and reached into its terrible mouth and pulled out my gory knife. I wiped it as clean as I could on the ground. Then we went to the door and used the key to exit, one at a time.

"I think you are a pretty brave mortal," Dana said to me. "That was an excellent shot with the knife and exactly what I needed to foster the illusion."

"I think you do have a soul," I replied. "If the key didn't prove it, the way you defended us did. An ordinary demon would have laughed and let the wolf spiders tear us apart."

"True. But I wasn't thinking about the proof of my soul at the time."

"Neither was I."

We smiled at each other. Then MareAnn summoned the winged horses, and we took off for Mount Parnassus.

We proceeded with the survey. Dana didn't even have to assume my form; she merely used the one she was comfortable with, which was an ethereally beautiful young woman, and interviewed the Maenads while we waited at the village. We would not have been able to fly to the Maenads anyway; it turned out that the oracle was as close to the mountain as we could go by air, because the Simurgh, the huge ancient bird who guarded the mountain and especially the great Tree of Seeds, did not permit other flyers there.

The Maenads had only one talent: vicious beauty. That did seem to make sense.

We surveyed the others in the region, and went on. In the following weeks Dana was increasingly helpful, both as interviewer and as guard; things we had feared before were no longer a threat, because it seemed that we had a dragon guarding us. Or worse.

In due course we returned to the South Village, and I made my first substantial report to King Ebnez. "So while there is much of interest in this region of southern Xanth," I concluded, "as yet I have found no Magician-caliber talents."

He nodded gravely. "There is much of Xanth remaining. Write up your report and save it, for the information will surely be useful in the future. Keep doing the survey until all of Xanth has been recorded. You are doing excellent work."

"Thank you, Your Majesty. There is one other thing."

"By all means. You wish riches or power?"

"No, nothing like that! I am getting the only thing I truly crave, which is information. I do have to share it with the oracle, but that turns out to be simple enough, though their Answer was useless to me. No, I have a plea to make for another person, which I fear you will not receive well."

"I will make the effort," he said with a gentle smile.

"A demoness is helping us. She has facilitated my effort greatly, and she saved my life at one point. She has a soul and wishes to be rid of it so that she can revert to the normal nature of her kind. But to do that, she must marry you."

Ebnez had been listening patiently and tolerantly, but at this point his jaw went slack. He coughed. After a moment he recovered himself. "I am afraid that is out of the question. Not only am I disinclined to marry this late in life, there is a proscription against the association of demons with kings, dating from—"

"I told her that, Your Majesty. But I promised to make her plea if she helped me, and she has helped me. She really seems to be a very nice creature."

"Perhaps some day there will be a King who has the confidence to vacate the proscription. It is within the kingly authority. But I am not that one."

"I shall tell her," I said unsurprised.

"Hold," he said in his kingly fashion. "You say she is truly helping you in the survey?"

"Yes. I fear I could not complete it without her."

"And if she receives an absolute refusal, she will have no reason to continue the work?"

"Yes, Your Majesty."

"Then it would not be expedient to turn her down absolutely. I will lift the proscription to the extent of allowing her to appear in my presence, but I will not marry her. Tell her only that I am considering the matter."

"But is that honest, Your Majesty? I mean, if you have no intent—"

"Perhaps she will change my mind. We can not be certain what the future holds."

I realized that this was a good compromise. The King had no intention of marrying Dana now, but perhaps next year he would see it another way. Dana was certainly winsome enough and had a nice personality. "Thank you," I said. "I shall tell her." I had learned another lesson about diplomacy and the ways of getting things done.

I told her. Dana was heartened, if that term could apply to a creature who had no heart. "This is more progress than I feared possible," she said. "I shall continue to help you, and perhaps I can meet the King when you next report to him. I know he has no interest in marrying a stranger."

So it was. We interviewed the fauns and nymphs, and the curse fiends of Lake Ogre-Chobee (I was later to forget about their existence, but that comes later in this narrative), and we penetrated the region of madness and interviewed the folk of the Magic Dust Village. We discovered a truly unusual creature there: a centaurpede, like a centaur but with a hundred pairs of legs. Her name was Margaret, and she was without price when the Dust Villagers had to travel somewhere; they could all ride a single steed. The winged horses were a great help, and the unicorns, and sometimes the sea horses of the ocean, and I loved and needed MareAnn both for the survey and as a man. But of course she valued her innocence, and I understood about that.

But Dana was a great help also, and I liked her too, and she had no compunctions about innocence. "If it weren't for my conscience and the practical matter of unicorns, I would seduce you in a moment," she told me candidly. "I know all about the Adult Conspiracy and could initiate you into it in approximately ninety seconds. But as long as you love MareAnn and she loves you, I will not do it."

"Thank you," I said, somewhat awkwardly. I was getting really curious about the secrets that the adults guarded so rigorously, and such easy access to them was quite tempting. But not if it ruined my relationship with MareAnn.

Meanwhile, we made periodic reports to King Ebnez. I found many interesting things, but no Magician-caliber talents, to our mutual regret. Dana met the King, and was very polite to him, and he was increasingly nice to her. It was possible that he was slowly changing his mind about the prospect of marriage. It was said that a demoness could make a man deliriously happy, if she chose, and Dana was eager to do just that for him. But he worried about appearances and propriety and just what she would do if she succeeded in getting rid of her soul, and remained cautious.

Three years went by, and I aged from late fifteen to early nineteen, and MareAnn did something similar. Dana did not change; demons are pretty much eternal. We tracked down the human folk living near the dragons, and near the centaurs of central Xanth, and near the five great Elements of northern Xanth. We also interviewed elves and goblins, for it turned out that they were of human derivation and had souls, and some did have individual magic talents. My notes were becoming voluminous, and also my collection of useful artifacts. My bottle of healing elixir was only the first of a multitude; I was filling a room with bottles, each containing something magical and moderately wonderful. Whenever King Ebnez needed an item or specialized bit of information, he asked me, and I was increasingly likely to have a vial of something that answered his need. Folk were calling me the Magician of Information, and both MareAnn and King Ebnez prevailed on me to hurt no feelings by disabusing them of this status.

We were in the final stage of the survey, going through the isthmus of northwestern Xanth, when we received a message: return to the South Village at once. Alarmed, we did so.

Our worst fear was realized: King Ebnez was dying. Dana was stricken as much as we were, for she had made a significant impression on him, and it seemed likely that in another year or so he would relent and marry her and allow her to make him deliriously happy after all. That fact that his life was nearing its end didn't matter; it only meant that he had less to lose if he was not satisfied with her delirium. Now it seemed he had waited too long, and her long effort would be wasted.

He insisted on talking to me alone. He smiled when he saw me, and I tried to smile back, but the signs of his demise were on him, and dark vultures perched on the roof of his house. "Please, Your Majesty, let me give you some healing elixir," I urged him. "Then I can go fetch some water from the Fountain of Youth, which I discovered serendipitously in the course of my survey, and that will make you young again."

IIe shook his head feebly no. "You must not give the water of youth to any other person not of your immediate family," he said. "Use it for yourself only. It is not right to interfere with the natural process."

I had to promise. Of course it would be a long time before I had any need of such water myself, considering my excellent health, though I had hoped that MareAnn would take some when she got old. But the word of a King must be obeyed, and besides, he was probably making sense. I would not give either youth elixir or information about the location of the fountain to any person not of my family.

But worse was coming. "Have you found a Magician?"

"No. Not even any talent close to it. You are the only one in Xanth, I think, Your Majesty."

"Then a desperate measure is called for. I shall be dead within the hour, and Xanth must have a king. More particularly, it must have a king who will carry on the proper traditions of the role, and who will continue the good works I have tried to do. We have the potential to bring Xanth out of the Dark Age, if continuity is maintained."

"Yes, it must be maintained," I agreed. The survey was only one of this King's endeavors; he was trying to see that every human being had a reasonable livelihood and was secure from the depredations of trolls and dragons. He was causing enchanted paths to be made, along which folk could walk in peace without molestation. Already it was possible to travel north and south from the South Village a considerable distance safely, and houses were being made along these paths, so that folk could come in to trade in the village without fear. The King hoped that such a network would be extended throughout Xanth eventually, and I liked the idea too. "There is so much good to be done! So you must live to do it, Your Majesty, and just a few drops of elixir—"

"No!" he said, showing uncharacteristic anger. "No, my time is done. Since we have no Magician to assume the throne, we shall simply have to make one. As king, I am the final authority on who is and is not a Magician. In due course we shall have to set up a committee or council of elders for this purpose; that is one of the reforms you shall see to."

"I don't understand, Your Majesty." Indeed, I was perplexed and feared he was becoming incoherent.

"I hereby declare—" he said, and coughed again, worse than before, sounding really bad, "that you are the Magician of Information, and as such the only person qualified to assume the crown."

"But, Your Majesty!" I protested, stunned. "I am not—"

His rheumy eye fixed me with its fading glare. "Do you charge me with lying, Humfrey?"

"No, of course not! The King's word is law! But—"

"Then take the crown. Use it well, until you find another Magician to whom to pass it along."

"But—" I said helplessly.

"Take it!" he said. His withered hand clutched mine. "Promise!"

I was stuck for it. His glare would not let me go. "I promise," I whispered.

Only then did his eyes close and his grip relax. He was dead.

Chapter 6

KING

I emerged from the death chamber carrying the crown in my hands. MareAnn and Dana and the King's attendants stared.

"The King is dead," I said. "I am the new King."

"The Magician of Information. Of course!" an attendant said. "He was grooming you for it throughout."

I looked miserably at MareAnn and Dana. They knew the truth. They could spare me this awful thing by speaking out.

But both bowed their heads. "Your Majesty," MareAnn said. Dana did not disagree. I was indeed stuck for it.

The burial arrangements were routine. In a day good King Ebnez was buried, and his house was mine. But my travail had only begun.

MareAnn approached me. "You must marry," she said. "It is a requirement for kings."

"That is true," I agreed. "And I want to marry you."

There were tears in her eyes. "King Humfrey, I can not. I love you, but I love my innocence more. I must depart, to free you to marry another."

"No!" I cried. "I need you!"

"You need my talent with equines," she said, with much accuracy. "But if you will marry another quickly, then I will stay and serve you."

I realized that to keep her near me, I would have to do as she said. "But who else can I marry?" I asked plaintively.

"Ahem." I looked. It was Dana Demoness.

Suddenly the meaning of the oracle's message came clear. "You have to marry a king! And I had to make a demon conquest. Why did you help me so loyally, Dana?"

"Because I love you, Humfrey," she said. "You did indeed make a conquest of me."

"But you had no idea I would become king! You had nothing to gain by loving me."

"Indeed I did not," she agreed. "And my conscience prevented me from making my sentiment known to you, because I would not want to disrupt your relationship with MareAnn. So I focused on King Ebnez, and I would have married him had he wished and made him deliriously happy, but my true love was always yours. So I had more patience with his slow progress than otherwise, because it gave me a pretext to continue working closely with you."

I had never suspected. MareAnn had been the only woman on my mind; my heart was numb with the shock of her refusal to marry me. I had really appreciated Dana's help, and perhaps had not questioned her motive because I did not want to disrupt the arrangement. *I had* willfully blinded myself to the obvious, and that, I realized, was dangerous. I would have to guard against that in the future, especially now that I was king.

"I suppose your soul enables you to love, as normal demons can not," I said, continuing to work it out. I was also postponing the question of marriage to a demoness, for the moment.

"Yes, friendship and love became possible for me," she agreed. "And I must say, they have their compensations. I was frankly bored much of the time before I got the soul, and sad after I had it, but loving you has made me happy."

I still found this hard to accept. I was of small stature and not handsome, despite my excellent health. I had helped MareAnn when she was injured, and I understood about her need to preserve her innocence, so the love between us seemed natural. But the demoness was a creature as spectacular as she chose to be, capable of impressing even a king. Why should she care about me? "When did—I mean, there must have been some event which—"

"When we worked together to fight the wolf spiders," she said. "We performed so well jointly! You understood how to do it, being very intelligent, and helped me to choose the right form, and then you supported me to make it effective, showing your courage. I felt really good about that, and it was wonderful, because I had never felt either good or bad before. Then at the end you said you thought I did have a soul, though we had both forgotten about that in the heat of the battle, and we smiled at each other. I never smiled at a man without ulterior reason before, or had one smile at me who wasn't looking at my body. We had true understanding and camaraderie, and it was such a thrill, and after that I had a similar thrill whenever I was near you. Maybe that's not love; I haven't had enough experience to know."

She was in her fashion innocent. She was old in the ways of the world, but young in the ways of love. That reassured me. I did need a wife. "Very well. I will marry you." I was as yet not completely certain that this was wise, remaining cognizant of the business about kings and demonesses, but she had certainly done her part and seemed worthy.

"Oh, thank you, Humfrey!" she exclaimed, delighted. "Is it all right for me to kiss you now?"

"Go ahead," MareAnn said, without complete grace. She had told me to marry someone else, but evidently retained feeling for me. That gratified me in a shameful way. "You're betrothed now."

Dana approached me and put her arms around me. She was taller than I was, but so was MareAnn. She brought her face down and put her lips to mine and kissed me. It was quite an experience! I had kissed MareAnn and really liked it, but I realized now that our kisses had been properly innocent. Dana's kiss was improperly experienced. Love might be new to her, but the ways of physical expression were highly familiar. I discovered that not only did she have remarkably soft and pliable lips, she had a tongue, and I had never imagined using a tongue that way. Meanwhile her body was pressing close to me, and her—her front was making my front tingle. I was beginning to get a hint of the kind of delight she was capable of giving a king. My doubt was fading.

I settled into the kingship with perhaps no more than the usual complications. There was a ceremony which the regular attendants got me through, and folk came from wide and far to pay homage and take my measure, and a new wardrobe was made for me. The crown was adjusted to fit my head. No one challenged my credentials as a Magician; apparently they accepted King Ebnez's judgment. Maybe they knew, as he had, that somebody had to be king, and that if there was no Magician, it had to be faked. But this aspect bothered me.

It was MareAnn who brought me to reality on this score. She was always near, because as king I needed to ride in state, and her ability with all equine creatures remained invaluable. So as she introduced me to one of the few regular horses in Xanth, we talked privately.

"I feel guilty—" I began.

"About me? Don't; you asked me to marry you and I declined. The demoness is a good secondary choice."

That, too. "Thank you. But also about the matter of qualification. You know I am no Magician. In fact, I may not have a talent at all."

"King Ebnez said you were the Magician of Information. The King's word is Xanth's law. So that's what you are. You can't change it just because he's dead."

"Yes, but he needed someone to carry on his good work."

"Aren't you going to do that?"

"Yes, to the best of my ability. But it smacks so much of convenience! I believe in the truth, and the truth is—"

"The truth is that you don't know what your talent is. You are smart, and you are curious about everything, and in the course of the survey you have collected more information and more incidental bottles of magic things than anybody else ever had before, and as a result you have more actual power than King Ebnez himself had. If you need to tally up the number of apples available to feed hungry folk, you have only to let your adder out of his bottle and that reptile will add up the total in an instant, and it will be exactly correct. If one of the Monsters Under the Bed outgrows the bed, and even starlight at night is too bright to allow it to come out, you can use the darklight you found in northern Xanth to flash darkness for it to travel to a larger bed. No one else recognized its potential as you did. If a maid loves a man who doesn't love her, you can give her a few drops of love potion from the bottle you had the wit to collect from that love spring we almost stumbled into. Not that it would have made any difference to us; we were already in love." Here she paused, perhaps wrestling once more with her problem of innocence. I knew the feeling. "All this is because you have been constantly in search of knowledge, and have achieved much. Who is to say that this is not your magic talent?"

"But anyone can look for things!" I protested weakly.

"But few can find them. Not only do you seem to find what you look for, you find what you aren't looking for, and recognize it for its potential immediately. So maybe that's a subtle talent—so who says a talent has to be obvious? Maybe you weren't a Magician before but now you are. And so you will continue, as long as others believe it."

She was making amazing sense, for an innocent. "Still—" I ventured with one last effort.

"Can you prove you are *not* a Magician?" she demanded.

I surrendered. I could not. From this time forward, I was the Magician of Information, and my qualms would simply have to find another home. I mounted the spirited horse, and MareAnn told it to make me look good before other folk. It was amazing what being mounted did for my appearance; I actually seemed kingly!

Dana brought me to another type of reality. We were married with due pomp, and she was beautiful as only an infernal female can be. I still loved MareAnn and wished she was the one in the wedding gown, but the knowledge of Dana's love was a considerable compensation, and I was truly curious about the supposed delights hidden by the Adult Conspiracy. In short, I was not exactly suffering.

The first night of our marriage, Dana initiated me into the whole of the Conspiracy, right through the Dread Ellipsis. I had mixed reactions. In one sense, I thought *is that it?* There just didn't seem to be anything worth concealing from anyone. Mainly, it was the rather straightforward act of signaling the stork, and it seemed to me that there ought to be an easier way to do it. But in another sense, it was like entering a land of perpetual wonder. I wanted her to show me the secret again and again, and she did so, and I knew that she had not been bluffing when she spoke of her ability to make a king deliriously happy.

But after that there was a barrier between MareAnn and me, for I was a member of the Conspiracy and she remained innocent. We pretended that nothing had changed, but it had. The love we had for each other became strained and began to cool, and there was nothing we could do about it.

After a time, when I was well established as king and was no longer dependent on her help, MareAnn asked to go to another village to live, and of course I agreed. It was the quiet end of our romance, and it hurt us both. That was the first of my several heartbreaks.

Dana did her best to console me, and she was very good at it, but the underlying sadness remained. I was paying a penalty for being king, and it was not one that others would understand. I had everything except what I had wanted most: a relationship with the woman I loved.

The business of being king was about like the Adult Conspiracy: clothed with immense mystery, grandeur, and aura but rather ordinary in its private realization. It consisted mainly of making long-term decisions about things most folk neither understood nor cared about, like crop rotation, so that the underlying soil was not depleted. "I've grown my cherry pie trees here for a generation!" the old peasant farmer would protest. "Why should I break in a new field from scratch? All I want is a better crop right here." No use to try to explain that there was only so much magic dust in the soil, which the pie trees drew on, and that it was becoming exhausted and needed time to replenish. That was not the kind of concept he could handle. So it had to be an imperious dictate: he would shift locations because it was the will of the King. That sort of nonsense he understood.

It was also largely ceremonial. The King was expected to officiate at celebrations, to cut the tape-worm at the opening of a new magic path and to express regrets when someone died. He also had to maintain a small force of soldiers, in case another Wave should wash in from Mundania, though the Shield guaranteed that there would be no such thing. In practice, it was a system for making employment for young men who were unwilling to forage for themselves. They got to don uniforms and look nice, and they were useful for harassing stray dragons that started bothering villagers. Of course the dragons soon realized that the soldiers were more show than substance, at which point I would have to go there with dragonbane and sprinkle it on the dragon's tail so that he would go away. Dragonbane was such vile-smelling stuff that I had to hold my nose as I uncorked the bottle, but it was worse for the dragon, who would go into uncontrollable fits of sneezing as long as he smelled it. He smelled it as long as any remained on his tail, which meant he would finally fry his own tail to get rid of it, and then he had to retire for a month or two of healing. Experienced dragons fled the moment they saw the bottle. So it was pretty routine, usually. The villagers took it as proof of my power as a Magician, but I knew better.

The truth is, I was soon just about bored into a gourd. Dana Demoness could distract me only so much, delightful as her distractions were. Thus, in the guise of inspecting the kingdom, I traveled. Actually I was resuming my quest for knowledge, searching out oddments along the way, adding to my growing collection. This had the effect of enhancing my power as the Magician of Information, so was a good thing. I listened to the complaints of villagers throughout the kingdom, and did what I could to alleviate them. I was surprised when Dana, who liked to turn invisible and float surreptitiously through villages and eavesdrop on conversations, informed me that I was becoming known as "Good King Humfrey." I really wasn't accomplishing much, but I was listening and responding, and apparently that was more than the folk were accustomed to.

In one village I encountered a young man who was quite smart. Like me, he had a passion for knowledge, but unlike me, he didn't care unduly about magic. The information he craved was historical: he wanted to know everything that had happened through the ages of Xanth. But no one else cared. Well, *I* cared! "I appoint you Royal Historian," I said. "Question the people about past events, and make a compilation of what you learn for the royal records." For this was what King Ebnez had done for me, with my survey of talents, and it had been a great employment. Too bad it hadn't enabled me to find a true Magician to inherit the throne! "Incidentally, what is your name?"

"E. Timber Bram," he said.

So it was that Bram commenced what was to prove a significant effort. He was the one who defined the dates of Xanth that I have used here. By his reckoning, I became king in the year 952, when I was nineteen years of age. Very well; I would note the dates of the subsequent events of my life. It provided a kind of framework that hadn't been there before. I was proud of instituting this, but I knew that no one else would care. People were so uninterested in dates that the task of keeping the holiday calendar had finally fallen on the ogres, who were too stupid to get out of it. Fortunately no one cared to argue about errors with ogres, so there were few complaints.

About two years into my kingship, Dana had news for me. "I tried to prevent it, Humfrey, but you were simply too healthy."

"Of course I'm healthy," I said. "I fell in the healing spring. If there is anything I have done which you regret, tell me and I will undo it."

She shook her head, smiling. "You can not undo this. We have succeeded in summoning a baby boy from the stork."

"Well, we sent several hundred signals," I said. "One of them was bound to reach the stork."

"Demons can dampen out those signals," she informed me. "This I tried to do."

"Why?"

"Because I wanted to remain longer with you."

"You may remain with me as long as you like! You have been excellent company, and I look forward to many more signals."

"But I fear that a delivery from the stork will complicate things."

"I will be a father and you a mother. That is wonderful news!"

She did not argue, but I could see that she was pensive. Fool that I was, I did not think to ask her why. I was too pleased with the notion of having a son. Even one who was half demon. The storks are very firm on this: they will not deliver a fully human baby to a mixed couple.

I had villages to visit, so this time I went alone, leaving Dana home to await the stork. The stork wasn't due for months, but delivery dates were never quite certain, and it would be a disaster if the stork came while the mother was absent. We didn't have any cabbage leaves growing around our house, so the baby might be set down anywhere. Unfortunately this left Dana with nothing much to occupy her attention, and she took to eating. Of course she had to eat some and remain solid, so as to build up enough milk to nurse the baby; milkweed pods were available, but it was considered better to do it personally. But she ate a lot and became quite fat. I didn't say anything, not wanting to have a bad scene before the stork arrived and perhaps scare it away, but I intended to put her on a diet once the baby was safely with us.

Then the stork did come, with a beautiful human/demon boy, and I discovered disaster. We had not understood the whole of the oracle's answer; we had forgotten Dana's original Question. She had wanted to rid herself of her soul. Now that soul went to the baby, and Dana was free of it.

She was abruptly also free of her conscience and her love for me. "Well, it's been fun, Humfrey, can't think why," she said. "Maybe some year I'll return for one last good ****; maybe not." She used a term which caused the curtains to blush, and which I think only an angry harpy would understand. It seemed to relate in a derogatory way to the process of stork summoning. Then she fogged into smoke and drifted away.

I was left with my half-breed baby, and no wife. Now I understood somewhat better than before why men were not supposed to associate with demons. It was a hard lesson, and my second significant disappointment.

I needed a new wife, because the King was supposed to be married and because what I knew about caring for a baby could be tallied on the fingers of one foot. As it happened there was a girl recently come of age who was smitten with the trappings of the kingship. She always smiled at me when I walked through the South Village, and lifted her hem in a manner that indicated that she would love to learn something of stork summoning from me. I was somewhat soured on storks at the moment, but I needed a woman in a hurry.

"Would you be willing to adopt my son, if I married you?" I asked her.

"I would adopt an ogret if that was the price of marrying you, Your Majesty," she replied.

So I married the Maiden Taiwan, and she took care of my son, Dafrey. She was really very good about it, and I came to like her well enough, though it would not be proper to say that I loved her. In due course I did do some stork signaling with her, but the stork, perhaps annoyed by the business with Dana, refused to acknowledge. I can't say I was unduly upset about it; perhaps I was afraid that she too would take off if she got a baby of her own.

I continued to travel, because I kept absentmindedly walking into hanging diapers at home. My wife was happy to have me travel; that left more room in the house.

In the North Village I discovered something truly significant: a six-year-old boy who could generate thunderstorms. I examined him carefully, asking him to make small storms and big ones, and he was glad to oblige. His mother didn't like him making storms inside the house, but was surprised and pleased to see the King taking such an interest in him.

Soon I was satisfied: this was a Magician-caliber magic talent. I had found my successor as king of Xanth. Of course he would need training, and it would be some time before he was ready, but it was a great relief to know that I would not be stuck with this chore forever.

Then a peculiar disaster struck. It related, ironically, to my own home village and to my family's farm. I had to hurry back to the Gap Village to get the story from my older brother.

"The tics have mutated," Humboldt said. "They no longer wait peacefully for harvesting and for their own clocks; now they scoot off on their own and make mischief elsewhere. We don't know what to do. But you're the Magician-King; *you* will know what to do."

I saw that I was stuck with an awful chore.

As it turned out, *awful* was far too slight a word for it. Perhaps a variant of the word the demoness had used would adequately describe my sentiment, but of course a king could never utter such an atrocity. You see, there were not just several mutated tics; there were several major families of them, each with many members, reproducing wherever they found fertile soil. That was all over Xanth. What had started in the Gap Village quickly spread to each cranny and nook. They disrupted every type of human activity and were extremely annoying.

We started by burning the field. Humboldt hated to do it, but it was the only way to be sure of eradicating the source of the mutant tics. The other farmers of the Gap Village had to do the same, to their extreme annoyance; I was not called Good King Humfrey in that region thereafter! Unfortunately, this was ineffective; the mutant tics only sprouted again. We had not realized that they had already escaped the neighborhood and were now sprouting in the inaccessible jungles all around. We had a major infestation.

I returned to the South Village and pondered the matter. I had a thinking cap I had found in my prior travels; I donned this and cogitated considerably. This produced an answer, but a difficult one: I would have to concentrate on each variety of tic separately and devise a way to eradicate it. The process might require years, but I was the king, so it was my responsibility.

I decided to capture one of the wild tics, so I could bring it home and study it and discover how to deal with its variety. I got a net of the type used on the tic farm and a collection of bottles, and mounted my trusty winged horse, Peggy. That was a legacy of MareAnn's association; she had told Peggy to stay with me as long as I needed her, and she was doing so, and we got along well. Perhaps the feeling I retained for MareAnn communicated itself to the mare, and so she was satisfied to be with me. Or maybe she was just a nice creature. She was technically a winged monster, but all that is technical is not necessarily true.

We flew back to the farm, because I thought most of the tics should be close by there. First I picked up a regular tic to use for comparison. Then I scoured the region, watching for wild tics, and managed to spy one. I chased it down and netted it. It jumped around madly. It turned out to be a fran-tic, always rushing around. Anyone it happened to land on would assume its characteristics and become similarly frantic. This one certainly needed to be eliminated.

I squeezed it into a bottle and put it in my pack. I flew home. I had a chamber I had set up as a magic lab; my main collection of items was there. This was where I could work without being disturbed.

I brought out the bottle. The fran-tic was a mere blur of activity buzzing around inside. Well, I had a cure for that: I brought out my vial of slowsand and sprinkled some on the bottle. The fran-tic slowed right down, because nothing moves rapidly around slowsand. I had to be careful not to get any on me, because it would slow whatever part of me it touched. There had been a time with the Maiden Taiwan when some of it had gotten on the bed, and it took us two days and nights to get an hour's sleep. I had had to cancel the effect with some quicksand, because it had gotten into the mattress and couldn't be removed. Now I was more careful with it; experience was a solid teacher. So now I used tongs to unstopper the bottle and slide the fran-tic out onto the table, where I had a little circle of slowsand. I was at normal speed, but the tic was slow.

It looked like an ordinary tic, with a round body and little legs. The only thing different about it was that it was dashing madly around, in slow motion.

I brought out the regular tic. It sat there and twitched in the normal fashion. Once it got into a clock and encountered the tocks it would turn to sound, becoming invisible.

What was the difference between them? What I needed to do was to find out how to change the troublesome one back into the normal one. I had thought that one might have longer legs or shorter antennae, but they looked the same. Only their actions distinguished them.

Actually, I realized, it wouldn't do any good to fix this one tic. There might be dozens of this variety out there, reproducing their kind, spreading out across Xanth. I couldn't catch them all! I needed a way to nullify every one of them, without having to bring them in to my lab. That meant finding a way to change them back in the field. So I had a greater challenge than I had thought.

I struggled with this problem for days. I analyzed those two tics every which way but loose. Their only real difference seemed to be in personality. Neither of them spoke my language, so I could not reason with the fran-tic and try to get it to change its ways and to persuade others of its kind to do likewise.

Then I started experimenting with elixirs, and this finally gave me the key. I mixed some healing elixir with some mute powder and doused the fran-tic with it. This slowed it down, and it became like the normal tic. I added some multiplier potion, so that it would keep increasing, making more of itself. Then I let the muted fran-tic go; It would associate with its own kind, and each time it did so, the other tic would be similarly muted by the multiplying potion. I hoped. It would take time, but in due course all the fran-tics should be quiet.

I went out again. This time I netted a cri-tic. This one was a real trial!

"So you're the nitwit who thinks he's a king," it said. I wished this hadn't been the one to speak my language! "You have been doing a despicable job! Whatever gave you the idea you could govern Xanth?! *I* could do a better job than you, with three legs and one feeler tied behind me. In fact I don't see why they didn't make *me* king, as I am so obviously superior to you, you poor excuse for a gnome."

This one really needed stifling! But the former mix of elixirs, powders, and potions had little effect on it. It criticized the mix with disdain. "I could make a better concoction than that!" it said.

"Very well, you do it," I said, giving it the ingredients.

But it refused. "I shall not soil my feet with common labor. In fact, I decline to do anything useful. It is my business to tell all others what incompetents they are, you first among them."

I could get to dislike this creature, if I concentrated. It had an attitude problem. Naturally, it thought it was the rest of Xanth with the problem, and was not about to listen to any contrary view. The only contrary views it tolerated were its own.

I feared I would pop a blood vessel or two before I was able to figure out a formula that would mute this cri-tic. For days it berated me for every evil its devious little mind could imagine. If I hadn't already known that tics are bugs, I would have realized it after being bugged by this one. But I finally fashioned a de-bug potion that turned it from a cri-tic into an an-tic, and that was the best I could do. I let it go, knowing that once the conversion had spread to all its cousins and they encountered people, the would-be cri-tics would perform an-tics instead. That was not ideal, but this had been one hard nut to crack.

Incidentally, I learned years later that some cri-tics had drifted into Mundania before being overtaken by an-tics. There they spread recklessly, and soon the whole of Mundania was infested with them. They had no natural enemies, you see, but they did their best to convert the rest of Mundania *to* enemies. They were having some success in this effort, the last I heard.

The next tic I caught was a roman-tic. I considered the matter, and finally let it go untreated. Xanth would not be harmed by its influence.

So it went, from tic to tic. There was the poli-tic, who infected those with ambition and the luna-tic, who made folk crazy. The hera-tic, who was concerned with matters of faith, and the dras-tic with its desperate measures. They would none of them be missed! Some were interesting and more or less harmless, like the aqua-tic and elas-tic. The gymnas-tic was one of the nimblest, but the acroba-tic was similar. The hardest one to figure out was the enigma-tic, the most difficult was the problema-tic, and the wildest was the orgias-tic. I was annoyed by the bombas-tic and bored by the pedan-tic. It was useless to argue with the dogma-tic or to try to calm the empha-tic. I managed to turn the spas-tic into a sta-tic. The largest was the gigan-tic, and the most interesting the fantas-tic. Some were nuisances mainly to children, like the arithme-tic and gramma-tic. The op-tic actually enabled folk to see better, so I let it go untreated. I had trouble distinguishing between the clima-tic and the climac-tic, but there was nevertheless a significant difference. I finally had to catch a characteris-tic to help me get them straight. It turned out that one affected the weather and the other affected great events. Sometimes these were similar, but not always.

The more tics I treated, the harder it became to locate and catch the remaining ones. It took me months roaming the countryside to catch up to the rus-tic, and then I didn't treat it, as it was pleasantly harmless. I had to search the upper floors of several houses before netting the at-tic, and that too was wasted effort, as it needed no cure. It merely liked to seek out the highest place of a house and stay there, getting pleasantly hot and dusty and forgotten.

When finally I had dealt with the last one, I danced madly for joy.

"Gotcha!" a little voice said.

"What?"

"You missed me. I landed on you instead. I am the ecsta-tic."

I was satisfied to concede that tic's victory.

I checked into the routine of things, and discovered that sixteen years had passed. My son, Dafrey, was now seventeen and was serving as an assistant to E.T. Bram. My wife, Taiwan, had filled out considerably; the trinkets she made in her spare time were now to be found all over Xanth. The Storm Magician was how twenty-two, with his powers at full strength.

It was time to retire. I had never much liked being king, and now there was a legitimate Magician to succeed me.

I went to see the Storm Magician. "You're it," I told him. "I quit!"

He accepted this with excellent grace. Arrangements for the orderly transfer of power were made. He preferred to remain in the North Village, and I had no objection; the only reason I had remained in the South Village was that had I moved home to the Gap Village, no one would have remembered my edicts, because of the—well, I forget why, but I'm sure I had good reason.

I assumed that the Matron Taiwan would accompany me to anonymity, but discovered otherwise. "But all my friends are here!" she protested. "I couldn't possibly leave them!"

I yielded to the persuasion of her logic, and we severed our marriage. I can't say I was heartbroken; we had gotten along well enough, but we shared few interests, and I no longer had a baby to be cared for.

So it was that I was uncrowned and went my way alone. Well, not quite; Peggy, my winged horse, concluded that I still needed someone to look after me, so she went along. I sincerely appreciated her loyalty; it made traveling so much easier.

Chapter 7

ROOGNA

At first I was exhilarated by my freedom from the responsibility of the kingship. This lasted about seven minutes. I was also depressed by my freedom from marriage, for I had become accustomed to the attentions of a woman. This lasted about nine minutes. Then I was bored.

I decided to do something interesting that I had never had time for before: locate the fabulous lost Castle Roogna. It had disappeared from history after King Gromden died and King Yang moved away from it because of his demon love. I now understood rather better than I liked how that sort of mischief happened. The plain fact was that the average man's brain dulled when he saw the average woman, and turned off completely when he saw a beautiful one. He hardly cared what was in her mind, except that he preferred it mostly empty. A demoness could present the most luscious body and emptiest mind of all. I had thought King Gromden to have been a fool, but now I knew that he was merely a man.

It was odd how Castle Roogna had disappeared, after being so prominent. It was almost as if some power didn't want it to be known. But who would object to the knowledge of a castle? Unless there was a concern that it would be pillaged in the absence of an occupying king. Well, I would not pillage it; I merely wanted to see it.

It was somewhere south of the—the—somewhere south of the center of Xanth. Not too far from the West Stockade, as I understood it, because that was where King Yang had gone, and it was said that he had not gone far. But Yang had been the Magician of Spell-crafting, who could have made a spell to jump him all the way across Xanth, so that was not certain.

Something about this chain of thought bothered me, and it was my nature to seek out any such bother because it could be a signal of something interesting. Yang? No, that wasn't it. Far side of Xanth? No. South Xanth? Maybe. South of what? I couldn't remember.

And that was it. I had surveyed all of Xanth. How was it that part of it was blank in my mind? I had no memory of ever being in the center of Xanth, yet surely I had been there many times. In fact I had lived there as a child. How could I have forgotten? Yet it remained blank: I could not remember where I had lived as a child.

"Peggy, fly north," I said to my winged steed.

She turned gracefully in the air and bore north. I continued to ponder, as was my wont. Could my forgetting about the center of Xanth have anything to do with the general forgetting of Castle Roogna?

Soon we came to a huge fissure in the ground. Amazing! How could such a thing be here and I not know it? The thing was hardly new; trees grew at its edge and down in its depths. Why, it would be virtually impossible to travel across Xanth lengthwise with this enormous natural barrier in the way! "Peggy, do you remember this chasm?" I asked.

She snorted no.

But now I was beginning to remember. My home village was on its north side. This was the—the—the Gap Chasm! It had been here forever, or something similar, and it—no one who didn't live here could—there was a Forget Spell on it! Now that I was here, I was recovering my lost knowledge, but when I left it I would forget it again.

Well, I could deal with that. I brought out my notepad and pencil and made a note: *Gap Chasm across central Xanth, Forget Spell on.* Next time I thought about what I couldn't remember, that note would help.

But now that I remembered, I knew that this was not associated with the disappearance of Castle Roogna. The Gap Chasm minded its own business. I added a note: *Castle Roogna not in Gap Chasm.*

"Turn south again, Peggy," I said, and the horse obligingly did so. Peggy was my only legacy of MareAnn, but a handsome one. I had never sought information about MareAnn after she left me, and that kept my memory of her clean: lovely and innocent. Probably, nineteen years later, she was no longer lovely, and her innocence was somewhat strained. An innocent woman of thirty-eight was not nearly as attractive as one of nineteen, for reasons that most men understood and most women didn't. But I had loved her, and loved her yet, in diminished degree. Had things been otherwise . . .

Where would Castle Roogna most likely be? Well, if it was unknown, it was probably hidden from the air or inaccessible. If Peggy and I canvassed southern Xanth, we should either run across it or discover a region we could not explore. Indeed, something like that must have happened when I surveyed Xanth before. I must have skipped by a region without realizing it. That was the place to investigate in more detail.

We canvassed. Peggy rather enjoyed it, I believe, for she lived for flying. I found it less delightful, for my posterior was getting sore from all the riding, and most of the territory we covered was already familiar.

Peggy curved in flight. Ordinarily I would not have noticed, for I trusted her judgment. But my recent experience with the—the—something or other had alerted me to unnoticeable things, and my attention focused. Why had she curved, when our normal pattern should have carried us straight forward? I saw no storm cloud or dangerous mountain, and no dragon was aloft nearby.

I was about to tell her to straighten out and fly right. But I really didn't feel like arguing the case; there was nothing interesting ahead.

Another warning nag bothered me. I was interested in *everything*; how could I find any unknown thing uninteresting? My talent was curiosity. This just did not figure.

"Peggy, fly over that boring jungle to the side," I said. She turned with an equine sigh and headed into it—only to turn away again soon.

There was now no doubt: there was an aversion spell here, just as there was a Forget Spell (according to my note) on the Gap Chasm. I had no memory of such a chasm, but trusted my note. An aversion spell would have similar effect: passing folk would not remember the region, because they never entered it.

I tried to have Peggy fly into it again, but she began to sweat and her ears turned back, and I knew she was becoming most uncomfortable. She did not have my ornery nature; she was a relatively innocent creature of the wild who stayed out of trouble by avoiding aversive things. It would not be kind to push her further.

"Land, and I will go on alone," I said. "If I do not return, you are free to do as you will. I thank you for your years of loyal assistance."

She cocked an eye at me, not liking this, but descended and let me dismount. She folded her wings and waited.

I assembled my pack, which Peggy had been carrying. I did not relish the notion of proceeding alone on foot into an aversive jungle, but I hoped that dragons and other monsters would also be avoiding it. "Happy grazing," I told the mare.

She pondered the matter, then lowered her head to the grass, which was rich here at the edge of the jungle. She had plenty to eat. That wasn't her concern. She knew I was being foolish, and she felt guilty for letting me do this. But she knew that she would have to let me get my own scrapes and learn my own hard lessons. She was a very maternal mare.

I turned and plunged into the jungle. I knew where to go, because it was where I felt least inclined to go. It had been a long time since I had done anything I less wanted to do. Yet, perversely, that was why I wanted to do it.

My orneriness paid off, because after a while the aversion eased. It was like diving into cold water: the first shock was the worst. I still did not like what I was doing, but I could tolerate it. I took things easy and kept going.

Then I saw something interesting. It was a snail. It was racing across a glade. Then I saw another, moving almost as quickly. This was remarkable; I had never seen snails move so rapidly. I realized that this was that rarest of all sports events, a cross-country snail race. Normally folk did not watch one of these from start to finish unless obliged to for some reason, such as punishment. But these swift snails would complete the course in a fraction of the time regular snails would.

The region darkened, and in a moment it was as black as night. There were even stars overhead, sailing along in their courses. They reached the other side of the welkin and came to rest. Then the sun came up again.

Something nagged my mind.

Slowly it came to me: why was everything moving so fast?

And slowly the answer came: because I had slowed down.

I looked down, in the time it took the sun to travel from quarter sky to half sky. Sure enough, I was standing on a patch of sand. That would be slowsand.

The world was proceeding at its normal pace. It seemed rapid to me only because my perspective had changed.

The aversion spell was not stopping me. Now I was encountering another type of magic. Someone had strewn patches of slowsand around, and I had foolishly stepped into one. I could step out of it, of course, but I would be a long time doing it. Meanwhile any other kind of mischief could be approaching.

I could try to step backward out of it or forward. There was three times as much sand in front. That would delay me a long time. But if I retreated, I might still have this barrier to traverse.

Fortunately I had the remedy. I had collected many useful things during my survey of Xanth and during my tenure as king. I had a fair assortment of them here in my pack.

I reached over my shoulder and fished for a bottle. I wasted no time, but the land darkened and brightened twice more while I did this. I found my quicksand and sprinkled some on my feet. It counteracted the slowsand, and I was able to step forward out of the patch.

But I had lost three days. Fortunately I wasn't on a schedule, as far as I knew, and I wasn't hungry, because my internal processes had been slowed too. Still, I would have to be more careful.

I now had little doubt that I was in the vicinity of Castle Roogna. I remembered that King Roogna, whose talent was adapting magic to his purpose had adapted many things to the defense of the castle. His talent was similar to that of the later King Ebnez, except that Roogna dealt with living magic while Ebnez adapted inanimate magic. Of course sand needed no adaptation; all it needed was to be there, and it had its effect. How the King had managed to move it here, far from its natural habitat, I hesitated to guess. But it had just about stopped my advance.

Well, onward. Time was not of the essence, but Peggy might be getting impatient for my return. I remembered how, so long ago, MareAnn and I had spent the night in the werehouse and been taken far afield. In fact, all the way across the—the—across somewhere, to the South Village. The poor unicorns must have dutifully returned to discover only a bare patch of ground where the house had been. Had they neighed soulfully, thinking us forever lost? Was Peggy now fretting similarly, having hoped for my return well within three days? I regretted putting her through that.

I brushed by a nondescript bush. There was a faint calling sound—and suddenly my gut boiled up. I grabbed for my trousers and yanked them down barely in time to let me squat. My nether innards blew out their contents.

Then I felt at ease, and I realized what had happened. I had touched a nature bush and been called by it. This was its way of getting fertilizer. A harmless ploy—but had I not reacted quickly, I would have soiled my trousers and been in a rather awkward situation. I had been careless again.

I reassembled myself and stepped forward again. There were other bushes, but not of the same type. Still, they were unfamiliar, and I preferred to avoid them. There was no telling what kind of magic they might have.

But there was a halfway solid line of them, the leaves of one touching the leaves of its neighbors. I could not pass without touching them.

So I took a running jump and sailed over them. My excellent health had never abated, and I could clear hurdles that would have been insurmountable in my youth before I fell in the healing spring.

The tip of one stem touched my foot. Suddenly I was spinning in the air, tumbling out of control. I came down turning like a wheel, rolling down a grassy slope toward a muddy pond. I had touched a tumbleweed!

I managed to stop my roll just before plunging into the mud. I lifted my face—and there was someone's bottom, huge and smelly. I wrinkled my nose against the odor of rotting cheese.

Then I got a better view, and realized that this wasn't a man's bare posterior, but a rounded stone with a vertical crevice. In fact it was a chink of moon rock, evidently fallen from the moon some time ago, because the green cheese was far from fresh. It had mooned me, as was its nature.

I got up and turned my back on the moonstone. I discovered that I had tumbled farther than I had supposed; I was not only near mud, I was surrounded by it, and beyond it was a ring of open water. In fact I was on an island in a pond! How could I have gotten here without getting wet?

Then I realized that this was another obstacle on the way to the castle. There was an enchantment of some sort that was trying to stop me or turn me back. Now it had dumped me on this island, possibly by flipping me through the air. It wasn't trying to hurt me, just to prevent me from going forward. Probably if I decided to give it up as a bad job, I would have little trouble making my way out.

That explained why the castle had been forgotten: someone wanted it left alone. But who? There weren't any Magicians or Sorceresses in Xanth, except for the Storm King, and no other person would have either the desire for such privacy or the power of magic to enforce it.

I had been more or less bulling through, and more or less not getting anywhere much. It was time to start using my mind, which was a good one when I gave it three quarters of a chance. How could I learn more about this situation so as not to blunder worse? After all, I didn't want to have to face Peggy's "I told you so!" snort.

I sat down on the moon rock, which emitted more strong cheese smell in protest. I took off my pack and rummaged through it for my small magic mirror. I gazed at it for a moment, considering whether to use it. I remembered the problem associated with it.

This was an excellent mirror I had found in a deserted graveyard. Most graveyards were deserted, of course; for some reason living folk did not care to spend much time in them. But this one was really deserted: even the ghosts were gone. I wasn't sure what could frighten off a ghost, and had hesitated to pursue the matter despite my curiosity; there was probably excellent reason for the fright. So I had picked up this little mirror.

"What is your nature?" I had asked it first.

"I am a magic mirror who can answer any question put."

Well, this was an excellent find! But I was suspicious of the circumstance under which I had found it, so I questioned it again. "What are the counterindications of your use?"

"I answer each question less accurately than the last, for each possessor."

That gave me pause. I could see that a living person might have used this mirror repeatedly, not thinking to inquire about its liabilities, and had his good fortune become bad fortune as the mirror gradually shaded from truth to lies. Finally it must have given him an answer that killed him, such as perhaps telling him that there was a fortune here when in fact there had been a ghoul lurking in its favorite place. That would account for the mirror being left in the graveyard.

But could this also account for the vanished ghosts? Yes, because they could have addressed the mirror as it lay on the ground near their graves, and they could have entertained themselves by asking it many questions— and finally it could have told them a ghost story which led them to a ghost town, from which they had been unable to escape.

So I had asked this mirror no more questions. But I had saved it, because it was probably still fairly accurate for me. When it became hopelessly inaccurate I could give it to someone else, with due warning.

I had asked it only two questions. How fast did its accuracy decline? If I asked it how to get safely to Castle Roogna, and it gave me an answer that was mostly *good*, but omitted news of one deadly threat, what then?

I decided to wait for a situation where the accuracy of the answer would be more evident. There were too many imponderables at the moment. So perhaps I had wasted my time. But that was my nature: to pause every so often and reassess my situation. It would be better if I did my pausing before getting into trouble so that I could assess instead of reassess, but such wisdom and caution came only with hard experience. I was not yet nearly as conservative as I would become in my maturity.

It had been better, actually, when I was married or with a female companion. MareAnn had sort of nudged me in right directions, and Dana had always given me good advice while she had her soul, and Maiden Taiwan had put things together for me very well. Even Peggy, my winged horse, had guided me by significant wiggles of her ears when I threatened to do something of more than ordinary stupidity. It had been a long time since I had been truly on my own, and by an odd coincidence the same time since I had been unusually thoughtless. It was evident that I needed management. In fact, I probably needed another wife. But after one love and two marriages, I was not eager to do it again. Not unless I could have both together. I really wished, in retrospect, that MareAnn had been willing to forgo her innocence and marry me. But she had preserved it, and the last I had heard of her she was in the business of providing mares for villages. She would summon a suitable female horse for a settlement, who would handle its affairs with such extreme discretion that they seemed nonexistent. Unicorns were able to serve only children's settlements, but any other mare could kick things off well enough. It seemed that every village wanted a competent mare. The mare of the West Stockade was said to have real horse sense.

But how could I have that? Where was the woman whom I could both love and marry? Someone who was lovely without being determinedly innocent or of demon origin or dedicated to status rather than the man? Where was the potential great love of my life?

I lifted the mirror, putting it away. I caught the flash of an image in it: the face of a beautiful young woman with a bright red rose in her hair. I quickly straightened out the mirror and looked more closely, but the image was gone. The thing had been teasing me.

Yet this was a question-answering mirror, and it could not do other than answer a question, correctly or incorrectly. I had asked it no question. So how had it flashed me a picture?

I cogitated a bit, realizing that there was a missing element here. By and by I ran it down: I had been thinking of my ideal woman. I had been holding the magic mirror in my hand. The thing must have flashed me a picture of that woman.

What the mirror wanted, of course, was to tempt me into asking a question. The more questions it could make me ask, the less accurate it would become, until it became useless to me. This was its way of getting rid of me, either by giving me bad answers or by getting given away.

"It won't work," I said. "I won't fritter away what accuracy remains in you by asking an irrelevant question. Once I locate Castle Roogna and am satisfied, then I can look for that woman. I don't want to know about her now, when the information may be at the expense of something I may need to know to save my life. So stop trying to distract me, you too-bright piece of glass."

Bold words. But in fact that glimpse had struck through to my heart, and I wanted to know who that woman was. Would I really meet her at some time in the future, or was this a false image? I was tempted to give up this foolish quest for Castle Roogna and go in search of the woman. What mischief that mischievous mirror had done to my fancy!

Well, on. Thinking was not doing me much good after all. I fished out a repulsive spell that would protect me from attack by serpents, allegories, basilisks, dragons, and anything else of the reptilian persuasion. I found another that guarded against insects of every type. Another that made fish lose their appetite. And one to wilt plants, from innocent poke berries to the huge deadly kraken weed. One more that would cause mammals below the humanoid level to retreat in disgust. That would spare me the awkwardness of bumping into a hypotenuse or worse. Finally, a spell to spook birds, from the cutest little hummingbirds through the ugliest big roc. The thing was, I could not know what threats lurked in the deep mud and water and did not care to find out the hard way. So I guarded against them all. It was a shame to expend so many spells at once when perhaps none were necessary, but it would be foolish to gamble with my life.

I took off my clothes, wadded them into my pack, held it high, and waded into the mud. I was prepared for any creature that might wish to molest me in the water. Of course elves, gnomes, trolls, ghouls, and ogres were humanoid, but I hadn't seen any of these in this vicinity, and I did have other spells that would be effective against them. This was the advantage of collecting magic things. It had occurred to me that some of them might eventually be useful.

The mud sucked up around my feet and ankles, and then pulled back with a disgusted sizzle. The repulsive spells were affecting the small creatures lurking within it and the reaching roots of plants. I continued slowly, giving the whole mud puddle time to spread the word, satisfied that most creatures would prefer to get out of my way before I got to them.

My leading foot came down into a sudden hole, and suddenly I was waist deep in mud. Yes, that was a standard ploy of mud puddles; they tried to look shallow, then they would snare someone who believed it. But it did this wallow no good, because nothing would touch me.

I forged on through the mud until it thinned and became muddy water. I was now chest deep, and my toes were sliding along the bottom. With luck I wouldn't encounter another hole; I hoped this muck had learned the futility of that device. So I could slowly forge through and out and finally scramble onto the far bank and be on my way toward the castle, which probably wasn't very far away now.

For somewhere in the course of my pondering a background thought had been percolating, and now it was rising slowly to the surface of my mind where it could be seen. It was this: it might be the castle itself that was trying to keep folk out. King Roogna had adapted a lot of living magic around the castle, and in the course of several centuries that magic could have coalesced into a halfway unified effort. Without King Roogna to tell it no, it had decided that any person who was not him was to be kept out. It had gotten quite effective, and I might be the first person to overcome it. That would be very nice.

Then something caught my ankle and pulled. What was this? My assorted spells should keep all enemies at bay!

I looked down, but could see nothing in the swirling opacity. This water was clear as mud, by no coincidence.

Now something was tugging on my other ankle. It did not feel like a tentacle. It was more like a webbed foot.

Then I realized what it was. My spells had not included the amphibians. This was an under-toad! A water-dwelling toad that crept along the bottom and hauled waders under. Here I was with my hands occupied holding up my packful of clothes and spells which I didn't want to get wet, and this thing was out to draw me down and drown me!

I tried to get away, but when I lifted one foot, the other was jerked out and I plopped down. I held the pack straight aloft and kicked my feet violently, managing to get one down onto reasonably firm muck. My head broke the brown surface, matted with bits of seeweed that must have gotten lost in this pond. Normally seeweed kept a sharp eye out for the sea, and draped itself over seeshells.

"Help!" I gasped involuntarily as there was another tug on my foot. The under-toad was only playing with me; soon it would get serious and drag me down for longer than a mere dunk. A lot longer.

A man appeared at the bank. He was purple. He caught an overhanging branch with one hand and extended the other to me. He caught me by a wrist and drew me toward him. Just in time, for my feet were going out again.

The toad hauled harder, not understanding why I wasn't going down. The purple man continued to pull me to the shore. In a moment he was joined by a green man, and the two of them got me up and out of the water, forcing the toad to let go lest it be brought to the surface. I had escaped with my pack undunked, my collection of spells complete.

"Thank you!" I gasped. "I needed that."

"Anything to help another colored person," the purple man said.

There I realized who my benefactors were. There were some folk whose colors were different from others, and those of the rarer hues tended to seek their own company, because the majority sometimes made fun of them. They had evidently mistaken me for one of them, because I was now mud and seeweed colored. How would they react when they learned that I wasn't? That *I* was not one of the guardians of this region but someone trying to sneak in?

I thought about it for a third of a moment and concluded as usual that honesty was best, though they would probably throw me back in the pond. "I'm not—"

"Look! There's a beach head!" Green exclaimed.

Purple and I looked to the side. There indeed was a head forming in the sand. This might be little more than a mud puddle, but it seemed to have a number of oceanic attributes.

"Quick! Fetch a beach comber!" Purple cried.

They charged into the jungle, foraging for combers. I had to admit that the beach head's hair was rather messy, so it was appropriate to comb it out. It was just my luck that the head had manifested right at this time.

I decided that three would be a crowd, as far as beach head combing was concerned. I marched on in the direction I hoped the castle was.

Interesting that there were human beings here. For colored people were human, despite the claims of some; they differed only in their hues. Apparently these ones had had trouble getting along elsewhere, so had accepted work here in the region that other folk avoided. It was too bad that they were not given the equal chance they deserved.

I squeezed through some foliage—and was abruptly facing a young blue woman. I remembered that I remained naked; my clothes remained in my pack. Fauns might run unclothed, but I was no faun, and this was no nymph. She was fully clothed.

I opened my stupid mouth. "I, uh—"

"Where is the beach head?" she inquired. "I have combs!"

"That way," I said, pointing to my rear. Let me rephrase that: I pointed back the way I had come.

"Thank you, Brown," she said, and dashed on.

I started to breathe a sigh of relief. But I had gotten no further than *si* before Blue paused, glancing back. Her gaze flicked to my midsection. She opened her pretty mouth.

"By the pond," I clarified. "Purple and Green are already there."

She nodded and ran on. I breathed my *gh*, completing my sigh.

Then I looked down at myself. I was not as exposed as I had thought. Several thick strands of seaweed were hanging from the region the woman had been looking at, like a codpiece.

Perhaps I should get dressed now. But my body remained caked with mud, and that would ruin my clothes. There seemed to be no suitable trees nearby, so I could not get a new suit. I decided to compromise by fashioning the seeweed (I wondered just what it was looking at) into a minimum loinpiece. That would have to do until I found water in which to wash.

But now night was closing in around me, and soon it would catch me. I would have to find a place to sleep. I was too tired to struggle on through darkness. My repulsive spells would protect me through the night, but I still needed somewhere comfortable to lie down.

I was in luck again: I spied bedrock. A nice big section of it, projecting from the ground. I went and touched it with one hand. It was genuine, no illusion, and wondrously soft, It was perfect. There was even a blanket tree nearby, with a fine heavy blanket just waiting to be harvested. That would ward away the chill of evening nicely.

I fished in my pack for a meal ticket, as I had not eaten all day. I tore the ticket in half, and the pieces formed into a fine loaf of bread and a flask of drink. I popped the cork and lifted the flask to my mouth. It turned out to be soft drink, which was fine; I did not care to tackle hard drink right now, because that had the side effect of making it hard for a person to keep his balance.

I completed my meal and lay on the bedrock. I bounced a little, enjoying the feel of the inner springs. Probably they contained more soft drink, but I preferred to let them be. If I bounced too hard, they might squirt out, and the bedrock would lose some of its softness. I relaxed.

Then the image of that face in the mirror returned to me. I knew that the mirror had no certain obligation to show the truth, especially since I had not actually asked it a question. It might have been the image of the most beautiful woman the mirror had seen in the past fifty years, and she could now be buried in that cute little graveyard where I had found the mirror. I suspected that the mirror didn't like me, so this might be its cruel joke. It was probably just trying to bug me, to deprive me of my peace of mind until I had to play its game and ask about the woman. I had known that all along. But if that was its game, it was working.

But I refused to give the mirror the satisfaction of knowing how effective its ploy had been. I simply let that image be in my mind, enjoying it. I knew that there was a whole lot more to know about a woman than just her face, and I hated being so moved so foolishly, but in this respect I was a typical man. So I would complete my present mission, locate Castle Roogna, then see what to do about that woman, assuming she existed. Then I slept.

In the morning I got up, used another meal ticket—they were quite handy when camping out—looked for water again, but only blundered into another nature bush. Thus I did not complete the particular function I had sought. I would just have to get clean when the opportunity came.

Before me was a dense forest of large trees. Now at last I was in familiar territory, as it were, for I knew that Castle Roogna was surrounded by just such trees. If these moved their branches to intercept an intruder—

I stepped forward. The trees on either side of the avenue I was going toward swung their branches around to bar the way. There was no doubt of it now: this was what I was looking for.

Excellent. I had come prepared for this. I had not known that there were other defenses around the castle, but the orchard was part of the history that E. Timber Bram had written up. In fact it was his history that had reminded me of this missing aspect of Xanth and aroused my ever-ready curiosity.

I retreated, removing my pack. I brought out a vial of elixir and anointed myself with it. This was a familiar potion: it made the wearer smell familiar. Since trees neither saw nor heard very well as a rule, they depended on ambience: the general odor and attitude of the creature who approached. If they smelled cold iron in the possession of an evil-smelling man, they became defensive, because the thing they hated most was the axe.

I approached again, whistling. This time the branches gaveway before me. I acted and smelled familiar. When it came right down to it, trees were generally not the smartest creatures in Xanth. But they did excellent service protecting the grounds.

I came to the inner orchard, where there were all manner of fruit, nut, pie, and other useful trees, surely the greatest collection of them in Xanth, because they had been assembled by King Roogna. It was a lovely place, and looked surprisingly well kept considering that it had been neglected

QUESTION QUEST

for almost three centuries. Technically, from 677 when Magician Yang assumed the throne and left the castle, until now, 971. It looked just as if someone had been tending this orchard yesterday. Roogna had certainly been a competent Magician.

Now I came to the grand old castle itself. What a sight! It was roughly square, with mighty square turrets at each corner and substantial round ones midway along the walls. It was surrounded by a formidable moat. To my amazement I saw that the water was clear, not scummy with neglect, and there was a moat monster there!

Could it be that Castle Roogna was occupied? This was astonishing. How could it be occupied, yet forgotten?

I walked up to the edge of the moat. A monster serpent lifted its head out of the water and hissed at me. My serpent repellent had worn mostly off by this time, but I had more if I needed it.

Then the drawbridge cranked down and landed with a clank. The portcullis lifted. The gate opened. A woman appeared, looking tiny amidst the huge fortifications. She was evidently a princess, for she wore a small gold crown set with tiny pink pearls and pink diamonds. There was a rather large square shaped pink crystal at her bosom. Her hair was like dew-bedazzled rose petals. Her skin was so creamy it seemed almost possible to drink it, and her eyes were shades of leafy green. She was attired in a low-necked gown made of translucent full silk gauze in wide stripes of deep rose and stripes of cream silk and cloth of gold. Her slippers and pantaloons were cloth of gold too, and seemed to be fastened together with delicate thorns. Her long cape and hood were of dated design but excellent quality heavy watered silk of deepest rose color, embroidered in seed pods made of pearls, musical shards of pink crystals, and small pieces of rose-colored jade carved in the shape of rose buds. There was a frog closure of shimmering gold in the shape of a living frog prince. These were all pretty good signs of royalty.

It was the woman of the mirror, every bit as lovely in life as in image, and the rest of her was as aesthetic as her face. "Don't hurt him, Soufflé," she said to the moat monster. "I know you can't let him in, but I'll go out to meet him." The huge serpent nodded and sank slowly back out of sight. It was evident that he regarded her as the mistress of the castle. That was another excellent recommendation, because moat monsters generally made very sure of their employers. It just would not do to make an error and swallow the proprietor instead of an intruder. It was against the code of guardianship.

Then she walked across the bridge toward me. I remembered that I was garbed in mud and a seeweed loin covering. I had had no idea that I would thus abruptly encounter the woman of my fancy. I tried to back away, but came up against a nearby gallan-tree that prevented me from withdrawing from the princess' exquisite presence.

"Uh, hello," I said, feeling very little of the intelligence I was supposed to have.

"Hello; Humfrey," she said. "I am the Princess Rose."

Somehow I had known that would be her name. But how had she known mine? "Uh—"

"I think I love you," she continued blithely. "And that presents a problem. I am here to marry a Magician who will become king, while you are the reverse: a king who will become a Magician. Castle Roogna is most upset. But I think we can make it work, if you are willing."

How did she know so much about me, even that I wasn't a true Magician but had been king? How could she speak of love, when we had only just met? "Uh—"

Then she smiled at me, and all my doubt wafted away. I was in love.

Chapter 8

ROSE

It was a bleak hour in the history of Xanth. Things had started to decline during the reign of King Gromden, who had been seduced by a demoness and sired a half-breed named Threnody, who was banned from Castle Roogna lest it fall asunder. She married Gromden's successor, King Yang. Therefore, King Yang set up residence away from Castle Roogna, to the castle's chagrin. He governed Xanth from the West Stockade. Four years later Threnody suicided and became a ghost, Renee. In life she had been banned from Castle Roogna, but in death she was able to enter it, and she kept company with her true love, Jordan the Ghost.

King Yang, not one to bemoan spilled milk pods, remarried, and two years later sired a son. The son lacked Magician-class magic, so could never be king. He was established at a separate estate, becoming Lord Bliss. He grew up and married the Lady Ashley Rose, and their child was Princess Rose Pax of Bliss. Her grandfather was an evil king, and her father an indifferent man, and Xanth was sinking further into its Dark Age, but Rose was a really sweet child. She had a talent for growing roses, and they were everywhere around her. A rose by another name did not smell as sweet as the rose that Rose grew.

When Rose was just fourteen, her grandfather Yang died. He had been evil but healthy; his sudden demise was a shock. Another Magician, Muerte A. Fid, took the throne. There was a suspicion that this Fid had poisoned Yang, for his talent related to alchemy, and he could make potions do sinister things. He was the most evil man known in Xanth. But there was no proof—and who would dare accuse the King? So those who had misgivings kept them mostly to themselves and muddled on. They really didn't expect much better from a Dark Age. Good kings limited their tenures to bright ages.

Lord Bliss, being the son of the former King and a halfway decent man with a wholly decent wife, did grumble a bit. That was perhaps his mistake. A grumble or two escaped the house and may have managed to reach the ear of the King. It was an evil ear, covered over by skin so that it did not project from his head, and most of what it heard was bad. The King's malicious mind may have started to percolate, and the results of such percolations were inevitably foul. The longer that brain oozed, the worse it festered, until at last the awfulness had to find its nefarious expression.

When Rose was sixteen, her father received a poisonpen letter. The poisoned thorn fell out of the envelope and pricked his hand when he opened it. *Gotcha!* the text of the letter said. It was unsigned, but only the King knew how to make such poison. So Rose had a notion who might have sent it, but no proof. There just never seemed to be proof for what most of Xanth knew was true.

The poison was slow but sure. At first Lord Bliss merely slowed down a bit, while his hand turned deepening shades of purple; but then he slowed down a bit more, and the pain of it showed around the edges of his face despite his effort to conceal it. Rose dedicated herself to helping him, for her mother was busy trying to maintain the household.

As autumn waned in a burst of rose-scented air and waxy white orange blossoms, Rose knew that her father did not have much time left. Each day the ruby and garnet colored sands of time slipped lower in the grand-father clock. That clock would stop entirely, never to run again, on the day he died.

Lord Bliss was resigned to his fate. If he had any regrets at all, it was that he was leaving behind one royal descendent, his daughter, the Princess Rose. She could never be king, because she was female and lacked sufficient magic, but she deserved better than what she faced. Even now as she sat beside his sickly bedside she was a great comfort to him and to the Monster Under the Bed. The monster was a childhood friend who had returned to keep him company during his last hours. The young and the old were similarly close to the ends of their lives, going in different directions, and monsters related well to that.

His dear and loving daughter kept her nimble fingers ever busy with her needle, working with the yarns and threads and needlepoint. He took her silence as a subtle reproach to the selfishness of his deep and abiding love for her, for Rose should have been married long ago. A beautiful Princess could readily find a match by the time she was seventeen, but she had remained single to better dedicate herself to his welfare. Now she was twenty, the blush of her youth past. Yet he had been unable to part with her, this child he loved above all people, and it was evident that she returned the sentiment.

But he could not forestall death further. "My daughter," he rasped with what was left of his dying breath. "You must marry. But I fear that marriage. The King—"

Rose was appalled. "The King wouldn't marry me!" she protested.

"Yes he would—to secure his seeming legitimacy. You are of the blood of the genuine King. Your grandfather was an evil man, but he had a good side. King Fid has none. He may seek to stifle objections to his terrible reign by requiring the support of the most beautiful, nice, and innocent Princess available."

"Father!" she protested, blushing in a beautiful, nice, and innocent fashion.

"You must hide from the King," he continued. "Only my life can protect you, and it is almost done. The moment I am gone, you must go too—to where the King can not find you."

"Yes, of course, dear Father," she agreed, chilled.

Then Lord Bliss expired. Rose knew it was so, because the big clock stopped ticking. She covered his face with the sheet and went to tell her mother about this and her need to hide. But as she did so, two royal soldiers walked up to the door. They had evidently been listening for the clock's final tick and tock. "No!" Rose cried, but Lady Rose was already opening the door, not realizing.

"We have come for the Princess Rose Pax of Bliss," the men said.

"But she has done nothing bad in her life!" the Lady Rose protested.

"Precisely. The King wishes to see her."

So it was that Rose had to go with the King's three horsemen of hate, fraught with trepidation. She had had no idea the King would act so swiftly. In fact, before the past hour, she had had no idea he even knew of her as other than nothing.

All too soon she was brought before King Muerte A. Fid. His presence was as ugly as his name. He was known as a black-hearted creature who delighted in giving pain. He would have oozed evil from his pores, had he had any pores. He derived his energy from the chaos that war and similar mischief brought.

His mouth was a cruel slit. He normally opened it only to lie, belittle, or harshly criticize. It was said that when he lost control and began to rant, bellow, and scream, his eyes would turn yellow and sparks would fly from them, while noxious fumes issued from his nostril slits. The prevailing theory was that he was the unnatural bastard son of a priestess who was into a lewd stage act with well-trained reptiles. It was quietly bruited about that no stork had brought him, all of them being too revolted by his aspect; he had been delivered by a large basilisk with a clothespin on its nose. Rose had not believed any of that, of course, but now, gazing into his cold black double-lidded eyes, she began to believe. She felt her innocent girlish heart thudding in her throat, and feared there would be an echo from the walls.

The King was naked to the waist. On his head, below a cap of greasy black curls, he wore a thin spiked crown of some unnatural metal, perhaps because gold would have eroded from the contact of that flesh. His skin gleamed everywhere with shades of purple, matching the hues of Lord Bliss's thorn-pricked hand. Glowing crystals were fastened to his feet, his chest, his neck, his face, and his tail. On his curls more crystals glimmered like baleful eyes: diamonds and purple dragon seeds.

He smiled, and this was worse. "We shall be married next week, when the preparations have been made," he said. "Too bad your father will not be able to attend."

Her worst fear had been realized. Marriage to this monster would be worse than death.

That realization gave her a perverted kind of courage. "It is customary to ask the lady first," she said, her voice sounding marvelously false: i.e., cool and controlled.

His eyes narrowed for an instant into snakelike slits. "Oh, did I forget that technicality? Rose Pax of Bliss, will you consent to marry your King?"

She nerved herself for her ultimate act of defiance. She opened her mouth and forced out the dread word. "No."

His lack of surprise was chilling. "You will return for the night to your home to reconsider your response. In the morning you will have your personal belongings packed and ready for transport here." He turned and swept away, literally: his tail made a sweep of the floor, stirring up an irritated cloud of dust.

"Oh, Mother, what is to become of me?" Rose wailed when they were alone at home. She had hardly been conscious of her trip back; doubt, indecision, misgiving, and uncertainty swirled around her pretty person, drawing it inexorably down into a gloomy quandary where brooding monsters of despair lurked. To have to marry the King—surely death would be kinder than this!

"Your father and I had thought to dress you as a farmer's daughter and place you in a distant village," the Lady Ashley Rose said. "But now that is impossible, for the King with ruthless cunning will have the paths watched. We may trick him for an hour or even a day, but not for longer. He will know if any farmer acquires a sudden grown daughter. No, we can not hide you among the people, and you would not like the life of a peasant maid anyway. The local yokels would treat you exactly as the King proposes to treat you. There is only one recourse: I will take you to the single place where the King can not go."

"Where is that, Mother?" It had not occurred to Rose that there might be some escape other than death, but the idea appealed to her.

"Castle Roogna."

"But that has been lost since Grandfather deserted it!"

"No, only largely forgotten. Your father and I have kept the memory. But we did not want to send you there, because there is a problem."

"A problem, Mother? Worse than the one we face with the King?" It did not seem that such a thing could be possible, but Rose's confidence in goodness had been severely shaken, and she feared that there might indeed be a worse horror, whose very mention might further pollute her maidenly innocence.

"No, hardly worse than that! It is that I can not accompany you there, and you can not leave it of your own volition."

"But that would be a prison!" Yet she was heartened, for to be imprisoned alone would be better than to be imprisoned with the

King. At least her tender body would not be savaged by his constantly evil gaze.

"Of a sort, dear. You will be excellently cared for, for you derive from the blood of the last legitimate King, as I do not. But you will be alone, until a good Magician comes to claim you and make you his queen of Xanth. That may be some time, unfortunately."

"Time? How long?" Rose was continuing to brighten, faintly. Good care? A good Magician to marry? That should be worth waiting for.

Her mother shrugged. "Perhaps ten years. Perhaps longer. We do not know. It depends on the Magician."

"But if I grow old, he will not want me to be his queen!" She suffered a distressing mental picture of a tall, handsome, robust young Magician striding up to the castle to discover a wizened old ancient hag of a maid. She could hardly blame her fantasy man for his reaction; it was well known that a woman's quality depended on her youth. Ten years would make her thirty, and at that moment her prospects would brutally decline. No woman had a right to pass thirty unless she was already married, and even then it was chancy. Some survived it with a certain grace, as had her mother, but they never spoke of it.

"You will not grow old, my dear. Now dress like the lowliest peasant, for we must sneak you rapidly out of here."

Rose was unable to question her mother further, understanding the need for haste. She dressed in the most ragged and dirty clothing she could find, but she still looked too pretty for her own good. Her face shone with muted beauty, her body pushed the shirt out here and here and the skirt out there, and they had to stuff her midriff with material to make her slender waist look ordinary. Finally her mother brought out the scissors and threatened her glorious swirling rose-petal-hued hair.

Rose screamed. "No, Mother, anything but that!" For it would hurt her physically to cut her hair. She knew, because she had severed a lock of it once as a child, and the cut end had oozed pained sap and the rest of the hair had darkened to brown for a day in distress.

Her mother sighed. "It would be a terrible shame, I agree. I shall do what else I can." She braided her daughter's long tresses, and bound the braids in a circle around her head, and poured ashes over them. This succeeded mainly in making the ashes pretty. Finally she applied a battered old man's hat, jamming it down over the works. She smudged some dirt on Rose's sweet red cheeks.

Rose looked in the mirror. She looked almost merely ordinary now, if not inspected too closely. It would have to do. Maybe she could hunch over to enhance the effect.

They looked out the window. There was a soldier watching the house. It seemed that the King was alert for attempted escape; that was of course the way his sinister mind worked.

"Your father, bless his bones, anticipated this," Lady Ashley said. "In an hour the men will come to carry him away in his coffin. You must be brave."

"Brave?"

Her mother led her to the room where the coffin had been set. Lord Bliss lay there in state. He seemed almost to be sleeping, but the ravages of the poison remained on him, and the atmosphere of death hung close. Rose felt her tears coming; for a brief time the dawning horror of her own situation had eclipsed that of his, but now she knew how terrible it was to lose the one who had loved her most. All because her dear father had grumbled legitimately about the terrible King, and a grumble had escaped to reach the evil royal ear and delve into the dire royal mind.

Rose glanced at the clock, but of course it no longer operated. Her world now seemed timeless, in an awful way.

Lady Ashley touched the base of the coffin. A panel slid aside. There was a shallow chamber beneath the main compartment.

"In there?" Rose asked, appalled.

"It is the one place they will not look," her mother said grimly.

Rose knew it was true. She nerved herself and squeezed into the chamber, and the Lady Ashley slid the panel back, shutting her in. There was a small pillow for her head, and a wan bit of light filtered in from a crevice; those were the only comforts she had.

Do not despair, my daughter.

Rose would have jumped, had there been room. It was no voice which had spoken; rather it was just a thought squeezing down from the corpse immediately above her.

It was a grisly business, but the thought did reassure her. Even in his death, her father had a care for her welfare. He would help her to escape the King. In fact, instead of feeling worse, she was feeling better, because of this realization.

She must have slept, for suddenly she woke to the jolting of the coffin, It was being picked up and carried away. Her mother must have had the bearers come in for it, one to each corner and two more for the sides. Strong men, who would not notice the extra weight. Or perhaps trustworthy men, who would not say anything if they did notice.

She heard the hard breathing of the men as they bore the burden and the voice of the Lady Ashley giving them instructions. The coffin lurched out of the house and into the village. It passed a soldier, who laughed callously.

"What, your fair daughter is not attending the burial? Maybe I'll go into that house and keep her some company. Haw, haw!"

"Do that," the Lady Ashley responded evenly. "And in the morning when the King learns . . ."

The soldier's laughter cut off so suddenly it was as if a sword had been run through his gut. That was of course a far kinder fate than what the King would arrange if the soldier interfered in any way with the King's pleasure. No one would go near that house, not even to verify Rose's presence there, for fear of being put under suspicion. The King's suspicion was deadly too.

There is a one-time enchanted path from here to Castle Roogna, *her father's thought came.* Follow it without fear, for though there are monsters along it, none will harm you. When you are challenged, state your name and business, and you will be allowed to pass. Do not turn back, for then the spell will be broken and you will be lost indeed.

"Thank you, my dear father," Rose said without voice. She had first thought he was helping her even in death; now she knew that he had planned this in life, and set up his death so as to enable her to be saved. The love she bore him was returned, and death had become an instrument of help, rather than a cruel separation. Still, she wished there had been some other way. Had she known the nature of the poison-pen letter in time, she would have stolen it and buried it unopened.

Thank you, beloved daughter.

They came to the burial place. "The spades!" the Lady Ashley said, sounding irritated. "Did no one bring the spades?"

"We shall fetch them," one of the men replied. He seemed somehow unsurprised that such a vital detail had been neglected, and of course it did not require all six men to fetch the spades.

Then the panel slid open. "Quickly, before they return," the Lady Ashley said.

Rose scrambled out. Farewell, my darling. In this manner I repay a bit of the care you so generously lavished on me. I know you go to great love, a long time hence.

"Farewell, beloved Father," Rose whispered, a tear in her eye again.

The Lady Ashley hugged her. "I must remain here for the burial. But you—"

"I know, Mother." And what of this wonderful woman, left bereft of husband and daughter, doomed to live out her declining life alone? Rose's other eye flowed a tear.

"Down that trail! It leads around the village. When you see an unfamiliar path with a slight glow, follow it without hesitation. Go, before the men return!"

"Farewell, beloved Mother." Rose disengaged and set off down the trail, not daring even to look back.

Already a man was returning with a shovel. She recognized him, but hoped he would not recognize her, masked as she was in dirt. She hunched her shoulders and tried to walk in the manner of a boy, crudely, instead of keeping her natural delicate gait. It seemed to work, for he did not give her a second glance.

Then she saw a bit of a glimmer on the ground. She was about to pass it by, before realizing what it was. She turned quickly onto the magic path, which headed directly away from the village.

The trees of the forest closed in about her, and in an instant the light shaded into gloom. It had been dusk, but this was more than that. The path ahead glowed ever so faintly," winding deviously through the jungle. Rose walked along it as fast as she could, fear of imminent pursuit lending her strength. But there was no sound from behind, and finally she slowed and glanced back—and saw nothing but trees and vines and foliage.

She almost paused, but remembered the warning. This was a one-way path, and if she took even one step backward it would disappear and she would be stranded in the wilderness, unable to fend for herself. So she settled for peeking back without stopping her walking. There was no doubt: there was no path behind. She looked down at her moving feet, and saw that the path faded out as her slippers left it behind.

How had her parents obtained this one-time path? The magic must have cost them dearly! They had not said a word to her about it until the time of its use. They had suspected that something like this would be required and had prepared. How fortunate she was for their loving foresight!

She settled into a steadier walk, not knowing how far she would have to go. The West Stockade was not very far from the ancient Castle Roogna, but neither was it very close. She would probably have to walk all night, and she really was not structured for that sort of thing.

A grotesque shape loomed ahead of her, blocking the path. He was huge, hairy, and unbearably ugly. He was an ogre!

"Me see a she!" the ogre boomed in stupid verse, because ugliness was his first nature and stupidity was his second nature. He lifted an arm in surprise. His ham hand accidentally brushed against a small tree. The tree snapped off and crashed to the ground, terrified. Strength was an ogre's third nature. Or maybe she had the order reversed. At any rate, she knew that ogres were justifiably proud of all three.

Rose remembered what she had been told. She stood straight and addressed the monster. "I am Rose, granddaughter of King Yang, and I am on my way to Castle Roogna to await a Magician to marry." She was afraid that if the monster reached for her, she would step back involuntarily and lose the path.

The ogre considered that. It was evident that a thought or two was forging through his brain, because steam rose from his head and fleas with hot feet were jumping off. At last the thought reached its destination just before the hair caught on fire, and the monster stepped off the path. "So go," he growled, disappointed. It was evident that he would have loved to crunch bones as shapely as hers.

Relieved, Rose resumed motion. She hurried by, wrinkling her nose where the air was fraught with the odor of boiled fleas and toasted bugs and the remnants of a scorched thought, and in a moment was well beyond. She glanced back and saw the hulk in the middle of the thickest possible tangle of trees. She wasn't sure that even such a monster could get through that!

Then she heard bashing, and her next glance showed splinters of wood flying up. The ogre could get through well enough, it seemed. She pitied the next person that ogre encountered and was sorry it was unlikely to be the King. But perhaps the creature would not care to crunch the King's foul bones; there were limits even to ogres.

She continued her walk. After a time, or perhaps slightly more, she smelled smoke. She hoped there wasn't a forest fire ahead! But it turned out to be worse: a dragon. A huge fierce smoker, lying athwart the path. If it even breathed on her, she would go into a choking fit.

She came about two steps closer than she dared and stopped. "I am Rose, on my way to Castle Roogna, and—"

The dragon's head turned to orient on her. The holes of its nose were emitting curlicues of dark smoke which drifted up to frighten the leaves of an overhanging branch. Rose almost stepped back, but caught herself. "And I will wait there for a Magician to come and marry me," she concluded.

The dragon sighed somewhat steamily. Then it hefted up its bulk and moved on. It would have no smoked maiden to gnaw this day. It was evidently somewhat disappointed. Or perhaps it was for some other reason that it turned its head and fired such a blast of smoke at a nearby tangle tree that the tree went into a coughing fit and its tentacles turned black with soot. Rose suspected that that particular tangler would not treat the next dragon it encountered very kindly. But perhaps she was being unfair to the tree; she really did not know it very well. She chided herself for possibly thinking ill of it or the dragon without proper cause.

She hurried on. She was glad that the magic of the path was in good order! It was now full night in the forest, but the glow of the path seemed to have brightened in compensation so that she could see her way.

Perhaps a time and a half later, her legs becoming deadly tired, Rose encountered another obstacle. The trees had grown larger, and now crowded the path unmercifully and extended their massive lower branches across it. She would have to scramble around and under and over those branches. This would not be very ladylike, but perhaps no one would notice.

But when she tried to pass the first one, it moved. Surprised, she stopped, not quite stepped back. How could a tree move its branch?

Then she remembered something she had heard. There was an orchard around Castle Roogna, and its outermost ring of trees were active guardians. She was getting near her destination!

She stopped again. "I am Rose, granddaughter of—"

The branches moved. They lifted and twisted like the tentacles of a kraken weed, clearing the path. It seemed that the trees had been expecting her. Maybe they knew that only she could follow this particular path.

It was a relief, for she was about ready to collapse. She had smeared on dirt to make herself look ugly; now she felt just as bad. She tramped on. In her more innocent time she would never have tramped, for it was completely unmaidenly, but right now she felt more like tramp than maiden.

The path wound on through the orchard, and the massive gnarled guardian trees gave way to fruiting trees of every type. In the darkness it was hard to see, but she saw a shoe almost overhanging the path, so knew there was a shoe tree here, and spied another extremely pretty branch arching over the path, which was probably part of an artis-tree. She was definitely approaching the castle.

Now at last it loomed into view, its imposing stonework silhouetted against the background stars. The castle was so tall she wondered whether any stars got snagged on the turrets. It was surrounded by a murky moat, but the path led to a drawbridge that was down. She kept moving, afraid that if she stopped she would collapse in fatigue and dirt where she was. That would definitely be out of character for a maiden princess.

The wooden planks of the drawbridge vibrated with her footsteps. Then she came to the front gate and found that it was open. This castle hadn't even been properly closed by the last person here! But as she entered, she heard squealing behind her and saw that the drawbridge was lifting itself. Then the gate closed, sealing her in. It was the castle opening and closing itself!

"Thank you, Castle Roogna," she said. Then, safe at last, she did collapse in what was probably not a properly maidenly swoon. Fortunately no one was watching.

She woke to sunlight. She was in a bed! It had wonderfully clean sheets and a truly pleasant soft pillow.

"But I'm a grimy mess!" she exclaimed, realizing how she must be soiling the sheets.

Something flickered nearby. "Nooooo," it moaned.

"*Eeeeek!*" Rose screamed in proper maidenly fashion. "A ghost!"

The ghost, frightened by her eeeeek, vanished. Rose realized that she had been impolite. "I'm sorry, ghost; I didn't mean to scream at you," Rose called apologetically. It just wasn't proper for a princessly maiden to be rude to anyone, even a ghost.

The shape reappeared. It was mistyish and amorphous, floating somewhat above the floor. It concentrated and became more like a human figure, female. "Noooo messs," it breathed.

Now Rose understood. "But I'm all covered in—and the sheets—" She looked down at herself, and her mouth dropped delicately open. For both she and the sheets were quite clean. "How—?" she asked, her chagrin changing type.

The ghost coalesced further, becoming shapely to the eye of those who might like that type. "Ffrienndss ccaaame," she said. "Yoou weere oon flooor—"

Now Rose remembered: she had collapsed on the stone floor just inside the door. Her legs still felt sore. Now she was not only in what was evidently an upstairs bed, she was clean and in a clean and fully princessly nightie. Someone must have—must have—

"What friends?" she asked, perhaps a fraction more sharply than was polite.

"Thhe zzombieees," the ghost replied.

"Zombies!" Rose exclaimed, horrified anew. But she realized that zombies, being dead, had very little human emotion and would not have cared a great deal about the exposure of her living body. They had not hurt her. So perhaps she would be best advised simply to forget that aspect. Selective memory was another maidenly trait, for it helped protect innocence. She had been dirty and now was clean, and the mechanism of it was no one's business.

"Perhaps we should introduce ourselves," she said, remembering her manners. "I am Rose, daughter of Lord Bliss and Lady Ashley Rose, granddaughter of King Yang and his second wife whose name escapes me at the moment."

The ghost made a floating curtsy. "I aam Millliee the Ghoosst, oonce a ssiimple mmaid, betrothed to the Zzombie Mmaster." Her speech was getting better as she practiced. So was her form; she was now about as shapely an apparition as Rose had seen outside of the mirror.

"So thrilled to meet you, Millie," Rose said, extending her hand.

The ghost extended hers. The contact was hardly tangible, just the feel of cool vapor. But it was enough for the formal introduction.

Rose inquired further and learned that Millie in life had had the talent of sex appeal and had expired by the magic of a jealous rival for the hand of the Zombie Master. After Millie's demise, the Zombie Master had zombied himself, so as to join her as well as he was able. It wasn't much of a romance at the moment, Millie confessed petitely, because he was rotten and she was insubstantial, but they hoped for improvement in the future. Meanwhile, Millie would be happy to serve Rose as she had served living folk when she had been a maid. She had a fair notion of the expectations of royalty.

Rose was hungry. Millie offered to have her friend the Zombie Master get a zombie chef in the kitchen, but Rose decided graciously that the zombies had done more than enough already, and she would not rouse them from their graves for something she could handle herself. She got up and followed Millie to the kitchen, where she found a collection of fruits and cookies with only a little zombie rot on them. She washed them without comment, realizing that it was not her place to be finicky, and had a good meal.

Thus commenced her life at Castle Roogna. She was free to roam the castle and the grounds, picking her own fruit and nuts, but not to leave: the outer ring of trees was woodenly firm about that. It was, she understood, protective custody; she was safe as long as she remained here, and no hostile party could get in. It was a pleasant life, with all the best of everything, except for the fact that she had no living company. Fortunately there seemed to be a sanity spell on the premises, so that she did not go crazy; she simply regretted that she was mostly alone, and comforted herself with the realization that company was as one defined it. Millie was excellent company, and so were the other ghosts: sultry Renee and her male friend Jordan the Barbarian, Doreen, the child Button, and one whose name she didn't quite catch. Even the zombies were tolerable from upwind, once she got to know them. She learned to play cards with the lady ghosts, though she had to deal the cards and hold theirs up facing away from her for them to see. But mostly she just napped, to wile away the boredom.

After a year, even napping became somewhat dull. "I need something to do!" she exclaimed.

"Perhaps some cross-stitching," Millie suggested. "It is dull for us ghosts too, and we can't do anything physical, but you can."

So Rose took up cross-stitching, starting with the image of a cross face, as it seemed appropriate. It seemed inadequate by itself, so She pondered a few days and devised a bit of verse to go with it. She would give it to the Magician who finally came to marry her and be king.

> These little stitches that were mine
> Had to be taken in time
> And so they grew cross
> For they counted it loss
> And decided they wanted to be thine.

She went on to do a great deal of fine needlepoint and tapestry, and this pursuit wiled away another year or two. But even this became dull without company; normally she made such things for others, and there were no others to give these to. She had offered to make things for the ghosts, but they declined, as they were unable to wear them.

"But do you know, you might like to see Jonathan's Tapestry," Millie said.

"Who is Jonathan?"

"The Zombie Master. He—oh, I can't talk about it!" But Millie did show Rose the Tapestry, where it had been carefully folded and put away in a drawer. Rose brought it out and hung it on a wall and gazed at it, and was amazed. For the pictures stitched into it moved.

In fact it was a historical presentation. It responded to her command, for she was a princess, and showed any pictures she desired. It had been made by the wonderful Sorceress Tapis, given to the Zombie Master in the form of a jigsaw puzzle, and hung on a wall of Castle Roogna after his death. It showed the history of Xanth. From it she learned exactly what had happened to Millie, a tragedy indeed, and even what had happened to Rose herself, for it covered everything through the present.

Rose lost track of the time she spent enraptured by the Tapestry. She learned everything about Xanth. But eventually even this palled. The one thing she refused to watch was her mother; she did not want to confirm her mother's loneliness and decline. Again she was up against the ultimate limit: she had no one to share this with. Doing things alone, no matter how interesting they might be, was incomplete.

She talked to the ghosts, but they spent most of their time fading out entirely. She sang and read poetry to the plants in the castle and garden. She made fancy meals for herself and an imaginary companion; since she had to eat the companion's food too, she made sure it was good, and because it was unprincessly to get fat, she made them small. She even forced herself to make and eat her most disliked food, sour kraut soup. A steady diet of that would make her thin as a ghost!

But mainly she planted and tended her beloved roses in the courtyard of the castle. This was her talent, and her roses were very special. They would live long after she was gone, and their precious magic would be available to anyone who requested it. The one thing that was forbidden was to cut any of them from their living stems. These roses had to be appreciated alive. They were a great comfort to her. Yet they could not make up for her lack of human company.

Then Millie had another suggestion. "The library—"

Rose checked out the musty castle library. There were volumes collected by King Roogna and his successors. They related to everything in Xanth, its history and magic and people. She had never been strong on reading, but how she got into it and spent a long time learning aspects of things the Tapestry hadn't covered. Much of the material was beyond her understanding, but of course it was not intended for her; it was intended for the edification of Magician-Kings. But she would be able to show it to the Magician who came to marry her and give him a good head start finding whatever type of information he might desire or need. In short, she was Making Herself Useful, before the fact.

One day when she was out picking new pillows for the beds, as she did every month to keep them fresh for the Magician—what a horror if

he arrived and was turned off by imperfect castle-keeping!—Rose spied a
monstrous serpent.

"*Eeeeeek!*" she screamed, affrighted.

But the creature made no hostile move. Instead it bowed its head as
if penitent. She realized that only appropriate folk were allowed through
the defensive trees, so perhaps she had misjudged this one. She hurried inside and fetched a translation book she had found in the library:
Human/Serpent. She wasn't sure how to use it, but hoped that she would
figure it out. She brought it out and came hesitantly toward the huge
snake.

"What do you want?" she inquired, primed to flee at the mere drop of
a bit of saliva from a fang.

The creature hissed, nodding toward the book. She opened the volume
and looked at the printing in it.

"Fear not, lusscious maiden," the print said. "I understand that this
casstle hass no moat monsster currently, sso I have come to apply for the
possition."

Rose was amazed and pleased. "This is true," she said. "The position is
open. But you have to promise not to eat me or the Magician who comes
to marry me and be king."

The serpent hissed again. "Of coursse," the print in the book said,
replacing the prior print. "Thiss iss SSOP.*"

Rose looked at the foot of the page. There was another asterisk with a
supplementary statement:

*SOP = STANDARD OPERATING PROCEDURE, SUCH AS IN THE CASE
OF MOAT MONSTERS NOT MOLESTING LEGITIMATE DENIZENS OF
THE CASTLE THEY GUARD.

"Right this way!" Rose said, thrilled. She walked toward the castle, and the
serpent slithered after her. "By the way, what is your name?"

There was another hiss, and the book printed "Ssoufflé Sserpent at
your sservice, ssisster."

"Soufflé? Oh, what a lovely name!" she exclaimed with maidenly
delight.

The serpent seemed taken aback. Later it occurred to her that it might have encountered less positive reactions to its name. But Rose loved soufflé, and sometimes splurged on soufflé pie when she felt naughty, for it was horribly fattening.

Soufflé took up residence in the moat, and thereafter Rose did feel safer. Also, the serpent was good company when she felt particularly lonely, because he had come from outside more recently than she had and had oddments of news. Of course she could get the news from, the Tapestry, but it was nicer when personal.

In such manner passed the first century.

Rose ceased to wonder when the Magician would come. She knew what was happening in Xanth because the Tapestry and a couple of magic mirrors kept her current, but it was now another world for her. She simply maintained herself from day to day, never aging or losing her wits. And she longed for the day it would end and she would be able to give all her love to the Magician. Someday.

The second century passed. All the folk Rose had known were gone. But Castle Roogna, forgotten by Xanth, remained, keeping itself in repair, waiting for the Magician who would be king and restore the former splendor of King Roogna's magnificent edifice.

After 246 years the Magician came—and Rose had a problem. For he was no Magician. She knew that, because the Tapestry showed his history. He was the former King Humfrey, twice married and twice deserted by his unfeeling or selfish wives. Also by his one true love, who had declined to marry him. This was a man thrice rejected. Not exactly ideal. But she was so desperate for company that she longed for his success. In fact, she might even have cheated just a tiny bit, to enable him to win through. After all, he was a good man, and by the time she had viewed his life history she loved him. It wasn't as if it mattered whether one more beach head appeared just in time to distract the colored men; it was their job to keep those heads combed regardless, as well as to question any intruders. So she had tried the spell she had found in one of the tomes and used the magic mirror to picture the place she wanted it to grow. Surely that was no evil thing, was it?

But now here he was, and she wasn't going to send him away and wait perhaps another two hundred and forty-six years for her Magician.

There was only one thing to do: she would have to see that Humfrey *became* a Magician. She had learned of a way from one of the tomes in the library. Then it would be all right.

She slipped on any old thing and went out to meet her hero.

Chapter 9

MAGICIAN

"So you see," Rose concluded, "I can't marry you if you aren't a true Magician. But if you go to the University of Magic, you can get a degree in magic, and then you will be a real Magician and Castle Roogna will have to let me go." She glanced obliquely at me. "Unless you are willing to be king again. Then you could live here."

"I don't want to be king again!" I protested. But if that was the price of marrying her, then I might have to do it. She was certainly my dream woman. It had taken time to love MareAnn—perhaps all of a day—and then it hadn't worked out. Rose had become my second love in all of a minute, and there was every sign it would work out if I cooperated. "Anyway, the Storm King is young yet, so Xanth won't have an opening for another king for perhaps forty years. Do you want to wait that long?"

"No!" she exclaimed with maidenly emphasis, her precious bosom heaving. "I want to marry you right now."

It was one of the oddities of our encounter that there had been no courtship or proposal; we had met and were in love, and we wanted to marry and remain with each other indefinitely. Neither of us questioned that. She had told me her story, and she already knew mine. So our only present concern was how to manage our association, when Castle Roogna would let her marry only a proper Magician and would not let her leave before she did. The castle had not anticipated the approach of a non-Magician who knew enough of magic to get through. It had tried to balk me and had failed, perhaps in part because it attuned to the kingly experience I had had and could not be quite certain that I wasn't a Magician. But it would not let Rose go. She was Rose of Roogna now, and the castle was in effect her parent. I really could not question that; it had taken good care of her for (almost) two and a half centuries. Had it not done so, I would not have met her, and that would have been disaster.

"Where is this University of Magic?" I asked. "I have learned of most magical things of Xanth, but not that."

"That's because it isn't of the human realm in Xanth," she said. "I read about it in an Arcane Text. It is a demonic institution. Most demons live under the ground somewhere; only a few bother to explore the surface, and then they aren't very serious about it."

"I know," I murmured, thinking of Dana. She had been caught with a conscience, so had had to endure the indignity of human fallibilities of conscience and love. She had been a wonderful wife in every respect, until she succeeded in getting rid of her conscience. Our son, Dafrey, was a good person too; I hoped he didn't lose the conscience when he married and sired offspring. Normal demons just didn't care very much about human beings.

"Yes, you do," she agreed, touching my hand. She had reviewed my relationship with Dana and did not hold it against me. Rose was my second true love, and would be my first married true love, because of MareAnn's determined innocence. "So you must go among the demons, and enroll in their university, and pass their courses and get your degree, and be a Magician, and then we can marry and be happy together."

"But I don't have a way to contact the demons," I protested. "And if I did, I can't think what would persuade them to let me enroll in their school."

"There is a spell for summoning demons in one of the tomes in the castle library," she said.

I realized that that library was something I had to see. I could probably spend years there, learning the things I had not been able to learn elsewhere. If I got to be a true Magician and married Rose, the castle would let me do that, even if it didn't let me stay overnight. "Maybe I could make some sort of deal," I said. I suspected that I would not enjoy whatever the demons demanded, but I was quite sure I would not enjoy life apart from Rose, so this was the lesser of discomforts.

"I shall go in and find that volume and learn that spell," Rose said. "Meanwhile, perhaps Soufflé will let you bathe in the moat."

The monster serpent hissed angrily at the notion, not wanting its nice moat dirtied by my grime. But Rose turned her head and looked at it with just a tiny hint of reproach, and the creature melted out of sight. I knew how that was.

So she walked gracefully inside, and I set my pack down on the bank and waded into the water. Soon I was clean and the moat was filthy. Soufflé retreated around to the back of the castle, but I could hear the monster sneezing.

Then I emerged and walked toward a linen tree to harvest a towel. At that moment Rose emerged and caught a full view of me. Oops!

But she smiled. "I have seen your healthy body in every state," she murmured. "The Tapestry conceals nothing."

That was true. I had known about the Tapestry only through history and hoped to get to see and use it when I became a Magician. Of course I had no physical secrets from Rose!

By the time I had gotten dried and dressed, Rose had set up the spell. It was an odd one, requiring a pentacle (a five-pointed star), a candle, and spoken words. "The words combine with the flame to summon the demon," Rose explained. "The diagram is to prevent the demon from reaching out to squish you, being angry about being summoned. It can't leave the pentacle until you let it go, and you won't let it go until it makes a binding deal with you."

"This is an interesting device," I remarked. I had thought I knew something about demons, but I had not known they could be summoned, and Dana had not told me. Even during her souled state, she had evidently had some caution. "What are the words of the spell?"

"There seem to be a number of variations," she said. "Some use terms which I, as a maiden, naturally do not understand. I suppose demons, being creatures of the nether regions, have a more explicit mode of expression. As nearly as I could tell, you can say what you want and it should work, as long as it rhymes. The more specific words are to isolate particular demons."

That gave me a notion. "Maybe Dana, the one to whom I was married, would be good to call. She would not pretend to misunderstand me."

"Perhaps so," Rose said, seeming not entirely pleased. That made me wonder just how explicit the Tapestry was about matters relating to the Adult Conspiracy. Since it evidently knew whether its watcher was of royal blood, it might also know whether the watcher was old enough. Was

Rose considered to be twenty or two hundred and sixty-six? What did it consider to be the fabled Age of Consent? I could not safely assume that she remained innocent, despite her reference to maidenly modesty. She could be jealous of Dana, for good reason. Yet I did not know any other demon by name.

We lit the candle and set it in the middle of the pentacle. Then I stepped out and said: "Dana Demon, passing by—come to me and don't be shy." The idea of a demon being shy was laughable, but the point was the rhyme.

The flame flickered. Then smoke curled out of it, looming larger until it almost filled the pentacle. Blazing eyes formed in the smoke and squirmy tentacles. What monster had we caught?

"I had understood your former wife to be beautiful," Rose murmured, with what in a less gentle person might have been taken as irony.

The smoke dissipated, leaving a firmer outline. The tentacles became arms and legs. The body shaped down into a roughly female figure with a head in the form of a swirling storm cloud. "What idiot put this firetrap here?" a voice reminiscent of a harpy's screeched.

Somewhat cowed, I nevertheless stood my ground. "Is that you, Dana? This is Humfrey, whom you have known." I wasn't completely satisfied with that phrasing; it was subject to interpretation. But this was the first time I had done this, and I was feeling my way.

The figure shaped up some more, becoming somewhat attractive. "Humfrey? I have heard that name before. But I am not Dana; I took her watch this month. Now let me go, dance, before I blow you away."

"Dance?" I asked. "Don't you mean dunce?"

"Whatever." The figure became quite appealing. "I think I recognize that voice. About a quarter century ago."

"Demoness Metria!" I exclaimed, remembering Dana's friend. The one with the slight problem of vocabulary, who liked to see what human folk did.

The figure turned luscious, and the face formed. "Well, now. You were good for a bit of entertainment, as I recall. What do you want this time?"

"I want to enroll in the University of Magic."

Metria's jaw dropped. But almost immediately she recovered her composure and squatted to pick up the fallen jaw. She set it back in place, where it worked as well as ever. "Are you crazy? Even for a man, I mean?"

"No. I'm in love."

"Same thing. Why would you want to get into anything as deadly dull as the university?"

"I want to get my degree and be a legitimate Magician."

"Well, you can't. Only demons can attend or folk sponsored by demons."

I had a bright idea. "Well, you're a demon. You can sponsor me."

She laughed, her torso shaking in interesting ways, while Rose frowned for some reason. "Why should I do a planetary thing like that?"

"What kind of thing?"

"Starry, solarian, cometary, moonish, cheesy—"

"Lunatic?"

"Whatever. Answer the question."

I pondered feverishly. "Because it would be amusing to watch me struggle through that system."

She considered. Her gaze focused disturbingly on me, then on Rose, who was standing back a way. "This is the creature you love?"

"Leave Rose out of it!" I snapped.

"I intend to. I'll make you this deal: I will enroll with you and be your companion. We shall share a room. If I can't distract you from your purpose before you get the degree, then you will have it."

"Listen, demoness," I said angrily. "If you think I'm going to mess with you as I did with Dana, forget it! All I want is an education."

"Then you have nothing to fear from me," she pointed out. "Safe in your desire for the degree and your love for Thorn, here—"

"Rose!" Rose said with an almost unprincessly sharpness.

"Whatever. So do we deal?"

I knew there was little I could do except deal or quit. I looked at Rose. "My marriage to Dana Demoness showed me that demons can be constant, when they have reason," I said.

"I know. But she had a soul."

"And the moment she divested herself of that soul, she took off. But she told me that Metria, here, always told the truth, except about her age. So maybe—"

"So I'm a smidgen over seventeen," Metria said, adopting the aspect of a teenage girl. "So does it matter?"

It had been twenty-two years since I had met Metria at the Key Stone Copse. I decided not to comment. But Rose did.

"Actually, I am a bit over seventeen too," she said. "I was born two hundred and sixty-six years ago. But the last two hundred and forty-six have been at Castle Roogna, and I haven't aged."

"Hey, I like this woman!" Metria muttered. "She knows about being ageless." She glanced at me. "Well, Humfrey, what is it to wasp?"

"To what?" I asked.

"Hornet, yellow jacket, buzz, sting, to exist or not to exist—"

"To bee?"

"Whatever. Are you in or out?"

I looked at Rose again. "I fear it is the only way, my love."

"I fear it is, beloved," she agreed. "Accept her sponsorship. I will wait for you. I know you don't have any future with a demoness."

"Ah, but what a past he has had with one," Metria said, "and what a present coming up."

"A what?" I asked.

"Gift, token, bonus, gratuity, alms—"

"You had the right word," I said. "I mean what are you going to give me?"

"You have a past and a future; I will make your present interesting. In fact, so interesting that you will be distracted from your studies and will flunk out of the U of M. Then your future will be without Rose of Roogna, here, and she will be tragically disappointed in you. That will be extremely entertaining."

I looked once more at Rose. "I'm not sure this is a good idea."

"It is a distinctly mediocre idea," Rose agreed. "But the best that offers. Prove her wrong, my love, and return to me with your degree."

Emboldened by that expression of confidence, I did it. "Sponsor me for the University of Magic," I told Metria. "I will succeed despite your distractions."

"Well, then, let's get it on," she agreed. "Smudge a hole in the pentacle and I'll take you there."

I scuffed a hole in the line with my foot. Metria became smoke and curled out through that gap, reforming as a flying dragon. The dragon's huge jaws snapped me up. Fortunately the teeth were more apparent than real and did not crunch me.

"I shall return!" I cried boldly back to Rose as the dragon launched into the air and bore me away.

"I'll be watching!" she called back. I thought she meant to say "waiting," but realized that she had the Tapestry, so could watch me as she had before. That would surely steel my resolve, should it ever waver.

The dragon winged southeast until it reached a large lake. That was Ogre-Chobee, where the ogres had once lived, until they set out for the Ogre-Fen-Ogre Fen. Then the dragon dived. It zoomed into the water, plunging through it, and finally a new world opened out. This was the realm of the demons; the dive into the water must have been merely to mask its location, since demons could dematerialize and reappear far distant in a moment. Did that mean I had done the same? That was an intriguing notion. But it could be that there really was an entrance to the demon realm under the water.

Metria had resumed her usual human form. I know it was no more natural to her than the dragon form was; *all* forms were unnatural for demons. But I preferred this one.

We were standing before a large desk piled high with meaningless papers. A demon with receding hair and heavy spectacles sat there. This was odd, because demons could assume any form they chose and did not suffer from the maladies of mortals. Evidently this one just happened to prefer this unprepossessing aspect. Beside him was a name plaque: BUREAUCRAT. "Next!" he said.

Metria nudged me. "Enroll, pull."

"What?"

"Yank, tug, wrench, lug—"

"Jerk?"

"Whatever. Do it."

I faced the desk demon. "I want to jerk. I mean enroll."

The demon yawned, showing a gullet that extended, literally, to his feet; he was hollow. He materialized a pencil and complicated form. "Name?"

"Humfrey."

He made a note on the form. "Species?"

"Human."

One bored eye oriented on me, while the other remained on the paper. "Sponsor?"

"The Demoness Metria."

Now the other eye left the paper and oriented on Metria. "Having fun again, female?"

"Well, it does get boring up there in man's land," she said defensively.

"To be sure." Now both eyes foeused on me. "You understand that she has no interest in your welfare, Humfrey? That your candidacy will be a joke among demons? That there are simpler ways to arrange to be humiliated?"

"Yes," I said, my mouth getting dry.

The eyes returned to the paper. "Major?"

"Magic."

"Are you sure?"

Suddenly I was uncertain. "I want to be a legitimate Magician among my kind. I understand that a degree in magic from this university will qualify me."

"Correct. Specialty?"

"Information."

Once more an eye aimed at me. "There are easier specialties, which are more dramatic."

"Information is power," I said.

"Motivation?"

"I want to become a true Magician so that I can marry the woman I love."

The Demon Bureaucrat's hand came down bearing a stamp. It pounded the form. "Proceed to your dormitory chamber. Next!"

"But—" I said.

One eye swiveled to cover me. "You wish to withdraw already?"

"No. But don't I have to pay for this? Demons don't do anything for nothing."

"You will pay." The eye left me.

"But *how* will I pay? I mean—"

Now both eyes returned, momentarily. "In the normal fashion. You will be entertaining us by your folly and failure. Did you expect otherwise?"

I realized that his candor was because he cared not even half a whit for my sensibilities. Everything I did here would be watched by the demons, whose greatest joy was the confounding of mortal folk. I suppose I might feel the same, if I lived for thousands of years with power to do anything I wanted and no need to eat or sleep. No, I should not have expected anything else. "Thank you," I said with what little dignity I was able to scrape up.

"Right this way, fool," Metria said, taking me by the hand.

"But don't you need to register too?" I asked belatedly. "You said you were enrolling."

"I enrolled five hundred—" She paused. "Hours ago. Now I'll get around to taking classes." She dragged me on.

We came to a bare stone chamber. I gazed at it, not pleased. The prospect of lying down on stone that was not bedrock did not appeal. Then Metria snapped her fingers, and abruptly the chamber had furnishings. There were curtains on the window that had not been there before—neither window nor curtains—and a plush rug on the wooden floor that had been stone, and rugs hanging on the walls, and sunlight slanting through the glass panel that was now the ceiling. In the center was a huge round bed.

"Well, let's get it on," she said, making a flying leap for the bed as her clothing misted away. She bounced, and her bare flesh bounced approximately in unison.

"Get *what* on?" I asked with greater naivete than I felt.

"Get your clothing off, and I'll show you."

Just as I had suspected. "Forget it, demoness! I'll sleep on the floor."

"No, you won't. You get demerits for acting uncouth."

This was new to me, but I had no reason to question her accuracy. "Demerits are bad for me?"

"Too many of them will wash you out."

"Then I'll sleep on the bed. But I'll ignore you."

"Ha!" she said confidently. But there was a tiny hint of uncertainty hovering in her vicinity. I knew what such hints were like; they hovered until they had the chance to magnify themselves enormously. It was good to see that the demons could be afflicted by them too.

I made it worse for her by distributing my few possessions appropri ately through the room while rigorously ignoring her. I could see from the edges of my vision that she was making scissor motions with her bare legs, but I never looked directly. Legs that were bare up to the waist could be a distraction, and I wanted her to know that I was having none of it. "Where do I eat?" I asked.

Demons didn't need to eat, but I did, so Metria took me to the mess hall. I wondered why it was called that, until I saw that it was the site of what might have been the worst food fight in contemporary Xanth. So that's what demons did with food! Mashed potato was caked on the walls, jam drooled from the ceiling, and puddings lay like mundane cow flops on the floor between pools of milk and beer.

"Serve yourself," Metria said, indicating the mess.

My reaction must have shown too plainly, because she dissolved into laughter. She melted right down into the biggest, brownest cow flop of them all, and I heard an echoing "Ho-ho-ho!" from the walls. It seemed that I was not disappointing the demons who wanted entertainment.

But I had a notion how such things were set up, because in my time of marriage to Dana Demoness she had let slip some hints. She had really been a good wife, while she had her soul. The funny thing was that the reason demons didn't have souls was that they *were* souls. It seemed that when a loose soul served as a body, it lost some of its finer properties, such as conscience and love. Evidently these were not properly things of the body, so the process of forming a body was hard on them. But when a soul occupied a body, even *a* body that was a corrupt soul, those qualities returned.

I walked to the counter across the chamber. There were tall stools there. I perched on one. Sure enough, a waitress appeared. She was another demoness, of course, playing a role, but roles were the perpetual delight of the demon species. "One slice of apple pie, please," I said. "*And* a pitcher of purple tsoda popka." I had discovered Lake Tsoda Popka near the North Village during my years of surveying and had developed a taste for the fizzy stuff.

She reached under the counter and produced these things. "Thank you," I said, and she smiled at me. The only problem was that demons did not feel pleasure the same way mortals did, so her smile was artificial.

I ate my meal, and it was *a* good one. Apparently the demons intended to play it straight as long as I did. I was here to try for my degree, and Metria was the one privileged to distract me from that effort. The others only served as supporting players. Perhaps they would get demerits if they failed to perform their roles aptly.

I finished in due course and stood. "Don't I get a tip?" the waitress asked.

Dana had not mentioned that detail. Very well. "When you smile at a customer, get your eyes into it as well as your mouth," I said. "Then it looks like genuine feeling."

"Oh, thank you!" she said, smiling with genuine feeling.

I returned to my room. Metria was there, in a stunning see-through blouse and skirt. She was very good with her emulations, and I might have been tempted despite knowing better. There was something about this kind of partial clothing that was more tempting than outright nakedness, perhaps because it gave the illusion that something hidden was being glimpsed. But I remembered three things. (1) She had no interest in me except my failure. (2) Other demons were watching, hoping that I would do something hilarious, such as trying to summon the stork with her. And (3) Rose was probably watching too, via the Tapestry. Suddenly I felt extremely Straight and Narrow.

Anyway, I had something else to do, after my meal. I looked around, but saw no place to wash or other. "Where is—?" I asked.

"Oh, that's right—mortals have natural functions!" Metria said. She gestured, and a door appeared in the wall.

I went to it and put my hand on the knob. I turned it, and the door opened. Beyond was a smaller chamber with the devices I required. I used them.

Then I heard the walls chortling. "Ho, ho, ho!"

Well, perhaps in time they would get tired of such entertainment. I was not about to suspend my natural functions for the sake of avoiding their ridicule.

I found pajamas hanging on a hook. I changed into them. They fit me perfectly. Demons could do things well when they chose.

I emerged and went to the bed. Metria was there, of course, wearing a clinging negligee. She rolled into me as I lay down, showing the deep cleavage of her bosom. "Show me what you did with Dana," she said.

I closed my eyes and breathed evenly. It was a significant effort, but *I* knew I had to succeed.

"That's what you did?" she asked, knowing considerably better.

"I associated with her for several years before we married," I reminded her. "Then I merely slept with her, as I did with MareAnn. Storks do not respond to mere sleeping. I am not married to you, so I am treating you similarly."

"Oh, fudge!" she swore, and a puffball of smoke flew from her pretty mouth.

"Ho, ho, ho!" the walls chortled. This time I knew that I was not the object of their laughter.

Next morning we went to the first class. There were a number of demons there, male and female, and they looked almost as nervous as I felt. It seemed this really was a university; the only unusual thing about it was that I, a mortal, was attending. I sat in the front row; at the next desk to my left was Metria, looking bored. At the next desk to my right was a demon wearing glasses; apparently some demons did need them for reading. This one's horns were vestigial, and his tail was a soft tuft. Taken as a whole, not one of the more ferocious specimens.

I decided to be positive. "Hello," I said to the demon. "I am Humfrey, here to learn to be a Magician."

"Hello," the demon replied. "I am Beauregard, here to study the liabilities of the living state." He blinked behind his glasses. "I say! Are you mortal?"

"That I am," I confessed.

"Why, you would be an excellent subject! May I observe you?"

"You might as well," I said. "Other demons are, and finding it humorous."

"We have our discourteous members, as do the mortal folk. I would never—"

I was coming to appreciate that all demons were not alike. I was getting to like this one, if he wasn't just pretending to be halfway decent. "Maybe you should insult me too, so you won't get in trouble with other demons."

"But that would be—" He paused, reconsidering. "You mean you won't mind?"

I smiled. "Not as long as you don't mean it. We can exchange friendly insults."

"Excellent, fathead!" he exclaimed, delighted.

"Think nothing of it, incompetent," I responded.

That was the way of it; thereafter we always greeted each other with insults, and we were friends. We were to have a long association. I was feeling better already.

The professor swept into the room. There was a sudden hush. He was an imposing figure of a demon, with gnarled horns and swishing tail, and his fangs made his mouth into a perpetual grimace.

"I am Professor Grossclout," he announced. "We shall now proceed to an exploration of the fundamentals of metamagic. What is a feasible definition of this concept?" he paused, glaring about. "Beauregard!"

Beauregard jumped. "I, uh, am not exactly sure, sir," he stumbled, looking ashamed.

"Metria!"

"Who cares?" she asked, shrugging. "I'm just auditing this class anyway."

The dread professorial eye spiked me next. "Humfrey!"

"I, uh, think that would be something alongside of or beyond magic," I said, terrified of being shown up as an ignoramus. "Maybe something that—"

"Inadequate!" he roared, cutting me off. He glared around the classroom. "You numbskulls come here with heads full of mush"—he glanced significantly at Beauregard, who cowered in his chair—"and bad attitudes"—he glanced at Metria, who was doing her nails—"but maybe, if you survive, you will eventually learn something about magic." He glanced at me, and I was electrified: *I had found faint favor!*

We listened, fascinated and terrified. What a creature!

"Simply put, metamagic is that magic which affects, or is defined in terms of, magic itself," the professor continued, edifying our mushy brains. "The one-time king of the human aspect of Xanth, Roogna, adapted living magic to suit his purpose. The other-time king, Ebnez, adapted inanimate magic similarly. Those are examples of metamagic. Someone who could emulate or otherwise affect the magic talents of others would be indulging in metamagic." The professor continued, and I was rapt; he knew more about magic than I had dreamed existed!

Hours later, dazed by the day's classes, I found myself back in my room with Metria and Beauregard. "What a monster!" Beauregard exclaimed.

"What boredom," Metria added.

"What genius!" I concluded.

The other two looked at me. "I can see why Grossclout likes you," Beauregard said.

"I can see I have my work cut out for me," Metria said, dropping into a chair.

"What work is that?" Beauregard inquired naively.

She spread her legs, giving him a good view under her short skirt so that he could see her panties. "To distract this tree-blood from his studies."

I had thought demons had seen it all, but evidently Beauregard hadn't. His glasses turned pink—the exact shade of the panties. There certainly *was* a difference between demons! "What?"

"Ignoramus, numbskull, blockhead, dunce, simpleton, nincompoop, fool, bumpkin—"

"Sap?" he asked, catching on at last.

"Whatever. I win if he doesn't get his degree." She closed her legs.

Beauregard's lenses began to clear. "I, uh, had better go," he mumbled.

"The toilet's there," she said, and the door to that chamber appeared.

"No, I mean—I don't know what I mean." He stumbled out. There was a "ho, ho" from a wall; apparently I wasn't the only entertaining figure here.

"That wasn't nice, Metria," I said reprovingly.

"Oh? What's wrong with it?" She opened her legs toward me. Now her panties were blue.

"What's wrong is that you're supposed to be tormenting me, not him—and I care a whole lot more about metamagic than I do about your faked-up underwear."

For once she was silent, but she looked ready to explode into a fireball. "Ho, ho, ho!" a wall laughed.

When, tired but exhilarated by learning at the end of the day, I came to bed, there was Rose of Roogna under the sheet. I froze, amazed. "H-how—?"

"Oh, my love, I just couldn't wait," she said breathlessly. "I had to come to you."

I got into the bed with her, hardly believing my fortune. "But how did you find your way here, Rose?"

She kissed me passionately on the mouth. "I looked in a tome for a period."

"A what?"

"Epoch, age, duration, era, term, time—"

"Spell?"

"Whatever. Clasp me close, my love! Make that stork jump!"

"Sorry, Metria. I have a hard course of study ahead."

She kissed me again. "Really goose that stork! I'm ready—" She broke off, realizing that I had seen through her little charade. "Peaches and cream!" she swore, turning into a fair emulation of the stork she had described.

"Ho, ho, and ho!" a pillow chortled, before getting smashed by a wing.

I did seem to be holding my own. I hoped Metria never caught on to how near she had come to fooling me.

The year passed in days, I mean a daze. I progressed rapidly, because I had already studied everything magical I could find and I was absolutely fascinated by the subject. Metria, unable to admit how badly she had misjudged the situation, settled into a polka-dot funk and finally drifted away, bored furious. I spent a lot of time with Beauregard; we did homework together. He was bright enough, just young for a demon. He would surely get his degree in time.

Before I knew it, I was embroiled in my dissertation: "Lost Human Castles with Magical Implications." I had a head start, because I had already found Castle Roogna, but now I had to run down the other great lost castle, that of the Zombie Master. It wasn't all that far from Castle Roogna, as the dragon flies, but it was a devious and messy distance as the magic student walked. I finally located it, and discovered that it was a rather nice place, now that the zombies were gone. In fact—

A light blinked over my head. This would be a fine place to live with Rose after we were married! I couldn't live in Castle Roogna, because I would not be king and was not of royal lineage. The castle, as I understood it, was quite strict about that. But once I married her, I could take her away with me. Castle Zombie was a fine and private place, ideal as a reclusive retreat for those without pretensions.

At last the grueling course was through. I knew more about magic than any living man before me, yet my thirst for more remained. Professor Grossclout was almost approving: "In another century you may be a credit to your species," he remarked gruffly.

I defended my thesis successfully, though the demon interrogators made me sweat. "What you have here is competent. But why haven't you covered *all* the lost human castles with magical implications?" one asked sharply.

"But there are only two," I protested, suddenly uncertain.

"What of the Ivory Tower?" he demanded. "What of New Castle Zombie?"

Professor Grossclout nudged him. "Those have not yet been constructed," he murmured.

"Oh. Well, what of the Nameless Castle?"

Grossclout nodded. "He did miss that. However, two out of three isn't bad."

Nameless Castle? I had never dreamed of such a thing. Where and what could it be?

So I made a C minus, but I passed, thanks to Grossclout's favor. It seemed that he appreciated having a student who was genuinely interested in the subject, even if some mush remained in his head.

I had my degree. I was now a true Magician of Information. I could marry Rose at last.

Chapter 10

HELL

To her great surprise, Rose found herself awakened by the delicious smell of hot coffee, though she had harvested no hot coffee mugs recently. What was happening?

Millie the Ghost floated in. "Good morning, sweet lady!" she cried, excited. "You looked so peaceful sleeping there that I hated to wake you, but it's past dawn and the wedding party starts by midmorning at the latest. Magpie is bringing you a drink to make you alert."

"Who?" Rose asked dazedly.

"Magpie. She's here to help get you through this day."

"But there's no other living person in Castle Roogna except me!" Rose protested.

"Yes. She's one of Humfrey's classmates."

Now Rose understood. A demoness. She had learned a lot about demons in the past year, and no longer feared them. She understood their nature reasonably well and was careful, but knew that demons were merely another of the formidable species of Xanth, like the dragons and basilisks.

Magpie came in then, carrying the coffee, which she must have imported from far away. She looked just like a bustling matron, with her gray hair under a white lace bonnet, and a black wool and feather dress. She set the mug down on the table beside Rose's bed, then went to poke her finger at the fireplace. A fire burst into being there, casting its warmth into the chill room. For Rose had chosen not to use any of the main bedrooms of the castle, feeling unworthy; she had taken a little attic chamber, and up here it did get cold at night.

Rose drank her brew while Magpie busily fetched the clothing. Actually it was more than the mug; the demoness had thoughtfully laid out a small breakfast of orange (or perhaps dark yellow) juice, fresh toasted breadfruit slices, and rose-hip preserves. This dainty meal would do until the wedding feast. "Thank you, Magpie; I am starving!"

"Call me Mag," the woman said, and continued her business. Rose realized that the woman's name was probably ironic; a magpie was a garrulous bird, but this one spoke only briefly.

Rose got up, wincing at the cold stone floor her tender warm feet encountered. She hugged her nightdress close about her and sat in the chair at the table. The day would warm in time; it always did. Meanwhile, the blazing fire certainly helped; that was an unaccustomed luxury!

While Rose ate, the realization washed over her. She was getting married! She could still hardly believe it. But Humfrey had completed the university program and now had his degree, which meant he was officially a Magician and eligible to marry her. She had seen it all in the Tapestry, and gotten the words from a magic mirror. Castle Roogna knew it too, and would not try to prevent the wedding. It believed that at some time in the future Humfrey would return and be king; a new prophecy had appeared in the Book of Prophecies to that effect. So it was half a loaf for the castle, but not even magic castles had everything their own way. The technicalities of the situation had been met.

Rose would have preferred to have the Wedding of the Century. But that would have attracted the attention of the Storm King, and there was another prophecy warning against that. "If the Storm King discovers activity at Castle Roogna, he will destroy it in a firestorm, for his successor will reside here," that prophecy said. It seemed that the Storm King was young and imperious, and resentful of anything that might conceivably threaten his authority. His correct action would have been to bring his retinue and live at Castle Roogna, but he was a homebody and preferred to remain in the North Village. Thus the very existence of Castle Roogna was an implied rebuke, and activity there would have suggested that a new King was being cultivated to replace him. So the wedding had to be quiet, and the castle had to remain anonymous. But in time there would come a new King, and it seemed likely that it would be Humfrey. After all, if the Storm King died and there was no other Magician in Xanth, Humfrey would have to take it. So Rose would settle for the quiet wedding, and wait on events. It wasn't as if she were inexperienced at waiting.

She finished eating and stood looking about. She discovered to her great delight that Mag had anticipated her desire for a bath, on this Day of all Days. To one side of the brick fireplace, aromatically burning crabapple shells and logs, the large wooden tub had been brought in and filled. Steam redolent with rose petals perfumed the room.

Soon Rose was settled in her tub, her curly rose-colored hair pinned atop her head. She settled herself deeply into the hot water. She could feel her dry skin soaking up the rose milk and becoming dewy and moist again. It was the beginning of the magic transformation that any wedding wrought: a pretty young naive girl would become a beautiful and competent woman. She had seen this transformation occur any number of times in the Tapestry history; now it was her turn.

"What a pity," Rose said, and burst out laughing. Mag jumped, and little Button Ghost, who had drifted in to watch the activity, spooked away in fright. There was a scramble as the Monster Under the Bed retreated farther into the darkness, and a rattle as the Skeleton in the Closet did the same.

"I only meant that it will be too bad to lose another innocent," Rose said contritely. "Marriage does that, you know; it sacrifices innocence." Actually, she had long since fathomed the key elements of the Adult Conspiracy; she had after all been twenty years old before coming here, and there were things she had seen in the Tapestry that—well, it had been an education. She had also noted the little tricks the Demoness Metria had tried with Humfrey; those had not been successful, but their general import had been plain enough. So in her case it would be more symbolic than actual; still, she was experiencing the mixed thrill and tragedy of it.

Rose washed her long, silky hair, pouring out warm water from a pewter pitcher. Little did she know that one day in the far future that pitcher would be stolen from the castle by a demon and used as the basis for a dreadful malignant mechanical thing called Com-Pewter that would be a constant menace to all things halfway decent in Xanth. This was just not the sort of thing innocent maidens were capable of knowing. Mag presented her with a cake of soapstone; it smelled of her natural attar of roses fragrance. When she finished, Mag offered her a huge fresh cotton-wood towel.

Now that she and her hair were clean, Rose was ready to be Attired in one of several glorious dresses she had harvested from the dress tree in the orchard for the occasion. One by one Mag handed her gossa-mer silken panties, pink creamy chemise-teddy, smooth stockings of gold thread, and a long whispering silken underskirt. Next came the overskirt and bodice of the gown. The central panels of the dress were embroidered in tiny seed pearls, crystals, and smoky topazes in a field of yellow roses upon the rich gold-colored silk. When she moved about the dress gave off a faintly rosy reddish gold glow. Her golden living frog sat in the middle of the rosette on her sleeve. The skirt of the gown came to the floor. The neckline was so low that Mag drew in her breath in a matronly gasp of disapproval. Rose's eyes widened to see her breasts exposed almost to the rosy nipples. She had not realized that the décol-letage was *quite* that daring! The gown was simply wonderful! With that deliciously low neckline Rose might even stand up to the competi-tion offered by those bare-breasted mermaids and all the other allur-ing maidens the Tapestry had shown her. Not to mention that horrible Demoness Metria!

Suddenly (it seemed) it was time for the wedding. It was held in the main ballroom of the castle, and if it was not the Event of the Century, it was hard for her to know the difference. The demons had turned out in force, for this was rare entertainment for them. Normally they were not wanted at weddings, for some reason. They were all solid, and behaved meticulously, with all the males being in tails and the females in float-ing gowns. Beauregard was best man and Millie the Ghost was maid of honor, and Button Ghost carried ghost flowers, and Professor Grossclout conducted the ceremony, having authority that no man or demon had ever dared question. Metria was there too, of course; she couldn't be kept out. She played the role of Former Girlfriend of the Groom, and was really quite effective in portraying resentment about the proceedings. One might almost suspect that there was just a bit of human feeling in that demon callousness.

But about all Rose noticed was that Humfrey, despite pushing forty, was clean and almost handsome in his own formal suit. He seemed truly glad to be there, which was a relief. It wasn't necessarily so with grooms, no matter how ardent they might be at other times.

They must have said their vows, because now there was an expectant hush. Humfrey faced her. "Take off your wedding cap and veil, Rose," he said.

She blushed meekly, made abruptly shy by his request. "You do it," she whispered.

He stepped forward and gently drew the heart-shaped spiderweb lace cap and diaphanous bridal veil from her head. Then his competent hands moved to undo the diamond and living golden frog hairpins that held her tresses in place. To his evident surprise the hair fell in a silken waterfall down, down to below her hips.

"It is a lovely lass you are," he murmured softly in her ear. "Your hair is indeed like rose petals." His hands slid through the perfumed mass of it. "I think it is time, Rose of Roogna, that we seal our marriage with a kiss."

He tangled his hands in her hair and drew her face forward. In his eyes she could have sworn she saw the images of flying storks, and she knew she was seeing through them into his mind. Then he closed his eyes and kissed her.

At once Rose felt as if the blood in her veins had turned to glowing golden lava from a volcano of love. She could not move. She never wanted to move again. She loved her husband, Humfrey. She would love him forever.

There was a sound as of the rippling of wavelets on a sandy beach. It grew to resemble the splash of the surf on firm rocks. Then it became the roar of the storm-driven sea against a stony cliff. No, it was not her heart, it was the applause of the audience. The marriage had been sealed.

Then it was done, and the demons were gone, and it was the Morning After. Standing on the ramparts of Castle Roogna, gazing down at the ruins of the gardens, Rose decided that she did not regret any particle of the prior day's proceedings. Not the wedding, certainly, and not the reception, and not the banquet. Not even the dancing under the New Baby Moon. And not the night of love, wherein they had tried so ardently to summon a phalanx of storks. That was only partially effective, as it turned out; only one stork came, in due course, bearing Rosetta

Bliss Humfrey, or Roy for short, whose power was to animate inanimate things for a while. But that was in the moderately near future; right now it was a beautiful day. The sky was spreading itself like a peacock's tail, turquoise blue, gold, and copper, luminous and brilliant. A spicy warm breeze was blowing in straight off the High C and Lost Keys. Everything was ideal.

She looked at her reflection in her maiden's mirror. Her romantic heart shimmered and softened. She did not *look* like an experienced woman who had been thoroughly indoctrinated into the practice of the Adult Conspiracy! She looked more like a maiden who had just begun to wonder about such things. Perhaps it took practice to develop the proper expression.

She went to her rose garden. She hated to leave it, but knew it would endure as she had, here at the castle, living without aging. Rose herself had to leave, of course, to be with her husband, and the spell would be off. But that was all right; how could a person truly live life, if she did not age? She wanted to grow old with Humfrey.

She sifted through the rose petals, ashes, and dust of the garden. There were pebbles, thorns, tiny gems, a small leather scroll documenting the marriage, and—UGH!—a long many-legged pennypede bug. It was harmless, unlike the larger nickelpedes, so she left it alone; it preyed on things that might otherwise attack her roses.

A shadow dimmed the light. It was Humfrey. "I have brought a magic carpet to the front," he said. "We can go, now, my precious wife."

She glanced at the roses, whose power was to test true love. That test had never been necessary, with Humfrey. "The scroll—I had it here with my darling roses. But if I am not to remain here—"

"Bring it along," he said, smiling. "The roses need no document."

So she tucked it into a pocket in her skirt. Then she went with her husband to the carpet.

They sat on it, she in front, he behind. The magic of the weave would keep them safe on it. "To Castle Zombie," Humfrey said.

The rug lifted smoothly and circled up. In a moment it was above Castle Roogna. Rose felt tears streaming down her face as she gazed down at the castle which had been her home for almost two and a half centuries. It had taken perfect care of her! But now she had her true life to live.

"Farewell, dear castle!" she cried, waving to it. "Thank you so much for everything!"

A pennant waved, which was odd, because there was no wind.

It was not far, as the carpet flew, to Castle Zombie. The thing was relatively horrible, with a muck-filled moat and decaying vegetation around it. But the zombies were gone or safely buried, and she knew it was a serviceable estate. The Zombie Master had died more than seven centuries before, so this castle had been deserted even longer than Castle Roogna. But it had been soundly constructed, despite its seeming decrepitude, and she knew it could be cleaned up.

Humfrey brought the carpet down in the rear of the castle. They got up and walked to a fence. He pushed open the garden gate made of driftwood and led the way into a small secret garden. Rose followed slowly down the narrow stone path. Tiny spiders had decorated every weed with their webs, and mice rustled under the leaves. Overall, there was a lingering smell of decay. "I thought you might have your rose garden here," Humfrey said.

Suddenly she was glad he had shown her this first. "Yes, I shall!" she exclaimed, delighted. She would make another rose garden! Roses would brighten this dreary region right up.

Then he led her to the front portcullis. Humfrey picked her up and carried her gallantly across the threshold, and set her down inside. Rose quailed; there was not a stick of furniture inside. Then he brought her to what she thought of as the captain's cabin: a large almost oval room so richly appointed that it was obvious that no human agency had done it. It had a fireplace with a malachite stone mantel with green ivy carved on it and great golden-winged lions holding the mantel shelf on their heads. Above it was a magic silvered mirror. On the mantel was a pair of magic pewter candelabra that burned without ever consuming their fine none-of-your-bees-wax candles. At the head of the bed was a rose window facing west that allowed the cabin to be flooded with light. The walls were hung with three well-worked moving crewel tapestries. The demons must have set this up during the night, and Humfrey had surprised her with it. What a delight!

Humfrey stood in the middle of their bed chamber, which had a priceless antique thick carpet on its wide wooden floor. The fireplace was lit with fireweed, and the air was fragrant with incense. "We can be very happy here, my wife," Humfrey said.

Rose was sure of it.

They settled into married life. Humfrey, nagged by the things he had not yet learned, embarked on his most ambitious project yet: he was compiling a Book of Answers. In it would be the Answer to every possible Question anyone might ask. He started by listing everything he had learned in his early survey of talents, which was considerable, and added whatever he could learn from the texts in the Castle Roogna library, which the castle allowed him to check out one at a time. He supplemented this with field trips, making copious notes. He kept himself so busy that some days Rose hardly saw him at all. But she wasn't concerned; she had lived alone for so long that it was not much of a burden, and she could contact him at any time by using a magic mirror, and he would always come immediately when she asked him.

In fact there was a certain delight to these brief separations, because every time she saw him again Rose experienced the intense jolt of feelings that seeing him always gave her. Love made him handsome to her, though she knew that this was not an objective judgment. She heightened the effect by dressing him well. She would send him out one day with shades of blue in his shirt, trousers, and cloak, complemented by sandy tan desert boots. Another day it would be shades of brown or gray. He always carried a battered bulging sack full of books, tomes, and spells over his shoulder; she could not do much about that, but she did tie matching ribbons to it. Sometimes he got caught out in the rain, and silvery rain drops sparkled like gems in his hair and on his driftwood staff. Then she would take him in and dry him off and comfort him with kisses, restoring his humor.

Meanwhile, she set the castle in order, eliminating the last vestiges of zombie occupancy. She started the rose garden; how could she endure without roses! She kept the kitchen filled with homemade soup and love. Sometimes she accompanied Humfrey on his field trips, delighting in the carpet rides and the picnic lunches.

But soon she had to stop this and stay home, because she was expecting the stork and it just wouldn't do to be *away* when it arrived. She had a horror of arriving home and discovering the baby deposited in the fireplace or somewhere, all dirty. Storks were notorious about their schedules; if the mother was not waiting for the stork's arrival, it dropped the baby off anyway, ready or not.

Fortunately she was present and alert when their daughter arrived, and after that she had little time for anything else. Roy did her best to live up to her masculine nickname from the start—Rose wondered in those harried moments she could squeeze in for thinking whether they would have been better advised to choose another name—and constantly made the stones of the floor and bricks of the fireplaces come to life and squirm vigorously. Fortunately they remained animate only while the baby focused on them, and Roy's attention span was brief. But it was hectic.

Humfrey's tome of Answers and Roy grew apace. Then, somehow, it seemed, in a few days Roy was grown into pretty childhood, and thence to girlhood, and thence to maidenhood, and suddenly she was marrying the son of a local forester named Stone, becoming Rosetta Stone, and moving away to start her own family. "But she's just a child!" Rose wailed through her tears of joy at her daughter's fortune. Stone was good at interpreting things and making sense of them, and that was bound to help their marriage.

"She's twenty-one," Humfrey pointed out gruffly. "Older than your physical age when you married me. That's old enough."

"But yesterday she was eleven!" Rose cried.

"And only one, the day before," he agreed. "Where's my soup?"

Rose might have been tempted to make a remark about insensitivity had she been less good-natured, but she was too princessly to deign. She fetched him his soup. She would not of course admit it, but he had grown twenty years older and grumpier in the past two decades, and looked more like a gnome than ever. It was a good thing she loved him.

But that was the thing about love in Xanth. When it was true, it was forever. In drear Mundania, she understood, love lasted only for a few years, and then marriages started breaking up. Humfrey had almost loved MareAnn, and that feeling had remained until he did love Rose. He had not loved Dana Demoness or Maiden Taiwan, though he had treated them courteously. It had been his misfortune to lack true love in his early life, but once they had found it together, they would keep it as long as they both should live.

That was good, because things were very quiet now with Roy gone. Rosetta and Stone had discovered that they could animate stones and make them tell what they knew, interpreting their confusing remarks? and sometimes they knew interesting or useful things. But that was there; things were dull here. Rose took a more active interest in her husband's work, and in the next six years his great Book of Answers progressed rapidly. Humfrey was excellent at discovering things, but not at classifying them or putting them in proper order. He couldn't even find his socks without help! Rose did that organizing of facts and cross-referenced them, so that it was possible to locate almost anything in the voluminous collection.

Little did she know that this would lead to considerable mischief. She had assumed that if she minded her own business and helped her husband loyally and was courteous to others, everything would be all right. It had never occurred to her that she could be the victim of outright deception and malice. That naivete was to cost her dearly.

It started innocently enough. Humfrey was cataloging seeshells, so she was gathering more of them while he was doing the paperwork. She would return later and properly index and cross-reference his notes, but he had to do the actual definitions. Peggy, the flying horse, had returned after a snit when Humfrey first got married and used the magic carpet; Rose had explained about things, and Peggy decided to forgive the transgression. Then Humfrey had used the carpet again, and the horse had got her feathers in an uproar. By the time Rose smoothed those feathers down, Peggy decided that she would give Rose rides instead of the fickle Magician. The two had been friends ever since. Humfrey, a typical man, had never noticed.

So today Peggy carried Rose to the Gold Coast of southeastern Xanth, where the sands and many of the plants were golden. It had been some time since Rose had been here. She had visited the region once as a child and played in the sand, and had retained a certain taste for the pretty stuff. Now she was dismayed to see a new development: there was a tower being built from ivory just offshore. Apparently it was to be a light house, and white ivory was lighter than gold. Rose would have preferred to leave die shore pristine, but realized that she could not stand in the way of progress. Perhaps if she ignored it, it would go away.

She told Peggy to go and graze where she wished, and the horse walked into the jungle, looking for tasty leaves and grass. Rose walked along the shore, picking up new varieties of gold seeshells. Their eyes were bright orange yellow, and some were very pretty. Humfrey didn't care much about that; to him an ugly shell was as good as a pretty one. But Rose preferred beauty without actually disparaging other conditions. It wasn't as if she would be beautiful forever; she was now forty-eight years old, in away-from-Castle-Roogna time. She had worked to keep her body in reasonable shape, and she still brushed out her hair each day to keep it luxurious, but on occasion a mirror was unkind enough to show a wrinkle. Rose had lost her taste for mirrors, coincidentally, and no longer carried one with her.

She came to a village of fishmen and fishwives. They had the heads of fish and human legs. Their village was in the water, but they came ashore to forage for food. Rose saw them using their upper fins to hold long poles from which descended lines, and on the ends of the lines were hooks which snagged on things of the beach. Sometimes small animals bit at the bits of candy around the hooks, and the hooks caught in their mouths, and the fishmen hauled them in by the lines and poles until they were dragged down into the water. It seemed like a cruel way to make a living to Rose, but she was cautious about criticizing the ways of other folk.

Then she saw a decrepit old woman hobbling along. The fishmen goggled at her and retreated into the water, evidently detesting her company. This disturbed Rose, who never liked to see any person excluded from things. She went to the woman, who was hunched over, carrying a heavy bag. "May I help you?" Rose inquired.

The woman gazed up at her. Her aspect was even more frightful from close up, and she smelled of something other than roses. Her clothing consisted of whatever rags and tatters she had picked up from trash heaps. "Well yes, lady," she wheezed. "If you would carry my heavy burden to my home, that would help me a lot."

"I shall be glad to," Rose said. She took the bag, which she was surprised to discover was filled with ivory horns and tusks. The woman evidently collected ivory! "If I may inquire, what is your name? My name is Rose."

The beady eyes flicked at her. "My given name is Peril, but the fishfaces call me the Sea Hag."

Rose was properly appalled. "How unkind of them! I shall certainly call you Pead."

"That's Peril, rose-hips!" the woman corrected her snappishly. Perhaps Rose might have had a hint about her nature then, had she not been so trusting.

Rose apologized for her error. It was very embarrassing to get a person's name wrong, for names were important indications to character. Everyone knew that.

The old woman set off at a brisk hobble, and Rose was constrained to keep abreast of her, because the odor behind her was barely to be endured. They proceeded downbeach to a spot directly opposite the half-completed ivory tower. "Oh, they have ruined my house again!" she exclaimed, her voice suggestive of a harpy's screech.

Rose saw a pile of driftwood, flotsam, jetsam, and seaweed. It was hard to imagine that this could ever have been a house. But of course it would be impolite to question the word of her companion. "Do you have any other place to stay?"

"There is one the fishfaces can't reach," Peril said. She hobbled to the edge of the forest. There was a huge dead tree trunk, rising above the height of Rose's head. Peril scrambled up it, remarkably agile for one in her condition, and squeezed into a hole in it. She disappeared inside the trunk. Then her face reappeared. "Well, come on, stupid!" she screeched imperiously.

Rose struggled to climb the trunk with the heavy bag of ivory. She was not good at this, because princesses were not supposed to climb trees, but somehow she managed. She wedged into the hole and hauled the bag after her.

She found herself squeezing down inside the tree, the bag pressing her down from above. Her nice dress was getting severely mussed. Then her feet lost purchase entirely, and she fell, screaming in an embarrassingly unladylike fashion.

She splashed into water. The bag splashed beside her. She flailed, and in a moment her feet found a sloping rock. She scrambled up it, out of the water. She was in absolute darkness.

Her first thought was for the old woman. "Peril!" she cried. "Are you all right?"

She was answered by a resounding cackle. "I'm horrible, but I will be much better soon," the voice of the hag came from above.

"Soon?" Rose asked, bewildered.

"Soon as I kill myself."

"I don't understand!"

There was another awful cackle. "Who cares! Rest easy, fool, until I come for you." Then the voice faded.

Rose looked up. Far above she saw a disk of light. It blinked out for a moment, then reappeared. She realized that it was the hole in the tree trunk. Peril had climbed back up and squeezed out of it, and was gone.

Rose realized that she was in trouble. It seemed to be a most unkind notion, and one she hesitated to entertain, but it almost seemed that the old woman had intended to trap her in here. There was no way she could climb up inside that trunk and escape; there was no purchase for her hands, and in any event she lacked the strength for such an effort. She was trapped in this awful dark pit.

She knew what to do: she had to call Humfrey, who would immediately come on the carpet and rescue her. Except that she no longer carried her magic mirror. What a problem her foolish vanity had made for her!

She heard a neigh. Peggy! The winged horse had found her! "Peggy!" she cried. "Get me out of here!" But even as she called, she knew it was impossible. The horse could not get in here and could not do anything to help from outside. So she did the next best thing. "Peggy, go fetch Humfrey! Bring him here! Quickly!"

The horse neighed acknowledgment. Rose heard the beat of her great wings. She would fly to wherever Humfrey was and alert him to Rose's problem. He could then use a mirror of his own and investigate, and he would take care of it immediately.

Then she remembered that she hadn't told Peggy where Humfrey was. He was checking references in the Castle Roogna library and would not be back until evening. Peggy would not be able to find him until then, for she could not go to Castle Roogna because of the aversion spell. Rose was stuck here for the full day.

She hunched herself with her back to the edge of this cave. There seemed to be just the pool and the sloping edge and the wall. The water was brine, so must connect to the sea, but Rose could not escape that way either. She was not that good a swimmer, and for all she knew it was too far for her to hold her breath. This place was some distance in from the shore, and any tunnel would have to connect under the surface of the sea. At least she had not been hurt in the fall; how lucky that there had been water there!

She thought about Peril. Now she realized the significance of the name. The woman was a peril to anyone who tried to befriend her! No wonder the fishfolk didn't like her. But why had she sought to snare Rose here? What could she gain by doing this to one who meant her no harm?

Rose remembered the Sea Hag's (for it seemed now that the name the fishfolk used for her was apt) parting words: she was horrible, but would be much better as soon as she killed herself. Whatever could that mean? Was the woman deranged? Why would anyone want to kill herself, and how would that make her feel better? Why would she want to trap another woman just before then?

There was a sob. Rose thought it was her own, then realized that it wasn't. It had come from across the pool. There must be another ledge there.

"Who is there?" she called.

"Me," a voice replied.

That was not phenomenally helpful. She realized that the other person could be young, and therefore thoughtless. "Please tell me your name."

"Dread," the answer came.

"Died? Are you a boy?"

"Dread Redhead, because I have red hair and I dread the darkness. I'm a ten-year-old boy."

Rose was much relieved to discover that she had company, yet horrified to learn that another person was similarly trapped. "Did Peril lure you in here too?" she asked.

"Sure she did," the boy replied. "Yesterday. But now she's got you, I guess she'll just let me die."

"What does she want with me?" Rose asked.

"You mean you don't know?"

"I have no idea. I was only trying to help her carry her bag of ivory, and she led me here and left me. She said something peculiar as she left."

"You sure *don't* know!" Dread said. "Well, let me tell you: the Sea Hag is a Sorceress who lives forever, because every time her body gets old, she kills it and her spirit takes over another body. Usually she takes a young woman, but if she can't find one, she'll take a boy. That's why she trapped me. But she'd rather have a woman, even an older one like you; that gives her a few more years to find a young one. So now she's got you, and in an hour or two she'll take it."

Rose was appalled. "But I don't want my body to be taken! How can she do that?"

"She traps a woman so she can't flee, and then her' spirit just comes in. That's her magic. You can't stop her. You have to get far away, so her spirit can't catch you. That's the only way to escape."

Rose realized that she was in twice as much trouble as she had thought. But rather than dwell on that awfulness, she focused on the boy. "What is your talent?" she asked, hoping that it was something that could help them.

"I pipe open doors. Even when there aren't doors."

"You mean you can make doors to places that don't have them?"

"Sure. With my hornpipe. It's fun, usually. I can get in or out of anything."

"But then why didn't you open a door out of here?"

"Because my doors open on the level, not up or down, and there's no light down here."

"No light? Why should that stop you?"

"I'm afraid of the dark."

"But it's already dark here!"

"Yes, and that terrifies me. But there's a spot of light from the hole in the tree, and I can watch that. But if I opened a door, it would be to an underground tunnel, and it would be dark. I can't leave the light!"

Rose began to get an idea. "Many children are afraid of the dark. But only when they are alone. They are never afraid when they are with their mothers."

"My mother isn't here," he pointed out with a certain accuracy.

"But *I'm* here! And I'm old enough to be your mother. I am a mother of another child. If I went with you, you wouldn't have to be afraid, no matter how dark it is."

"Say, maybe so," he said.

Her heart beat faster. He was accepting her logic! "Can you open a door in your wall?"

"Sure. Come over here and I'll do it."

Rose did not waste time. She slid into the water and swam across. She found a similar sloping ledge on the other side and climbed out. "Do it," she said breathlessly.

Music sounded. How lucky that Dread had his hornpipe with him! There was a creaking, as of a door opening.

Rose felt in the darkness. Sure enough, there was a door, with a dark passage beyond. "Come on!" she said. "Maybe this tunnel intersects a cave, and we can follow it to the surface where it's light." The tunnel was heading directly away from the sea, but that was fine; that was also away from the Sea Hag.

"You first," Dread said.

She didn't argue. She knew he would follow, rather than be left alone. She felt her way into the tunnel, proceeding on hands and knees. She heard the scuffle of the redheaded boy following.

The tunnel went straight ahead, on the level. She was afraid it went nowhere, but then it came to a faintly glowing underground stream. Her eyes had become adjusted to the gloom, and now this faint light was quite bright enough to see the path of the river.

It was breathtakingly beautiful. The rock surrounding it was crystalline, and each small stone at the bottom was a rough-cut gem, and above it hung stalactites of glossy sardonyx. Now there was sound, too: the stream sang as it wended its way through and around these crystals. At the bottom of the stream small plants were growing, and these plants produced tiny fruits, and there were fish eating the fruits.

But they could not linger to enjoy the scene. "We must move on," Rose said. "There seems to be no way out from here. Open another door."

Dread raised his pipe to his mouth and played. A new door opened in the wall. They entered the new tunnel, leaving the lovely river behind.

This tunnel was tall enough for them to walk upright, which was a relief, but soon it narrowed so that they had to go single file. The darkness became complete again; Rose could not see anything in front of her. She had to stop, yielding to the primitive fear of banging her face into something disfiguring.

Now the boy squeezed ahead of her and began cursing. His curses lit up the dark and dim pockets of the cave. Rose, about to object to such language, realized that it was better to stifle her ladylike sensibility for the nonce; they needed this bit of light. Yet how was it that the boy had not thought to do this before and so escape before she arrived?

"We're almost there," Dread said confidently.

"Almost where?" Rose asked. But before she could inquire further, she heard a screech echoing down the tunnel. The Sea Hag!

As one, they charged down the tunnel. Now there was a glow from another wall. Dread whipped out his hornpipe and played another brief melody, and another door opened.

But if the Sea Hag had killed herself so that her spirit was coming after them, how could there be a screech? That was the Hag's living voice!

"Hurry!" the boy cried urgently, taking her arm. He jumped through the door, hauling her after him.

They were on a water slide. It carried them down and around through more darkness. Then they landed in some kind of—well, it felt like a basket. A huge wicker basket, with a high arching handle. It was swinging from a rope tied to that handle. As they landed in it, it started moving, swinging down into yet further deep depths.

"What is this?" Rose cried, alarmed. "Where are we going?"

"This is a handbasket," the boy replied. "We are going to Hell."

"Please don't swear anymore," she reproved him. "It offends my matronly sensibilities. Where are we really going?"

"To Hell," he repeated. "I am a demon from there. It is a dull place, so we decided we needed some pretty flowers, but they won't grow. Your talent is making roses grow, and they are nice flowers, so we are bringing you there."

Rose was upset and bewildered. "But the Sea Hag! What about her?"

"Oh, she was going to take your body, all right. That's why we had to act quickly. Some talents go with the souls, and some with the bodies.

Yours goes with your body, so your soul would have been no good to us, and anyway, it is far too good for us. So we had to have your body, and get it before the Sea Hag did. We had only a few hours before she killed herself and came for you."

"But it took only minutes to flee her cave!"

"Yes, we couldn't let you stop to think too long, or you might have found a way to escape. But now you are in the handbasket to Hell, and we have you."

She stared at him in the growing light of the flames that were appearing outside the basket. "You're no more an innocent boy than the Sea Hag is an innocent woman! You were out to trap me too!"

"And succeeded," he agreed, well satisfied.

She peered down over the side of the big basket. There was nothing but licking flames and roiling smoke there. She could not escape.

Rose sighed. This was just not a good day!

Chapter 11

LETHE

I returned late front Castle Roogna. Our own reconditioned castle was quiet. Rose was not there. Where was she?

Then I saw a parchment on the table. It was in my wife's hand. It was a letter from Rose! I read it wonderingly.

Dearest Husband Humfrey,

Where are you, my beloved? If you do not rescue me soon from this Hell, I fear for the consequences. Each day I walk the Castle Walk, in the lonely Silver Rain, from the Sand Castle Inn to the Castle in the Sky, but you do not appear. I told the demon in charge of this Hell that at long last I am prepared to give anything to see you and love you one more time. I have talked to the trees here and they whisper that my banishment from Xanth will not be one times nine years, or two times nine years, but ten times nine years, unless you rescue me immediately. Why have you not come? I have only one more Day of Grace, and then I am locked here for the full term.

Oh my love, everywhere I walk Forget-Me-Nots in thyme spring up to cover my footprints of blood in the white snowsand. My soul is being tugged from me; it will be encased in rose quartz in the rose garden of Castle Roogna unless you rescue me today! It shames me to confess it, but I have bribed a demon with a kiss to deliver this letter to our home. I beg you, if you love me as I love you, come take me away from all this before it is too late!

Rose of Roogna

As soon as I finished reading it, the letter burst into flame. It was a missive from Hell, all right! It was gone.

I glanced at the calendar an ogre had left. I remembered the date on Rose's letter. I had evidently gotten more deeply embroiled in the research at Castle Roogna than I had realized. Four days had passed.

I was one day past Rose's deadline. I had already missed my chance to rescue her. I could not redeem her from Hell, I was the Magician of Information, not of Power, and I knew I lacked the power to bring her from that infernal region. Maybe if I had been able to learn more—but she had been helping me to learn, and without her I knew I could not research well enough to find out how to free her, assuming that there was a way. So she was lost.

I could not live with that. I would have to kill myself and join her in Hell. I knew I would not mind it much, in her company.

I started to put the castle in order for my departure. My vials of potions, my collected spells, my almost-complete Book of Answers—it would not do for these to be left out for any passerby to take! Suppose they fell into evil hands? But where could I put them where they would be safe?

Castle Roogna, of course. So I carried the flying carpet out to the landing place beside the moat and began loading it.

Soufflé lifted his head from the water. He had moved here from Castle Roogna when we did, because it was pointless to defend an empty castle that needed no additional defense, he claimed. Actually, it was because he liked Rose. She looked good enough to eat.

I gazed into the monster's eyes. How could I tell him that Rose was gone and that I would be too? I realized that I had commitments here that I could not simply desert. For one thing, I had to be ready in case I was needed as king again, much as I loathed the thought. The arrogant Storm King had put in a law that all human citizens of Xanth had to demonstrate a magic talent by age twenty-five or be exiled. That was oppressive and unfair. If I didn't want to be king again myself, I had at least to keep looking for another Magician and train him, so that when he became king he would abolish that law.

No, I could not desert my post, even for Rose. Yet I could not endure without her. I couldn't even find my socks, alone! I would need a woman for that—and how could I marry again, loving Rose as I did? The answer was that I couldn't. Not as long as I remembered my love for her.

There was only one thing remaining to do. I stepped to the cupboard and fetched my vial of Lethe elixir. There was enough in here to make a man forget something for eighty years. By that time I should be safely dead and with Rose in Hell. For this potion affected only the living mind, not the dead mind. It was ideal.

"Rose!" I cried, naming the thing I had to forget, and lifted the vial to my mouth. I drank down the whole of it.

I looked around, bewildered. What was I doing here? I stood in the middle of an arcane study with a vial in my hand. The last thing I remembered was discovering Castle Roogna. I had been approaching the ramparts, and I had seen a moat monster. Then—nothing.

Was I inside the castle, having hit my head during the entry? No, I had no bruise, and anyway, this wasn't Castle Roogna; the smell of it was different. This was somewhere else. More must have happened than simple entry; somehow I had been transported elsewhere.

Maybe that was the castle's last defense: it used magic to move anyone who entered to a different castle. Maybe the—a memory glimmered from the fog—the Nameless Castle. The castle of which I had not heard, which ignorance had cost me a good grade. Somewhere, sometime. But I could not remember more of that matter. I seemed to have forgotten a lot.

I peered more closely at the vial. Now I saw a label, on it: LETHE.

I had just drunk the elixir of forgetfulness! Whatever had possessed me to do that?

Slowly I figured it out: there was a period of my life missing. I must have entered Castle Roogna, then traveled here and set things up to suit myself, and then taken a drink of potion to forget it all. Why?

I didn't know but was sure that if I had done it voluntarily there had to have been excellent reason. So my best course was not to inquire into the matter. In due course the elixir would wear off—there was no telling how much had been in the bottle—and then I would remember. Meanwhile, I should go about my business, awaiting that revelation.

Just how much time had been wiped out by the elixir? I looked at the calendar again, this time checking the year. My mouth fell open. It was the Year 1000! It had been 971 before. I had lost twenty-nine years of my life! Instead of being thirty-eight years old and fresh from my stint as king of Xanth, I was now sixty-seven years old and not fresh at all. Indeed, the weight of those extra decades now came down on my shoulders, and I felt stooped.

But there was no sense groaning over squished milk pods. I would simply have to make the best of it, hoping that it wasn't unbearably bad. It had obviously been bad enough to make me take Lethe, though.

I explored the castle, which turned out to be not the Nameless Castle, but the ancient Castle Zombie. I must have discovered this in my travels, after leaving Castle Roogna, and decided to patch it up and live in it. But it was too well kept; there seemed to be a woman's hand in this. I must have had a servant maid. What had happened to her? She was certainly not here now. Whoever she was, she had been highly competent, because everything was in far better order than I was capable of managing.

I located the bed chamber, and found therein only one bed, large enough for two. On one side were my things, such as a lost sock; on the other were a woman's, such as the perfume of roses. Obviously we had been close.

I spied a magic mirror on the wall. "What woman was here?" I demanded of it.

"You told me not to answer that, Magician, before you took the Lethe elixir," it replied.

"Well, now I'm telling you to answer," I said shortly. I tended to be shorter now than before being shortened by those extra twenty-nine years.

"But then you were in command of your faculties," it responded with a sneer. "None of the magic items here will answer you now."

I realized that it was true. I would not have taken Lethe if I had wanted to remember what I was trying to forget.

I also discovered in a closet a fat tome labeled BOOK OF ANSWERS. Now this was interesting. Where had I gotten this? But as I turned the pages, I recognized the handwriting: it was my own, with cross-references by some other party, evidently an assistant.

Well, maybe this would help me. I needed a woman to find my socks; where was she? I tried to use it to ascertain what woman had been here, but it balked me, as I had expected. I had been routinely thorough, before, as befitted me. But I should be able to use this and the other magic items in other ways so that I could get on with my life.

I thumbed through the pages. Soon I located WOMAN. There were pages of types, but there was no SOCKS subheading. Too bad. So I checked for the next best thing, and there it was: WIFE.

I discovered that this was a spelled entry: it changed as I watched it, listing names and descriptions of marriageable females. I could fix it on any one who interested me by touching the entry with my finger; when I removed my finger, the entries started rotating again.

But I didn't want to choose randomly. So I tested its resources. "I want the best sock finder available," I said, and stabbed my finger down without looking. If this worked the way it should, that name would be the one.

And there it was: SOFIA SOCK SORTER. Her description was ordinary, and she lived in—

Oops! This was a problem. She lived in Mundania.

Well, either I wanted the best or I didn't. Of what mettle was I made, today? I decided to go fetch Sofia, regardless.

I packed those spells I recognized from my early days of collecting. I found a magic carpet I seemed to have acquired in my missing years. I carried it outside, looking for a suitable place to launch it.

There was the moat monster, whose name, I had learned, was Soufflé Serpent. No doubt because that was what he would make of any intruder. "I am going to find a woman," I announced. "I shall return. Guard the premises well."

Soufflé nodded and settled back into the water.

I unrolled the carpet, set my things on it, sat on it myself, and gave it the standard takeoff command. It lifted smoothly; it was a good piece of work.

I flew north and slightly west—and soon discovered below a monstrous chasm. Where had that come from? I remembered nothing of the sort in Xanth! I fetched up my notepad—and there was a note: GAP CHASM—FORGET SPELL ON. Oh. That explained it. I admired the scenery, continuing my flight across the varied landscape of Xanth until I reached the isthmus. There I landed and hid the carpet away in a tree, putting a routine invisibility spell on it from my collection. Then I used a temporary neutrality spell on the Shield that enclosed Xanth, and walked safely through it. It was evident that my hiatus of lost memory had not impaired my routine skills; I seemed to be about as good as ever, apart from being older.

There was a peculiar thing I remembered about Mundania: it had little if any magic. However, I had found a vial of magic dust I had gotten from somewhere, and that would enable me to do such magic as I required, if I didn't waste it.

I set out on foot across drear Mundania. It would be pointless to recount my experience there; no one cares to learn any more about that boring and backward place than the absolute minimum. I shall just say that I found Sofia the sock sorter at the mundane company she worked for. She was about thirty years old and plain, but her hands sorted socks of all types with marvelous dexterity.

I sprinkled some magic dust and then used certain other spells, to set up the interview. This made me imperceptible to other Mundanes and made my words intelligible to Sofia. Take my word: such steps are necessary when operating in such a region, silly as they may seem to ordinary folk.

"I have come to take you away from all this to a realm of magic," I told her.

She considered a moment. "Okay," she agreed in the Mundane *way*.

So we walked back to Xanth, chatting as we went, and got to know each other as well as necessary. We passed back through the Shield and I fetched the carpet. We sat on it, and it lifted.

Sofia screamed and almost jumped off. "What's the matter, woman?" I demanded with justified irritation.

"It's magic!" she cried.

"Of course it is. I told you this was a land of magic."

"But I didn't believe you."

"Then why did you come with me?"

"Because anything is better than being an old maid in Mundania."

She had a point. "Well, you will just have to learn to live with magic, because I am a Magician." I had found a scroll attesting to my degree from the demon's University of Magic, so knew that in my missing years I had become a certified Magician. In fact, when I saw that, I remembered an entire year-long episode with Professor Grossclout, Beauregard, and Metria. The demoness had for some reason wanted to seduce me, but had failed (which was even less explicable), and I had completed my studies. That was good.

Sofia decided that she would live with it. But she seemed quite nervous about the height and exposure of the carpet, until I uncorked a relaxation spell and she relaxed.

We came to the castle. "Oh, it's beautiful!" she exclaimed. "Just like a fairy tale!"

"No fairies here," I corrected her. "They live elsewhere in the forest."

She glanced at me, then laughed, though I wasn't sure what she found funny.

She seemed somewhat in awe of the castle, especially its appurtenances like the moat monster, until she saw my mound of unsorted socks. "Now that I understand!" she exclaimed. "There's enough here to keep me busy for years!"

Precisely.

We settled into what she termed a common-law marriage. She was good in the kitchen, once she learned how to use simple spells and how to harvest ripe pies from the garden. She was good with clothing, once she learned about shoe trees and such. She discovered a rose garden in back, and tended to it carefully, for the flowers were similar to those she knew at her home. Actually, that rose garden seemed to be magic, flourishing with no care, but the roses bloomed more readily when someone paid attention to them.

But she did have one problem. It seemed that she felt I should at some point break off my study of the fascinating Book of Magic and do something with her on the bed. It seemed to be some sort of custom in her land.

Perplexed, I went to a magic mirror, one which gave straight answers. It showed a flying stork.

"Oh, you want to summon the stork!" I exclaimed.

She laughed, again finding something mysteriously funny.

So I put a place marker in the book and went to make this sacrifice. She was in some kind of nightie, and actually looked somewhat fetching; I hadn't really looked at her before. It must have been some time since I had indulged in this activity, because I became quite interested in it once I got started and wound up spending the rest of the night with Sofia on the bed. Apparently she had learned to be dextrous with more than mere socks during her prior dull life.

The next time she was interested in this activity, I was quicker to catch on. I was in my seventh decade, but my dunking in the healing spring kept me healthy, and I felt more like thirty-nine, which was the age I was when I got my degree in Magic, and my last memory until my jump into the present. So, in my experience, I was that age, and perhaps that counted for something.

The following year our son was delivered. Sofia named him Crombie, after an obscure relative of hers who had been a soldier, once she got over the shock of seeing the stork land with the bundle. Apparently she had expected another manner of delivery. There's no accounting for the expectations of Mundanes. Then she shrugged. "When in fairyland, do as the fairies do," she said. I didn't bother to try to understand what she meant by that. Just so long as she was satisfied with the baby. He did seem to have a certain Mundanish cast, but this sort of thing happened when one married a Mundane.

Meanwhile, I was getting involved in something new. I did not recognize its implications at the time. A farmer approached the castle. "I hear tell you are a Magician," he said.

"So?" I agreed noncommittally.

"Do you have a spell I could use to make the most beautiful girl in my village fall madly in love with me?"

I looked at him. He was a rare bumpkin, smelling of manure. Only a cow flop could love that kind. But as it happened, I had found a number of bottles and vials on my shelf, and one was labeled LOVE, so I presumed it contained elixir from a love spring. I did not know how long it had been there or whether the potency of such water faded with time, so it would be good to test it.

I poured a few drops of it into a smaller container. "Put this in her drink or simply sprinkle it on her," I said. "Make sure that you are the first man she sees thereafter."

"Hokay," he said. "Whatcha want for it?"

It hadn't occurred to me that this was a trade, but I realized that it did make sense. I didn't want the whole village coming to get free love potion! "We do have a garden plot to dig," I said, remembering that Sofia had expressed the desire to try growing some Mundane plants here. Why she should want to do such a thing was beyond me, but I attributed it to the mysteriousness of women. I knew from my limited experience with her that it was best to humor her whims. Otherwise she might mismatch my socks.

So the farmer took his spade and did what he did best, and in a day had a nice garden plot dug. Sofia was thrilled, and not only were my socks extra sweet for the next week, so was she. Good deeds had their rewards. The farmer went back to his village, and later we heard the village wedding gong sounding, and I knew that the potion had been effective.

After that more villagers did come. Some wanted healing, which my supply of healing elixir did, and others wanted curse spells for their neighbors, and sundry others had sundry other requests. I was able to accommodate them all, for the needs of rustics were elementary, but in an effort to discourage such business I gradually increased my demands for trades. This process continued for years, and finally it reached to the point of equilibrium: there would be three formidable challenges for each person just to gain admittance to the castle, and then he would have to give me a year's service or something equivalent, before I would answer his Question. Then the flow of folk finally diminished, and I had no more calls than I wanted, which was on the order of one a month. Sofia agreed with this policy; as a Mundane she did not feel entirely at home in Xanth and preferred seclusion for the raising of her son.

That turned out to be more complicated than anticipated. Remember, Sofia was Mundane; she was learning about magic but it wasn't natural to her, and she had no magic talent of her own. She did not understand the pitfalls of it. I was busy with my own pursuits and did not think to inquire, and in any event Sofia would not have been able to tell me what was happening, because she had no basis for suspicion. The consequence of this was to be unfortunate. Had I the chance to play that portion of my life over, I would pay better attention and spare my son grief and alienation. But all I can do now is tell what happened, with my regrets.

When Crombie was three years old, an eight-year-old boy came for an Answer. I knew instantly that he was a Magician, and in the guise of making him serve me a year, I trained him in certain necessary things. I was quite excited, and my enthusiasm spread to Sofia, who had never seen magic like this before. In fact it was about at this point that she became a believer. Thus we were both distracted and did not think of the effect on our son. That was my error, one of a number whose memory forever plagues me. Sometimes I am almost tempted to take Lethe again, to abolish such embarrassments. I will discuss the business with the other boy in the next chapter; this one is for Crombie.

When Crombie saw our attention taken by the other boy, who was resident at the castle for that time, he was jealous and resentful. He had an excellent talent of his own, but it was not close to Magician level, while the other boy's was. Crombie was somewhat annoyed with me for being distracted, but he had little contact with me in the best of times, so that was not the problem. It was when Sofia also got involved that Crombie's helpless rage overflowed. She was *his* mother; how could she be neglecting him in favor of this stranger? A few words could have eased his passion, but we were not alert, and they went unsaid.

So Crombie did what made sense to him: he sought another mother. A better one. One who would pay him fall attention, to the exclusion of all other children. Oh, the subtle mischief of that quest!

His talent was to find things. All he had to do was fix a thing in his mind, close his eyes, turn himself around, and point, and his finger would be pointing in the direction that thing was to be found. It had been interesting discovering this; at first he had been a baby, too small to point, but once he started walking Sofia kept finding him into the cookie jar, no matter where she hid it, and finally discovered that he was Finding it. He could find anything, even intangible things, but could not be sure how far away they were. He was sure only of the direction. Since he wasn't allowed out of the castle alone, he didn't have much opportunity to use it for more than cookies.

But this time, in his rage, he broke the rule. He spun around, pointed, and opened his eyes. Then he walked in the direction he was pointing.

Into a wall. His Finding sense took no note of intervening obstacles, it merely pointed the way. So he walked through the doors and out of the castle and tried it again. This time he was pointing across the moat.

He knew he shouldn't cross it, but his rage pushed him on. If he got out into the jungle and got lost, it would serve his mother right. Maybe he would never return home; it would serve her right. But of course he could find home by using his talent, if he changed his mind.

So he crossed the drawbridge. Soufflé lifted his head from the water and hissed warningly; he knew the boy was not supposed to go out alone. But Crombie ran on across, and the monster couldn't stop him, for he certainly wasn't going to bite my son.

Crombie did his Find routine again, and followed his finger into the jungle. Soufflé, alarmed, slid out of the moat and into the castle, coming to warn us. But Sofia would have none if it. "You're getting my carpet wet!" she screamed. "Get out of here this instant!" And Soufflé, cowed, slithered hastily back out. There are rare times when it is a disadvantage to be unable to speak the human way, and this is one of the few examples I can muster.

The serpent then crossed die moat and slid after Crombie. But it was slow, sniffing out the lad's trail, and soon he lost it in the welter of odors around the castle. Defeated, he returned to the moat and sank down under the water, miserable. He could only hope that the boy returned safely of his own accord.

Crombie, undaunted by the big outside world, followed his finger. It led him through forest and dale, until he came to a big pot of honey. There was candy around its rim. Well, now! He walked up and ripped off a gumdrop.

The gumdrop clung to the pot. Crombie pulled, and it came off, connected to the rim by a thinning string of gum. He yanked harder, and the connection stretched and thinned further.

Then he put it in his mouth and chomped down on it.

The honeypot exploded into smoke. "Yow!!" The gumdrop became smoke too, and curled back into the main cloud.

Somewhat daunted, Crombie nevertheless stood his ground. He was a fighter, even at the age of three. It wasn't as if he had never seen magic before.

The smoke coalesced into the figure of a woman. "Who the abyss are you?" she demanded.

"Who the what?" Crombie asked, confused.

"Sheol, Hades, inferno, blazes, hot underworld—" She broke off, examining him more closely. "Wait an instant! You're underage! I can't use that word around you."

"What word?"

"The word I can't remember. What's a little tyke like you doing out here alone? Where's your mother?"

"She's too busy for me. So I'm finding a better mother, and you're it."

The demoness considered. "Who is your busy mother?"

"Sofia. She's Mundane."

The demoness considered again. It had been a long time since she had considered anything twice. In fact it hadn't happened since she tried to seduce me. For this was indeed *that* demoness, who was somehow always near when there was mischief about to break loose. Perhaps demons do have talents, and this was hers.

"And who is your father?"

"The Magician Humfrey."

"Now this is abruptly interesting. You are Humfrey's son?" She evidently wanted to be quite sure.

"Yes. Only he's busy too."

"Indeed. I remember when he was too busy for me. And what is your name?"

"I'm Crombie."

"And I'm Metria. What makes you think I'm a better mother for you?"

"I pointed to you."

"You bit me, too, right on the—never mind." She rubbed the farthest out spot on her bosom. "This is your magic?"

"Yes. I Find things. So I Found a better mother."

The demoness nodded. "That is an interesting way to put it. That certainly is a nice talent. You recognized me despite my deceptive configuration."

"Your what?"

"The way I looked. You weren't fooled."

"Nothing fools my talent," he said proudly.

"Why are your folks too busy for you?"

"There's an older boy there now. They like him better."

Metria considered. "You know, I used to know your father, but he treated me as shabbily as he is treating you. I even showed him my panties."

Crombie was young and innocent, but not *that* innocent. "You were his wife?"

"Not exactly. That was the Demoness Dana, who sensibly departed after having her way with him. I wanted to summon the stork with him too, but he didn't cooperate. He was just too dam—uh, darned busy for me." She frowned, aggravated in retrospect.

"Yes," Crombie said, understanding perfectly.

"Well, your talent must be right. Tell, me, what is your idea of the perfect mother?"

"She'll pay all her attention to me and nobody else," he replied, for he had done some thinking on this subject. "She'll give me candy, and never make me take a bath, and never make me sleep alone. And she won't like any other children, not even a little bit."

Metria nodded. "I can do that."

"Sure. My talent Found you."

"It certainly did. Well, Crombie, this should be most entertaining."

"What?"

"Let's find some candy."

It was obvious they were going to get along.

Metria picked Crombie up and carried him swiftly through the air to the bank of the With-a-Cookee River, where cookies of all types grew in abundance. Crombie was delighted. He picked cookies galore and stuffed them into his mouth. Then she took him to Lake Tsoda Popka, and he sampled the fizz. He didn't like the first taste, but she showed him how to put some in a bottle she found, and shake it until it squirted all over everything, and then it was tame enough to drink.

But after a bit she became more serious. "Crombie, this stuff is very good, but if you eat too much right away it can give you a tummy ache. You have to get used to it. I would not be a perfect mother if I did not warn you of this. So I will take you home now, but tomorrow you can come out again, and you will be able to eat more without getting sick. Eventually you will be able to stuff yourself with impunity, and that is the ideal state."

"But I don't want to go home!"

She frowned. "I understand your position. But if you don't return, they will know how you sneaked out, and then there will be censored to pay."

"What to pay?"

"Worse than seeing panties."

That set him back. "I don't want to be censored!"

"Just what is so bad about spending the night home?"

"I'm stuck in this dark room all to myself, while they do fun things somewhere else. There are spooks just waiting to grab me if I even peek out from under the covers. And I have to have castor oil, because it is Good For Me."

Metria made a face. "You're right. That's a fate worse than whatever. But I have an idea. I can't go in that castle, because your father has spirit levels out that flatten any spirit. But maybe if I make myself very small, you can sneak me in. Then I will keep you company and help you avoid the bad things."

"Great!"

The demoness became as small as a gumdrop, and he put her in his mouth. "Now don't swallow me," she warned, a little mouth forming on the drop. "Because then I would have to turn crepuscular to come out, and you wouldn't like *where* I came out."

"Turn what?"

"Hazy, indistinct, impalpable, vague, smoky, gaseous—

"Poopy?"

"Close enough."

He was careful not to swallow her or even to bite on her, though she tasted very good. His tummy was already feeling just enough queasy from the cookies and tsoda popka so that he didn't want any ill wind in there.

Soufflé Serpent was greatly relieved to see him return safely. Crombie knew that the creature would not tell on him, now. Moat monsters never told, when it would only get them in trouble too.

No alarms went off. It seemed that the magic of the castle couldn't detect an evil spirit when it was inside a good person.

Crombie hadn't even been missed. That certainly seemed to justify his attitude.

Soon it was time for supper. He wasn't hungry. But Metria curled out of his mouth, an invisible vapor, and made the food disappear. She did the same for the oil from the castors, and that was an even greater relief.

When he went up to his lonely room, she was with him. He had company. She formed herself into the nicest pillow he could imagine, with two extremely soft mounds, and he rested his head on her and felt wonderful.

Then in the dark, a spook came. It leaned over the bed. "Look!" it exclaimed. "He forgot to hide under the covers! Now we'll get him!"

Suddenly the pillow opened a big long mouth with one-and-a-half squintillion teeth. "Oh, yeah?" it breathed with supreme menace and snapped at the spook's nose. The spook was so surprised it dropped to the floor, where Missile-Toe, Crombie's Monster Under the Bed, fired a spike into its foot. "Owoooh!" the spook cried, and shot out of there so fast a piece of it tore on a nail in the wall. After that no more spooks came. Crombie laughed until he almost cried, sheerly happy.

Then the pillow formed arms, and they hugged Crombie and stroked his hair, and there was a soft sweet humming until he drifted to sleep. Metria was the perfect mother, all right.

After a year, the other boy went away. But Metria stayed. Usually she assumed the form of Crombie's jacket, and he wore her around the house, but she could be anything he wanted. Indeed, she *was* all he wanted; he hardly cared about anything else. When Sofia made him study things he Ought to Know, he paid no attention, knowing that Metria would provide the answers for him when they were required. And often they sneaked out to the With-a-Cookee River and gorged. His miserable life had become totally happy.

What none of us knew, then, was that Metria was learning all my secrets, for she was an enemy in our midst. A number of my spells went wrong, causing great inconvenience and annoyance, and we didn't know why. What a joke the demoness was having at our expense!

Then Crombie turned thirteen. The moment he was a teenager, he became aware of the female of the species. He was still too young to join the Adult Conspiracy, but he had notions about it, and chafed at being kept in ignorance. In short, he was a typical teenager.

Here he ran afoul of Metria herself. She was a creature of mischief, but she knew there was more mischief in maintaining the Adult Conspiracy than in abolishing it, so she maintained it. So when Crombie sought to put his hands on her in an aware way, she told him no. He had never been balked by her before and was at first incredulous, then furious. He grabbed her—and she dissipated into smoke and floated away. While it disturbs me to agree with that confounded demoness, I have to say that she acted correctly in that instance. Any woman who gets grabbed in a manner she doesn't want should depart with similar swiftness.

After that she was no longer with Crombie. He had to sleep alone. He was now too big for the spooks to harm, but he hated losing his womanly-soft pillow. Now his almost complete ignorance of the things Sofia had been teaching him manifested. He was a spoiled-rotten teenager, and that was a condition not even he could live with. Metria had done him the worst of favors by enabling him to escape any discipline in childhood. He was so angry he had to keep blinking to keep the red glare of rage from burning his eyes. He cursed all older women, for of course he was incapable of blaming himself.

He stormed out of the castle, now having more freedom because we were under the impression he was worthy of it. He whirled and pointed, uttering the syllable "Girl!"

He followed his finger—and came across a girl his age, sitting in the very glade where he had first found the honeypot. She was exquisitely pretty, and he fell in love with her right away. This, too, is the manner of teenagers. Since he hadn't grabbed her, she was responsive. The two of them had a marvelous time dancing and kissing and sharing secrets. Then he became too demanding: "Show me your panties."

She laughed. Annoyed, he grabbed at her—and she dissolved into smoke and floated away. Only then did he realize that she had been merely another aspect of the Demoness Metria, having her fun with his innocence.

That was when he swore never to trust another woman. Any age, any type. They say there is no fury like that of a woman scorned, and Metria is a perfect example, but surely the fury of a teenager balked comes close. (I have, of course, long since forgotten that I was ever a teenager, not that this is relevant.)

By the time I discovered what had happened, it was way too late. My son was hopelessly embittered. There was nothing to do but send him away to be a soldier, for hate is an asset to that profession. I had in effect lost my son. Sofia was not particularly pleased, either.

I revised the castle defenses, to make sure that never again could a demon sneak in unobserved. It was not that I was prejudiced against demons; some of my best friends were demons. But Metria was sheer naughtiness. She never acted with outright malice, and indeed sometimes seemed to act decently, but there was no telling what the final cost of her mischief would be. Obviously she remained annoyed by her failure to corrupt me, so had corrupted my son instead. Corrupted him, ironically, with kindness: she had enabled him to avoid the necessary disciplines of growing up. That lack of discipline might be typical for demons, but was disaster for humans.

Yet it was my fault too. I should have been alert. I should have taken a hand in the upbringing of my son. I, too, had been spoiled, for the Maiden Taiwan had brought up my first son. I resolved that if I ever had another son to raise, I would be a true father to him, not leaving his upbringing to others. To that resolution I was true.

But let me now return to the matter that so preoccupied me at the time my son was going astray. It was not, as will be seen, a thing of little consequence. Let's make that a separate chapter.

Chapter 12

TRENT

One day Sofia came, to me, surprised. "There's an eight-year-old boy approaching the castle!" she exclaimed. She, in common with most mothers, could tell a child's age and state of health at a glance.

I pulled my nose from the Book of Answers. I had been studying it for five years now, and was beginning to understand its use. It was evident that I had made the original entries and someone else had organized and cross-referenced them. There were so many entries that without such organization the tome would have been useless, but even with them it could be a job to discover exactly what I wanted. Now I could generally get a desired Answer in a few minutes, and with further practice might make that even faster. Much of the time I had simply read through the entries in whatever order they came. What a tremendous amount of information I had accumulated in those missing twenty-eight years!

"Well, doubtless he has a Question," I said. "There is no age barrier. Let me see what challenges are best."

"You will make a child do the challenges?" she asked, appalled. She was odd in certain ways, but of course that was her Mundane heritage.

"I don't want to be overrun by children any more than I want to be overrun by bumpkins," I said reasonably.

I looked in the book—and was surprised. It said NO CHALLENGES. So I researched for the reason, and it said POLICY. Growing frustrated, as often happened when dealing with this book, I investigated that, BECAUSE QUERENT IS A MAGICIAN.

I stared. Then I looked up at Sofia. "Let him in," I said gruffly. "He's a Magician."

Delighted, she hurried off. Meanwhile, I did further research in the book, but it couldn't tell me what the Magician's talent was. This was because its Answers had all been researched years ago; it was not a predictor of the future. It was attuned to the signals of Magician-class magic, because that had always been a prime matter with me, but that was the limit.

I closed the book. A Magician! In all my years of searching, I had found only one Magician before, and now he was the Storm King. The more I saw of the Storm King's reign, the less I liked it; the man was a Magician, true, but an incompetent administrator, and Xanth was sliding back into the Dark Age instead of climbing out of it. We needed a better king: one who would bring vigor back to the throne and who would restore Castle Roogna to prominence. Maybe this boy was that future-king.

Soon the lad was ushered into my presence. "Good Magician," Sofia said formally, "this is Trent."

I concealed my excitement. I needed to know a lot more about this boy before I let him know his importance. "A greeting, Trent. Why are you here?"

"I'm a Magician," he said. "I should be king. But Mom says the Storm King will kill me if I go and ask him for the throne."

"She's right," I said.

Sofia made a stifled exclamation. The very notion of harm to a child upset her. "Go fetch this young man a cookie," I said, to get her out of the room for a while. She disappeared.

"But I don't need a cookie," Trent protested. "I can make my own."

"By means of your magic," I said, trying to ascertain what his magic was.

"Sure. Want to see?"

Yes! "If you wish."

He looked around. There was a speck of dust on the table that had somehow managed to escape Sofia's destructive attention, and in that dust was a flea. He pointed to it. "Cookie," he said.

Instantly there was a plant. A fine fresh chicolate chop cookie plant, by the look and smell of it. He had transformed the flea into this. That was certainly Magician-class magic, if he could do it across the board.

But it might be illusion. I had to be sure. "May I?" I asked, reaching for a cookie.

"Sure. It's your dust."

I took the cookie and bit into it. It was perfect.

"Want a different kind?" Trent asked. "I can make it any kind I know."

I held the bitten-into cookie. "What about a glass of milk?"

He pointed. Suddenly the plant was a milkweed, with several full ripe pods. "I can't make glasses," he said. "Only living things."

"That is good enough," I said, suitably impressed. I was satisfied that he was a Magician of Transformation of living creatures. "So you have come to find out how to become king without getting killed first."

"Right."

I heard Sofia returning. "Spot lesson in diplomacy," I said. "Don't mention cookies; just accept hers."

"Okay."

Sofia had brought a plateful of cookies. Trent thanked her and took one. He was evidently a quick learner. That was good.

"I do not have an easy Answer for you," I said. "There are only two ways you can safely become king. One is to wait until the Storm King dies—"

"But that'll be forever!" he protested.

"And the other is to prepare yourself so that you can take power, displacing him. But you will have to be well trained, and adult, because such displacement is not a gentle matter."

"Oh." He looked disappointed. "You mean I have to pay a year's service to you, for that?"

"In the course of that service, you will learn how to prepare yourself," I said. "I would not, of course, advise you to bother the legitimate king, but I will teach you how to be alert and defend yourself."

"Oh." His disappointment was fading. As I said, he was a bright boy.

So it was that Trent did a year's service for me, moving into a spare room in the castle, and I taught him how best to use his power. The strategy was simple: to transform any menace to something that was not a menace. When a mosquito came to suck his blood, he changed it into a harmless purple fly. When a dragon reared up before him, he transformed it to a dragonfly. When a tangle tree grabbed at him, he transformed it to an acorn tree. The key was to rehearse things so that he could handle any living thing and not be surprised. Some creatures could hurt him from a distance, while he had to be within arm's reach to transform them, so he had to figure ways to nullify them from afar. Usually it was possible to transform some nearby creature into one which was a natural enemy of the attacking creature. But some natural enemies were also enemies of man. So if a dragon were about to blast out a long tongue of flame, he wouldn't transform a nearby worm into a monstrous fireproof serpent, because that serpent would find him easier prey than the dragon. But he could transform that worm into a huge sphinx, which wouldn't care about a man but would object strenuously to having its hide scorched by the dragon.

I also showed him how to sleep safely by transforming something into a mock tangle tree. Then he could sleep in the branches of that tree, while other creatures did not know it was harmless. Because he had to be on guard at all times, if he wanted to tackle a resentful king. Even so, I urged him not to do it—knowing that he would not follow this advice. We understood each other.

Between sessions, we discussed philosophical matters. "It has occurred to me that the Shield is a mixed blessing," I remarked.

"Is it? But doesn't it protect us from invasion by the Mundanes? It stopped the Waves!;

"It stopped the Waves," I agreed. We were referring to the series of wavelike invasions made by the Mundanes, which had wrought much havoc until halted by the deadly Shield King Ebnez had adapted. "But it also stopped colonization from Mundania. There are actually more human people in Mundania than in Xanth, and the Waves served to renew the human stock here. Without that irregular renewal, our species has been dwindling in Xanth. Today the villages are smaller and farther apart, and there are fewer magic paths between them, making travel more hazardous. We need more people—and we can only get them if that Shield comes down."

"But the Mundanes are terrible folk!" he said, repeating the standard lore. Children were frightened into good behavior by threats that the Mundanes would get them.

"Is Sofia terrible?" I asked.

Sofia had been very nice to him throughout. She had come to under-

stand as well as I the importance of a potential future king of Xanth, and
had treated him royally. "No. But—"

"She is from Mundania."

He gaped at me. This subject had not come up before. This was the beginning of a change in his attitude. Never again did he speak ill of Mundanes.
In fact, the time would come when he would marry one, as I had.

But I made one mistake in training him. I did not sufficiently stress
the importance of integrity. I assumed that he already understood it, and
I was preoccupied by practical matters. That error, as with the one I made
by neglecting my son, was to cost us all dearly. How late we learn wisdom!

Another visit was from a harried woman. The Book of Answers cut short
the challenges again, though she was no Sorceress. Why? I had to interview the woman to find out.

"It's my daughter," she said. "She's six years old, and it's impossible to
discipline her or anything. She's out of control! I'm at my wit's end!"

I could see that. Normally folk were right in the middle of their wits,
but she was off to the end of hers. "She talks back?" I asked.

"No, she doesn't have to. She just uses her illusion."

"She has illusions? Many girls do."

"Not like this! Iris has illusions that—oh, how can I describe them?
They're so real!"

I began to get a glimmer. The Book of Answers knew something
about this, and it warned me only when there was Magician-class magic
involved. "Do you mean she makes illusions you can't penetrate?"

"Well, not exactly. But it's so difficult, we just can't—it's so easy to be
fooled—"

Gradually I got the story from her, and I understood what was happening. Her daughter Iris was Sorceress of Illusion. A Sorceress was the
same as a Magician, only female. There was this foolish distinction, making it allowable only for a Magician (and therefore a man) to be king. That
was one of the things about Xanth that needed changing, and that the
current King *wasn't* changing.

I knew what I had to do. "Send her here to do your year's service for
you. We shall teach her how to use her power beneficially and return her
to you with better manners."

"Oh thank you, Good Magician!" she exclaimed tearfully.

So it was that six-year-old Iris came to spend a year with us, a year after Trent left. Crombie was a year younger than Iris, but kept mostly to himself; we did not knew then how he had found comfort with the demoness, and he and Metria were careful never to let us find out. So there was not much interaction between the two children. Iris discovered early that Crombie had ways of getting back at her if she teased him with her realistic illusions, and she left him alone. I believe she crafted an illusion of a dragon coming to eat him up, and that night she climbed into bed only to discover a gushy meringue pie there first. It was no illusion. She had to wash the stuff off her feet and change the sheets. She didn't even tell the adults, sharing the Juvenile Conspiracy. So only now, in distant retrospect, can I say that probably it was Metria who placed that pie. Who says the demoness never did anyone a favor? It taught Irismanners in a hurry.

Iris did have a wondrous talent. She could make anything appear and be believably realistic, complete with sound and smell. Only touch was missing; if you walked into the illusion, you went right through it. But who would just walk into a fire-breathing dragon, on the chance that it wasn't real? Who would do it if the chances were only one in ten it was real? But for those who liked to play the odds, she could make a counter trap: by placing the illusion of a dragon over a deep pit. Thus if someone walked into it, he would fall in the pit and be in as much trouble as ever. In fact, she could cover the pit with the illusion of innocent level ground. Or she could cover a real dragon with that illusion of level ground. So a person could not be safe by avoiding the apparent illusions. Anything could be an illusion, and that meant that anything could be dangerous in an unexpected way.

But we did not have trouble with Iris, for two powerful reason's. First, we were delighted with her talent. This was the second Magician-class talent I had encountered in two years; was a trend commencing? Even if she could never be king, she could be a power in Xanth. So while her family had been driven to distraction by the illusions, we delighted in them, and Iris was flattered by the attention. Flattered girls are generally not difficult girls. Second, I knew a good deal about magic myself, having studied at the University of Magic and collected spells all my life. I could not be fooled the way others could. I could tell illusion from reality immediately.

I proved this early: Iris made illusion duplicates of herself, and little girls ran all around the castle, screaming. But I always spoke only to the true one. She did not know that I had had to take a potion to enable me to do this. She was impressed. Children respect adults they can't fool.

So I taught her new ways to use her talent, and how to craft ever more glorious illusions. When she came, she could make a realistic dollhouse; when she left, she could craft a realistic castle. At the start she could make a miniature storm cloud that seemed to rain on the rug, to Sofia's distress. At the end she could make a storm that wailed all around the castle. And perhaps most important, she learned to make real food that was dull look and taste like the most elegant meal. The feel of a glass of water was cool liquid; so was the feel of exotic wine. So she could get around her limitation, deceiving even herself. She could drink nothing but green and orange tsoda popka, and share it with the rest of us—yet it was only water. She could eat spicy dragon steak, yet it might be mere fruit from a stake plant. Best of all, she could forget to brush her hair, yet have it look eloquently coiffed.

I explained to her how she could do even more than that, when she grew up. She could be as slovenly as she wished in person, yet always appear beautiful and well dressed to others. Then she showed me how well she was learning, for she became a beautiful adult woman with a low decolletage. Then her dress dissolved, and she was bare breasted. "Am I sexy now, Good Magician?" she inquired coyly.

"No," I informed her.

She pouted. "Why not? Aren't my bosoms big enough?"

"The term you intend is breast," I said. "You are showing two breasts. Only one bosom." This discussion would have been chancy for a boy, but not for a girl, as it covered Necessary Information and so was partially exempt from the Adult Conspiracy. There was a portion of male anatomy that was similarly proscribed for girls.

"Whatever," she said. That gave me pause for just a moment, but of course this was not the wily Metria. It was a coincidental use of the term. "How big do they have to be?"

"There is no actual correct size," I said. "The problem is that yours lack nipples." This time the air clouded and there was a distant rumble, for that word was really pushing the limit of what the Conspiracy allowed. But again I was able to plead Necessity. Things can be uttered in the guise of Education which can not be even thought of elsewhere.

Iris looked down at her illusion. "Oh." Two nipples abruptly sprouted.

Then there was the sound of footsteps in the hall, and the entire illusion vanished, leaving the girl in her ordinary dress. "Tell me more about the illusion of beauty, Good Magician," Iris said brightly as Sofia entered with sandwiches. By that token I knew that she understood well enough the limits of the Conspiracy. Sofia, despite being Mundane, would have called a foul instantly, had she seen what I had seen. The Adult Conspiracy extends wide and far, and few truly comprehend its intricacies, but the mothers of children come close.

So in due course we sent Iris home, and she was by then a perfectly behaved little girl of seven. I had impressed on her that there was more to be gained by pleasing others than by teasing them. Instead of putting up walls of illusion to avoid taking her castor oil, she could thank her mother and make it taste like vanilla syrup. I knew that her family would be most pleased with her improved attitude.

Sofia decided to visit her folks in Mundania, so I gave her a Shield-passing spell and took her to the border. I expected her to return with a new appreciation of Xanth, having been reminded just how dreary Mundania is. But she surprised me by returning almost immediately, excited.

"It's gone!" she exclaimed.

"Mundania? It can't be."

"Yes it is! There's just a nothingness there:"

So I had to go look. She was right; where Mundania had been, across the isthmus, there was a mere void. Mundania had disappeared.

Now of course this could not be considered much of a loss. Nobody likes Mundania anyway, especially the Mundanes who have to stew in it all the time. Depression is rife among them, which they seek to ameliorate by taking all manner of mind-zonking drugs. But Sofia was adamant: her homeland had been lost, and I would have to find it. So I sighed and got to work on the problem.

It turned out that the various parts of the geography of Mundania were defined by peculiar numbers called "zip codes." Every year or so a new directory of zip codes was made. This year someone in their arcane Post

Orifice, whose mascot was a fierce big snail, had forgotten. Thus there was no longer any way to find anywhere, and Mundania had disappeared into formless glop. No one in Xanth had noticed the difference in the neighboring realm, of course, assuming there was one.

I had to write a letter and powder it with magic dust and send it to the main office, which the letter could reach only because there was nowhere else for it to go. In it I explained the problem, and urged that the forgotten directory be remembered and issued.

The snail moved as slowly as ever, but in a year my advice was heeded, and Mundania came back into findability. Sofia was finally able to make her visit home. The odd thing was, she reported on her return, that nobody in Mundania seemed to have been aware of the missing time. Apparently that world had been suspended, and resumed only with the appearance of the new directory. What a strange business!

Iris had left at age seven, in the year 1008. When she was the maidenly age of seventeen, she returned. This time, she was ready to do service for an Answer on her own behalf. She wanted to know where she could go to have everything her own way. That was, for a teenage girl, a reasonable wish.

I looked it up in the Book of Answers. There was such a place. It was an isle off the east coast of Xanth, about half way down, just beyond the place where the—the—well, I forget what, but anyway, where it intersected the ocean. Few folk ever went there, yet it was a nice enough place. All it needed was some fixing up—which Iris could readily do, by means of her illusion.

So she went there, and named it the Isle of Illusion. She crafted the entire island into one big illusion, which she changed at her whim. Everything there was indeed all her own way. There she remained for some time, gradually discovering that what a person most desires is not necessarily what she really wants.

In 1021, at the age of twenty-four, Magician Trent grew tired of waiting for the aging Storm King to blow out, and started organizing to take over the throne directly. I was in favor of this effort, but could not say so; I had to maintain overt support of the existing regime. Trent did not consult me, which I appreciated; I remained aloof from the politics of the day. But I used my spells to watch events closely.

Trent decided that he needed to have a major constituency, so as to have a base from which to move against the King and force his abdication. He chose the centaur community of central Xanth. (The centaurs of Centaur Isle were out of the question; they would not touch human politics, considering it almost as dirty as human magic. They had a point.) But they refused to join him.

He made a demonstration of power: he went to Fish River and changed all its fish into lightning bugs. This was an amazing feat, because that was a magic river which guarded its waters and sought to nullify any threat against it. Only an extremely powerful and versatile Magician could have overcome that river.

But centaurs are ornery folk—some say stubborn—and do not yield readily to demonstrations. So Trent proceeded to the second part of his program. He sent those lightning bugs to harass the centaurs. He did this by changing gnats to huge rocs, and requiring the birds to anchor themselves to the ground and flap their wings, generating a wind to blow the lightning bugs into the centaur village. The birds did it because it was the only way they could get changed back to gnats; after they blew the lightning bugs, Trent did change them back.

The lightning bugs, irritable at finding themselves flying in air instead of swimming in the river, descended on the centaurs in a raging mass. They hurled their little lightning bolts at any flesh they found. When the centaurs tried to swat them, they made a flanking attack, and really zapped those flanks. The centaurs smashed at them with their tails, but there were so many clouds of bugs that it did little good. Trent no doubt figured that the centaurs would yield, then, but he had misjudged them. Instead they came to me, asking for some way to get rid of this scourge. Their leader, Alpha Centauri, made his way through my castle challenges and put their Question.

Now I did not want to get involved in this, because of the political background, so I set a price I thought would make them balk: one year's service for each centaur my advice rid of the scourge. That would be three hundred centaur years, an unimagined total. But they amazed me by agreeing!

So I told Alpha to go to the hate spring in north Xanth, dip out a single drop if it, dilute it with a thousand parts of regular water, and spray the mix on the herd. Hate elixir is dangerous to the user, but highly diluted it merely makes the user detestable for a while. The lightning bugs couldn't stand the sprayed flesh, and could neither shock it into submission nor feed on it, and soon died out.

Now I had three hundred centaurs committed to work for me one year. What was I going to have them do?

Well, I found things. I had one crew build some bridges across the—the—well, anyway, some useful bridges. One was one-way and another was invisible so not just anyone could use them. They required fine design, craftsmanship, and workmanship, and these were centaur strong points. This was a real service to the community, though no one remembered it.

The main crew worked on renovating my castle. There had always been a certain rotten odor about it, dating from the zombie time, and that distressed Sofia. So we replaced much of it, and converted it to a very special design: a simple command could cause the rooms and walls to shift position, and the moat to change its shape and depth (Soufflé almost sailed into the air in alarm, the first time that happened), and the trees around it to assume new positions. The access paths could change and change again, and the entire aspect of the castle could alter. In short, it was like having a completely different castle, outside and in, in about two and a half moments. That made spring cleaning a delight for Sofia; she could change everything to be almost unrecognizable. It was a woman's dream come true.

The centaurs completed their labors exactly on schedule, one year after the deal had been made, and departed. I made a note: not to try to bluff out a centaur next time.

Meanwhile Trent, now called the Evil Magician, had lost his ploy to enlist the support of the centaurs. But he was stubborn too. He plowed ahead anyway. He marched on the North Village, employing the simple expedient I had taught him: he transformed anyone who tried to interfere into something that couldn't interfere. If someone tried to kill him, he transformed that man into a fish and let him flop in the ground until he found water or died. Mere nuisances he changed to harmless animals or plants. A man named Justin got in Trent's way, and was converted to a tree in the middle of the village. Some folk became odd creatures: pink dragons, two-headed wolves, land octopi, or moneypedes. One girl tried to give him wrong directions; he transformed her into a winged centaur filly. She was an attractive specimen of her kind—but the only one of her kind. Chagrined, she fled to the Brain Coral and begged for sanctuary in its pool. It was granted, of course, and she was soon forgotten. Others saw the way of it, and decided to join the Evil Magician. There was a revolution developing and gaining force.

The Storm King had to use his talent in his own defense. He summoned a phenomenal storm. But he was now seventy-three years old, and his powers were failing. The storm turned out to be hardly more than wind and rain and a few hailstones.

It looked as if nothing could stop the Evil Magician from cornering the Storm King and turning him into a rooster roach. But the king was cunning. He bribed one of Trent's trusted associates to cast a sleep spell on him. This was effective, and Trent fell asleep in the midst of his final advance.

His friends hastily bore the body away. Now the supporters of the King became bold in a way they had not been before, and pursued. The only way to save the sleeping Magician was to get him out of Xanth. The keeper of the gate at the Shield decided to let him through; it was, after all, one way to be quite sure he would never return.

Indeed, it seemed that he would not. The affairs of Mundania are largely opaque to ordinary folk, and it, was only twenty years later that we were to learn his fate there. He settled, married, had a son—and then lost both to an evil Mundane plague. This was to have a significant consequence for Xanth, which is why I mention it. Otherwise I wouldn't have bothered.

So the revolution was ended, and the Storm King was victorious. I know I was not the only one who regretted that. Xanth was destined to continue its mediocrity.

Things continued in their petty pace another dozen years or so. Then Sofia, now about sixty-five years old, decided she preferred to return to Mundania to die. I tried to dissuade her, pointing out that I was a hundred and two, but that did not change her mind. So I had to let her go, after thirty-five years of marriage, with regret. She had been a very fine sock sorter, and it really wasn't her fault that our son went wrong.

Thereafter things were pretty quiet at the castle. My son was long gone, my wife was gone, and I was even more grumpy alone than in limited company. I had thought that all I wanted was to be left alone with my studies in magic, but I found that this was too much of a good thing. And my socks were piling up horrendously.

A young woman came. Her name was Starr, because she twinkled like a double star; that seemed to be her magic. At this time I was lonely enough so that I was glad to see anyone, even someone with a Question, so I let her in with only token challenges. Her Question was what could she do with three hummingbirds she had befriended? Her family objected to the constant music as the birds hummed in chorus, so she had to get rid of them. But she couldn't just cast them out into the jungle. For one thing, they always flew back to her. Where could she leave them where they would be happy and not follow her home?

For this she was willing to undertake a year's service? Yes, it seemed she was. She really cared about those birds.

I took Starr and the birds to the little rose garden in the back. The roses were magic, dating from my blanked-out period, and were always red and sweet. Near them were other flowers, more seasonal but still nice. The hummingbirds were delighted; they hovered near the roses, humming a very pretty melody. "They will like it here," I said. "There is plenty to keep them fed and happy."

"Oh, thank you!" the young woman said. "Now what is my service?"

"How are you at sorting socks?"

Starr wasn't great at that, but she learned, and the mountain of socks began to be reduced. She also fixed me meals, which was just as well, because I had forgotten to eat for several days and needed reminding. Good health could go only so far, at my age.

The three hummingbirds turned out to be good company themselves. Their names were Herman, Helen, and Hector, and they delighted in humming in three-part harmony for any person willing to listen. The flowers seemed to like them too. I felt almost guilty, making Starr do a year's service, because she had really done me a favor by bringing those birds. But I had no one else to sort my socks, so I said nothing.

I had been answering Questions as a kind of burden, because they distracted me from my studies. But now I looked forward to visits, because they distracted me from my loneliness. The greater the problem, the more interesting it was for me.

One case almost stumped me. This was a centaur who felt somewhat ambivalent. He called himself AmbiGus. He said he felt as if his personality wanted to split. I checked everything about him, and he seemed normal. It would be bad form not to provide an Answer; I had a reputation to maintain, for what little it was worth. What was wrong with this creature? Was it a mere complex of the type that Mundanes experienced?

Mundanes. I tried one more thing. I took Gus to the border and spelled us through the Shield. Sure enough, when he walked away from the magic ambience of Xanth, he separated into the basic centaur components: a man and a horse. That was why he felt like splitting: his talent was to split, in the absence of magic.

Unfortunately he could not do it in Xanth. So his choice was either to reside apart in Mundania or together in Xanth. He thought about it while performing his year's service for me.

One case was interesting for another reason: who it was. It was Trojan, the Horse of Another Color, otherwise known as the Night Stallion. He governed the realm of bad dreams, which was accessible only through a hypnogourd. He came to me in a dream, as he was not comfortable outside the gourd. But he had a legitimate Question: what was a suitable bad dream for writers who wrote about the dream realm? Such folk were almost immune to ordinary bad dreams, because they were constantly devising bad stories themselves and were jaded. But they could not be allowed to mess with the dream realm, because that could dilute the potency of the dreams.

I sweated over that one, partly because our dialogue was in the form of a bad dream. But finally I came up with a satisfactory formula: the guilty writer would be taken into a dream which seemed like reality, so that he did not know he was dreaming. In that dream he would be led into the Night Stallion's very own study and shown a lion. This was not a fearsome lion, for writers wrote about that kind all the time, seeming to enjoy the crunch of bones and splatter of blood. No, this was an old ill lion, its pride gone. Its teeth were so worn and weak that it could survive only on a diet of soggy puns. The writer was required to produce such puns, to the satisfaction of a grim person called Eddie Tor, lest he be guilty of letting the lion die. If the lion died, there would be a real stink. But if he failed to make Eddie Tor's unreasonable standards, Eddie would do beastly things to his prose, putting him farther behind. There was also a cursed block on his desk, which constantly interfered with his vision so that he could not concentrate. Somehow he had to get around that writer's block before he was faced with the dead lion.

The Night Stallion was pleased. He was sure this would torment any writers enough to prevent them from messing with any more dream stories. In fact, it might drive some of them out of the trade entirely. It was an excellent punishment. He repaid me by granting me a bye on future bad dreams for myself, no matter how much I might deserve them. After that I did sleep easier.

So my life went in its petty pace for about seven years. Then the Muses of Parnassus started writing volumes of history of Xanth, apparently just as a matter of record, and my life became infernally complicated.

Chapter 13

BINK

Trouble came in the form of a seemingly innocent young man of about twenty-five. He trudged up to the castle, having somehow managed to cross the—the—to get through a difficult section of Xanth and avoid the inherent dangers of the countryside. He evidently had a Question, so I had AmbiGus spread the word and retire. I really didn't want to be bothered at this time.

But the man was determined. He rode the hippocampus through the moat, refusing to be bucked off by the water horse or to lose his nerve and quit. The hippocampus had not been trying too hard, of course, and had he succeeded in throwing the man, he would have arranged to not-quite trap him in the water, allowing him to beat a hasty escape. But the man had prevailed. That spoke for his stamina.

Then the man explored the huge facade door and found the little door set within it, and climbed in through that. AmbiGus had carefully crafted the inner door to be invisible but to yield readily to a push, its panel falling out. The man located it quickly. That spoke for his intelligence.

Finally he encountered the manticora, which was a creature the size of a horse with the head of a man, body of a lion, wings of a dragon, and a huge scorpion's tail. The monster had come to me to ask whether it, being only partly human (there must have been quite a gathering at a love spring when he came to be!), had a soul. I told him that only those who had souls were concerned about them. Satisfied with that obvious Answer, he was now serving his term of service, his instructions being to scare visitors without actually hurting them. If he could scare them off, good enough; if he could not, he had to arrange some un-obvious way of letting them pass. The visitor passed, which spoke for his courage.

Well, I would have to see what he wanted. Sometimes I knew well ahead of time, but this one was curiously opaque, with no reference in the Book of Answers; I would just have to ask him. But I wasn't pleased at the prospect. I had produced too many love potions for country hicks and beauty potions for girls who hardly needed them, and this certainly seemed to be more of the same. How I wished a real challenge would appear, instead of these nothings!

The oaf yanked on the bell cord. DONG-DONG, DONG-DONG! As if I wasn't already on my way. And I still didn't know his name. I didn't want to ask it; I didn't want to admit that I, the Magician of Information, had not found it listed in my references. "Who shall I say is calling?" I inquired.

"Bink of the North Village."

Ha! Name and origin in one breath, both about as unheroic as it was possible to be. Naturally someone this dull wouldn't be named Arthur or Roland or Charlemagne! But I remained annoyed, so I pretended to mishear. "Drink of what?"

"Bink!" he said, getting annoyed himself. Good. "B-I-N-K."

I looked up at him, for this disgustingly healthy young man stood about twice my century-gnarled height. I was healthy too, but the years had gradually twisted me, and I never had been tall or handsome in the way he was. What conceivable problem could he have that might ameliorate the dullness of my existence for a moment?

"What shall I say is the business of your master Bink?" I asked, still needling the hayseed.

He clarified that *he* was Bink, and was looking for a magical talent. He was ready to deliver a year's service. "It's robbery, but I'm stuck for it," he confided, not yet catching on to my identity; he assumed I was a servant. This was getting better as it went! "Your master gouges the public horrendously."

This was actually beginning to be fun. I played it for another laugh. "The Magician is occupied at the moment; can you come back tomorrow?"

"Tomorrow!" he exploded in a manner that warmed my heart. "Does the old bugger want my business or doesn't he?"

He had dug himself in deep enough. It was time to wrap it up. I led him up to my cluttered study and seated myself at my dcsk. "What makes you think your service is worth the old gouging bugger's while?"

I watched with deep satisfaction as the realization slowly percolated through his thick head. At last he knew to whom he was talking! He looked suitably crestfallen. "I'm strong," he finally said. "I can work."

I couldn't resist turning the screw just a bit more. "You are oink-headed and doubtless have a grotesque appetite. You'd cost me more in board than I'd ever get from you." Probably true, but it might be fun having such a naive lunk around.

He only shrugged. At least he had the wit to know how unimportant he was.

"Can you read?"

"Some," he said doubtfully.

So he wasn't much at that. Good; that meant he wouldn't be prying into my precious tomes. "You seem a fair hand at insult, too; maybe you could get rid of intruders with their petty problems." Would he catch the implication: that his own problem was as petty as any? I could readily ascertain his talent; it was probably the ability to make a stalk of hay change color or something similarly banal. The Storm King required every person to have a talent, but most of them were so slight as to be barely worth it. That *law* was barely worth it, too.

"Maybe," he agreed, evidently determined not to aggravate me further.

I had had enough of this. "Well, come on; we don't have all day," I said, getting down from my chair. Actually we did have all day, if that was what it took. One advantage of boredom is that all-day distractions can be welcome, especially if they happen to become interesting.

I decided to try Beauregard on this one. The demon was still working on his paper, "Fallibilities of Other Intelligent Life," after several decades, and had finally come to me to ask for some kind of help. I had suggested that if he spent a decade or two in the bottle, helping me answer the Questions of living creatures, he should have a rich lode of fallibilities to analyze. He had agreed, merging service with research and snoozing between times. He pretended to be confined to the bottle and to the pentacle, though by our agreement neither was tight; it was for show so that the visitors wouldn't be terrified by the manifestation of a genuine demon. Why disabuse them? Demons were not nearly as horrendous as represented, and some, like Metria or my ex-wife Dana, could be surprisingly winsome at times. But it could be tricky to deal with them, even unknowingly, as my son Crombie had learned the hard way.

I lifted the bottle from the shelf and shook it to alert the demon that a show was coming up. It wouldn't do to uncork him and have him go right on sleeping. I set it in the middle of the five-pointed star painted on the floor. I gestured grandiloquently and stepped back out of the figure.

The demon put on the show. The bottle's lid popped off and smoke issued impressively. From the resulting cloud the figure coalesced. About the only thing that detracted from the effect was the pair of spectacles perched on the demon's nose. But the fact was that demons varied in temperament as men did, and this one felt more comfortable using spectacles to read small print, just as I did.

"O Beauregard," I intoned dramatically. "I conjure thee by the authority vested in me by the Compact," which was nonsense; the only compact was our deal to observe dull visitors without frightening them off. "Tell me what magic talent this lad, Bink of the North Village, possesses." I could see that the hayseed was suitably impressed by the rigmarole.

Beauregard played it like a pro. He oriented impressively on the man. "Step into my demesnes, mortal, that I may inspect you properly."

"Nuh-uh!" Bink exclaimed, drawing back. He was accepting it all at face value.

Beauregard shook his head as if regretting the loss of a tasty morsel. Of course demons don't eat people; they don't eat anything except in rare situations when they have to pass the food along, such as when nursing half-human babies. The Demoness Dana had not even done that; she had lost her soul, and *bbrrupst*! she was gone. "You're a tough nut."

My turn. "I didn't ask you for his personality profile! What's his magic?" For Beauregard was good at fathoming such things with cursory inspection.

Now the demon concentrated—and evinced surprise. "He has magic—strong magic—but I am unable to fathom it." He frowned at me, and proffered our usual insult. "Sorry, fathead."

"Then get ye gone, incompetent!" I snarled just as if meaning it, clapping my hands. The truth was this was getting considerably more interesting. If Beauregard couldn't fathom the talent, it had to be well beyond the minimum level.

The demon dissolved into smoke and returned to his bottle to resume his nap. No, this time he was reading a book; I could see him in miniature in there, turning a page. Bink, evidently quite impressed, stared at the bottle.

Now I got serious. I questioned Bink, but he was ignorant, of course. So I tried another device: the pointer and wall chart. I asked questions, and the pointer pointed to either a cherub, meaning yes, or a devil, meaning no. This only confirmed what Beauregard had said: strong magic, undefined.

I was really getting interested now. This was indeed turning out to be a challenge and was brightening my day.

I tried a truth spell on him. It wasn't that I thought he was being dishonest—he lacked the wit—but that this device addressed the magic within him, requiring it to clarify itself. But when I asked him his talent, the manticora abruptly roared. It was his feeding time. I had been at this chore longer than I had realized; time was passing.

So I went down to feed the manticora, who turned out not to be that hungry. "I don't know what came over me," he said. "Suddenly I just had to roar as loud as I could."

Curious. I returned to Bink—who had, like the simpleton he was, broken a magic mirror during my brief absence by asking it a question beyond its competence. I was disgusted. "You're a lot more trouble than you're worth."

I restored the truth spell and started to ask him about his talent, again. Just then the cracked glass fell out of the mirror behind me, breaking my concentration. What a nuisance!

I tried a third time. And the whole castle shook. An invisible giant was passing close by, his tread making the earth shudder.

I realized that more than coincidence was operating here. Some extremely powerful enchantment was preventing me from getting the answer. That had to be Magician-caliber magic! "I had thought there were only three persons alive today of that rank, but it seems there is a fourth."

And, indeed, the joke had turned out to be on me, for I had assumed that this was a nothing situation. Why had my Book of Answers failed to warn me of the approach of this odd Magician?

"Three?" he asked stupidly.

"Me, Iris, Trent." I did not count the Storm King; he had been a Magician, but his talent had dwindled with age. He was way overdue for replacement. But Iris was a woman, and Trent exiled these past twenty years, and I certainly didn't want to be stuck with the chore again. But if we had here a genuine new Magician—this was now fascinating in its implications!

"Trent!" he exclaimed. "The Evil Magician?"

I explained that Trent had hot really been evil, any more than I was good; it was just a popular misconception. But I doubted that Bink was getting it. He still thought in stereotypes.

And so I had to turn Bink away without an Answer, for it was not safe to probe further. It was unsatisfactory in one sense, but exciting in another. A new Magician—with undefined magic! Something interesting would surely come of this!

At this point I suffered a coincidental realization: now I understood why a creature like the Demoness Metria was always alert for new mischief. If I, as a man hardly over a century in age, was so eager for something interesting to pep up my boredom, how much worse it must be for a demon, who existed for many centuries without any responsibilities or vulnerabilities. That didn't mean that I liked Metria, but I could hardly blame her for her incidental mischief. I had been acting a bit like a demon when I tormented the loutish young Bink of the North Village.

After that I watched that young man. At first he was a severe disappointment. All he did was go straight back to the North Village, crossing on the invisible one-way bridge I had told him about. There he was exiled by the Storm King, who refused to heed the paper I had sent with Bink attesting to his undefined magic. The Storm King didn't like me any better than I liked him; my note was probably slightly worse than nothing. Maybe the notion that there might be significant magic here frightened the King, who was now, with the fading of his magic, technically an impostor. Bink was deemed to have no magic and was exiled and sent out of Xanth, beyond the Shield. That irritated me something awful, but all I could do was watch. Had I realized that the Storm King would be that petty, I would have looked for some way to bypass him. That was a Magician the idiot had exiled!

Or had he suspected the truth, and that was *why* he had exiled Bink—as a possible rival? My irritation progressed into something like anger. What a fool I had been to give up the throne to that broken wind!

Meanwhile, I had another client. This was a young woman who called herself Chameleon. She was plain, bordering on ugly. Her talent was intriguing, because it was involuntary: in the course of each month she changed gradually from average appearance to beautiful, and back through average to ugly. The magic mirror showed her physical phases: she was truly sublime when on, and truly hideous when off. Her intelligence and personality shifted in the opposite direction, counterpointing her appearance. Thus she was smartest when she was ugliest, and stupidest when she was beautiful. I verified this with my sources, and looked again at pictures of her extremes in the magic mirror. At her best she was a creature to make any man, even an old grouch like me, stop and stare, as I was doing now. At her worst she was a young crone, with a caustic tongue, whom no man would tolerate.

She wanted, of course, to be rid of her talent, as it was doing her no good. She was in constant danger of being seduced in her stupid-lovely stage or stoned in her smart-ugly stage. Only her neutral central stage was suitable. She also wanted to win the man she liked—who, coincidentally, was Bink. It seemed that she had encountered him twice recently, once in the—the—somewhere dangerous, when she was in her lovely phase, and they had been separated because of his heroism. The other time was in her neutral stage, and he had been in the company of a woman-hating man named Crombie. So she had followed Bink here, and now was begging me for help. For a spell for Chameleon;

I did not tell her of my relation to Crombie, but I felt responsible. For Bink had liked her all right, in her neutral stage, but Crombie's animosity had driven her away. Crombie had made up some story about how his mother had been able to read minds, and had driven his father loco. He probably believed that nonsense, by now. Or maybe that was his interpretation of his family life: concealing the shame of the Mundane mother and a crotchety Magician father.

I had bad news for Chameleon: her magic was inherent, and could not be eliminated without eliminating *her*. But I did have an Answer, for which I accepted no payment, because it was probably worse than the malady: she could go to Mundania. There she would revert to her neutral state and remain there, being neither lovely nor ugly, smart nor stupid.

"Where is Bink going?" she asked.

"Probably to Mundania," I said heavily.

"Then that's where I want to be."

I stared at her, but it did make sense. She could have her neutral state and her man, together, by that grim expedient. So I told her of the magic path available, and the magic bridge, and warned her about not trying to turn back on either, and sent her on her way after Bink. Perhaps it was for the best. She could gain on him, if she hurried, and perhaps catch him before he left Xanth. Or, better, right after, because by then she would be into her awful-smart phase and would need to get out of the magic before showing herself to him.

It would be nice for them if they could be happy together in Mundania. It was not a completely dreadful place, I knew, when properly understood. After all, I had had thirty-five years of satisfaction with a Mundane wife. But I still hated the idea of the loss of that Magician-caliber talent Bink had; it was such a colossal waste.

So I watched Bink go, glumly. I think I was glummer than he was.

But when he passed beyond the Shield, it suddenly became more interesting. For there was a Mundane army—and Magician Trent was leading it! My magic mirror could show me scenes as far as the magic went, and that was for a certain distance beyond the Shield. Xanth did not end at the Shield; it was merely circumscribed there. Trent had returned, and in that limited section between Mundania and the Shield, his magic talent was operative.

Things got complicated after that. Trent captured both Bink and Chameleon and tried to coerce them into joining his effort to invade Xanth from Mundania, but they refused. They tried to escape, but Trent pursued them, and an improbable coincidence got them under the Shield where it was damped out by deep water, and further coincidences got them through assorted hazards. Then—

I was amazed. The three, now reluctant allies because of the adversity of the Xanth jungle, made their way to Castle Roogna itself! The castle accepted them, even encouraged their progress—*because two of them were Magicians.* It didn't care about the legal structure of Xanth; it just wanted a Magician to be king and renovate the structure and the status of the castle so that it would once more be the center of Xanth. And that was no bad thing.

Then the three went on from Castle Roogna, remaining together under a truce though Bink and Chameleon still opposed Magician Trent. The two remained foolishly loyal to the existing order. I shook my head, watching them in the mirror.

It became even stranger. The two factions agreed to settle their differences by dueling. It was, in effect, Magician against Magician, and that was dangerous. But in the course of the almost unbelievable coincidences that kept Trent from transforming Bink into something harmless, Bink's talent became evident. *He could not be harmed by magic!* Not even Magician-class magic. That explained why magical threats had always somehow missed him. That was perhaps the most devious and wonderful talent in Xanth.

But Trent, realizing this, was undeterred. He simply changed to the use of his sword. Bink's talent did not protect him against purely physical attack. But he was saved by the intercession of Chameleon, who took the strike intended for Bink, because she loved him.

At that point Trent had had enough. He concluded that he did not want the throne at the price of these two young lives. He helped Bink come to me, to fetch healing elixir for Chameleon. This is a simplification, but it will do. The full story has been duly recorded by the Muse of History.

Then the Storm King died, and suddenly the entire complexion of things changed. The elders naturally asked me to assume the throne, and I naturally pointed out that there was now an alternative.

So it was that Magician Trent became king after all, and Castle Roogna was indeed restored to its former glory. Trent married the Sorceress Iris and made her queen, to keep her out of mischief, and Crombie took up service as a soldier for the King. Bink married Chameleon, being satisfied with her as she was, changes and all. He was made Official Researcher of Xanth, so he could explore whatever interested him, especially things magical. It was in fact a happy ending.

But things had hardly settled down for me, before Bink was getting into more complications. His wife, Chameleon, was expecting the stork, but her phases of beauty and ugliness continued as before. She was not pleased, having discovered she didn't really want a baby, now that it was too late, and she compensated by eating a great deal and growing unreasonably fat in the tummy. Many women did that. Normally the arrival of the baby thinned such women down in a hurry, because they were kept so busy taking care of it. But Chameleon in her ugly-smart stage was surely no joy to be near.

That was why Bink elected to go in search of the source of magic. He set off on the adventure with two other dissatisfied males. One was Chester Centaur, whose ugly nose was farther out of joint because the arrival of his foal, Chet, had completely distracted his mare, Cherie. The other was Crombie the Soldier, my now-unacknowledged son, who was fed up with the imperial female ways of Queen Iris. Actually, I really couldn't condemn him for that; even a normal man would have found her burdensome if constantly exposed. His talent for finding things was being put to excellent use, pointing the direction they had to go to find that source. King Trent transformed him into a griffin, however, so that he could fly and fight and guard the party. They were on their way, Bink riding the centaur.

They promptly ran afoul of a dragon and a nest of nickelpedes. Unfortunately, those did not turn them aside, and all too soon they arrived at my castle. They wanted advice for their quest, and I knew what they meant. This was no innocent jaunt; they were seeking the source of magic, and that meant they would have to have a fully functional Magician along. Otherwise they would have no chance of success and would probably just get themselves killed. Even Bink himself; he could not be harmed by magic, but there were plenty of nonmagical dangers in Xanth too.

I hoped to discourage them, but Bink fought his way into my castle and I had to talk with him. When I explained that he would have to take a Magician along, he misinterpreted it completely.

"You old rogue!" he exclaimed. "You *want* to come!"

"I hardly made that claim," I said with restraint. "The fact is, this quest is entirely too important to allow it to be bungled by an amateur, as well Trent knew when he sent you here. Since there is no one else of suitable expertise available, I am forced to make the sacrifice. There is no necessity, however, that I be gracious about it."

So it was that I mothballed the castle and joined the quest. I brought along a number of my magics folklore claimed I had a hundred spells, but that was an understatement—and Grundy Golem, who was doing his service for me. His talent was translation, and the obnoxious little string man was good at it. I should know; I had animated him four years before for this purpose, only to have the ungrateful twerp run away. He had returned when he discovered that he wasn't real, and asked me how to become real. Like many ignorant folk, he hadn't cared for my Answer: "Care." It would take him time to fathom it, of course.

Unfortunately Grundy took pleasure in doing misleading translations of the griffin Crombie's words, stirring up trouble between him and Chester, who was a pretty ornery centaur to begin with. For example, he translated "centaur" as "horse-rear" and "ass," and professed confusion as to which end of the centaur it applied to. I stayed out of it; as far as I was concerned, Crombie was a stranger to me until he chose to be otherwise.

We did not reach our destination by nightfall, and sought shelter. Crombie's talent indicated the house of an ogre as a suitable place. Distrusting this, I invoked Beauregard. We exchanged the usual friendly insults, to the probable amazement of the others. "Of course it's safe," he assured me. "It's your mission that's unsafe." He explained that the ogre was a vegetarian, so would not crunch our bones. This ridiculous assertion turned out to be accurate; Crunch was a veritable pacifist among ogres.

So we enjoyed the hospitality of Crunch Ogre, after a bit of repartee, and he served us a good meal of purple bouillon with green nutwood. Then he told us his story, rendered into crude rhyming couplets by the golem. He had met and loved a curse fiend actress who was playing the part of an ogress, and was therefore exquisitely ugly. He had snatched her and hidden from the other curse fiends, avoiding their massive destructive curse by becoming a vegetarian. The curse had oriented on a bone cruncher. It was a surprisingly neat ploy, for an ogre; probably the actress had thought of it. For one thing, that would prevent him from ever crunching *her* bones.

But the mock ogress now lay stunned in a dead forest. Crunch wanted to know whether to fetch her from there. Crombie, Chester, and Bink recommended that he do so (Crombie had thought he was doing the opposite, not realizing that ogres *liked* being made miserable by their females). Beauregard, participating in their dialogue, learned the rest of what he needed about the fallibilities of intelligent life on the surface of Xanth, and returned to his realm to write his dissertation.

Next day we continued on along a magic path to the Magic Dust Village, which was inhabited exclusively by women of many humanoid species. This was because their men had been lured away by the melody of the Siren. There were trolls, harpies, wood nymphs, sprites, fairies, elves, centaur fillies, griffin cows, and even a female golem to keep Grundy company. That last startled me; someone must have made that one recently, because there had been no females of his species before. Now the women were eager for male company. Indeed, they just about buried us in their eager softness. The males were of mixed feelings about this, some of them being otherwise committed, and one being a woman hater.

Then the Siren sang—and all of us were lured to go to her, losing our volition. The women tried to hold us back, but could not. Until Crombie the woman-hater rebelled and pecked in his griffin form at a tangle tree we were passing. That got us into a fight with the tree. Its tentacles wrapped around us. Crombie fought his way free, flew away—but then returned with the women of the village, who attacked the tree with torches. Fifty of them went after its tentacles, under the direction of the woman hater. They were grimly determined and courageous. I think that was the beginning of the end of Crombie's problem with women, though it would take time for the end of the end to come.

But before that battle had been concluded, the song of the Siren came again. It mesmerized us; we males could not resist its spell, though it had no effect on the women.

But an incident with a battering ram caused a pineapple to explode by Chester's head, deafening him. As a result, he could no longer hear the Siren, and was freed from her spell. He fired an arrow through her heart, and her music stopped.

We approached her. She was not yet dead. She lay on her little isle in a lake. She was the loveliest mermaid I had seen in a century, with hair like flowing sunshine and tail like flowing water and bare breasts that the Adult Conspiracy prevents me from describing, just in case a juvenile male should happen someday to see these words. She was soaked in blood from her wound, yet she pleaded only love.

Perplexed by this, I consulted my portable magic mirror. It confirmed that she intended us no harm. So I brought out my vial of healing elixir and healed her. She was instantly healthy again; that type of magic is beautiful to see.

We learned that though the Siren summoned men, they inevitably were drawn on to her sister the Gorgon at the next isle. The Gorgon's gaze turned men to stone, but had no effect on women. Later, as the Gorgon matured, that changed, and she stoned men and women and even animals. Perhaps she should have been recognized as a Sorceress for that phenomenal power. But for a reason I shall get to in due course, I am not objective about that.

Meanwhile the Siren was good company. She was a mermaid, but she was able to make legs so that she could walk on land. A certain number of merfolk can do that, though they seldom bother. She made us a dinner of fish and sea cucumber, and a bed of soft dry sponges, and we spent the night there.

Next morning we went on to brace the Gorgon. The others had to be blindfolded, and I used the mirror, because the stoning spell could not reflect from it, while the rest of her did. This was special magic called polarization.

The Gorgon turned out to be as lovely as her sister. She was fully human in the sense that she had no fish tail, but her hair consisted of little serpents. It was surprising how prettily they framed her sweet face. She was also as innocent as the Siren, having no notion of the mischief her magic was doing. All around her island statues of men stood; she thought these were gifts, not realizing that they were what remained of the men themselves.

I tried to explain this to her, but was handicapped because her loveliness in the mirror distracted me. I wanted to turn and face her directly, and did not dare. "Men must not come here anymore," I said. "They must stay home, with their families."

"Couldn't just one man come—and stay awhile?" she asked plaintively.

"I'm afraid not. Men aren't, er, right for you." What a tragedy! Any man would love this lovely woman, if not turned to stone before he had the chance.

"But I have so much love to give—if only a man would stay! Even a little one. I would cherish him for ever and ever, and make him so happy—"

The more I talked with her, the worse I was feeling. "You must go into exile," I said. "In Mundania your magic will dissipate."

But she would have none of it. "I can not depart Xanth. I love men, but I love my home more. If this is my only choice, I beg of you to slay me now and end my misery."

I was appalled. "Slay you? I would not do that! You are the most attractive creature I have ever seen, even through a mirror! In my youth I would have—"

"Why, you are not old, sir," she protested, and her smile seemed genuine. "You are a handsome man."

The three blindfolded males squawked, coughed, and choked. That irritated me for some reason. "You flatter me," I said, being flattered. "But I have other business." I knew I had better get on with it quickly, because I was in danger of being smitten by this devastating woman in two respects: my body turned to stone, my heart turned to mush.

"Of all the men who had come here, you alone have stayed to talk with me," the Gorgon continued passionately. Even the little snakes of her hair looked at me beseechingly in the mirror. "I am so lonely! I beg of you, stay with me and let me love you always."

I started to turn my face toward her, charmed by this maidenly appeal, but my companions warned me in time. I demurred, though the idea of being loved by such a woman was becoming increasingly attractive. I had been alone too long. "Gorgon, if I were to look at you directly—"

"Come, close your eyes if you must," she said urgently, not yet comprehending the danger she represented to men. "Kiss me. Let me show you how much love I have for you. Your least word is my command, if you will only stay!"

Oh, my, what temptation! Suddenly I realized how intense my own loneliness had become, these eight years since my fourth wife had departed for Mundania. (Fourth wife? Then why could I remember only three?)

Young women had approached me in this time, but I knew it was my power as a Magician that appealed to them, not my body, which was wizened and gnomish, or my personality, which was grumpy. Certainly not for my mountain of used socks! So how could I trust their motives? But the Gorgon knew nothing of my background. She asked only my presence.

"My dear, I think not," I said with real regret. "Such a course would have its rewards—I hardly deny it!—and I might normally be inclined to dally with you a day or three, though love be blindfolded. But only a Magician could safely associate with you, and—"

"Then dally a day or three!" she exclaimed, her bosom (containing two breasts, I was sure) heaving in a way that made me feel forty years younger. "Be blindfolded! I know no Magician would have interest in me, but even such a Magician could not be more wonderful than you, sir!"

She really didn't know! She was trying to flatter me one way, and succeeding in another. "How old are you, Gorgon?" I asked, wickedly tempted.

"I am eighteen! I am old enough!"

And I was a hundred and ten. What was I thinking of? This was the sort of game Metria liked to play with men. That healing elixir had preserved me remarkably, but how could I think of any dalliance with this virtual child? "I am too old," I said with deep regret. "Not all your flattery can change what I know to be true."

Her lovely face clouded over in the mirror. The snakes hung limply down as if completely suppressed. Tears overflowed her eyes and trailed down her cheeks. "Oh, sir, I beg of you—"

I sighed, yielding to an impulse I might later regret. "Perhaps, after my present quest is over, if you haven't changed your mind, if you would care to visit at my castle—"

"Yes, yes!" she cried eagerly. "Where is your castle?"

"Just ask for Humfrey. Someone will direct you. But you will have to wear a veil—no, even that would not suffice, for it is your eyes that—"

"Do not cover my eyes!" she protested. "I must see!"

"Let me consult." I rummaged through my collection of spells. I found one that might do the job: invisible makeup. "This is not ideal, but it will have to do. Hold this vial before your face and open it." I held it over my shoulder.

She did so. There was a pop as the cork came out, and then the hiss of the expanding vapor. It shrouded her face and disappeared—and her face went with it. There simply wasn't anything showing where it had been.

I lowered my mirror and turned to her. "But you said—" she protested, not realizing how she had changed.

I held the mirror up, facing her. She took it and held it up, gazing at her reflection. She made a little gasp.

Then she returned the mirror and stepped into me. She kissed me. How sweet it was! Her face was there, touchable, just not seeable.

"How long I have longed to do that, with someone," she murmured. "How I thank you, marvelous man!"

Then she stepped away, and I recovered as much of my equilibrium as was feasible. "Companions, you may now remove your blindfolds," I said. "The Gorgon has been nullified." That was a highly misleading statement; she had a greater effect on me than ever now.

The others cleared their blindfolds and gazed at the Gorgon for the first time. They were obviously impressed. I felt a certain suppressed pride.

I used my magic mirror to contact Castle Roogna and report on progress. Queen Iris answered, using her power of illusion to make her voice heard directly from the mirror. Her talent had certainly matured, but she showed scant appreciation for the training I had given her in her girlhood. That was the problem with power: it corrupted.

The Gorgon, hearing the Queen call me Good Magician, finally caught on to my status. It dampened her ardor not half a whit. She flung her arms around me and planted another invisible kiss on my mouth. Her hair-serpents, caught by surprise, hissed and snapped at my ear lobes. Fortunately they were too small to do much harm, and they weren't poisonous.

We made our way back to the Magic Dust Village and assured the women that no more men would be taken. Unfortunately I lacked the power to revert the stone men to life. The Gorgon might not be a full Sorceress, but her power was strong enough to withstand any spell I knew. That, perhaps, was part of her appeal. Certainly I remained somewhat distracted, after so unexpectedly encountering so intriguing a creature.

The ladies provided us with a griffiness as a guide. We were going on through the region of madness, where thick magic dust made things strange. This was the way Crombie's talent pointed. On the way we passed a marvelous region of bugs, and I discovered a new species: a Crayon-Drawing Picture-Winged Beetle. I was thrilled, and made careful note of it.

Unfortunately, this' region of intense magic had mischief for us. A midas fly buzzed us, getting set to land on me. Knowing the danger, I ducked so low I fell off Crombie. The fly was about to land on him instead, when the female griffin knocked him aside and intercepted the fly.

They touched—and suddenly she was a solid gold statue. She had saved us by sacrificing herself. Crombie was evidently shaken; how was the woman hater to react to a female who had given up her life for him? Her action was surely a considerable enigma to him. Of course she might not have done it had she realized that he was not the griffin he appeared, but I did not see fit to point that out.

Now we were without our guide, and we all understood the danger of our situation. It was late, so we had to camp for the night. We found the bones of an ancient sphinx, and made camp within their protection. Crombie's talent indicated that this was the safest place for us to be.

But our travails had hardly begun. Looking for food, Bink brought me something to check. I made an effort to freak out; probably only my age prevented me. "That's Blue Agony fungus!" I exclaimed. "Get rid of it!" For one bite of that would turn a person's whole body blue, and he would melt into a puddle that killed the surrounding vegetation. Yet Crombie's magic had indicated it was the best possible thing to eat. A second check caused him to indicate that it was the *worst* possible thing to eat, which was more accurate. What was going on?

After some confusion, we discovered that we were being confused by a chip of what was to become known as reverse-wood, that reversed the magic of the person who touched it. What a deadly effect that could be! I made a note. This variety of magic must have evolved after I did my survey of talents, as I had passed through this region without encountering it before.

Then, in the night, things became more interesting. The constellations of the sky came to life. Chester got into a duel with a centaur constellation. Soon we were all climbing into the sky—until Grundy brought the reverse-wood and nullified some of the illusion. We were actually climbing a tree! This was certainly the region of madness!

Seeing our retreat, the constellations came down to the ground to attack us. When we fought them off, they dumped a sky river on us, trying to drown us. This was probably a thunderstorm in real life, but the effect was the same: we were drenched and miserable.

We were saved in the end, perhaps, by that same reverse-wood, because it caused Grundy Golem to reverse his selfish nature and care about us and help us make our way out. There was a certain irony in that, but we were beyond caring.

We proceeded on toward Lake Ogre-Chobee, where the curse fiends dwelt. I wanted to save a bit of that reverse-wood, because it could be useful, but when I tried to conjure it into a bottle, it reversed the spell and put *me* in the bottle instead. The others found that very funny. But after several tries I did manage to secure the wood. Then I investigated the source of the mysterious mounds of dirt that kept popping up near us. These turned out to be the work of squiggles, one of the branches of the great family of voles. The creatures zipped along just under the ground, leaving the dirt behind. Was it spying on us? If so, why? My magic mirror was not providing a clear answer. Perhaps the underground habitat of the creature obscured the image.

To safely approach the curse fiends, who it seemed were on our route to the source of magic, we had to diminish our number. I conjured Crombie and Grundy and me into a bottle, which Bink and Chester would carry. They would take water-breathing pills I had provided, so as to be able to walk on the bottom of the lake. I was not entirely sanguine about this arrangement, but we had to chance it.

Thus we found ourselves in a nicely carpeted chamber. The outside world seemed far removed. "Say, we're traveling in style!" Grundy remarked.

The griffin squawked. "Well, you'd think so if you were in manform, beak-brain!" the golem retorted, understanding Crombie perfectly.

I liked the magic mirror, which I had similarly shrunk. It showed what was happening outside the bottle better than the glass wall did, because the mirror lacked distortion and was not confined to Bink's pocket.

Bink and Chester walked under the lake and encountered the curse fiends. Wouldn't you know it: they managed to aggravate the fiends and had to plunge into the central whirlpool which traversed the underwater city. The bottle we were in was flung free and went rushing out of control in the fierce current. We were in for it now!

It was a horrendous ride. I was trying to watch the outside realm in the mirror so that I could keep track of where we were, assuming we survived. But the violence of the water made our chamber whirl around dozens of times. It banged into a wall or stone, and I went banging into the floor of our chamber. The mirror flew from my hand and shattered against the wall.

Then the motion ceased. I picked myself up, and Grundy and Crombie picked themselves up. We were shaken but not hurt. It could have been another story, had the bottle we were in smashed. As it was, the furniture was scattered and overturned, and part of the carpet had been wrenched askew.

"Next time, let's not let idiots carry us," Grundy said, and the griffin squawked agreement. I would have been hard put to disagree.

I picked up the largest fragment of the mirror. It remained operative; the magic was in the glass, not the shape or frame. I held it carefully. It remained oriented on Bink.

Bink was at this moment rousing from his strewn condition at the edge of the lake our bottle floated in. He dragged himself up, and found Chester Centaur. He picked up a shard of glass—and it was from the magic mirror! It must have flown right out from the bottle, though the bottle remained sealed. I wasn't sure exactly how that was possible; I would have to investigate the phenomenon when I had leisure.

Bink saw me in the shard. He waved. I waved back. We had established contact.

But already our bottle was being carried along in the current, and the lake was becoming a river. We had not been all that close to Bink and Chester to begin with, and now we were moving away from them.

"Well, we don't need to hide anymore," Grundy said. "Let's pop the cork and come out into the real world, before we get worse lost."

"Not applicable," I said, now tuning the fragment to the water around us.

"Why not?" he demanded in that obnoxious way of his.

"Several reasons. One is that I can't, as you so quaintly put it, pop the cork from inside. This bottle is designed to contain what is in it, whether it be hate elixir or a demon. The spell on the cork makes it impervious to pressure from inside. Another is that if we did get out, we would abruptly resume our full size, and quite possibly be stuck in a channel that is less than that size." I showed him a flash of the outside, where the river boundaries had constricted considerably. "A third is that the water may be poisonous. A fourth—"

The griffin squawked. "I agree," Grundy said dourly. "Three's enough."

There was nothing to do but ride along, hoping that Bink would in due course find us. Since he had the other shard from the magic mirror, this was possible. Then he could open the bottle, and we would be reunited.

"What's the idiot doing now?" Grundy asked, evidently suffering a similar thought.

I reoriented the shard,. Bink was now scrambling through a hole in the cavern wall. He came to a streamlet, and was about to wangle a drink from it.

"The fool!" I exclaimed.

"Aw, he must be thirsty," Grundy said.

"That's the flow from a love spring," I said. I recognized the glint of the water, from long practice.

Helplessly we watched Bink drink, then encounter a nymph who was typical of her species: long of leg, pert of bottom, slender of waist, full of bosom, and large-eyed of face. She was sorting through a keg of jewels which represented enormous wealth, for those who cared for that sort of thing. There were diamonds, pearls, emeralds, rubies, opals, and other precious stones of many colors and sizes.

"Hoo!" Grundy exclaimed. "What I wouldn't give for that nymph and that tub of gems!"

Precisely. And Bink had just taken a love potion. His talent protected him from magic harm, but didn't define love as harm. It didn't care that he was married. His talent was happy to let him have a little un-innocent fun with an innocent nymph.

I checked a reference, for I had reduced my collection of tomes and had them with me in miniaturized bottles. This was Jewel the Nymph, perhaps the most important rock nymph in Xanth, for she it was who placed the precious stones for others to find. Her barrel was never end-

ing; no matter how many she removed, it remained full. She probably
had a soul, unlike the useless nymphs whose sole purpose was to run
around barelegged and tease men. Jewel even had a talent: she smelled
the way she felt, whether this was of fresh pine needles or burning gar-
bage. Many women did smell, but they had to apply perfume; Jewel did
it naturally. Of all the folk for Bink to encounter, she was perhaps the
worst, because she was a nice person with a necessary job who should
be neither hurt nor distracted. She was bound to suffer both fates, now.

Jewel helped Bink and Chester travel. She summoned a giant of the
vole family of creatures, a diggle, who worked for a song. Chester's magic
talent had manifested by this time: he could conjure a silver flute, which
played beautiful music by itself. This flute now charmed the diggle, so that
it was happy to carry them through the solid stone.

Then they encountered the demons. There was Beauregard! Suddenly
I knew what I was in for. Sure enough, he just couldn't resist conjuring me
out of the bottle. Fortunately he didn't make me do anything bad; we had
Crombie point out the direction of our bottle from where Bink was, so he
could find it.

Meanwhile the bottle was floating down to the deepest subterranean
lake. My references could not get a line on where it was going; there was
powerful evil magic here. I did not like this at all.

"You know, something's been spying on us as we travel," Grundy
remarked. "I've got the feeling we're floating into its clutches."

That was my own impression. I had not discussed it because it seemed
pointless to alarm the others.

"But maybe I could get out of the bottle, and then pull it to safety and
wedge the cork off," Grundy continued.

"No living thing or inanimate thing can pass the cork from inside," I
reminded him grimly.

"Yes, but that shard of glass got out, maybe because it's a nonliving
yet animate thing: it animates whatever picture you want to see. I'm not
exactly living or dead; I might be able to get out too."

I was amazed. He could be right! "See if you can pass," I agreed.

He went to the neck of the bottle and pushed against the cork. It didn't
budge, but he went on through it. In a moment he was out. He resumed
his normal size, which wasn't much larger than the bottle.

But the bottle was floating in the dark pool, and the golem could not get to solid land. His body was made of bits of wood and cloth and string; he would not be able to swim well enough. So we would still have to wait for the bottle to get close enough to land for Grundy to do anything.

Bink and Chester and Jewel the Nymph arrived, riding the diggle. They spied the bottle and headed for it. We were about to be rescued!

Then the trap sprang. Grundy's little mind was taken over by a hostile power. Now he wrapped his string arms around the cork, braced his feet against the neck of the battle, and hauled out the cork. "By the power of the Brain Coral, emerge!" he gasped.

Oh, no! He was Summoning me and Crombie—in the name of the enemy. For suddenly that hostile force overwhelmed my mind, and I knew that this was the thing that had opposed us and spied on us. It was the Brain Coral, a creature that could not move, because it was locked in its subterranean pool, but had tremendous magic and intelligence. It correctly regarded Bink's magic as a threat to its interests, so had done everything it could to eliminate him as a threat. It had to act through other agencies, but was quite facile in that respect. It had sent a magic sword to kill Bink, and the dragon, and had caused the Siren to lure him to the Gorgon, but Bink's talent had foiled all these threats, seemingly coincidentally. The midas fly had been intended for him, and the great curse of the curse fiends, but only with the spell of the love potion had it been able to compromise him at all. That he had actually turned to his advantage, because instead of dissipating his energy chasing the nymph, he had enlisted her help.

But now it had found a way to accomplish its purpose. It had taken over the golem, and caused the golem to invoke Crombie and me from the bottle. We now had to serve the Brain Coral. That meant that all my magic and knowledge and intelligence were ranged against Bink, and that was the most formidable challenge he had faced since his duel with Magician Trent.

Other facts came into my mind as I assimilated the tremendous information of the Brain Coral. The cork had been partly dislodged from our bottle before, a seeming coincidence that would have enabled me to rejoin Bink, but the Coral's magic had arranged to have it jammed back. Grundy had escaped then, and clung to the bottle, but the Coral had made it seem that he remained inside. I should have realized that if one shard of glass could get out, so could other things. The real battle had been over control of this bottle, and Bink had almost recovered it, but the Coral had just managed to take it as it floated into the center of the Coral's region of power.

Now my resources were at the disposal of the Brain Coral. I had to try my best to make Bink give up his quest for the source of magic and go away. For that was the Coral's objective: to prevent Bink from accomplishing his mission. This I told Bink, urging him to depart immediately.

I had to admire his stubbornness. He refused to quit, though it meant open combat between us. I opposed him directly, while Crombie-Griffin would nullify Chester Centaur.

It did come to combat, unfortunately. After a horrendous fight, Crombie succeeded in knocking Chester into the pool, where the Coral quickly took him under and in. Meanwhile Bink had been able to nullify or avoid my myriad spells; that talent of his was truly amazing! Perhaps it was the strongest talent in Xanth, for all its subtlety.

But now it was two against one, and the griffin could attack him physically. Still he did not yield. He had once been relatively clumsy with the sword, but Crombie himself, in human form, had trained him, and now that sword was deadly. Bink managed to injure the griffin and hurl him into a crevice where he could fight no more. This, despite the distraction of the spells I was hurling against him. That was too impressive for comfort.

And, in the end, Bink actually won. I think the Brain Coral was as surprised as I was. I had to yield to him. He had the nymph sprinkle healing elixir on the sadly wounded griffin, who jumped up as if to attack Bink again. The nymph jumped between the two. "Don't you dare!" she cried with the odor of burning paper. That was an extraordinary act for a nymph, as the breed is generally pretty empty-headed. It was, in retrospect, a significant event, yet another aspect of Bink's extremely powerful and subtle talent.

The Brain Coral reconsidered. It agreed to show Bink the source of magic, now believing that if he knew the truth, he would come to agree with the Coral's position.

The source of magic was the Demon X(A/N)th, who resided in the nethermost cave and whose thoughts were in the form of fluxes through the cave. He was one of a number of such extremely powerful entities. The very rock near him was charged with magic, because of the trace leakage of it from his body. When this rock welled out to the surface it became the magic dust, which spread the magic to the rest of Xanth. He did not like to be disturbed.

The Demon was playing a game with others of his kind, which was the only way to alleviate the boredom that came to otherwise omnipotent creatures. Its rules were obscure to those of us with merely mortal comprehension. One aspect of this game was that a mortal such as Bink could by a single word free the Demon from his self-imposed captivity.

Now it was clear why the Brain Coral, one of the most powerful entities of Xanth because it was closest to the source of magic, had labored to keep Bink away. Coral was afraid Bink would do something unutterably stupid, such as releasing the Demon X(A/N)th who would then depart, leaving Xanth without magic. That would be disaster.

Sure enough, Bink wrestled with his concept of honor, and did the most stupid imaginable thing: he freed the Demon.

Instantly X(A/N)th was gone, and with him the magic of Xanth. There followed the most unpleasant few hours in the history of Xanth, for it was a sorry place without magic.

Yet, somehow, it all worked out, for the Demon returned. After certain incidental complications, he made Grundy Golem fully real and gave Bink a special gift: all his descendants would have Magician-class magic. In return, it was agreed that the ordinary creatures of Xanth, including man, would be barred from access to the Demon, so as not to bother him further.

So Bink had come out ahead after all, just as if his talent had planned it that way. Which was impossible—yet maybe not.

And my son Crombie, as a result of his experience with Jewel the Nymph, who had sprinkled the healing elixir on him and stood up to him when he threatened to attack Bink again, because she loved Bink—he had realized that if only such a creature were to love him, Crombie, she would be worth marrying. So he set aside his hatred of women and took a love potion to use on her, and they were in due course married. Thus my most significant failure was abated; my son had become a family man. All because of Bink.

I shook my head, reflecting on that. How phenomenally I had misjudged that young man, the first time I encountered him! He had enabled Magician Trent to return and become king, and he had discovered the true source of the magic of Xanth, and he had restored my son to a proper life. And, as it turned out, he had virtually single-handedly ended the dearth of Magicians and Sorceresses in Xanth, thus helping to usher in what might prove to be the Bright Age, so soon after the Dark Age.

Yet even then I had underestimated Bink's impact, for he had also affected my own life most significantly. It merely took another sixteen years for that to become fully apparent.

Chapter 14

GORGON

I returned to my comparatively dull existence at the castle. Somehow it no longer satisfied me as it had before. Something was missing from my life, but I wasn't sure what.

Meanwhile the chain of supplicants continued, at the rate of about one a month. Most were routine; I solved their problems, made them serve their year, and sent them on their way. But one nymph surprised me. She had come to ask me for a spell to turn off a faun who was pursuing her. She lived outside the main encampment of her kind and did not forget each day as it passed, though most nymphs did. Every day this faun came after her, remembering nothing, and she was tired of it. So I dug in my collection of spells and found a faun repellent. She could use this on him early in the day, each day, and be free for the rest of it. That was ideal, she said; she was quite satisfied with this remedy.

But as it happened, there was no useful service she could do for me for a day, let alone a year. I had someone to fix my meals, and someone else to sort my socks, and someone else to figure out a suitable set of challenges for the next person who came with a Question. I didn't want to let the nymph go without service, because that would set a bad precedent, but neither did I want her hanging around the castle doing nothing. What was I to do?

I asked the magic mirror. I now had several of these, having long since gotten rid of the one that became unreliable with time. This one merely showed a cherub falling over with laughter. No help there. The problem with competent mirrors was that they also tended to be too bright, and found ways to express themselves that I did not necessarily appreciate. But even so, a bright mirror was better than a dull one.

So I did what I didn't like: I told the nymph that I had no use for her, and she was free to depart. I asked her not to bruit the news about, lest others be dissatisfied by unequal treatment. But to my surprise she refused; she had her Answer, and she intended to pay for it. She wouldn't leave until her year was done.

That was exactly what I didn't want. But there wasn't much I could do about it. So I assigned her a room, and hoped something would turn up.

That night, when I finished my researches and went to my hard cold lonely pallet to sleep, I discovered it occupied. The nymph was there. "I think I have found something I can do for you, Good Magician," she said. Then she clasped me and kissed me and lay down with me. And somehow my pallet was no longer hard, cold, or lonely.

I had forgotten what nymphs were for, but in the course of that year I remembered. A man could not summon the stork with an ordinary nymph, for they were not subject to that call, but he could do a heroic job of imitation. Jewel the Nymph had not been ordinary; she had a soul, and could do anything a normal woman could. But regular nymphs were made for pleasure without responsibility, so die storks ignored them. How could a person take proper care of a baby, if she did not remember her activity from one day to the next? This one wasn't interested in marriage, just in completing her service. I had to agree that I was satisfied. In fact, when her year was done, I was sorry to see her go.

After that, when a similar creature elected to serve in that manner, I did not protest. I now knew what was missing from my life. It was a woman. But who would want to marry a century-plus old gnome of a man?

Then in 1054, eleven years after our meeting, the Gorgon came with a Question. She was now a marvelously developed woman of twenty-nine, and to my eye the most ravishing creature imaginable. But of course I couldn't tell her that; this was business.

We had set challenges, of course. When I can, I tune them to the individual person, but sometimes they are all-purpose for whoever comes. We had a foghorn guarding the moat, and it was lovely to see it operate. When the Gorgon tried to cross in the boat provided, the horn blasted out such columns of fog that she couldn't see or hear anything. In that obscurity her boat turned around and came back to the outer shore. That was the boat's magic; it had to be steered, or it returned to its dock. One of my prior querents had built it for me during his service. When the fog cleared, the Gorgon was a sight; her snake-hair was hissing with frustration, and her dress was plastered to her body. I had thought that body to be voluptuous; now I knew I had underestimated its case. I remembered our dialogue and how she had seemed to dote on me in the brief time of our encounter. Naturally she would have forgotten that, but it was a fond reminiscence. If only—but why be foolish?

The Gorgon was no dummy. She pondered a moment, then set out again. This time she steered the boat directly toward the foghorn, the one thing she could hear. Since it was inside the moat, she soon completed the crossing. I think I would have been disappointed had she not figured this out.

She navigated the other two challenges successfully and entered the castle. I braced myself and met her. She was even more impressive from aclose than she had been from afar. Her face was heavily veiled, including her deadly eyes, but the rest of her was nevertheless stunning. I was now a hundred and twenty-one years old, but in her presence I felt more like eighty-one. I remembered the surprising delight of our first encounter, when I had made her face invisible so that she would no longer stone any man who met her gaze. That spell would have been aborted at the Time of No Magic, of course; all the men she had stoned had returned to life then, and of course she had let them go.

I knew I should tackle her Question and give her an Answer, but I was reluctant to terminate our second contact quickly. So I dallied somewhat. "What have you been up to, Gorgon?" I inquired in as close an approximation to sociability as I could manage. It was an effort, but less of one for her than for others, because I didn't care about others.

"After the Time of No Magic my face was restored, and since I didn't want to make any more mischief in Xanth, I went to Mundania, where there is no magic, as you recommended. I hated to do it, for I love Xanth, but because I love Xanth I had to leave it, so as not to do it any harm." Her face went wry behind the veil; I could see the outline of the expression. "Mundania was colossally dreary. But what you had told me was true: I was normal there, and my face did not stun anyone. So I bore with it, and found employment as an exotic dancer, for it seems that Mundane men enjoy the appearance of my body."

I tried to wrench my eyes from that same body, embarrassed. "Mundanes are odd," I mumbled, feeling like the hypocrite I was.

"But in time I got to miss Xanth too much to bear," she continued blithely, taking a breath that threatened to pop a button on her décolletage or a lens on my spectacles. "The magic, the magical creatures—even the ogres and tangle trees had become fond memories. I realized that I had been born to magic; it was part of my being, and I just couldn't endure without it. But I also did not want to do harm. So I have returned and come to the man I most respect, and that is you."

"Um," I said, foolishly flattered.

"But when I returned to Xanth after several years, I discovered that my talent had matured along with my body," she continued, sighing. It was some sigh; my old eyeballs threatened to overheat. "Originally I stoned only men; now I stone men and women, and animals, and even insects. It's much worse than it was!"

Obviously she wanted another invisibility spell for her face. I could readily give her that. Then she would perform some service and be gone. And I would be twice as lonely as before. But I had to do it. "Evidently your talent is not far short of Sorceress class," I said. "Ordinarily that would be an asset."

"Perhaps when I'm a mean old woman, I'll enjoy stoning folk," she said. "But now I am in my prime, and I don't."

She was certainly in her prime! "What is your Question?" I asked, knowing too well what it was.

"Would you marry me?"

"I do have another vial of invisible makeup," I said. Then something registered. "What?"

"Would you marry me?"

"That is your Question?" I asked, dumbfounded.

"It is."

"This is not a joke?"

"This is not a joke," she assured me. "Understand, I'm not asking you *to* marry me; I merely want to know whether you *would*, if that were my desire. In this manner I seek to spare us both the unpleasantness of rejection."

Oh. I had to stall, because suddenly my heart was beating at a rate somewhat beyond my age. "If you really want my Answer, you will have to give me a year's service."

"Of course."

"In advance."

"Of course."

I was amazed at the readiness of her agreement. It was evident that she had thought this out, and preferred a considered Answer to an extemporaneous one. Perhaps she believed that I would be more likely to be affirmative if she associated with me for a while. In that she was grossly mistaken: I was locked into affirmation the moment I saw her approach the castle. The reason for my delay in answering was other than my private preference.

So the Gorgon worked for me a year. I made her face invisible again, of course, because otherwise her veil might have slipped sometime and made a nuisance. Now she could go around unveiled, which was easier.

The first thing she did was tackle my mountain of socks. She was good with them, which was an excellent sign. Next she tackled the castle, getting it organized and cleaned up. She went through my study and put all my papers and vials in order. When my meal-fixing maid completed her service and departed, the Gorgon took over that too. She even tended the roses in back. She was good at everything she tried, and I was better off than I had been in decades. I no longer needed other assistance around the castle; the Gorgon was running it.

I treated her in a cursory manner. In fact I was downright grumpy. I called her "girl" and I was never quite satisfied with what she did.

Now you might wonder about this. My reason was simple: I had been intrigued by her when she was a maiden of eighteen, and fascinated by her as a woman of twenty-nine. Her mere proximity caused my pulses to pulse. There was, it has been said, no fool like an old fool, and the Gorgon's competence, appearance, and power of magic had made a conquest of me in a matter of moments. I had loved MareAnn, I had loved Rose of Roogna; now I loved the Gorgon.

She was considering marrying me? Then she deserved to see what marriage to such a gnome was like. I was showing her the worst of me, deliberately. If that didn't alienate her, nothing would.

Surely it *would* alienate her! But it had to be done, in fairness. The Gorgon, with her face masked, was simply more of a woman than I deserved.

Yet she survived even that challenge of mistreatment, and when her year of service concluded I gave her my Answer: "Yes, I would marry you, if you asked." I would go to Hell for her, if she asked.

She considered that. "There is one other thing. I shall want a family. I have too much love for just a man; it must overflow for a child."

"I'm too old to summon the stork," I said.

"There is a vial of water from the Fountain of Youth on your shelf," she said. "You can take some of that and be young enough."

"There is? Fountain of Youth elixir? I didn't know that!"

"That's why you need a woman around the castle. You can't even keep track of your socks."

She had me there. "Still, I would have to be a great deal younger to—" For the truth was that, pleasant as it had been to have the company of certain nymphs in the past, I had seldom gotten to that stage with them, knowing that it made no difference. If I should have to do it for real, would I be able? I had realistic doubt.

"Why don't we find out? I will spend the night with you, and you can take drops of elixir until you are young enough." She was nothing if not practical, which was yet another trait I liked.

The notion intrigued me. It might require more elixir than I had, but I could go fetch more tomorrow; I of course knew where the Fountain of Youth was. So that night she came to me with the vial, and she wore a translucent nightdress. Suddenly I felt forty years younger, and wished it were eighty.

She kissed me. Her face was invisible, but solid; I could feel her lips on mine. My feeling of age reduced another twenty years. I hadn't yet taken a drop of elixir.

Of course feeling is not the same as being, and my body did lag somewhat behind. I might have the aspirations of a younger man, but lacked the capacity.

Rather than go into tedious detail, I will say that each drop of youth elixir took ten years off my age, and that two drops turned out to suffice. At a physical age of a hundred and two, with close proximity to that gorgeous creature, I discovered I was young enough. Health, youth, and love carried the night. I knew it would have taken several more drops with any other woman, however.

And so we were betrothed, though we did not rush to marriage, and thereafter every decade or so I took another drop of youth elixir so as to keep my physical age at about a hundred. With one exception I will cover in due course. The happiest period of my later life was upon me. I hope this was true for the Gorgon, too.

Meanwhile, less interesting events continued. Bink's son, Dor, was of course a Magician, thanks to the Demon's largess. He could talk to the inanimate and make it respond. But he was dissatisfied, because he lacked the physical stature of his father and was bullied by other boys. So he went on a Quest to the past of eight hundred years before, to fetch the elixir of restoration that would enable Millie the Maid (formerly a ghost) to restore her zombie friend Jonathan to life. Dor was now twelve years old, which was young, but he was a bright boy, and of course his status as Magician enormously expanded his capabilities.

Naturally much of this had to be explained to him, and he came here to inquire. Because he was a Magician and probable future king of Xanth, I did not charge him a year's service; instead I made a deal with him. I would enable him to undertake his Quest, and he would bring me information on a period in the history of Xanth whose details were somewhat obscure.

But I did set up challenges, as a matter of form. Dor came with Grundy Golem, who was now a real live person, but still small and with a mouth larger than the rest of him. They came to the moat and found it guarded by a triton: a merman with a triple-tipped spear.

Dor used his talent to make the water of the moat talk in his voice, leading the triton astray while he swam under the surface. By the time the triton caught on, Dor was safely inside. That had been an elementary challenge, and an elementary response.

The next challenge was a needle cactus, ready to shoot its needles into anyone who passed by. But Dor pretended he was a fireman, who would burn anything that touched him, and cowed the cactus into letting him pass unheeded. That demonstrated the lad's cleverness.

The third challenge was one of courage. The Gorgon stood where he had to pass. Dor was terrified, but barged ahead blindly, literally: he kept his eyes closed, so that he could not meet her gaze and be stoned. And that was his victory: he had gone forward instead of back. Courage, as I understand it, relates not to fear but to how a person handles the fear he has, and Dor handled it as well as could be expected for a boy his age.

So I helped Dor make a deal with the Brain Coral, who was no longer our enemy. The Coral used Dor's body during Dor's absence, and Dor went back to occupy the body of a grown barbarian hero, or so it seemed. This is an aspect that few understand: Dor was visiting the image in the Tapestry, rather than the original setting, so the setting was much smaller than it seemed. He was not man-sized, and neither were the other folk; he was tiny. But this had no affect on his activity, which was independent of size, with one exception.

Dor had quite an adventure; the Gorgon and I kept track of it all. He encountered what he took to be a giant spider, Jumper, who in our realm is a tiny arachnid, and they were great companions. That was the exception: Dor's interaction with the spider on an even basis. Jumper had gotten snagged by the adaptation spell and been brought into the adventure life-size. To Jumper it had seemed as if he had entered a realm where human folk were his size.

Dor encountered Millie the Maid in her seventeen-year-old youth, and of course was somewhat smitten by her. Her talent, remember, is sex appeal, and even at the age of twelve he felt its potency. He helped King Roogna save his castle from encroachment by the goblins and harpies, who were at war with each other. He met Evil Magician Murphy and Neo-Sorceress Vadne, who in a fit of jealousy rendered Millie into a book. That was why Millie became a ghost; when the book was found and restored in contemporary times, Millie became a maid again. In the end Dor learned something about manhood, and brought back the elixir of restoration, and used it to restore Jonathan the Zombie, who turned out to be the Zombie Master who had first occupied this very castle.

Thus Dor had an effect on my life too, for Jonathan and Millie married and moved in with us. There was nothing to do but share the castle, as the Zombie Master did have a prior claim on it. Later he built a new Castle Zombie and moved there with his family, so we were no longer so crowded.

You may wonder how all this came to pass, when Dor had entered only the Magic Tapestry of History, rather than the real period of Xanth's history. The answer is that there are intricate connections between the two, and the magic worked to make what Dor did have real effect. He might not have been there physically in the way he thought, but what he did was real. A fuller understanding is impossible for anyone not well versed in esoteric magic.

Millie's talent was sex appeal, remember, and she was certainly the sexiest creature I encountered. Naturally it took almost no time for her and Jonathan to summon the stork, and the effort was so effective that the stork brought two babies. Those were Hiatus and Lacuna, with the talents of growing eyes, ears, and noses on things, and of changing print. They were cute tykes, but capable of enormous mischief. In fact they performed remarkably when the Gorgon and I got married four years later, in 1059. Prince Dor was then sixteen and serving as temporary king while King Trent was visiting Mundania, so it fell on him to perform the ceremony of marriage for us. The Zombie Master and Millie handled the details. For all that, it was accomplished, and thereafter the Gorgon and I settled down to married life. She was my fifth wife, though at that time I suspected she was the fourth, because of the period blanked from my memory by the Lethe elixir.

In 1064 the stork brought our son Hugo, named after the combination of the first syllables of our names. We waited until we determined Hugo's talent before announcing his arrival, and that took a while, and then it was an imperfect talent, so word was slow to get around. Hugo could conjure fruit—but because his magic was flawed, the fruit was often of poor quality, or even rotting. That was an embarrassment. Nevertheless, the Gorgon lavished her love on him, and he had a gentle character. I made it a point to pay some attention to him, because of what had happened to my son, Crombie, and tried to involve him in my activities when possible. Later the Princess Sorceress Ivy was to associate with him, and in her presence he became all that any family could wish for. Unfortunately, he relapsed to normal in her absence.

Meanwhile, things were proceeding elsewhere. Crombie and Jewel the Nymph's daughter, Tandy, grew up to the age of nineteen, suffered the attentions of the Demon Fiant, and managed to flee on a night mare. She came to this castle in the year 1062, asking how she could be free of the demon, and served as a house maid for a year awaiting my Answer. I did not mention the fact that she was my granddaughter to her; that was not relevant to the issue. Presumably Crombie would inform her when he deemed it appropriate. But I must admit that I rather liked her spunk. She was a pretty girl, with brown hair and blue-green eyes, and her personality was pleasant. I wanted to do right by her, so that she would not think ill of me, at such time as she learned. I must admit it: I was proud of her.

Now some Answers are more complicated than others. Those involving demons can be troublesome, because demons are more or less immortal and are difficult to bar from any place. My castle was specifically spelled to exclude them, but when Tandy departed it she would be subject to the attentions of her demon lover again. I did not have any spell which would adapt to a particular person to discourage demons. What could I tell her?

Then the following year, just as Tandy's term of service finished, Crunch Ogre's son, Smash, arrived with a Question he had forgotten. Ogres are not the brightest creatures. Fortunately I knew what was bothering him: he was dissatisfied with his life.

You see, Smash was not an ordinary ogre. His mother was a curse fiend, which is a euphemism for human stock. So he was half human. Regular ogres, remember, were justly proud of three things: their outrageous strength, their grotesque ugliness, and their horrendous stupidity. Deep down inside, where it was so well hidden that even Smash was not aware of it, he had a certain human weakness, human handsomeness, and human intelligence. He would have been so embarrassed to learn of these qualities that his blush would have fried all the fleas on his hairy body. But these subterranean qualities nevertheless were having their muted effect, polluting his pristine ogre nature and making him vaguely dissatisfied. He wanted to know how to restore his satisfaction as an ogre, and I had no good Answer, because I knew that this half ogre could never be satisfied unless he recognized his true heritage and came to terms with it.

Smash had grown up near Castle Roogna, and was a friend of Prince

Dor and Princess Irene. (Dor was considered a prince because he had Magician-caliber magic which qualified him to be king in due course; Irene was a princess because she was the daughter of the King and Queen. Definitions are somewhat loose in Xanth.) Thus he had picked up certain human sensibilities which further compromised his ogrehood. No ordinary ogre would have thought to come to me for an Answer.

So there I was, stuck for two Answers simultaneously. How could I free Tandy of the attentions of a demon, and how could I make Smash satisfied to be what he was?

And the solution came to me with such a flash that the edges of my assorted tomes turned brown and the magic mirror winced. I had to blink for several moments before my sight was fully restored. These two problems canceled each other out! If Tandy kept company with an ogre, even a demon would think two and a half times before molesting her, and if Smash got to know a human/nymph girl well, he would discover the rewards of being partly human. She would be protected and he would be satisfied.

So I gave them both my Answer, which of course neither understood: they were to travel together. In Smash's case it was both Answer and service; he was to protect Tandy.

Smash was too stupid to formulate his protest well, but it was obvious that keeping company with a human girl was somewhere near the top of his limited list of things not to do. Tandy was more specific: "If he gobbles me up, I'll never speak to you again!" she told the Gorgon.

They had what I found to be an instructive adventure, because Smash did something so stupid only an ogre could have managed it: he looked into the peephole of a hypnogourd. He got locked into the realm of the bad dreams, but remained too stupid to be afraid, and did significant damage to the dream settings. He terrorized the walking skeletons, who were not accustomed to having their tables turned in this manner. One of them, by the name of Marrow Bones, got lost at this time. Finally the Night Stallion himself had a showdown with him, and Smash lost half his soul. He also encountered a number of females of other species, and in his fumbling way managed to help them find husbands. Notable among these were Blythe Brassie, of the realm of the gourd, and Chem Centaur, Chester and Cherie's filly. Maybe that was later; no matter.

But in the end Smash did protect Tandy, and she did impress on him certain advantages of being a man. They married, and when Tandy was twenty-one the stork brought them their son Esk, my great grandson. They called him an ogre, but technically he was only a quarter ogre, and looked human except when he got really angry. He was to grow up to marry Blythe Brassie's daughter, Bria, who like most of her kind was as hard as brass but could be surprisingly soft when she wanted to be. I was sorry I never got to meet Esk in person, because there were aspects of him that might have favored me. But I was otherwise occupied at the time when a meeting would have been convenient.

However, the female who had more direct impact on my life was Night Mare Imbrium. She was an ancient creature; a sea of the moon had been named after her. But she looked just like a small black horse. In the confusion surrounding Smash Ogre's dealing with the realm of the gourd, she got half of Chem Centaur's soul and did not turn it in. As a result she was corrupted by it, and became too softhearted to remain effective in delivering bad dreams. Finally she was allowed to go out into the regular world of Xanth to do two things: to bear a message to King Trent, "Beware the Horseman," and to see the rainbow.

But things seldom go right when minor characters of this drama become major ones. The Horseman was a creature who could assume the aspects of both man and horse, not in the manner of a centaur, but as one or the other separately. His talent was the making of a line of sight that could not be broken between a person's eye and the peephole of a gourd. He used it to connect King Trent to the gourd, making him unable to function. This occurred just as the NextWave came, for the Shield no longer protected Xanth; the Horseman was working with the NextWavers. It was a bad time for Xanth.

When Dor assumed the crown of Xanth, the Horseman did the same to him. Then the Zombie Master assumed the role, and he too was taken. Then it was my turn. I had to do the thing I detested and be king again. All because Mare Imbri had not been able to deliver the warning message in time to avert disaster. I was properly disgusted.

It was Grundy Golem who rode the night mare to bring me my bad dream. I was not exempt from this one, because it was real. My castle defenses were useless against Mare Imbri, of course; she galloped right through the walls and stepped out of my bookshelf.

I looked up from my tome. "So it has come at last to this," I grumped. "For a century I have avoided the onerous aspect of politics, and now you folk have bungled me into a corner." Technically it was only ninety-six years since I had quit the throne of Xanth, but I had not meddled in politics for the last decade of my kingship, leaving that to the Maiden Taiwan.

"Yes, sir," Grundy said with seeming humility. "You have to bite the bullet and be king."

"Xanth has no bullets. That's a Mundane anachronism." But that wasn't quite accurate, because there before me on the shelf was a row of magic bullets. "I'm not the last Magician of Xanth, you know."

But they would have none of it. They did not realize that Bink was a Magician, and Arnolde Centaur wasn't human, and Iris and Irene were female. So I was stuck with it. The worst of it was that I knew I would fail, because I was destined to do something calamitously stupid. That's what really bothered me: making that mistake.

For it was written in the Book of Answers: IT IS NOT FOR THE GOOD MAGICIAN TO BREAK THE CHAIN. The chain of lost kings, obviously. I had prepared by removing the spell from the Gorgon's face; now she was heavily veiled, so that her aspect would not stone any creature who gazed upon it. But if she encountered the enemy, she would whip that veil aside.

Well she knew the danger. "Oh, my lord," she said with unaccustomed meekness. "Must you go into this thing? Can't you rule from here?" She had packed my lunch and a change of socks, knowing my answer. I had already told her to fetch her sister the Siren for this encounter, and I had restored the Siren's broken dulcimer so that she could summon Mundanes to their doom. But I knew that I would not be the king for whom they served; it would be one of my successors.

I told Grundy to watch my castle while I was gone. The Gorgon would use my magic carpet to fetch her sister and reunite her with her dulcimer. Meanwhile, I mounted Mare Imbri, who was solid by daylight now, and we headed for Castle Roogna. How I hated all this! I was too old for such adventure, but it had been thrust upon me.

Mare Imbri, being female, was naturally curious about what was none of her business. She formed a dreamlet which showed her as a black-gowned and rather attractive human woman, her hair in a long ponytail.

"Why didn't you let the Gorgon be with you?" this dream woman asked me. "She really seems to care for you."

"Of course she cares for me, the idiot!" I snapped. "She's a better wife than I deserve. Always was. Always will be."

"But then—"

"Because I don't want her to see my ignominious doom. My wife will perform better if not handicapped by hope."

"That is a cruel mechanism," the dream woman said as the mare carried me into the eye of a gourd for rapid transit.

"No more cruel than the dreams of night mares," I retorted. But of course Imbri herself had lost that meanness; that was why she was no longer a night mare by profession.

We arrived at Castle Roogna. I made clear to Queen Iris that Bink was to be the next king after me. His talent of not being harmed by magic might be useless against the Mundanes, but he was a full Magician, and that was what counted. After that, I informed her, it would be Arnolde Centaur.

"And after him?" Iris asked tightly.

"If the full chain of future kings were known," I pointed out, "our hidden enemy might nullify them in advance."

"What can I do to help save Xanth?" she asked. She evidently thought I was getting senile.

"Bide your time, woman. In due course you will have your reward: the single thing you most desire." For so that too was written, though I had forgotten what it was she most desired.

Then I took a nap, and Mare Imbri trotted out to the zombie graveyard to graze.

Later we went to the place of my ignominy: the baobab tree. There I met Imbri's friend the. Day Horse, a handsome white stallion. And there it was I performed my most colossal act of folly: I failed to recognize my enemy when I saw him. For the Day Horse was the equine aspect of the Horseman, and he connected my vision to the gourd, and I was gone.

I found myself locked in the realm of bad dreams, instead of passing through it as I had when riding Mare Imbri. I was in a castle chamber, which was pleasantly appointed with tables, chairs, and beds. There were Kings Trent, Dor, and Jonathan the Zombie Master.

"So good to see you again, Humfrey," Trent said. "What's the news?"

I was taken aback. How could he be so casual? Then he laughed, and I knew he was teasing me in his fashion. I shook hands with him and Jonathan, and then with Dor, who was no longer a child at age twenty-four and had served honorably as king. He seemed slightly taken aback, which gratified me. We were all now recent kings, with a certain morbid camaraderie.

"The wives are mourning," I reported. Dor had just been married to Irene, after a betrothal of eight years duration; they had not seen fit to rush things. Irene had finally taken a hand and tricked him into the ceremony. But she had played it too close; the sudden duties of the kingship had occupied him in the crisis, and they had had no wedding night. "I told Iris that Bink and Arnolde Centaur were to follow me as king. Meanwhile, I failed to recognize the Horseman when I met him." Actually I'm not quite certain now exactly when I figured out the identity of the Horseman; it was some time ago. But the scene was something like that, I'm sure.

"Didn't we all!" Jonathan agreed.

I caught them up on the recent events of the battle against the Last-Wave, and they nodded. All of us were wise too late.

Then we settled down to a game of poker, a game Trent had picked up in Mundania. One might think that this consisted of poking a nymph, but this was not the case. It consisted of dealing out cards and bluffing about the values of our holdings. It was a fitting occupation for kings. Dor, being of a younger generation, merely watched. We used our closest approximations to Mundane value, as this was a Mundane game: lettuce; clams, and bucksaws, all provided by the dream realm. We were of course, all sharing a sustained dream; our bodies were lying in their various places, comatose, being tended by our assorted women. We knew that if we were not rescued in a few days, our bodies would die, and then we would have no escape from this realm, except perhaps into the neighboring ream of Hell. It seemed best not to dwell on that; the decision was out of our hands.

We were comfortable enough, aside from the boredom. We did not feel the discomforts of our bodies. Our bodies seemed solid here, because we were all spirits, none of us having any more solidity than the others. The Night Stallion checked in on us every so often and provided anything we wanted within reason. But he could not provide us with our freedom.

In due course Bink showed up. We welcomed him, especially his son, Dor, acquainted him with our situation, and learned the latest details of the battle of Xanth. Bink had met the enemy leader Hasbinbad in single combat, and was getting the better of it, but they had had to break off because of darkness. So they had made a truce for the night and retired. Then Hasbinbad had treacherously attacked in the darkness, but Bink had been ready for him, avoiding the trap, then pursued him to the brink of the Gap Chasm. We were all able to remember that cleft, now, because the Forget Spell worked on our physical bodies, not our souls. He had been wounded, but had forced Hasbinbad into the Gap, where he had fallen to his death. Then a white horse had come, and the Horseman had locked Bink into the gourd.

"But you cannot be harmed by magic!" Trent protested.

"I wasn't harmed by magic," Bink pointed out.

"But if we all die here—" Dor said, worried.

"We are unlikely to," I said. "If Bink's talent allowed him to join us, we must be safe."

The others nodded agreement. We were all comforted.

Then Mare Imbri showed up. The Night Stallion gave her a tail-lashing for her tardiness and brought her in to us. She projected her communication dreamlet, and the pretty young woman in black informed us how King Arnolde had performed a truly centaurian series of interpretations of Xanth human law, concluding that the distinction between Magicians and Sorceresses was purely cosmetic, and that the definition of king did not necessarily indicate male. Thus he was able to designate Queen Iris and her daughter, Princess Irene, as the next two kings in the line of succession. Queen Iris had been somewhat antagonistic to the centaur, but for some reason had suffered a swift change of sentiment. And now it was clear to me what my reference had written: what Iris desired most was to rule Xanth, and now she was very likely to have her chance.

Then Mare Imbri departed—but returned later with a visitor. It was Irene. "You can't skip out on me this time!" she told Dor. "We started our marriage in a graveyard, and we'll consummate it in a graveyard."

"The skeletons won't like that," he demurred, perhaps awed by the prospect, as has sometimes been the case with men.

"The skeletons don't have to participate," she assured him.

But the Night Stallion had prepared for them a separate chamber filled with pillows. When last seen, before the door closed, they had a full-scale pillow fight going. I had a suspicion that it wouldn't last the night. Indeed, there came a silence for a time, and I suspect a stork took notice, if the signal was able to get out of the realm of the gourd. Then later still they emerged, both looking satisfied, and started throwing pillows at the rest of us. Soon we were all in it: the Pillow Fight of Kings. I had forgotten, in the course of the last hundred and twenty years or so, what fun pillow fights could be. Too bad the Gorgon wasn't here; I was sure she could handle a pillow well.

Then Arnolde joined us. He had sent out *a* contingent of fifty centaurs from Centaur Isle to fight the Mundanes, and they had fought a great battle and greatly reduced the strength of the Wave, and then the Horseman had taken him out too. Iris was now King of Xanth.

But all too soon King Iris herself showed up. She had crafted a horrendous army of monsters and tricked the Mundanes into walking into the Gap Chasm, decimating their number again, and taunted the Horseman via her illusion image—and he had made a gesture at that illusion and taken her out. "What a fool I was!" she said.

"Join the throng," her husband, Trent, said.

Irene was now king.

"How long can this continue?" Iris asked.

"Through ten kings," I said, remembering what I had read. "The chain is to be ten kings long."

"And I was number seven," Iris said ruefully. "Irene is number eight. But who next? We are out of Magicians and Sorceresses."

Then King Irene arrived, having tried to lull the Horseman while her plants encircled Castle Roogna and sealed him in. But he had caught on too soon and banished her to the gourd. She had designated Chameleon as her successor—but in only two minutes more, King Chameleon arrived too. She was in her smart-ugly phase, and had planned a course of action to destroy the Horseman. She had designated as the final king—Mare Imbri.

And the King Mare killed the Horseman and destroyed his magic ring of power by throwing it into the Void. That freed us all. But she lost her body in the process, for the Void took her too. Fortunately she retained the half soul she had gotten from Chem Centaur, and that maintained her existence. She became a day mare, bringing pleasant daydreams to folk.

After that King Trent retired, turning over the throne to King Dor. The rest of us faded back into our quiet existences. I returned to my castle and to the Gorgon, who had performed well in battle, stoning a number of Mundanes. It was good to revert to normal.

Chapter 15

IVY

The stork brought Ivy to King Dor and Queen Irene in 1069, two years after their marriage and their assumption of the throne. She was a Sorceress, thanks to the continuing largess of the Demon X(A/N)th's gift to Bink, and therefore in line to become king of Xanth someday. I made a note in my references, for it behooved me to keep track of all Magician-class magic. As it happened, Ivy was to have an impact on my quiet life almost from the start of her career.

Her talent was Enhancement. She could increase the power of the magic of any creature. But that was only part of it. The creature itself tended to become what Ivy chose to believe it was. If she thought an ogre was gentle, that ogre would be gentle; if she thought a mouse was vicious, beware of that mouse! Thus she had an insidious effect on those around her. Indeed, her mother, Irene, had been classified as Neo-Sorceress, her talent of growing plants not being of Magician caliber. But after Ivy arrived, (or perhaps before; I lose track) Irene was recognized as a full Sorceress, by no coincidence; her daughter perceived her that way, and so she was.

It occurred to me that Ivy's magic could be useful in my business. Suppose she Enhanced all my spells? Suppose she met my son Hugo, and perceived his talent as strong instead of marginal? He might then be able to conjure fresh fruit instead of rotten fruit. That would do wonders for the smell of our castle. Hugo was also a bit slow—some said retarded—and if little Ivy happened to see him as smart, that too would be nice. So I looked for a pretext to meet her, without being obvious. She was *a* cute, bright child, by her perception and therefore in reality, so that even at the age of three was impressive.

So it was that I elected to make a personal appearance at a function to which Ivy was invited. That was the debut of the Zombie Master's twins, Hiatus and Lacuna, then just sixteen. Actually there was business too, because the dread Gap Dragon, the terror of the chasm, had somehow found a way out of the Gap and was menacing the neighborhood of southern Xanth. Perhaps this was a result of the fragmentation of the Forget Spell on the chasm. That spell had been detonated by Dor in his youth, when he visited King Roogna, to make the goblins and harpies forget their war and not overrun Castle Roogna. It had been permanent—until the Time of No Magic. That had shaken the spell, and indeed had abolished most of it. But it had been soaking into the chasm for eight hundred years, and now that residual forgetting was sifting out and drifting away in whorls and eddies, causing any creatures who walked through them to suffer amnesia. This represented more mischief. And my tomes suggested that a wiggle swarm was about due. Wiggles were always trouble, because they zapped through anything in their path, leaving wiggle-sized holes. Actually there was evidence that we misunderstood the nature of the wiggles, but I had not yet gotten around to researching that. In addition, I had run out of youth elixir, and the Gorgon had hinted that it was time to get more. So I planned to make a side trip to the Fountain of Youth, which was in easy carpet distance from the new Castle Zombie, and refresh my stock. I think, all in all, there was enough business to justify a few hours away from my tomes, though I remain uncertain about that.

Thus it was that my wife stayed home to tend the castle, and I took Hugo, then eight years old, on the carpet to New Castle Zombie. Little did I know the mischief that would result from that excursion!

Somehow it is impossible to start any trip on time; there seems to be a hostile spell which prevents it. Thus we were an hour late taking off. We were flying somewhat slow and uncertain, because I was trying to teach Hugo how to operate the carpet. Then we encountered some unfriendly clouds and an adverse wind, and were further delayed in the air. I picked up a suitable eddy current near the ground and zoomed along it. But there was a dragon obstructing the current, and I had to slow until it got out of the way. Always some idiot making a left turn when you're in a hurry! So we were well behind schedule by the time we reached New Castle Zombie.

Well, I would just have to condense things. So we flew into the window where Dor, Irene, the Zombie Master, and Arnolde Centaur were gathered. "We have another chore," I told them. Then I spelled out the problems: the Gap Dragon had to be contained but not hurt, for it was necessary to the welfare of the Gap; and the forget whorls had to be sprayed with fixative and moved out to Mundania where they would do less damage. "Take it up, Hugo," I said. And, narrowly missing the wall, we lurched up and sailed out of the window.

In retrospect, I fear I was too brief with them. The Gap Dragon bore down on the castle, and in the resultant confusion little Ivy got lost in the jungle beyond the castle. I should have warned them about the proximity of the dragon, but forgot. It's hard to keep every detail in mind when you're in a hurry.

We flew on to the Fountain of Youth, landing a short distance from it. It had once been a full fountain, but had worn down into a more ordinary spring over the course of centuries, or perhaps the rocks around it had youthened into sand. The Zombie Master had known its location and informed me, and I had found it useful. But naturally I did not tell others about it. What would Xanth come to, if everyone used this elixir to stave off old age, and so no one ever died? I had never used it myself, until the Gorgon suggested it, and gave me reason to want to be younger.

I left Hugo and the carpet a safe distance away, because it wouldn't do to have him reduced in age, or it accidentally youthened into a doily. I brought out a disk, freed a catch, and it sprang out into a ten-foot pole suitable for touching unpleasant things. Why anyone should want to touch ten feet I'm not sure, but I did need a good long shaft.

I tramped to the edge of the spring. It wasn't actually a fountain in the sense of water sailing up; the water merely welled out continuously, always young and fresh. The vegetation at the verge of the pool was of course very small, mere seedlings, becoming older only with distance. Any animal who came to drink here departed considerably younger than it came. Most were smart enough to sip; those who drank deeply had to start their lives over.

I fixed a bottle to the end of the pole, and extended it, dipping carefully from the spring. When it was full, I twitched it so that its flip-top lid snapped into place. I shook it dry, then brought it in and wrapped it in cloth. I retreated from the spring. Someone watching me might have thought my exaggerated care foolish, but youth elixir is dangerous. I returned to the carpet and handed the wrapped bottle to Hugo, with an admonition, so that I could condense my pole to packable length. It resisted in the manner of the inanimate, but finally I got it back into cylinder form and then into its original disk, and put it in my pocket.

There was a sudden roar, and the ground shook. I looked up—and there was the Gap Dragon steaming toward us. It must have continued to run after visiting Castle Zombie. My spells were on the carpet with Hugo. I would have to get my portable dragon net and fling it over the monster, subduing it. "Hugo!" I cried. "Toss me my bag of spells!"

But Hugo fluffed it. He grabbed at the fringe of the carpet instead, and it mistook the gesture as a command and took off. Hugo, unbraced, rolled off. The carpet sailed into the air, carrying my bag of spells with it. I was suddenly without my magic, except for the compressed ten-foot pole, and the dragon was still bearing down on us. That pole was too clumsy to serve as a weapon, and the dragon could probably steam us from beyond its length anyway.

Then I saw the wrapped bottle of elixir. It had fallen beside Hugo. "Hugo!" I called. "I'll distract the dragon. You unwrap that bottle, lift the cap, and sprinkle some elixir on its tail." For the youth elixir did not have to be imbibed; it would work on any body it touched, in the manner of the healing elixir. We could make the dragon young enough to be harmless. No younger than necessary, of course, because it was needed in the Gap Chasm. Perhaps even trace youthening would confuse it, so it would leave us alone.

Hugo, never clever with his hands, struggled to get the bottle unwrapped and the lid off, while I dodged about as briskly as I could, avoiding the steam-snorts of the dragon. There were larger dragons than this one, and there were flying dragons, while this one had only vestigial wings, and there were fire breathers and smokers who were frightening to see in action. But this was nevertheless one of the most ornery and fearsome creatures of Xanth, because it normally hunted in the Gap Chasm and its prey could not escape it. That steam could cook prey where it stood. Worse, this dragon could not be spooked or frightened; it pursued its prey relentlessly until catching it. I *had* to neutralize it in some fashion or it would steam and eat us both.

I glanced back at the fountain. Could I lead the dragon to that? No, it was between me and the pool. It had to be the elixir from the bottle. "Hurry, Hugo!" I yelled. I was in excellent health for my age, but my age was old.

The boy finally fumbled the bottle out and the lid open. But in his haste he did not pour a few drops on the dragon's tail; he held the bottle and made a throwing motion that sent an arc of elixir flying toward the dragon and me.

"No!" I cried, too late. The elixir scored all too well. It wet down the dragon solidly, and some of it also splattered against my skin.

Disaster! The dragon youthened rapidly, becoming smaller, with brighter green scales. But so did I. We were both overdosed, and were losing a century or more of age. As it happened, we were both over a century old; otherwise we might have dwindled all the way into pre-delivery. But it was bad enough. The dragon became a baby dragon, and I became a baby man.

I saw us both changing rapidly, and I saw Hugo gaping at the sight. I tried to call out something to him, but my youthening prevented me from making much sense, even to myself. Perhaps I was even speaking backwards.

Hugo, dismayed and confused, began to cry. The baby dragon shook itself, then scooted away, evidently as alarmed as I. But I could do nothing, for I was now too young to talk.

Then abruptly I was back at the castle. The Gorgon had evidently been watching us in the magic mirror, seen the disaster, and used the emergency conjure spell to bring me home. Unfortunately it, like the mirror, was tuned to me only, and she did not know how to retune them. That meant that Hugo remained out in the wilderness, alone.

The following years are a bit vague for me. I aged at the normal rate, except when Zora Zombie, whose talent was accelerated aging, came to baby-sit me. My wife managed somehow, and worked with Queen Irene to keep things in order. But it was three-year-old Ivy who did the most. It seems that she, lost in that region of the jungle, encountered the Gap Dragon and used her talent to tame it. Then she met Hugo, and her talent made him a virtual night in shiny armor, as she put it. The three had a great adventure, and in the end even managed to help Glory Goblin, the young-est, prettiest, and sweetest of Gorbage Goblin's daughters, unite with her lover Hardy Harpy, and also to defuse a wiggle swarming.

Then, when Ivy was five, she came to ask me a Question. She had, she felt, been Grounded, for no reason at all. Actually she had gotten into such mischief that the entire chapter of that volume of the Muse of History's record had been censored out. The missing chapter turned up years later in a *Visual Guide to Xanth*, where no one would notice it. These things happen, in Xanth. All children got into mischief, but Ivy could Enhance mischief to an excitingly new level. Now she was compounding it by sneaking out to visit me.

I had managed to age rapidly, and was now about seven years old, physically, and the same actual size as she was. Ivy had had considerable effect on me, because she Enhanced Zora's aging talent, enabling me to age much faster than otherwise. However, I was now old enough to remember my principles, so I made her go through the challenges.

Ivy used stepping stones to step across the moat. She used a dark lantern to get through a region of intolerable brightness. She nullified a flying kitty hawk by intensifying its hawk and kitty aspects until the two got into a fight with each other, and the fur and feathers really flew. Then she encountered a headstone who sounded the alarm so that she would get the brush-off, and that huge flying brush really terrified her. But she buried a dead moth by the headstone, so that it become silent like a moth, and could not alert the brush. So she won through, as I had known she would. I couldn't turn her in, of course; that would have been in violation of the Juvenile Conspiracy, to which I technically belonged until I got old enough to rejoin the Adult Conspiracy.

"Okay, okay, what's your Question?" I inquired graciously.

"I need something to clean up the Magic Tapestry so Jordan the Ghost can remember."

Another person might have had difficulty grasping this, but I was the Magician of Information. I knew that she referred to a ghost of Castle Roogna who had died in the year 677, and been dead for 397 years, approximately, and who was now trying to tell her the story of his life to alleviate her boredom while she was Grounded. They were using the Tapestry to show pictures and refresh his memory, but the Tapestry was somewhat dirty after 838 years, approximately, and its crewel stitchery needed cleaning by caustic lye. So I gave her the recipe for the crewel lye, and she took it back to use the caustic on the yarn. The Tapestry brightened immediately, and Jordan the Ghost was at last able to tell his sad tale of an unkind untruth. It was replete with Swords and Sorceries and Goods and Evils and Treacheries and Thud and Blunder, and Ivy of course loved it, even though some of the juicier parts got censored out. After she heard it, Ivy managed to get Jordan restored to life, and then his girlfriend Threnody, who was half demon (I knew the type). Everyone was happy, except maybe for Stanley Steamer, her pet little Gap Dragon, who had gotten accidentally banished by a misinvoked spell.

So naturally that led to more mischief. Ivy was going to send her shape-changing little brother, Dolph, out to find the dragon. But Dolph was only three years old when she decided this. To stave this off, Grundy Golem did something unusually caring, and volunteered to go on this search himself. And of course the first thing he did was come to me for an Answer.

I told him to ride the Monster under the Bed to the Ivory Tower. I had of course already researched it. Little did he know, then, that the Ivory Tower contained the maiden Rapunzel, Ivy's pun pal, who was the distant descendent of Jordan the Ghost back in his Barbarian years and Bluebell Elf, who had used an accommodation spell to have a rather special tryst with him. As a result, Rapunzel could change sizes, being of elf stature or human stature or anything between or around. But her magic was in her hair, which was marvelously long. Rapunzel was to become the love of Grundy's life, as there were not many suitable female golems, and anyway he was no longer a true golem, having been rendered real. I did not bother to tell him all this, of course; he hadn't inquired. Suffice to say that he did rescue Stanley Steamer from a fate considerably better than death, and brought the dragon back to Ivy.

Incidentally, Grundy said something that changed my life again. He suggested that I use reverse-wood in conjunction with youth elixir to age myself instantly to any level I wished. Now why hadn't I thought of that? As a result, I was able to restore myself to the physical age of a hundred, or perhaps a bit less, to the pleasure of the Gorgon. We lived happily ever after—for three years.

Then it was 1080, and the Lethe elixir I had taken in 1000 abruptly wore off, and I remembered Rose of Roogna. Naturally I departed immediately. My wife and son insisted on coming with me, so the castle was deserted.

But this chapter is about Ivy and the ways her life related to mine, so I shall complete that discussion before getting into my more private continuation.

My great grandson, Eskil Ogre, encountered that most mischievous of demons, the Demoness Metria. It seemed that she was seeking a convenient and comfortable place to relax away from the hummers which infested her home region, and so she intended to take over Esk's private retreat. Perhaps she had an affinity for his family, having been a surrogate mother for his grandfather two-generations before. Esk decided to come and ask me for a solution to this problem.

Meanwhile Chex Centaur, the winged offspring of Chem and Xap Hippogryph, was unable to fly, so was coming to ask me how to do it. She was only seven or eight years old at the time, but had matured rapidly because of her animal parent, and was now a young adult. It helped that she was a centaur, for even the youngest of centaurs is uncommonly intelligent, educated, and poised. So she met Esk on the path leading to my castle.

Finally, Volney Vole was coming from the region of the Kiss-Mee River, to ask how the once curvaceous and friendly river could be restored to its natural state, because the Angry Corps of Demoneers had pulled it straight. Now it was known as the Kill-Mee River, and was hostile to normal life. Volney encountered the other two on the path.

So it was that the three of them traveled together, getting to know each other and overcoming the hazards of the route. I had seen them coming in my mirror, of course, and was readying a series of challenges calculated to dissuade them from entry to the castle. Because the truth was that each of their Questions represented a problem for me. I did not want to tangle with the Demoness Metria again, knowing that she would find a way to make me regret it, such as telling the Gorgon too much about my prior wives, and that Esk was my great grandson. Esk was also scheduled to meet Bria Brassie, the love of his life, in the course of his search for

Volney's answer, and I did not want to deny him that. I did not want to tell Chex how to fly—it was simply a matter of flicking herself with her magic tail, which made what it touched get light—because centaur pride was such that she would never forgive herself for not figuring it out on her own. She was destined to play a part in something truly significant for Xanth, and to meet Cheiron the winged Centaur, the love of *her* life, in the course of this quest, so it was best for me not to interfere at all. And the solution to Volney's problem was elementary: the hummers who were bothering the demons would go away if the demons restored the curves of the Kiss-Mee River. All he had to do was tell the demons that. But my tomes indicated that Volney could find lasting happiness if he solved his problem the hard way—a happiness he would lack if I made it easy for him. This was because in the course of searching for the answer, he would encounter Wilda Wiggle, who was both to educate Xanth on the true nature of wiggles and to become the love of Volney's life (wiggles being another branch of the great family of voles in Xanth). So I had excellent reason to avoid giving the Answers. But how was I to accomplish this, if they made it into the castle and insisted on asking their Questions and agreed to pay their year's services, to their mutual loss? The sound of tearing hair reverberated through the castle, and I hadn't even started doing that yet.

But something suspiciously like fate solved my problem, because about a day before the dread trio arrived, the Lethe wore off and I remembered Rose. So I was gone and the castle was vacant. In our rush to depart we forgot to shut down various ongoing activities, which was a nuisance. One of them was an amnesia ambrosia, ironically, that I was brewing in the cellar. That stuff could be extremely awkward to handle.

The trio arrived and navigated the reduced hazards of the defunct castle. They were perplexed, but of course unable to ask their Questions or get their Answers. So they went on to Castle Roogna to inform the King of the mystery of my disappearance. There they met Princess Ivy, now just about eleven years old, and the growing Stanley Steamer, her pet Gap Dragon. Ivy insisted on helping them in their quest, for they had decided to work with Volney to save the Kiss-Mee River. Thus Ivy got involved in this adventure. Because her talent of Enhancement can be devious, it is not possible to say to what extent she changed things. But by the time their adventure was done, they had explored new aspects of the gourd, and brought out Marrow Bones, one of the walking skeletons, who was to remain as one of the solid (or at least bony) citizens of Xanth, Remember, he had gotten lost when Smash Ogre bashed up the dream realm.

But they did not figure out what had happened to me. So three years later Prince Dolph, then nine years old, decided to go on his own Quest to find the Good Magician. It was Ivy's fault, really, because at age fourteen she was an insufferable nuisance to her little brother, and he felt he had to Prove himself. His mother, Irene, insisted that he be accompanied by an adult—mothers are funny about things like that—so he took Marrow Bones. First they checked my deserted castle. There they found a message I had set up for another purpose and put in storage until needed: SKELETON KEY TO HEAVEN CENT. It was for Dolph, actually, but only when he came of age and had to go rescue *a* sleeping princess. Unfortunately he found it early, and that complicated things.

In fact, by the time he was through his adventure, not only had Prince Dolph faded to find me, he had gotten himself betrothed to two nice girls: the wrong one and the right one. They came to live at Castle Roogna for several years, while he tried to make up his mind which one to marry, because his mother was being unreasonable again and said he couldn't marry both. They became fast friends of Ivy. Thus her insufferability to her little brother had resulted in her gaining two excellent companions, which was surely a miscarriage of justice. And Dolph's misadventure had resulted in Queen Irene's Dictum: One Wife at a Time. This was to complicate things for me in yet another way, because it meant that I could not bring Rose of Roogna back to life while married to the Gorgon. But that complication must wait for the end of this narration.

Three years later, at age seventeen, Ivy got into it with both feet. *She* decided to look for me. She invoked the Heaven Cent, which was a magical device that sent the user where most needed, assuming that that was where I would be. That was specious logic, of course, but one does not expect common sense in a princess.

The Cent sent her to Mundania, where lived the one who really did need her most: Grey Murphy. He was the son of Evil Magician Murphy and neo-Sorceress Vadne, who had escaped the Brain Coral's pool in the Time of No Magic and fled to Mundania. It took the Brain Coral so long to complete its inventory after that shake-up that it never knew they were gone and was still claiming to have both of them in storage decades later. Grey and Ivy made their way back to Xanth and looked up my temporary address in the gourd. That was a real nuisance. You see, I was down here in the anteroom of Hell, waiting to see the Demon X(A/N)th, and I did not want to be disturbed. My body was resting peacefully in a coffin at the address on Silly Goose Lane where no sensible person would ever think to look, and protected by a spell of illusion. But Grey Murphy's talent was the nullification of magic. His parents had signaled the stork before leaving Xanth, so he had magic despite being delivered in Mundania. In fact he was a Magician, and as a result was able to penetrate the illusion hiding my coffin. Thus Ivy had finally succeeded in disturbing my peace by the devious route of causing her brother to find the Heaven Cent and then using it to bring Grey Murphy to Xanth.

So they braced me at my physical body, and I had to risk a moment away from Hell's antechamber to talk to them. Grey lifted the lid. "Hey, Magician Humfrey!" he said boldly. What a brash young man!

I opened an eye. "Go away," I said politely.

"But I need an Answer," he said.

"I am no longer giving Answers." I had to get rid of him quickly.

But he persisted. "How can I void the service I owe to Com-Pewter?" he demanded.

Suppose the Demon chose this moment to check the anteroom? I had to get back! "I'll give your Answer when I'm done here."

"How long will that be?"

"If you want an Answer," I said with enormous patience, "serve me until I return."

"But I must serve Com-Pewter!" he protested.

"*After* you complete your service to me." I pointed out the obvious.

"But how can I serve you if you're asleep?"

Would he never give over? "Go to my castle. You will find a way."

Finally he lowered the lid, and I zipped back to the antechamber. What a relief: there was no trace of the Demon's recent presence. I had not missed him.

I had, of course, given Grey Murphy his Answer. It was his destiny to be my apprentice. His magic was the nullification of magic, which was not at all the same as information, but my own status as Magician derived from something other than inherent talent too. He could do the job, if he put his mind to it and blundered through. He would have Ivy to Enhance him, and that counted for a lot. So he would be the Good Magician pro-tem, until I finished my business here. He did not have to worry about the service Com-Pewter demanded of him, because his service to me took precedence. Thus he could remain in Xanth until I returned, whereupon I would tell him how to vacate his commitment to Com-Pewter. It was simple enough.

He did go to my castle, and finally did manage to catch on, thanks in large part to the effect of his father's curse. His father had returned to Xanth after renouncing any claim to the Xanth throne, and his talent was to make anything go wrong that could go wrong. He cursed Com-Pewter's effort, with the result that it did go wrong in the most devious way, and Grey Murphy escaped the onus of having to serve an entity hostile to the welfare of Xanth. That also, incidentally, made Ivy happy, for she had every intention of marrying Grey.

So it was that Ivy brought my replacement, and occupied my castle herself. That was her greatest impact on my existence, and actually it was not a bad one.

The history of Xanth continued apace. Three years later Prince Dolph married Electra and gave Princess Nada Naga her freedom, which was the decent thing to do. At the same time a new character came to Xanth: twelve-year-old Jenny Elf, from the World of Two Moons. She helped res-cue Che Centaur, the winged foal of Cheiron and Chex, and joined that family as a guest child, along with Gwendolyn Goblin. Great things were getting ready to happen in the goblin realm, and I realized that it would really be better if I returned to take a hand. Grey Murphy meant well, but was relatively inexperienced and might bungle it. So I hoped the Demon X(A/N)th would come soon, so I could settle with him. But that belongs in the next chapter.

Chapter 16

MEMORY

So at last I come to my departure from the normal realm of Xanth in 1080. I confess it was a surprise, for I had completely forgotten a section of my life, by no coincidence.

The day started normally, which was to say, all fouled up. There is an endemic curse on households called snafu that accounts for this; one simply learns to live with it.

I was working in my study, of course, poring over my treasured tomes. The Gorgon was in the kitchen making gorgon-zola cheese by staring at milk through her veil. I had not rendered her face invisible again, after the action of the NextWave invasion; we had decided that a heavy veil, spelled to remain in place, sufficed. Hugo, now sixteen years old, was supervising the placement of a cage of little dragons on the drawbridge over the moat. There was an elf doing his service, today setting up a holy smoke generator. I would use that smoke in a future challenge; the querent would have to figure out that he could get through it only by stepping through one of the holes in it. The holes could lead anywhere, but in this case would lead to the inside of the castle. The person who fled the smoke would not get inside, and that would save me the burden of yet another Answer.

I had the magic mirror tuned to Hugo, knowing that he would foul up at some point. Only when he was with Ivy did he become truly competent, because Ivy had never quite lost her image of him as a night in shiny armor. How I wished we could borrow a bit of her talent and permanently. Enhance our son, so that he would be all that he sometimes was with her. My tomes said that Hugo had a good destiny and that he would find special happiness and do something really nice for another person; we just had to wait for that to occur. I knew that sometimes the most promising of children went astray, and that at other times the least promising turned out well. Time and hope would show the way.

But it wasn't Hugo who fouled up this time. It was the elf. I missed it because I wasn't watching him. Hugo finished with the dragons and retired to his room to practice conjuring his fruits, and the mirror remained on him. The Gorgon finished making her cheese and started on a petrified cheese salad which also used some of Hugo's fruits. Because the fruits were of all types but tended to be overripe, a bit of petrifaction improved them. All was reasonably well, there, as it was with assorted other creatures working around the premises. But not with the elf.

Holy smoke is tricky to handle. It is best made in small quantities and bottled; then the bottles can be opened separately, keeping the amount measured. When it is actually being manufactured, there has to be a strict containment spell, similar to those used to confine summoned demons. The elf forgot that. He simply set a chunk of knothole wood in the brazier and ignited it with a lightning bug. He assumed it would burn slowly, allowing him to siphon the smoke into the bottles.

Instead, the entire chunk of wood burst into flame. Suddenly there was a rapidly expanding billow of smoke. The elf should have doused it immediately with a bucket of unholy water, but he panicked and retreated, coughing. He was afraid the smoke would surround him and send him through a hole, and the holes were not yet defined. He could wind up anywhere in Xanth!

The smoke expanded, filling the chamber. It was enjoying this. The inanimate is always perverse, but holy smoke is more perverse than most, with more power of mischief than most. It was out to catch the elf and send him through that hole regardless.

The smell of the smoke reached the Gorgon's sensitive nose. She perked up, sniffing. She recognized the smell and screamed, warning to me.

Now I reoriented the mirror and saw what was happening. I hurried down to deal with it. Hugo came down, bearing a bunch of blue-speckled bananas he had just conjured.

The smoke did not wait on our convenience. It doubled its effort and coursed from chamber to chamber, filling them all, hot on the trail of the fleeing elk. We converged, meeting the elf, who gesticulated wildly as he explained. "The wood—it all caught fire at once—the smoke chased me out—"

"Cease babbling, elf!" I snapped, justifiably annoyed. I searched through my memory for a smoke containment spell, but naturally couldn't remember the formula at the moment.

Meanwhile, the smoke, with inanimate cunning, circled around to fill the chamber behind us. I couldn't remember my free-breathing tunneling spell either. A curse on my aging mind! There was nothing to do but step into the one remaining clear chamber, to give me a breather while I cudgeled my memory for the spell I knew was at the tip of my brain.

We clustered in the center of the chamber. The smoke, knowing it had us trapped, encircled us in a smiling wreath. Then it expanded inward, filling the room. I focused on the errant spell, about to remember it. I did a brief exercise to enhance my memory. In a moment I would have us free and the smoke under control.

That was when the Lethe wore off. It had been wearing thin anyway, and my effort of memory banished the last of it. "Rose!" I cried, stricken.

"I have a banana, not a rose," Hugo replied.

"The Love of my Life!"

The Gorgon turned to me. "What?" she inquired with somewhat more than ordinary interest as the smoke swirled up to enclose us in a constricting bubble of air.

"My third wife. She's in Hell!"

"Don't you mean your first wife, the demoness?"

"No. Rose was human. A princess. I must go to her!"

"If you go, I go too," the Gorgon said firmly. I can't think why she was interested.

"Hey, don't leave me behind!" Hugo protested.

Now the smoke was filling in the last of the air around us. But that was no problem. I uttered a spell to orient the nearest hole. Then I took hold of my wife's hand and my son's hand, and we stepped through. What was to be one of the great temporary mysteries of Xanth was commencing: our abrupt disappearance from the scene.

***

We stood on a nearly barren terrain. Nearby we heard the surge of ocean breakers. There were a few trees and a great many weeds. Ahead was a tumbledown shack.

The Gorgon peered around. Her vision was not good, because she had to look through her thick veil. "Where are we?"

"The Isle of Illusion," I said. "It is fallow, since the Sorceress Iris left to become queen.

"Her fabulous residence? No more than this?"

"No more than this, when stripped of its illusion. I sent her here long ago, and she used her talent to make it a region of wonder."

"But you were going to see your third wife! Is she here?"

"I have come here to have a suitable place for my body," I explained. "It has to be well hidden, so that I will not be disturbed while I'm in Hell."

"I don't want to go to Hell!" Hugo protested.

"Nobody asked you to, son," I pointed out. "You are free to return to the castle or to go anywhere else you choose."

He looked disgruntled.

"Let me make sure I have this straight," the Gorgon said. "You are going to sequester your body here and send your soul to Hell?"

"Precisely."

"To be reunited with your third wife, who died some time ago?"

"Rose didn't die. She went to Hell in a handbasket in the year 1000. I lacked the means to rescue her from Hell, so I took my full supply of Lethe, which happened to be eighty years' worth. I assumed I would be dead before it wore off."

"It seems you miscalculated," she noted. "Do you have the means to rescue Rose now?"

That set me back. "Not exactly. But I have more experience now, and should be able to figure out a way."

"And if you bring her back to life, and she is your wife again, what of me?"

I began to get her drift. "Why, you are my wife too! I wouldn't give you up."

"That's nice to learn," she remarked to no one in particular.

"The two of you can divide the tasks. One can cook while the other sorts the socks."

"A fair division," she agreed, but she seemed to lack conviction.

"But that can be settled at the time," I said. "First I must recover Rose."

"Perhaps Hugo and I will wait for you elsewhere," she said. "We do not care particularly for Hell."

"It's too hot," Hugo agreed. "Fruit must spoil very quickly there."

He had a point. "Perhaps we can make a deal with the Night Stallion to fashion a nice dream for you, until my return."

"Perhaps," the Gorgon agreed doubtfully. I realized that she might not consider the dreams of the gourd to be very pleasant. "How long do you expect to be?"

I hadn't considered that. "Perhaps a day," I opined.

"We can survive a bad dream for a day," she said. She looked around. "We shall have to find a sheltered place. Then we shall have to devise a strategy."

"A strategy?"

"Dearest husband, dealing with the Night Stallion is one thing; he does owe you a favor or two. But Hell is not strictly part of the dream realm. It is, I understand, administered directly by the Demon X(A/N)th. He owes you no favors."

She had another point. "I shall just have to reason with him. Surely we can make a deal."

"What kind of a deal? You know he isn't much interested in the affairs of lesser creatures like us."

"Don't pester me, woman!" I snapped with righteous ire. "I will figure that out on the way down there."

She knew better than to argue with me. "Very well. Let's find a place to sleep, and then we shall see the Night Stallion. Once Hugo and I are comfortable, you will be free to proceed without worrying about us."

"Exactly." She had always been a bit quicker to formulate my thoughts than I was.

So we cast about on the isle, and to our surprise found a sheltered place with a collection of coffins. Evidently the Sorceress Iris had used them to form the walls of her residence when she lived here before becoming queen. Her power of illusion would have made the structure seem like a palace or anything else she wished; it didn't matter what she used in the real world, as long as it was solid enough to last.

"Why all the boxes?" Hugo asked.

I had never thought to do a survey of this island, or any other, so I didn't know. But I could conjecture. "Evidently I am not the only one to regard this as a suitably private spot. Someone must be storing coffins here." Indeed, they seemed quite solid and were evidently resistant to weathering, because they remained in good condition.

Hugo tried to lift the lid of one, but it was nailed on. "There may be someone in it," the Gorgon said, with her veil suggesting a smile. Her facial expressions were evident when one learned to interpret the configurations of the veil; she could even wink. She had been able to do that while her face was invisible, too, though I can't be quite certain how it showed.

Hugo hastily left the coffin alone. He was no more eager than others to peer into the face of a dead person.

"There should be some empty ones," I said.

We found several, together with their lids. We dragged them to a separate spot, packed them with pillows from a pillow bush, and tried them out for size. They were suitable. "Now the two of you don't have to do this," I reminded them. "I expect to take only a day or so. You may wait here or return to the castle—"

"While you go to Hell to fetch your former wife," the Gorgon said. Somehow I could tell she was going to be unreasonable about this. "I shall go along, at least as far as the dream realm."

"Me too," Hugo said.

"Then I shall put you both to sleep with a spell, and take it myself," I said. "It will endure until I invoke the antidote spell. But I really doubt it is necessary, for such a brief time. This is a very powerful spell, and I dislike wasting such magic when—"

The Gorgon only stared at me through her veil, and I felt the tingle of her power. Sure enough, she was being unreasonable. I ceased arguing. It was better than getting slowly stoned.

They got into their coffins and made themselves comfortable. I invoked the sleep spell, and they sank down in it. Not only would it keep them asleep, it would maintain them at the same age as now, no matter how long it endured, without the need of food or water. It suspended their animation, leaving only their minds free to dream. I used this spell because I knew it would enable me to go as far in the dream realm as required, and there was no sense in using a different one on them.

I set the lids on their coffins, so that they would be protected in case it rained. They would not need to breathe either, so it was fine if the lids were tight.

Then I climbed into my own. Just before I invoked the spell on myself, I had a thought. I got out and traced a message in the dust on the outside of my coffin: DO NOT DISTURB. I muttered a spell which caused the words to sink into the hard wood, becoming permanent. Then I climbed in again, hauled up the lid, let it settle down into place, and uttered the sleep spell.

I found myself standing in a pavilion. My wife and son were waiting for me. "If this is the dream realm, it is much the same as the waking one," the Gorgon remarked.

"Only superficially," I said. "There should be a path leading to the other aspects."

As I spoke, it appeared: a gold brick road. I could have wished that the dream realm have something more innovative than that, but of course I did not run the dream realm. I suppose most folk who spent a lot of time here were not interested in working very hard.

We set off down it. But it wound around interminably, extending far beyond where the island had originally been; we were no longer on an island. "I wish I had my magic carpet along," I said impatiently.

The carpet appeared before us. We were all startled. Then Hugo caught on. "You can do anything you want to in a dream," he said. "I wish I could conjure a perfect fruit."

Suddenly there appeared in his hand a perfect apple. He bit into it. It was evidently good. But when his attention went elsewhere, the apple faded out. Dreams had only seeming substance. It might not be safe to ride this carpet.

"I wish we were already there," the Gorgon said.

Suddenly we were there. Her practicality had simplified things again.

Where we were was at the edge of a rather pleasant village. The road went through the center, and the houses were pretty colors with nice little gardens around them, with flowers and fruits and decorative shrubs. There were people, too, and in a moment they spied us.

"Oh, newcomers!" a girl exclaimed happily. She hurried up to meet us. She was about ten years old, with pigtails and freckles. "Hello, I'm Electra. Who are you?"

"I am Good Magician Humfrey," I said, surprised that she did not know of me. I might be a recluse, but I understood that everyone in Xanth knew about the wizened old gnome who gouged the public horrendously. "And this is my wife the Gorgon, and my son Hugo."

"Is he a prince?" Electra asked.

"No, merely a boy," I said.

She studied Hugo. "You must be close to my age."

Hugo was startled. "I'm older than I look," he said gruffly. "I'm sixteen."

"Oh, I thought you were thirteen. I'm older than I look, too; I'm twelve, in real time. I know how it is. Wira's sixteen. Would you like to meet her?"

"I'm looking for Hell," I said: "Tell me where that is, then introduce him to Wira."

"Okay," the girl said brightly. "You have to take the handbasket." She pointed, and there was a huge basket swinging along on the end of a rope which faded out somewhere above. "But usually only dead folk go down there; it's really not part of the dream realm."

I walked to intercept the basket, which dropped low for me. I climbed in. "I shall return," I said as it lifted and bore me away. Hugo and Electra and the Gorgon waved.

The basket bore me swiftly down through the various dream sets and into the nethermost regions, bringing me finally to Hell's anteroom. I got out, walked to the door, and knocked. The door did not open; instead a sign flashed on it: NO ADMITTANCE.

"But I have business here," I protested.

THEN SEE THE DEMON X(A/N)TH, the sign printed.

"Where is the Demon?"

HE WILL STOP BY SOMETIME.

Several questions' and prints later I understood the situation: The Demon would meet with anyone here in Hell's waiting room when he stopped by. It was in the rules of the Demon's game. But if a person happened to be out when the Demon came, he lost his chance forever. So it was best to remain right here, no matter what. Because I was in the dream state, this was possible; I had nowhere I needed to go and did not need food.

So I settled down to wait. The chamber was small and bare, absolutely uninteresting, as if designed to discourage anyone from waiting. But I was not anyone; I was the Good Magician, and I had a wife to rescue from Hell. I focused on the problem, pondering ways to get the release of Rose from this unpleasant confinement.

Time passed. After a while I wished for my magic mirror, and it appeared in my hand, and I oriented it on the innocent dream realm above, where Hugo and the Gorgon waited. As it turned out, they were doing something interesting.

The Gorgon had always felt that Hugo needed female companionship. She had encouraged little Ivy to visit, but Ivy was into everything in Xanth, Enhancing it to her heart's content. Right now (my mirror showed in an inset view) Ivy was meeting Chex Centaur, Esk Ogre, and Volney Vole, doing her best to help them. She was similar in her girlish way to Electra, who was now leading Hugo to meet Wira. So the Gorgon (I knew how her mind worked) was hoping that Wira would be a Nice Girl who would interest Hugo, even if this was only a group dream.

Wira turned out to be in the Deer Abbey, petting the deer. They were pretty little things, friendly but shy.

"Hey, Wira, here are new dreamers!" Electra called.

Wira was a reasonably pretty young woman in a nice pink dress and brown slippers. She looked up, and her eyes matched her dress, which was mildly startling. "Hello," she said, seeming as friendly and shy as the deer. But the deer did not stay for the visitors; they trusted Wira but not strangers.

"This is Hugo," Electra said eagerly. "He's sixteen too."

"How nice," Wira said, smiling sadly. She extended her hand. "Are you here long, Hugo?"

"Not long," Hugo said, taking her hand. It was evident that he liked the look and feel of her. But of course no girl took him seriously when she realized how gnomish he looked and that his magic talent wasn't very effective. That was his tragedy. Then, of course, he said something stupid: "I'd sure like to meet you by a love spring!"

I winced, but Wira was not disturbed. "It wouldn't have any effect on me," she said. Which was an odd statement. "I am immune."

"Oh, that's your talent?"

"No, my talent is sensitivity. I can sort of tell how things are, when they're close. That's why I can pet the deer. They're sort of lonely, because there isn't much for them to do here. Bad dreams seldom need little deer."

Hugo nodded. He had forgotten that this was the realm of dreams. "But they aren't all bad, are they? I mean, this isn't the gourd."

"But most of the interesting things are in the bad dreams," she said. "Those are the ones that have the most careful settings so as to make folk feel worst. So when the Night Stallion comes recruiting, lots of the people here volunteer for bit parts. It relieves the boredom. But the little deer don't get the chance. So even in their sleep, they aren't very happy. I try to help them, but I'm not very interesting either, so there's not much I can do."

"*I* think you're interesting," Hugo said.

"You do?" Wira blushed, turning almost the color of her eyes, and they both were silent. I remember how the Demon Beauregard had blushed the color of Metria's pink panties, long ago. It was an interesting effect.

"And this is his mother, the Gorgon," Electra said.

The Gorgon stepped forward as Wira turned toward her. But Hugo, stepping back at the same time in typically clumsy fashion, brushed against her, and his jacket snagged against her veil. The veil, less secure in this dream, was pulled down, exposing her eyes—just in time to meet Wira's gaze. The Gorgon froze with horror, for her face was no longer invisible. Any person or creature who met her direct gaze was immediately stoned.

"So pleased to meet you, Mother Gorgon," Wira said, extending her hand.

The Gorgon hastily drew up her veil before anyone else could see her face. As it was, two butterflies directly behind Wira plummeted like the little stones they now were, striking the ground with separate plinks. "You—you're alive!" the Gorgon exclaimed.

"Asleep but alive," Wira agreed. "Is something wrong?"

"You looked into my face—and didn't turn into stone!"

Wira blinked. "I'm sorry, I didn't mean to offend you. I didn't see you."

"You what?" the Gorgon asked, confused.

"Oh, I guess I forget to tell you," Electra cut in. "She's blind. She can't see you at all; she goes by your voice."

"Blind!" the Gorgon exclaimed. Now it was coming clear why the girl's eyes were pink: it was the albino hue, the blood vessels showing their color through the colorless lenses. That could be a factor in her lack of sight. This also explained why a love spring wouldn't affect her: it would make her love the first man she saw after touching its water, but she would never see a man. She would be similarly immune to a hate spring.

"I'm sorry," Wira said. "I did not mean to mislead you. I understand why you're upset."

The Gorgon recovered most of her somewhat scattered wits. "My dear, I'm not upset! I'm astonished! Your lack of sight just saved your life!"

Wira shrugged. "It wouldn't have made very much difference, I think. I am of no use to anyone. That's why my folks had me put to sleep."

The Gorgon was taken aback again. She had the most fearsome power in Xanth and the gentlest heart; I happen to know. She was becoming increasingly interested in this young woman. "Do you mean to say it wasn't an accident or bad fortune? Your family wanted to get rid of you? Because you are blind?"

"They didn't exactly say that. But I knew. They were tired of always having to take care of me, and they knew I would never be able to take care of them. They saw how the boys avoided me, so I probably wouldn't get married. So they decided to have me put to sleep until they could find a better situation for me. I'm sure they looked for one."

"Of course they did!" the Gorgon said righteously. "Surely they will find it any time now and come to wake you up. You are one of the folk in the coffins on the Isle of Illusion?"

"Yes. We are all here because we have a problem in the real world of Xanth. Electra's been here longer than any of us."

The Gorgon turned to Electra. "Is this true? How long have you been sleeping?"

"About eight hundred and fifty years, I think," Electra said. "I tend to lose count, there are so many of them. I'm waiting for a prince to come and kiss me awake."

"A prince!" Then the Gorgon stifled that line of reaction, remembering that Xanth was short of princes at the moment. The only one was six years old. She turned back to Wira. "And how long have you been sleeping, dear?"

"Twelve years."

Hugo gaped, chagrined. He had thought she was his age, and she was actually twelve years older.

The Gorgon understood her son's thoughts almost as well as she understood mine. "But you don't age while you're sleeping," she said quickly to the girl.

"Yes, I do age," Wira said. "My folks could afford only a cheap potion. It makes me sleep, and stops my body from wasting away, but it doesn't stop aging. So if I woke now, I would be twenty-eight. I'm afraid my folks didn't find—"

"It doesn't matter," the Gorgon said firmly.

"But, Mother—" Hugo began, appalled. He had evidently liked this girl, but a twenty-eight-year-old woman would be quite another matter.

"Remember that potion your father OD'd on?" the Gorgon asked him. His face brightened; she was referring to the Fountain of Youth elixir, which could take years off any person in a hurry. Wira could be sixteen again, if she woke. If Hugo wanted her to be. "Why don't you go and tour the garden with this young woman? Perhaps you will have something in common."

Hugo's thoughts were not the fastest in Xanth, except when Princess Ivy wanted them to be. But he was beginning to picture the presence of a pretty young woman in our castle, who would have no concern about catching an accidental glimpse of the Gorgon's face, and who just might find him interesting. "Yes, let's see the garden," he agreed. Then he realized that he had blundered again. "Uh, not see—I mean—"

"It's all right, Hugo," Wira said. "You certainly see, and I also see, in my own way."

"You do see? But—"

"By touch," she said. "Give me your arm."

Awkwardly, he put out his arm. She heard the cloth move, and put her hand on it. She guided him down the path through the abbey. They walked on through the ferns and flowers.

"Do you think maybe I could pet a deer?" he asked.

"Certainly, Hugo, if you want to. I will introduce you. But you have to be patient, for they are very cautious."

The Gorgon watched them depart. "My, don't they make a nice couple," she murmured.

"Yes, she's a nice girl," Electra agreed beside her. The Gorgon jumped, having forgotten her presence.

Now the Gorgon focused on Electra. "You say you must sleep until a prince comes. Are you a princess?"

"No! I'm more like an accident."

"Tell me about it."

So Electra told her story, which was a complicated one involving a curse by Magician Murphy that caused her to take the long sleep instead of the princess who was supposed to. Electra's coffin was the other side of Xanth, on the Isle of View. She had come here to join the others, in her dream, because it was pretty dull being alone. Now she had to marry the prince who kissed her awake or die. That was awkward because she was only twelve years old and looked ten, and wasn't a princess. But she hoped to do her best.

Meanwhile Hugo was getting to know Wira. She showed him how she could see him with her hands, by lightly touching his face and body. Then he managed to do something stupid again, when she was close: he kissed her. But it turned out not to be as stupid as it might have been, because she rather liked having someone like her.

Time passed, while I waited for the appearance of the Demon X(A/N)th. I realized that this was not a daily matter, with him, but I didn't dare depart even for a moment lest I miss him. In fact I realized that he was probably aware of my presence and waiting for the moment I did step out, so he could step in and miss me. The Demon hated being bothered even more than *I* did. So it was a war of endurance, and I intended to endure.

Three years later Electra was abruptly called away: her prince had come. It was really too soon, because he was still only nine years old and already had a bethrothee. But eventually that did work out, in its devious fashion.

The Gorgon answered one of the Night Stallion's casting calls, and landed a nice role in a bad dream intended for someone who had been mean to snakes. "Ssso," she hissed in sinister fashion, while her snakehair writhed enthusiastically. "You have assssked for it." Then she started to remove her veil. That was where the dream cut off; the purpose was to scare the dreamer, not to actually turn him to stone.

After that she was able to obtain a number of nice roles and developed a fair career as an actress in the dream realm. She was actually enjoying it. That was just as well, considering how the years were passing. I had thought we would be here only for a day or so, but this business was running a trifle overtime.

Hugo and Wira became great friends. It turned out that she could sense when he was going wrong, and correct him with a word or nudge so that he went right instead. When he conjured fruit she guided him so that it was good fruit. Of course it was dream fruit, of no lasting substance, but it was evident that the principle would apply in waking life as well. He told her of the youth elixir, so that she could remain sweet sixteen when they woke, if she wanted to, and she said that if he woke her, she would want to be any age he wanted her to be. Meanwhile, it hardly mattered whether they were awake or asleep, or sleeping in the dream realm. They enjoyed each other's company.

Ivy and Grey Murphy came to disturb me, and I managed to get through without losing my appointment, as mentioned before. The years continued, and I continued to watch what was going on both within and without the dream realm. I knew that the time would come when the Demon came, and then he would have to let me take Rose out of Hell, because she really didn't belong there. If he could admit to making a mistake, which of course he couldn't. However, I had used my long time in the waiting room to devise a plan.

Then, ten years after the start of my vigil, you arrived, Lacuna. You brought me news I had overlooked, which complicates my situation: Xanth law no longer allows a man to have two wives. I have mentioned that complication here as a result of your information. But perhaps that plays into my hands.

Now I shall proceed to tell my future history, if the Demon does not come. So put a dash on the end of this sentence, Lacuna, and we shall start the next chapter, which we shall title—

Chapter 17

BARGAIN

Lacuna looked at the wall, where the final words remained printed: "And we shall start the next chapter, which we shall title—" followed by "'Chapter 17: Bargain.'" Then she looked inquiringly at the Good Magician.

"Keep writing," he told her. "But make it third person. You're in it too, now, but it would be confusing to have the 'I' switch from me to you."

"But your story is finished," she protested. "I mean it's all caught up to the present."

"And going on into the future, exactly as I said it would. So the Demon will have to come or lose by forfeit."

"Of course," she agreed with such doubt that it sounded like a denial. But she kept the print printing on the wall. Already the last words of the prior chapter were disappearing into the ceiling. But they could be recovered at any time; all she had to do was reverse the scroll.
scroll.

Oops! In her distraction she *had* reversed the scroll, and the bottom line had moved down to bump the floor, where it had bounced and duplicated itself. She re-reversed the scroll, but it was too late to erase the repeat line; it was stuck as a flaw in the text.

Meanwhile, the Hell-bent handbasket swung into the anteroom, and two children scrambled out. They appeared to be twins, about six years old, a boy and a girl.

"Don't let go of the basket!" Lacuna cried. But she was too late. They landed on the floor, and the handbasket swung away. Now the children, too, were stranded here.

They looked at the adults, turning shy. "Hi, folks," the little boy said. He wore blue shorts and an off-white jacket and socks.

"Who're you?" the girl inquired. She wore a pink dress and off-white hair ribbon and socks.

Humfrey shrugged, so Lacuna had to do the introduction. "This is the Good Magician Humfrey, and I am Lacuna. Who are you?"

"I'm Jot," the boy said.

"I'm Tittle," the girl said.

"We're twins," Jot added.

"We're going to Hell," Tittle added.

Then they both ran to the door to Hell, keeping in step with each other. They stopped before it, side by side, and pounded on the door. "Let me in!" they cried together.

WAIT FOR THE DEMON X(A/N)TH, the sign on the door printed. It looked like Lacuna's print, but was more authoritative.

"Oh, pooh!" Jot exclaimed, disgusted.

"Oooo, what you said!" Tittle reproved him.

"I didn't say 'poop,' I said 'pooh,' dummy!" he snapped.

"Well, you shouldn't have!"

Jot tried the doorknob, but it turned in his hand without effect. Tittle tried it next, with no better effect.

Frustrated, they turned to the adults. "Hey, when's the Demon coming?" Jot asked.

"Yeah, when?" Tittle echoed.

"I don't know," Lacuna said. "The Good Magician's been waiting for him for ten years. But we think he will arrive soon."

"Well, we can't wait," Jot said.

"We're too little to wait," Tittle agreed.

They walked in step away from the door.

"Stay," Humfrey said suddenly.

Lacuna and the children were startled. "Surely you don't want to keep them here!" Lacuna said. "They should get on home to their mother."

"I came here to talk to you," Humfrey said firmly to the children. "And now I shall, Demon X(A/N)th. You can not depart until you have settled with me."

The two children looked resigned. "You have named me," Jot said.

"What gave me away?" Tittle asked.

"Two things. First, I knew that you had to appear very soon, if you were going to, so any arrival was suspect. Second, you used a term only a member of the Adult Conspiracy can use. You said the word 'Hell.'"

"But this *is* Hell," Jot protested.

"Its waiting room, anyway," Tittle added.

"That doesn't matter. Only an adult can use the term. Therefore it was obvious that you were not a child, or children. Not of our culture, anyway, and since you are speaking the human language, you must be pretending to be human."

"I shall be more careful, next time," Jot said.

"Well, out with it," Tittle added. "What do you want?"

"I want to free my wife from Hell," Humfrey said. "The woman I love. She does not belong there and must be released."

"You have a wife who is not in Hell," Jot pointed out.

"And you can only have one wife," Tittle reminded him.

"I shall have to choose between them," Humfrey said. "If Prince Dolph was able to choose between his two loves, I can do the same. But first things first: release my wife."

"I have to listen to your plea," Jot stated.

"But I don't have to do your bidding," Tittle finished.

"But you *do* have to deal with me," Humfrey said. "You have to satisfy me that you have given my plea fair consideration."

"Why do I have to do that?" Jot asked.

"Yes, who says I have to?" Tittle added.

"*You* said it," Humfrey said. "You laid down the rules of your game, and this is a footnote to those rules."

Jot sighed. "I said too much."

"You've done your homework," Tittle said.

"Well, I *am* the Magician of Information, and I have had some intercourse with demons. I have a notion of their nature."

"You can't say a word like that to a child!" Jot cried.

"You have violated the Adult Conspiracy!" Tittle added.

Lacuna kept her mouth shut, but found that she was rather enjoying this dialogue. She knew that the business at hand was deadly serious, but the children were little darlings, even if they weren't what they seemed.

"There are no children here," Humfrey reminded them. "Only facsimiles. Anyway, that demoness was my wife."

The twins considered. "I will make you a deal," Jot said.

"Yes, a fair deal," Tittle said.

"But if it is not fair, I don't have to make it," Humfrey said sternly.

"I will complete your Question Quest," Jot said.

"I will ask you the one Question you can't answer," Tittle added.

"There is no honest Question I can't answer."

"If you answer it correctly, you will win," Jot said.

"And if you don't, you will lose," Tittle said.

"But it must be a fair Question," Humfrey said.

"It's an *easy* Question," Jot said.

"Anybody could answer it," Tittle agreed.

Lacuna knew that it would be nothing of the sort; Humfrey had explained that at the beginning. How did he plan to handle it?

"Let me be the judge of that," Humfrey said. "Tell me what the Question will be, should I choose to answer it."

Lacuna knew that trick wouldn't work. The Demon would require him to agree to answer it before he gave the actual Question. But she was surprised.

Jot said, "It will be this—"

"What is the color of Mela Merwoman's panties?" Tittle asked.

"Objection," Humfrey said. "If you ask me that one, I will be unable to answer it because she doesn't wear any panties. So that is a Question with no Answer, and therefore unfair."

"But she *will* wear panties," Jot argued.

"When she makes legs to walk on Xanth," Tittle continued.

"Why would she ever walk on land?" Humfrey demanded. "She prefers to swim in water."

"In search of a husband," Jot said.

"In the next volume of the History of Xanth," Tittle finished.

Humfrey nodded, as if persuaded. "So you will ask me to name the color, when she does don them."

"Yes," Jot said.

"When," Tittle agreed.

"And the correctness of my Answer will determine whether my wife is released from Hell."

"Right."

"True."

Lacuna knew that Humfrey knew that the Demon would see that Mela chose panties of a different color than Humfrey predicted. So how could he possibly win?

"That seems fair," Humfrey said after a bit. "But it would be tedious to have to wait for her before recovering my wife. It will be a year before she walks on land."

What was he doing? How could he agree to the fairness of a manifestly unfair Question?

"You will just have to wait," Jot said.

"Not that it makes any difference," Tittle added.

Humfrey arched a wrinkled eyebrow. "I was not speaking only of me. I was speaking of you. It will be tedious for you to have to keep this matter in your mind for that year, when it would be preferable to dispose of it immediately."

"I have demonic patience," Jot said.

"I can wait forever," Tittle agreed.

"Unless there is a shift in the fortunes of your game, and you are called away from Xanth in the interim," Humfrey said. "Then you would not be able to attend the panting."

Lacuna was perplexed, then realized that he meant the donning of the merwoman's panties. Which meant the Demon could not dictate their color, and Humfrey would win. Of course in that event the magic would be gone from Xanth, because of the absence of the Demon, changing everything. But the Demon still would have lost, which would probably gripe him somewhat.

"You have a point," Jot said.

"But only one point," Tittle said.

"I should think you would prefer to avoid both the inconvenience of keeping the matter in mind and the chance of missing the event," Humfrey said. "Considering that there is an easy way to accomplish that avoidance."

"What?" Jot said, caught by surprise.

"How?" Tittle asked.

"By plea-bargaining," Humfrey said. "It is obvious that if I answer the Question, we shall both have to wait a year before verifying its validity, to mutual inconvenience and annoyance, despite knowing the outcome. But if we compromise now, we can each get part of our desire without further nuisance. We can skip the Question and Answer."

"You are beginning to make sense," Jot said.

"For a human being," Tittle amended.

He was? Lacuna could not quite see how. But she was neither a Magician nor a Demon.

"Let me reside in Hell for a month," Humfrey said. "Then let Rose out for a month. The average attendance will be the same. Naturally I would rather have Rose out without penalty, and you would rather keep her in, but this may be a feasible alternative."

"No, you're too smart to live in Hell," Jot said.

"You would get the denizens all worked up," Tittle agreed.

"But who else would be willing to fill in in Hell?" Humfrey asked. "It has to be me."

"There is another."

"Yes, another."

"Who?"

"The Gorgon," Jot said.

"Your other wife," Titde clarified.

"But I wouldn't ask her to do such a thing!" Humfrey protested.

"But I would," Jot said.

"Yes, I would," Tittle agreed.

The two of them gestured with their four little hands. Suddenly the Gorgon stood in the chamber, regal in a black dress and veil. "Humfrey!" she exclaimed. "Are you finished here yet?"

"I am plea-bargaining with the Demon X(A/N)th," he said, "to mitigate the sentence on Rose. I have offered to spend time in Hell equivalent to the time she is released from Hell, but—"

The Gorgon's veiled eyes narrowed. "So you can spend time with her both in and out of Hell?" she asked. "Neither of you much noticing where you are?"

"Yes, that's it," Jot said.

"He's a cunning one," Tittle said.

The Gorgon's veiled gaze focused on them. "Children?"

"They are the present form of the Demon," Lacuna explained.

The Gorgon refocused on Humfrey. "Well, I'll have none of this. *I'll* visit Hell instead."

Humfrey looked surprised, but Lacuna was catching on to his ways. He had anticipated this, too, and was maneuvering both the Gorgon and the Demon into agreement with his compromise. "I would not ask you to—"

The Gorgon looked at the children. "If I resided in Hell, would I be allowed to pursue my career in dream pictures?"

"If the Night Stallion asked for you," Jot said.

"Hell is a bad dream, after all," Tittle agreed.

"But—" Humfrey said.

"Then I'll do it," the Gorgon said.

"I agree," Jot said.

"She can sub for you," Tittle agreed.

Humfrey looked amazed. "If that is the way you feel—"

"I will make the bargain," Jot said firmly.

"The Gorgon can sub for your wife in Hell," Tittle added, nailing it down.

"Then I am constrained to agree," Humfrey said, spreading his hands as if outflanked.

Lacuna saw that Humfrey's plan had worked. He had avoided the rigged contest and obtained the release of Rose half time, without running afoul of the problem of having two live wives in Xanth at the same time. He had outsmarted the all-powerful Demon.

Jot turned toward her. "I wouldn't say that," he said.

Tittle also turned toward her. "I would say he just makes sense," she said.

Lacuna was aghast. The Demon knew what was in their minds! So Humfrey had not prevailed by trickery but by offering the Demon a good compromise.

Jot extended his hand, and a rolled scroll appeared in it. "Here is the Agreement," he said.

Tittle extended her hand, and a huge feathered quill appeared in it. "Sign it," she said.

Jot unrolled the scroll and held it against the wall, covering part of Lacuna's ongoing printed narrative. Tittle gave Humfrey the feather.

Lacuna peered over Humfrey's shoulder to read the scroll. It said, in script more elaborate than she could render:

It is hereby Agreed that Good Magician Humfrey shall be allowed to exchange one wife for another in Hell, et cetera and so forth.

There was a decorative line below, separating the text from the space for signature. Humfrey squinted at it through his spectacles, then shrugged and signed.

Then Jot took the quill and signed: *Demon.*

Tittle took it and signed *Xan*th. Then she handed the quill to Lacuna.

"But I'm not part of this!" Lacuna protested.

"You have to witness it," the Gorgon explained. "I can't; I'm a relative."

Oh. Lacuna brought the quill to the paper. But something nagged her. "I'm not sure that—"

"Sign it," Humfrey said shortly.

So, doubtfully, Lacuna signed it too.

"Well, that's that," Jot said.

"Yes, that's that," Tittle agreed.

"So let's get on with the exchange," Humfrey said.

"What exchange?" Jot asked.

"Yes, what?" Tittle added.

"The exchange of wives," Humfrey said. "As agreed."

Jot and Tittle exchanged one glance. "I think he didn't read the small print," Jot said.

"Yes, I think he didn't," Tittle agreed.

"Small print?" the Gorgon asked, her veil twisting in perplexity.

Jot extended his hand, and a big magnifying glass appeared in it. "Use this," he said.

"Yes, read the small print," Tittle said.

Humfrey took the glass and held it over the decorative line. The line expanded, and turned out to be two lines of very small print, now legible:

But only in the Changes of Moon
On days beginning with Letter *N*

"'But only in the Changes of Moon, on days beginning with Letter *N*,'" Lacuna read aloud, getting it right for her own text. "But when does the moon change?"

"And what day of the week begins with the letter *N*?" the Gorgon asked. She looked at Humfrey. "Dear, this is nonsense."

"Tough udder," Jot said smugly.

"You signed," Tittle said smugly.

Humfrey shrugged. "Did you suppose I got to be the Magician of Information without understanding the concept of small print?" he asked. "It can merely modify, not reverse the contract; that's according to the rules demons follow. We have only to interpret it."

"Well, go home and interpret it," Jot said.

"Yes, and stop bothering me," Tittle added.

Humfrey waggled a finger at them. "Not until I have completed my mission. If I leave beforehand, I will default." He turned to the Gorgon. "You interpret the Changes of Moon." Then he turned to Lacuna. "You find the days beginning with *N*."

Lacuna exchanged two glances with the Gorgon. Then both fell to concentrating. Lacuna thought about the days of the week, and found none that began with *N*. There were two beginning with *S*, two with *T*, and one each with *F*, *M* and *W*. There was a month beginning with *N*, No Remember, but no day. Yet it seemed that there had to be a day. What could it be?

Then she suffered a blinding inspiration. There were *N* days—if the days of the month were numbered alphabetically! The ninth and the nineteenth.

"Lacuna has gotten her notion," Humfrey remarked, blinking as the flash of light faded.

Then a flashbulb went off just above the Gorgon's head, making Lacuna blink. The other part of it had been solved.

"The moon changes every month, just like a woman," the Gorgon said. "So it's every month."

"On the ninth or nineteenth," Lacuna added.

"And what is today?" Humfrey inquired as if bored.

"The ninth of OctOgre," Lacuna said.

"Then what in Hell's annex are we waiting for?" Humfrey demanded irritably.

Jot and Tittle exchanged half a glance and half a shrug. It was evident that the Demon's little trick had been found out. He had tried to outwait Humfrey and not succeeded; so he had tried to fool him with the appearance of the little twins, and not succeeded; so he had tried to pose an unanswerable question and not succeeded. This contract was the fourth trick which had failed, thanks to Humfrey's determination and insight. Would there be another trick? If so, what would it be?

Lacuna looked up. The others were looking at her. Oh, no—she had been automatically transcribing her thoughts, and they were now being printed on the wall. There were no secrets here!

"There will be one more trick," Humfrey said. "But it will be possible to navigate it, if we are sensible. The Demon can not actually cheat. There must always be a way through, however devious, or he defaults."

Only one more trick. That was a relief! Lacuna turned away from the wall, preferring not to see her thoughts displayed. Fortunately she was such a dull person that no one else was really interested in her thoughts anyway.

"Right you are," Humfrey agreed absently.

"Don't mind him, dear," the Gorgon murmured. "He only speaks when he's interested, even if only to grump."

That made Lacuna feel better. But she tried to cut off her thoughts, without much success.

"Well, let's go," Jot said, walking toward Hell's door.

"Yes, let's make the exchange," Tittle agreed, pacing him.

And the Demon, she realized: he must have wanted this also. Perhaps because the Gorgon was in her way as great a prize as Rose in her way. Rose could grow flowers in Hell; the Gorgon was now a successful actress. The Demon must want to keep her, but could not unless he made the deal. What a cynical bargain!

The two children paused at the door. As one, they glanced back at Lacuna, knowing her thoughts. So did Humfrey. She felt a chill, not of danger but of understanding. These folk were frighteningly intelligent and cynical. How could any ordinary person compete?

"We don't try, dear," the Gorgon murmured, walking beside her. Then Lacuna realized that the Gorgon, too, was getting something she wanted: instead of waking and returning to her life as a housewife, she would get to continue her dream career, at least half the time. Hell, it seemed, was not much of a specter to one who was making a career in bad dreams.

The twins pushed open the door. "Come on," Jot said.

"All of you," Tittle said.

They walked through the door: the twins, Humfrey, and the Gorgon and Lacuna. The print followed along on the wall and when necessary the floor, recording the scene.

Hell turned out to be a barren, smoky, windy place. Everything was soiled gray: the ground, the walls, the sky. Lacuna coughed as she breathed the bad air, but the Gorgon's thick veil seemed to protect her.

The path led upward. Then abruptly it was too hot and dry, with a blazing sun and withered trees.

They followed the path on around and down into a gulch—and here it was clammy wet, with greasy dirty water forming on the skin.

Farther along, it was cold, with grimy snow on the ground and a storm approaching. But when the storm arrived it was mostly just violence, threatening to blow them off the path.

Lacuna was beginning to understand the nature of Hell: the weather was always wrong.

Then they came to a garden, and there were roses. The air became sweet with their fragrance, and the climate was almost nice. Red, yellow, and blue: the rarest roses known. This had to be the magic of Princess Rose, making even Hell become pleasant in this one limited region.

An there she was, a woman of middle years, kept at the age she had been when brought here in the handbasket: Rose. Now she was somewhat plump, her hair becoming ash gray, but even so, more attractive than Lacuna herself, because she was interesting rather than dull. She was in work clothes, but these were well tailored and well cared for. She did not see the approaching party, being intent on her work.

"Hey, Rose-hips!" Jot called.

"Someone to see you, petal-ears," Tittle added.

Rose looked up from the orange-striped rose bush she was tending. Her mouth curved into a rose-petal bow of surprise as she peered past the twins to fix on Humfrey. "My husband! You have come at last!" Then she saddened. "Or did you die?"

"I did not die," he said, walking up to her. "But I had to compromise. I can free you only part time."

She brushed herself off and embraced him. "Part time is better than no time. But how is it that you have come now, after ninety years? You don't look ninety years older."

"I've been using youth elixir. I could not rescue you before, so I took Lethe elixir. When it wore off, I came here. However, there is a complication."

"There always is," Rose said wisely.

"I remarried."

"I know. Sofia is here too."

"But she was Mundane!"

"Yes, she was surprised to find herself here when she died, but not, unduly dismayed. She said it wasn't much worse than Mundania in bad weather. Taiwan is here too, and even MareAnn."

"MareAnn!" Humfrey echoed.

"Sofia is your wife too," Jot said.

"And the Maiden Taiwan," Tittle added.

Lacuna began to see the trap being sprung on Humfrey. He had made a deal to get his wife out for a limited time—but there were three wives here. How could he rescue one and not the others?

"And who are your friends?" Rose inquired, becoming aware of the remaining two women.

"This is Lacuna, who is recording my history," Humfrey said. "And this is the Gorgon, my fifth wife."

Rose frowned. It was almost as if she were becoming aware of a problem. But she kept it to herself. "So nice to meet you, Gorgon. Are you alive or dead?"

"I am alive," the Gorgon said. "I have agreed to take the place of a wife here, so that that wife can return to life for a time."

Rose smiled, and it was like the blossoming of a new rose. "Then you are generous! I knew my husband would marry only a good woman."

Surprised, the Gorgon smiled too, under her veil. "Yes, that is true." Lacuna knew they were complimenting each other, not themselves.

Just then another figure approached. It was a much younger woman, quite shapely in her revealing dress. "Are you collecting wives, Humfrey?" she inquired.

Humfrey looked at her, and was chagrined. "Oh, no!" he muttered.

"And who is this?" the Gorgon asked.

"The Demoness Dana—my first wife," Humfrey said.

"If you are now dating your wives, I qualify," Dana said.

"But you left me when you lost your soul!"

"True. But on reflection, I realized that I was happier when I was with you. You must admit that I was a good wife, while it lasted. I can be so again."

Meanwhile three more women were approaching. "Ah, here are MareAnn, Maiden Taiwan, and Sofia," Rose said, spying them. "We have all become great friends, having one interest in common."

Humfrey looked somewhat befuddled. Perhaps he had reason.

All the women were beyond youth, but none was unattractive. There was a circle of greetings. Then the Gorgon asked the obvious question: "How is it that you are here with the wives, MareAnn?"

"Because I always did love Humfrey," MareAnn said simply. "I would have married him, had I not feared it would cost me my innocence. Now, in Hell, I have had much of my innocence taken from me, so there is no further barrier between us except that of death. I would be happy to marry him now."

"So which wife are you going to take?" Jot inquired smugly.

"Or will you marry MareAnn and take her?" Tittle asked.

So it was to be a choice among six. No wonder the Demon had decided to compromise; he had of course known that this was coming. Demons of any kind had little care for the affairs of man, but great interest in complications. This was a rare complication! Lacuna did not see how Humfrey was going to find his way out of this one.

"Let's consult," the Gorgon said in a businesslike manner. "Since I'm the one who is making it possible, I think I should have some say in the decision."

"Yes, maybe you will change your mind," Jot said.

"Maybe you won't let any of them out," Tittle added.

So that Humfrey, having made his compromise, would be denied the benefit of it, Lacuna realized. The Demon X(A/N)th must have seen to it that all of them appeared here, including Dana Demoness. What a great joke, for the demons!

Jot gestured, and a round table appeared with ten chairs. Tittle gestured, and ten place settings appeared. Then Rose fetched a decanter of rose wine and a kcy lime pie with rose petals decorating each piece; evidently the petals made the pie good despite its origin in Hell. The wine turned out to have rose petals floating in it too.

When they were all served, the discussion began. Jot and Tittle gobbled their pie slices and gulped their wine as if it were milk, in exactly the manner of children. The others sampled theirs more cautiously. Lacuna found both the wine and pie to be very good; Rose evidently had a talent for preparing such things. Probably this was a trait shared by all his wives and girlfriend.

"All five of you wish to share moments of Humfrey's life?" the Gorgon inquired. She was eating especially carefully, lifting her veil aside without uncovering her eyes.

The other nodded. "Perhaps we wish also to experience life again," Rose said. She glanced at Dana Demoness. "Or to simulate it." She glanced at MareAnn. "Or to indulge in a manner not possible before."

"But I can take only one," Humfrey protested. "And the only one I want is—"

"Is it?" MareAnn inquired.

That evidently set him back. Lacuna knew from his life history that he had loved only three times: MareAnn, Rose, and the Gorgon. The other three had been essentially business relationships, however well they had fulfilled them.

"I have discovered things of interest in the dream realm," the Gorgon said. "I have no objection to spending more time in it. Suppose we give each wife or love a month, in turn, before I take my turn? In six months the cycle would be complete, and we could start again."

The women exchanged fifteen glances. Lacuna thought that there should be twenty-five glances as each woman met the eyes of the five others, but some magic made fifteen enough.

"Hey, don't I have any say in the matter?" Humfrey inquired grumpily.

"Of course not," the Gorgon said, and the others nodded agreement. "It took you ten years to get this far; do you think we want to wait another ten for you to figure it out?"

"What, no big fight?" Jot asked, disappointed.

"No screeching and hair pulling?" Tittle added.

"This may be Hell," the Gorgon said, "but we aren't hellions. So it seems we are agreed. What should be the order of visitation to Xanth?"

"Alphabetic," Dana said. That would put her first.

"Age at death," Sofia said. That would put her first, because three had not died and so couldn't compete, and the other two had evidently died younger. "That's when our assets were frozen, as it were."

"Chronologic," MareAnn said. That put her first.

The others considered. They nodded. Chronologic did seem to make sense.

"So it seems we are agreed," the Gorgon said. "MareAnn will go first. Now if you will excuse me, I have a curtain call by prior appointment." She glanced at the twins. "You are honoring the deal, I presume."

Jot grimaced. "I have to."

Tittle scowled. "More's the pity."

"Let's do it, then," the Gorgon said as she faded out. This was, for her, only a dream, so she had dreamy powers, and evidently enjoyed them.

"But I think we owe a vote of thanks to Rose, who made this possible by bringing Humfrey here," MareAnn said.

The other applauded. Rose blushed rose red. "Have some candied rose petals," she said.

Humfrey looked at MareAnn. "I suppose you're going to want a ceremony," he grumped.

"A little one will do," MareAnn said shyly.

Try as he would, Humfrey did not manage to look entirely displeased. She had, after all, been his first love.

"Fun's over," Jot said.

"Until the panties," Tittle agreed.

Lacuna glanced at the twins as she followed Humfrey and MareAnn down the path toward the exit. "I realize that you are merely figments of the Demon's imagination, but you are cute and I'm almost sorry I won't be seeing you again."

At that they both burst into wild laughter and dissolved into smoke. That bothered her. What was so funny?

The handbasket was waiting in the waiting room. The three of them climbed in. "Won't you be sorry to lose your unicorns?" Humfrey inquired.

"There are no unicorns in Hell," she replied. "I haven't seen them in ages anyway. I will still be able to summon other equines."

They continued to talk as the basket swung up and away, oblivious of Lacuna. She was glad for them, but what of her own life? Would she really be able to change it?

The basket slowed. Lacuna saw that it was not proceeding straight back the way she had come. Now another type of dream realm was opening out, with a yellow brick path below. Humfrey had described that.

They reached a pleasant community. There was a handsome young couple standing on the path, evidently waiting for them. It was Hugo with Wira, his blind love.

"This is where we get off," Humfrey said. "Lacuna, you ride back to the castle. Tell them we're coming."

"Yes, of course," Lacuna said, surprised. But now she realized that her body was at the castle, while the other bodies were at the Isle of Illusion. They would have to take turns riding the magic carpet back after waking up.

The others got out. Introductions were proceeding as the basket bore Lacuna away. MareAnn had never met either Hugo or Wira, of course; now she would be a temporary stepmother for Hugo. It should be all right.

Then the castle came into sight. Lacuna had a lot to tell Grey and Ivy!

Chapter 18

CHANGE

Lacuna saw her body lying within the temporary coffin. She climbed out of the handbasket and let go. She dropped to the coffin, through its lid, and on down into her body. She was back.

Suddenly she felt stifled. She lifted a hand to pound on the closed lid. In a moment it lifted, and there was Magician Grey Murphy peering down. "You're back!" he said. "We didn't see you."

Lacuna sat up, feeling a bit disoriented. "I've been to Hell and back in the handbasket," she said. "I have a whole lot to tell you. But first I have to warn you that Good Magician Humfrey is coming back; he's on his way now with his girlfriend, MareAnn, and—"

"What?" Ivy asked.

Lacuna saw that this was not going to be a simple explanation. So she plunged in. She just had time to cover the main gist and part of the minor gist (gist was the sort of stuff that needed to be covered quickly) before Humfrey's magic carpet arrived. He had evidently used a lightening spell, because all four were on it together.

Then Lacuna had to perform the introductions, because she was the only one present who had had personal contact with everyone, though some of it only through her printing of Humfrey's history. Wira was now a woman not a lot younger than Lacuna herself, but Humfrey located his youth elixir and gave her a dose; then she became her real age of sixteen. Lacuna wished she could do that! But of course youthening wouldn't do her any good; it was her whole life that was blah, not just her physical age.

She felt awkward now, for she was not really part of this group. "I should go do my service for Magician Grey now," she murmured. "And—"

Grey took note. "But it will take time to research your Answer."

Humfrey snorted. "Oh, I'll do it. I don't like reunions much anyway." He stalked off toward the study, and Lacuna followed.

Humfrey squinted at the old pages. "Ah, here it is. You must take the Key to Success and go to the Mountain of Change before the Statue of Limitations runs out." He went to a shelf and picked up a large wooden key. "Bring this back when you are finished with it." He handed it to her.

"But—" Lacuna said blankly.

"Nonsense. The magic carpet will take you there after you deal with Com-Pewter. Be sure to return it, too." He walked out of the study.

"But—" Lacuna said, following helplessly.

"Oh, by the way," he said, pausing. "Thank you."

"You're welcome. But—"

"Here's the carpet. Get on it."

She did so, bemused. Then it took off.

"But—" she protested one more time, despairingly, to no better avail than before. She was on her way.

The carpet seemed to know where it was going. It flew out a window and looped around the castle before heading north. It soon went out over the awesome Gap Chasm, but instead of crossing it, it turned to fly west along it. Then it flew south a short distance to a small mountain and looped down to a cave in the base. It entered this cave, flying unerringly in the sudden darkness until reaching a large, bright chamber. It landed.

Before Lacuna was a rather junky metallic box with knobs on the front and a pane of glass sticking up at the top. Part of it was fashioned from a pewter pitcher, which Lacuna now realized the Demoness Metria had sneaked from Humfrey's castle to bring here. It was amazing how things integrated, now that she knew Humfrey's life story. This was Com-Pewter, the dread nemesis of Xanth.

A GREETING, the pane printed.

"I think you don't know who I am," Lacuna said, nerving herself for her effort. She had spoken blithely of changing its print, but she knew that the evil machine had a lot of power, and a doubt was starting to nag at the edge of her mind, with a qualm, a twinge, and even a compunction waiting in line behind. Com-Pewter's power was to change reality in its vicinity by printing the reality it preferred on its screen. She could change its print—but would it remain changed? Why hadn't she thought of this problem before?

I DON'T EVEN CARE WHO YOU ARE. YOU ARE OBVIOUSLY SUPREMELY DULL. I WILL USE YOU AS A SERVANT.

"I don't think so," she said, and concentrated on the magic formula she had rehearsed to dominate the device.

The print on the screen changed. Now it said: COM-PEWTER IS REPROGRAMMED TO BE A NICE MACHINE. IT HAS NO USE FOR THE SERVICES OF GREY MURPHY, AND RENOUNCES THEM. SAVE AND COMPILE. The last word was the key; that constituted a special spell that would change Com-Pewter's nature.

The pane of glass blinked, HUH? it printed, with something less than machinelike precision.

Lacuna had had the sense not to get off the magic carpet. "Well, I'll be going now," she said.

Print rolled across the screen, WOMAN DECIDES TO REMAIN LONGER. And Lacuna found that she couldn't tell the carpet to go; she had indeed changed her mind. The evil machine was fighting back. In a moment it would decree that she decided to reverse the reprogramming she had just accomplished, and she feared she would not be able to deny it.

But she could fight back too. Even as the print appeared, she changed it: WOMAN IS SENT ON HER WAY BY COM-PEWTER, WHO PREFERS TIME ALONE TO MEDITATE ON ITS NEW NICENESS.

It worked! The carpet lifted and sailed down the cave tunnel, out of the mountain. Not only did Com-Pewter's print change the local reality, it changed the evil machine's mind. Once it was printed, it was so, even if the machine didn't like it. And it seemed that Com-Pewter could not reprogram itself. It was stuck with her new prime directive: to be nice and to renounce the services of Grey Murphy.

Lacuna had accomplished her mission. Now she had only to get her reward. She stared at the wooden key she still held in her hand. What had Magician Humfrey said? She had to take this Key to Success to the Mountain of Change before—before what? Something was going to happen, but she didn't remember what.

She looked around. The carpet was moving over unfamiliar territory. Lacuna had not been paying attention and was now lost. It didn't matter, because the carpet knew where it was going, but she would have preferred to know also. Was this north or south of the Gap Chasm?

The carpet circled down by a curious walled park. Somehow Lacuna couldn't quite see what was inside the park; it was obscured by trees and bits of mist. This must be where the Mountain of Change was. But what was she supposed to do there? It was all so unclear. She wished it had been Grey Murphy who had researched her Answer, because he was young and inexperienced, so tended to explain things carefully. Humfrey just assumed that everyone knew things, and had no patience. But of course he had lived a long time and experienced many things, as she well knew after printing his life history. He had a right to be short with ignorant folk.

She got up and stepped off the carpet. It rolled up behind her, but did not fly away. That was a relief. She did not want to be stranded in this strange place. It wasn't that the loss of such a dull person as she was would harm Xanth in any way, but she preferred to be dull in her own home rather than to bore folk she didn't know.

She approached the large wooden door to the park. She lifted her wooden key and fitted it into the keyhole. She turned it. The lock resisted. She turned harder, but it was no use; the key would not work.

Lacuna stepped back and looked at the park. What little she could see was not attractive. The wall was worn and the nearby trees were wilting. She saw a word printed along the wall: FAILURE. Oh, no! She had come to the wrong place!

But the carpet wouldn't have done that. This must be the right place—or maybe it could become the right place.

She focused on the word, and changed it: SUCCESS.

The wall brightened. The foliage of the trees hanging over it became greener.

She approached the door again. She tried the key. This time the lock clicked. Now this was the right place, thanks to her talent.

She tried to close the door after her, but the hinges tightened up and it no longer budged. It remained firmly open. Curious, she stepped back outside the park to see if anything else was approaching, waiting for this opportunity, but no one was.

Then the door slammed shut behind her, making a bang. She jumped. Was she locked out?

She tried her key once more. It turned, and the door opened. But again it refused to close—until she stepped outside. Now she understood: it would not close until the one who had opened it and entered the park went back out. That was a fairly neat magical device—but to what purpose? Why should the door care whether she was inside or outside? She shrugged; it was a harmless mystery. If it should close while she was inside, she could use the key to unlock it again.

She gazed around the park. Inside she saw a statue of a naked running man. He was a fine-looking specimen in every respect—muscular, handsome, and well endowed in a fashion a maiden was not supposed to understand. But of course it was only a statue; they were always idealized. She really didn't care about that particular detail; her desire was for a man who was good in his head and heart, and for good children. One of the problems with men was that they put more store by a woman's anatomy than by *her* head and heart. Fortunately, women had more sense, so used their minds to choose the more sensible men. But it did help if the men were handsome.

Then she became aware of something else. The statue was changing. Ever so slowly, it was moving. The forefoot, was coming down and the body was shifting forward, and the hair was blowing back as if he were racing through the wind. Maybe on her scale he was barely making progress, but on his scale he was sprinting.

Where could he be going? She looked the way he was looking, and saw that it was the open door. Oh. Evidently he hoped to get out before it closed again. How lucky for him that she had happened to come long just before he reached it.

Lucky? Lacuna had learned to distrust coincidence. Maybe in Mundania chance governed, but this was Xanth. There might be more to this than appeared.

She pondered, then tried an experiment. She scuffed a mark by the man's leading foot, so she had a record of exactly where he was. Then she stepped out of the park again. The door slammed shut behind her.

She took a walk around, exploring the region. After a few minutes she returned, and used her key to open the door again. She entered, and as usual it froze in the open position. She walked to the statue.

Sure enough, he had not passed her scuff mark, though he had had time to do so. In fact, he was even a bit behind it. He had retreated during her absence, or perhaps been reset to his original position. He raced for the door only when it was open, and he had to start a certain distance from it.

But what was the point? Coincidence was not the only thing Lacuna distrusted. Pointlessness was suspicious too, especially in a magical place.

She peered more closely at the statue. Now she saw what she had overlooked before: it was on a low pedestal. Evidently the man started there, and ran off it to the door. On the pedestal was the legend: STATUE OF LIMITATIONS.

That was the other thing Humfrey had mentioned! She had to go to the Mountain of Change before the Statue of Limitations ran out. Before he ran out the door, obviously. If he got there first, the door might close behind him—and then perhaps her key would no longer work, and she would be confined in the park. Perhaps she would have to strip naked and get on the pedestal, ready to run out when the next person entered. And she might have to move as slowly as the man did, being rendered statuesque.

What an awful fate! But now she knew: she would have to complete her business at the Mountain of Change quickly, because the man was not all that far from the door. If she took too long, she would surely be lost.

So where was the Mountain of Change? It had to be here somewhere.

She spied a path behind the statue, and quickly followed it. The park was not all that large, so this had a fair chance of leading where she wanted.

She was right. Soon the mountain hove into view. It was not large as ordinary mountains went, but it glistened oddly. As she came closer, she saw that its slopes were rough with shiny little stones. Then she came closer yet, and discovered that those weren't stones, they were disks. In fact, they were Mundane coins, gold and silver and copper and brass. What was called small change.

The Mountain of Change! She had assumed that it would be a mountain where things changed, and perhaps her life would change too, so that she could somehow be fulfilled instead of deadly dull blah. She should have known better.

Still, this was supposed to represent the solution to her problem, so maybe it was both kinds of change. What was she supposed to do here?

Well, what did anyone do with a mountain? Anyone climbed it, simply because it was there. Everyone knew that. So she would climb it.

She started climbing it, but the moment her feet got on the coins, they lost purchase. Her legs did not exactly sink into the surface; it was just that she could not climb. Instead, the coins gave way below, so that she remained pretty much where she was.

But she *had* to climb, or the Statue of Limitations would run out before she got where she was going. She surely couldn't afford that.

She stepped back and pondered the situation. What would freeze these loose coins in place, so she could climb them?

She remembered something Humfrey's Mundane wife, Sofia, had said in passing. Frozen assets. It seemed irrelevant, yet she almost had a notion.

Her notion clarified. It turned out to be a naughty one. But she was pressed for time; that statue might reach the door at any moment. She had to try whatever might work, and quickly.

She stepped back onto the change, held her skirt tight about her legs, and sat down. The surface of the mountain was surprisingly cold; she was chilled right through the hips. Then she touched the coins around her. Sure enough: they did not budge. They were frozen in place. They could not handle this particular type of contact.

She knew she could not afford to stand up again. It was not her feet which froze the change. So she pushed with hands and feet and scooted as well as she could up the slope. It was uncomfortable and tiring, but she made decent (or perhaps indecent) progress, and the mountain was small. She was glad it hadn't been composed of large change!

Finally, somewhat soiled of skirt—she hadn't realized that Mundane change was such dirty money—and numb of rear, she reached the top of the Mountain of Change. She got to her feet and stood in the loosening coins. What now? Humfrey had not told her what to do once she got here.

Well, maybe she simply had to make her wish. That might be so obvious to Magician Humfrey that he thought it was unnecessary to mention. So she would try it.

"I wish I had married Vernon twelve years ago," she said.

She waited. Nothing happened. Her excursion had, it seemed, been for nothing. She must have gotten here after the Statue of Limitations ran out. Her effort had not been enough, because she was no heroine, just a drab woman.

Lacuna sighed. It had at least been worth a try. She had, for a little while, had a glimmer of hope.

She slogged down the mountain, her feet half sliding on the massed coins. She walked forlornly back the way she had come. There was nothing to do but fly back to the Good Magician's castle and return the magic carpet and the Key to Success.

But when she reached the door, she discovered it closed—and the statue still inside. What had happened? That door had been wedged open; had someone else come and managed to close it?

She saw that the statue had almost reached the exit; he must have had the door slam in his face. She knew how that felt. But there was no other person.

Lacuna shrugged and used the wooden key to unlock the door from inside. It opened, and she stepped through. The door closed immediately behind her.

"Hi, Mom!"

She jumped, surprised. There was a blue-haired boy with a water ball in his hand. It was Ryver, the guardian of the moat, who had almost prevented her from entering Humfrey's castle at the outset of this story. What was he doing here?

"Did you get your wish, Mom?" Ryver asked politely.

"I'm afraid it just wasn't—" She broke *off*. "What did you call me?"

"What's the matter, Mom? You look spooked! Did something bad happen in there?"

She stared at him. He had wanted to be adopted into a human family. But she wasn't a family, she was just a middle-aged maid. "Something odd may have occurred, yes," she agreed cautiously. She preferred not to speak further on the subject until she had a better notion what had happened *outside* the park.

"Well, we'd better get back before Dad misses us," Ryver said. "I got the carpet; let's go." He indicated the magic carpet, which was now spread out on the ground.

They got on. Ryver sat in front, to direct it. He handed her his water ball, which she accepted as if used to this. It did not break in her hand, to her faint surprise.

She sat behind the boy on the carpet. It took off. Soon they were sailing over the landscape.

"Your father—he's worried?" she inquired, hoping to elicit further information.

"No, it's not that," he said cheerfully. "He just isn't much of a hand at taking care of the kids. Also, he's curious what you were wishing for. He says it isn't as if you had a bad life or anything."

Lacuna stared into the ball of water as if it were a magic crystal, wondering just how good or bad her life was supposed to be.

In due course the carpet descended. It came to rest just outside the moat of the Good Magician's castle.

Two blurs of motion came charging across the lowered drawbridge. In two moments they flung themselves into Lacuna's embrace, causing her to drop the water ball, which splattered on the ground. They were Jot and Tittle, whom she had encountered in Hell's annex.

"Great to see you again, Mom!" Jot exclaimed, planting a somewhat slobbery kiss on her left cheek.

"Yes, great to have you back, Mom!" Tittle agreed, planting a slightly more dainty kiss on her right cheek.

These were now her children?

Then a man crossed the drawbridge at a more sedate pace. He was oddly familiar. In fact he was the statue—that perfect specimen for running. No—now she saw that he was older, but still in excellent physique. It was Vernon, who had grown considerably more handsome in the past decade or so, as if a good woman had seen to his health and happiness. "Did you have a good trip, dear?"

Lacuna tried not to stare at him. Could it be that he really was her husband, now? "I may have," she answered.

He reached down to help her get off the carpet and out of the entanglement of children. He brought her to her feet and drew her in for a kiss. Then she began to believe. The Mountain of Change *had* changed her life! Yet why was she the only one who realized it?

Vernon rolled up the carpet and carried it back across the drawbridge. Lacuna and the children followed. She noticed that there was now a regular moat monster in the water, who let them pass without challenge.

She paused, looking more carefully at the creature. It seemed somehow familiar, though she was sure she had never seen it before. Had she heard of it? Then she made the connection: she *had* heard of it! "Aren't you Soufflé Serpent?" she asked it. "Who guarded the moat for Princess Rose of Roogna?"

The monster nodded his head in agreement. Evidently more had changed around here than her life! When Ryver stopped being the moat guardian, Soufflé must have resumed the post. If her change of life had made Ryver's life change, then this had been necessary. How many other ripples had this thing set in motion?

MareAnn met them at the castle entrance. She stepped forward to embrace Lacuna. "I see that you did get your wish," she murmured. She, at least, recognized the change which had occurred, perhaps because she had been in Hell with Lacuna, and therefore apart from normal Xanth.

"What wish?" Vernon asked.

MareAnn answered for her. "Hers was the same as mine: merely to return to her loving family."

"But you were away from yours," Vernon said.

MareAnn merely smiled. "We women have our little ways. They come with our loss of innocence."

Vernon shook his head, perplexed. Lacuna decided that it would be best to let him remain that way.

They returned the carpet and key to Magician Humfrey. He was already deep in his beloved Book of Answers. "That confounded foreign elf," he was muttering. "Now she wants to find her way back to the World of Two Moons, and she's going to arrive here right at the worst time."

"Worst time?" Lacuna asked, curious though she was sure it was none of her business—or perhaps *because* it was none of her business.

"Portrait Day," he grumbled. "All my wives will be given passes from Hell to attend, because such a melee will amuse the Demon X(A/N)th, and I'll have to have my portrait done too, and if there's one thing I hate worse than a gaggle of women, it's posing for a portrait."

"Maybe Jenny Elf's appearance will give you a pretext to get away from it all for a moment by addressing her Question," Lacuna suggested.

Humfrey brightened. "Maybe it will." Then he realized that someone was actually in the room with him. There was the key beside his tome. "Oh. You're back."

"Yes, thank you. Your Answer worked. But—"

"Of course it worked," he snapped. "How could it be otherwise?"

"But there is one thing—" Lacuna began.

"Is that another Question?" Humfrey inquired.

For another service? She would have to let it go. "No. Thank you for the use of the carpet and key."

He glowered at her. "I hate it when dull folk are too nice. Very well, I will make an incidental remark: certain people are not directly affected by certain events, when they are the focus of those actions. They are, as it were, the movers rather than the moved. But in time you will pick up your intervening history by listening to the comments of others, and you will gradually come to accept this as your own memory. Your present life is as it seems."

"Thank you, Magician," she said gratefully. Now she knew why she, almost alone, remembered her other life. She was the one who had changed it. Some few others who had interacted with her before that change, and who had had their own lives changed by her actions, also remembered. But the rest of Xanth would not realize what had happened; to them, the present situation was the one which had always been true.

Humfrey nodded. Then he did an extremely rare thing: he smiled. Lacuna returned the smile, while Vernon looked confused.

"It's nothing to worry about, dear," Lacuna told him, taking his arm. "Let's go home and find something interesting to do." She nudged him in a way that suggested all manner of wild creatures, such as lovebirds and storks. She had dreamed for years of doing that, but had never before had the opportunity or courage. What a joy it was!

His eye glinted. "You have always been the most interesting person in my life," he said.

Lacuna intended to remain so.

HISTORY OF XANTH

(SIMPLIFIED) BY E. TIMBER BRAM

−4000   Presumed arrival of the Demon X(A/N)th, plus or minus ten thousand years or multiple thereof, causing magic to slowly infuse the region from the trace leakage of his essence.

−2200   Around this time, a colony of human folk arrives from Mundania. It grows for a while until Magicians and Sorceresses manifest. One of the early Sorceresses is the Sea Hag, mostly unknown to others because of her frequent change of bodies. She survives until 1077, when she is banished to Brain Coral storage. The Hag apparently forgot her history, remembering only that she is thousands of years old.

−2100   About this time, Xanth is cut off from Mundania, becoming a true island.

−1900   The human colony fails, with the humans becoming assorted magic species through interbreeding or change by magic. Harpies, merfolk, naga, sphinxes, ogres, goblins, elves, fauns, nymphs, fairies, and other crossbreeds and variants may derive from this; they tend to be closemouthed about it, evidently preferring not to admit the debasement of their lineage by human stock. Thus this colony is unknown to history, except by the mute evidence of the surviving species.

-1000   The isthmus is restored and limited contact with Mundania is resumed.

-800   Centaur species begins around this time.

-85   Prince Harold Harpy delivered.

-73   Prince Harold Harpy exiled to Brain Coral storage.

0   First Wave of human colonization arrives in Xanth, establishing current permanent settlement.

1   Civilized voles leave their main camp near the Gap Chasm.

35   Second Wave occurs, killing men and children of First Wave.

200   Third Wave occurs several generations later.

202   Magician Roogna delivered to Third Waver.

204   Fourth Wave occurs. Women surviving the Third Wave kill their rapist husbands and bring in better men.

216   The Princess is delivered to the King preceding Roogna.

219   Millie the Maid delivered in West Stockade.

224/225   Electra delivered to West Stockade.

228   Roogna crowns himself king.

233   Electra goes to the Isle of View to help the Sorceress Tapis by making the Heaven Cent.

236   The Princess goes to Tapis to have a coverlet made for her sleep.

—   Altercation between Magician Murphy and Sorceress Tapis at the Isle of View. Murphy's curse causes Electra to bite the apple and start the 1,000 year sleep scheduled for the Princess.

— Fifth Wave advance scouts enter Xanth.

— Dor's adventure in Fourth Wave Xanth, wherein he detonates the Forget Spell in the Gap Chasm.

— The great Goblin/Harpy War occurs.

— Prince Harold Harpy released from Brain Coral storage, and the spell on goblin females is revoked.

— Topological transformation of Millie the Maid into a book titled *The Skeleton in the Closet*. Neo-Sorceress Vadne exiled to Brain Coral storage. The Zombie Master zombies himself.

— Tapis and the Princess go to Castle Roogna, and the Princess marries King Roogna.

237 Magician Murphy retires to Brain Coral storage.

— Fifth Wave proper begins.

286 King Roogna dies in battle with the Sixth Wave.

367 Zombie Jonathan encounters a phantom at Specter Lake.

378 Seventh Wave.

591 Stork brings Magician Gromden.

623 Magician Gromden assumes the throne.

657 Stork brings Magician Yin-Yang.

658 Stork brings Threnody as the result of the mischief of a demoness with King Gromden.

659 Stork brings Jordan the Barbarian to Fen Village.

677 Jordan commences his adventure in medieval Xanth.

— Jordan has a tryst with Bluebell Elf.

— King Gromden dies; Castle Roogna deserted.

— Magician Yang assumes the throne.

—	Jordan becomes a ghost.
—	Threnody marries King Yang.
681	Threnody becomes a ghost.
682	King Yang remarries.
684	Stork brings Lord Bliss, son of Yang.
689	Stork holds nose and brings Evil Magician Muerte A. Fid.
698	Eighth Wave.
704	Lord Bliss marries Lady Ashley Rose.
705	Stork brings Rose of Roogna to Lord Bliss and Lady Rose.
719	King Yang assassinated by poisoning.
—	Muerte A. Fid, Magician of Alchemy, assumes the throne.
721	Lord Bliss receives poison-pen letter.
725	Lord Bliss dies. Rose sent to Castle Roogna for safety.
753	Ninth Wave.
797	Tenth Wave.
866	Eleventh Wave.
883	Stork brings Magician Ebnez.
897	Mare Imbrium foaled as night mare.
909	Magician Ebnez takes the throne.
917	LastWave (Twelfth).
932	King Ebnez adapts the Deathstone into the Shieldstone to protect Xanth from Mundane Waves.

933	Stork brings Humfrey.
—	Stork brings MareAnn.
949	Stork brings Storm Magician.
—	Humfrey hired by King Ebnez to do a Xanth census of talents, as Royal Surveyor.
952	King Ebnez dies.
—	Humfrey declared Magician and assumes throne.
—	King Humfrey marries Dana Demoness: wife 1.
953	E. Timber Bram appointed Historian of Xanth.
954	Dafrey delivered to King Humfrey and Dana Demoness; Dana takes off.
—	Humfrey marries Maiden Taiwan: wife 2.
955	Tics mutate.
971	Humfrey abdicates throne. Matron Taiwan abdicates their marriage.
—	Storm Magician assumes the throne.
—	Humfrey rediscovers Castle Roogna.
972	Humfrey achieves degree from University of Magic and becomes a true Magician of Information.
972	Magician Humfrey marries Rose of Roogna: wife 3.
973	Rosetta Bliss Humfrey—"Roy"—delivered to Magician Humfrey and Princess Rose.
975	Storm King decrees that any resident without a magic talent will be exiled from Xanth.
994	Rosetta marries Stone.
—	Cherie Centaur foaled south of North Village.

997   Stork brings Magician Trent to North Village.

1000   Rose goes to Hell in a handbasket.

—   Magician Humfrey takes eighty years' worth of Lethe elixir.

—   Magician Humfrey marries Sofia Mundane: wife 4.

1001   Stork brings Sorceress Iris to an unwary family.

1002   Crombie the Soldier delivered to Magician Humfrey and Sofia.

1005   Magician Humfrey trains Magician Trent.

1007   Magician Humfrey trains Sorceress Iris.

1017   (Magician) Bink delivered to North Village to Roland and Bianca.

1021   Magician Trent transforms the fish in Fish River into lightning
             bugs; also others, including a winged centaur filly who flees to
             Brain Coral's pool.

1022   Evil Magician Trent attempts a coup d'état. Transforms Justin
             into a tree. Is betrayed and exiled to Mundania.

1025   Stork brings Gorgon and Siren, twin sisters.

1027   Bink loses the middle finger of his left hand in a nonmagical
             accident.

1033   Herman Centaur exiled from the herd for having magic.

1035   Sofia (wife 4) returns to Mundania.

1036   Sea Hag takes over her last body.

1039   Grundy Golem animated by Good Magician Humfrey.

1040   Donald becomes a shade.

1042   Bink travels to the Good Magician to learn whether he has a magic talent. Encounters an aspect of Chameleon, Donald Shade, Sorceress Iris, Magician Humfrey, has missing finger restored by healing spring, and is exiled to drear Mudania.

—   Bink, Chameleon, and Magician Trent return to Xanth and find Castle Roogna.

—   Wiggle swarm; Herman the Hermit Centaur dies.

—   Storm King dies.

—   Magician Trent becomes king and deactivates Shieldstone.

—   Magician Trent marries Sorceress Iris.

—   Bink marries Chameleon.

—   Chester Centaur marries Cherie Centaur.

—   Thirteenth Wave: Trent's former army settles peacefully.

—   Chet Centaur foaled near North Village to Chester and Cherie Centaur.

—   Grundy Golem goes to Magician Humfrey to learn how to become real.

1043   Millie the Ghost restored to life.

—   Time of No Magic.

—   Magician Murphy and Neo-Sorceress Vadne escape from Brain Coral storage and make deal with Com-Pewter: get them safely to Mundania and their child will serve the evil machine, if he ever comes to Xanth.

—   Brain Coral starts inventory of stock in pool. This requires two or three decades to complete, so Murphy and Vadne are not yet missed.

—   Crunch Ogre marries curse fiend ogress.

—   Demon X(A/N)th makes Grundy Golem alive.

—   Magician Dor delivered to Bink and Chameleon.

—   Crombie marries Jewel Nymph.

1044	Princess Irene delivered to King Trent and Queen Iris.
—	Smash Ogre whelped north of Magic Dust Village to Crunch Ogre and pseudo ogress.
—	Tandy delivered to Crombie and Jewel.
1046	Goldy Goblin delivered to Gorbage Goblin.
1047	Chem Centaur foaled to Chester and Cherie Centaur.
1051	Stork brings Xavier in South Xanth to the witch Xanthippe.
1052	Stork delivers Wira into an undistinguished and probably undeserving family.
1054	Gorgon returns to Xanth and asks Good Magician Humfrey a Question: "Would you marry me?"
1055	Dor goes to Fourth Wave Xanth to get the zombie restorative formula from the Zombie Master. Uses it to restore Zombie Jonathan to life as the Zombie Master.
—	Zombie Master marries Millie the Maid.
—	Hardy Harpy hatched in South Xanth.
—	Gorgon, having served a year, gets her Answer: Magician Humfrey would marry her. She's not surprised.
1056	Hiatus and Lacuna, twins, delivered to Zombie Master and Millie.
—	Stork brings Glory Goblin to Gorbage Goblin.
1057	Zora dies of grief for her false true love, and is zombied.
—	Stork brings Rapunzel. She is raised in the Ivory Tower by the Sea Hag.
1057	A centaur and winged horse happen to drink at a love spring.
1058	Cheiron Centaur foaled: a winged centaur.

1059	Dor becomes king during King Trent's trip to Mundania.
—	Gorgon marries Good Magician Humfrey: wife 5.
—	Zombie Master assumes the throne . . .
—	. . . while Dor, Irene, Arnolde Centaur, Smash Ogre, and Grundy go to Mundania to rescue King Trent and Queen Iris.
—	Ichabod Mundane learns of Xanth.
1062	Tandy rides a night mare to Humfrey's castle.
1063	Chem Centaur maps central Xanth.
—	John Fairy and Joan Fairy married.
—	Siren marries Morris Merman.
—	Smash Ogre marries Tandy.
—	Goldy Goblin marries nonentitous goblin chief.
1064	Stork brings Cyrus Merchild to Water Wing to Morris Merman and the Siren.
—	Eskil (Esk) Ogre delivered to Smash Ogre and Tandy.
—	Hugo delivered to Magician Humfrey and the Gorgon.
—	Zombie Master and Millie the Ghost move south and build New Castle Zombie.
—	Prince Naldo Naga delivered to King Nabob in Mount Etamin.
—	NextWave (Fourteenth).
1067	Princess Irene marries Magician Dor.
—	Chain of kings during the NextWave:

> Trent
>
> Dor
>
> Zombie Master
>
> Humfrey
>
> Bink
>
> Arnolde Centaur
>
> Iris

Irene

Chameleon

Mare Imbrium

—   Mare Imbrium becomes a Day Mare.

—   King Trent abdicates and retires with Iris to North Village.

—   Dor assumes throne.

1068   Wira put to sleep at age sixteen.

—   Stork manages to bring Magician Grey to Magician Murphy and Sorceress Vadne in Mundania.

1069   Sorceress-Princess Ivy found under cabbage leaf by King Dor and Queen Irene. (Sometimes the stork can't get into a castle and can't wait for it to open.)

—   Princess Nada Naga delivered to King Nabob in Mount Etamin.

1072   Gap Chasm Forget Spell, shaken by the Time of No Magic, fragments, spinning off forget whorls.

—   Magician Humfrey and the Gap Dragon (Stanley Steamer) youthened to infancy in a slight mishap.

—   Chem Centaur has an informal liaison with Xap Hippogryph.

—   Lady Gap Dragon, Stacey Steamer, takes over post.

—   Wiggle swarm.

—   Hardy Harpy marries Glory Goblin.

—   Xavier marries Zora Zombie.

1073   Chex, a winged centaur filly, foaled by Chem Centaur. Because her sire is of the animal kingdom, she grows and matures quite rapidly for a centaur.

1074   Magician-Prince Dolph found under cabbage leaf by King Dor and Queen Irene.

—   Jordan the Ghost and Threnody (Renee) restored to life and married.

—   Stanley Steamer accidentally banished by a leftover spell.

1077	Grundy goes with Snortimer, the Monster Under Ivy's bed, on a Quest to find Stanley Steamer.
—	Stacey Steamer changes her name to Stella.
—	Grundy rescues Rapunzel from the Sea Hag, with the aid of the Monster of the Sea.
—	Snortimer remains to protect the fauns and nymphs, in lieu of Stanley Steamer, who returns to Ivy.
—	Grundy Golem bests the Sea Hag, who is banished to the Brain Coral storage. Grundy shows the Demon X(A/N)th how to play to win.
—	Godiva Goblin marries Chief Gouty Goblin.
—	Grundy marries Rapunzel.
—	Gwendolyn Goblin delivered to Gouty and Godiva Goblin.
—	Jenny Elf born in the World of Two Moons.
1078	Lacuna marries Vernon, retroactively.
1079	Gobble Goblin sneaked to Gouty Goblin and a tart.
1080	Good Magician Humfrey's dose of Lethe elixir wears off, and he remembers Rose of Roogna and goes to rescue her from Hell. The Gorgon and Hugo join him in the dream realm.
—	Latia Curse Fiend leaves Gateway Castle in Lake Ogre-Chobee to help Esk Ogre and the voles.
—	Esk finds Marrow Bones and Bria Brassie on the Lost Path in the gourd.
—	Vale of the Voles and the Kiss-Mee River restored. (Unfortunately the Kissimmee River in Florida, Mundania, remains hostage to the will of the Armed Corps of Engines, so is not affectionate.)
—	Esk Ogre marries Bria Brassie.
—	Ryver retroactively delivered to Lacuna and Vernon.

1083   Prince Dolph undertakes a Quest to find Good Magician Humfrey, accompanied by Marrow Bones.

—   Vida Vila wishes to marry Prince Dolph, but he is too young.

—   Marrow and Dolph find Gracile (Grace'l) Ossein on the Isle of Illusion.

—   Melantha (Mela) Merwoman captures Dolph. To win free, Dolph undertakes to recover the firewater opal from Draco Dragon.

—   Cheiron Centaur marries Chex Centaur in a ceremony performed by the Simurgh before the winged monsters. All present swear to protect the foal of this union, whose life will change the course of the history of Xanth.

—   The goblins of Mount Etamin raid Draco's nest and abduct Marrow Bones.

—   King Nabob Naga betroths his daughter, Princess Nada, to Prince Dolph, making a naga-human alliance. The naga rescue Marrow and the dragon's treasure.

        Marrow and Dolph return two firewater opals to Mela.

—   Dolph and Nada enter Mundania through the gourd and meet Turn Key, who provides a way to locate the Heaven Cent.

—   Marrow, Grace'l, and Dolph use a hypnogourd to enter the realm of dreams and find the sleeping Princess. Only it turns out to be Electra, awakened after 847 years; she got time off for good behavior.

—   The Night Stallion puts Grace'l Ossein on trial, with Dolph as defense attorney. Dolph succeeds, barely, in vindicating her, and gains the respect of the Stallion.

—   Jot and Tittle, twins, delivered retroactively to Lacuna and Vernon.

1085   Che Centaur foaled to Cheiron and Chex Centaur.

—   Com-Pewter acquires a Castle Roogna magic mirror from a traveler.

1086   Princess Ivy, Princess Nada, and Electra recover the magic mirror from the evil machine.

—   Ivy invokes the Heaven Cent and is transported to Mundania, where she meets Grey Murphy and brings him to Xanth.

—   Grey and Ivy encounter the Goblinate of the Golden Horde led by Grotesk Goblin, and rescue Donkey Centaur. Ivy affiances Grey.

—   Grey learns his talent at Mount Parnassus: he is a Magician of Nullification.

—   Com-Pewter's plot to take over Xanth using Grey Murphy is revealed.

—   Magician Murphy and Sorceress Vadne return to Xanth, and Murphy lays his curse on the geis on Grey to serve Com-Pewter. The geis is thus fouled up, and Grey is freed to work for Magician Humfrey.

1089   Che Centaur is foalnapped by the goblins of Goblin Mountain.

—   Jenny Elf and Sammy Cat come to Xanth from the World of Two Moons and give comfort to Che.

—   Siege of Goblin Mountain, resolved when Che agrees to be Gwenny Goblin's companion, and Gwenny and Jenny go to live with Che's family.

—   Prince Dolph marries Electra as she turns eighteen in normal-living time.

1090   Humfrey rescues five and a half wives from Hell, in a fashion.

—   Lacuna's change of life.

AUTHOR'S NOTE

I try to discourage my readers from sending in puns and notions, because I have an adequate imagination of my own and the letters piling in take time to answer. I answered 553 in the first three months of 1990, and that slowed the start of this novel. But because the story of Good Magician Humfrey covered over a century of Xanth's history—to be precise, 157 years, from his delivery in 933 to his return in 1090—and because he is the Magician of Information, there was occasion to see more aspects of Xanth than usual. So this time *I* used more reader notions, and I have a bundle of credits to give. Just bear in mind that I am unlikely to be this free with reader notions again and that I am turned off by fans who pester me with ideas or puns in the hope of getting their names in print. Indeed, I tend to favor notions by folk who are not seeking that kind of recognition.

Here are the names of the contributors, roughly in the order of the appearance of their notions:

Jessica Timins—talent of making others experience vertigo, Tyler Stevenson—Ryver the water boy. Eileen Kelly—the lie berry. Colette Bezio—Lacuna's ability to free Grey Murphy by changing Com-Pewter's print. Karen Tsai—literal figures of speech. Miles T. Grant—tics to tell time; marshmallows, wolf spiders, adder, tumbleweeds, beach heads, bedrock. Cheryl Eisler—MareAnn, who summons equines. Frank Shaskus—dumbbell. Chris Swanson—werehouse. Anonymous—Chrissy Centaur. (Yes, it *is* you, Chrissy, but he won't admit to sending in your name. Ask him and he'll deny it. See? Proof!) Asia Lynn—Dana, the demoness with a soul. Theresa M. Brown—Key Stone Copse. Amanda Wagner—darklight. Eva Piccininni—Maiden Taiwan, Deer Abbey. Margaret T. Price—the centaurpede. Margaret is gone from Mundania, but her nice drawing of this creature remains for Xanth.

While Barbara Hay Hummel sat in her wheelchair and waited for her pain medication to take effect, she diverted her mind with fancies of Xanth. From this diversion came almost the whole of Rose of Roogna and her times: her description, her clothing, her nemesis, Muerte A. Fid, her wedding, her distraction by Dread Redhead, and her sad letter from Hell. Thus it was that I discovered why Humfrey so suddenly disappeared from Xanth and who had planted the enchanted roses of Castle Roogna.

Phillip Mangum—cross-country snail race. David Davis—moon rock. Stephanie Erb's father—the underload. (Stephanie's own suggestion, the talent of Erasure, is slated for Xanth 16, *Demons Don't Dream*.) Margaret Love—the Cross-face stitch and related poem. Mark A. Mandel—meta-magic. Stephen "Bigfoot" Hasanbuhler—the talent of animating a thing briefly. Beth Stackpole—realized that magic makes love last in Xanth; it has a harder time in Mundania. Chris Progar—realized that magic dust can bring magic to Mundania. Yes, that accounts for a lot. Stephen Neal— asked for the background of Crombie the Soldier. That turned out to be a surprise. Colette Bezio—the problem Iris' parents had raising the Sorceress of Illusion. W. G. Bliss—Mundania's zip-code directory snafu. Starr Treumiet—the hummingbirds Herman, Helen, and Hector. Tonya Espedel—centaur who splits. Susan Teitelbaum—the Night Stallion's dream for writers. I wonder how she knew about that? It has hitherto been part of the Literary Conspiracy, hidden from nonwriters, who think that writing is fun. Amy Pierce—Hugo's blind girlfriend, immune to love and hate spring. J. D. Norris—Key to Success. Ken Wheeler—Statue of Limitations. Chris and Natalie—Mountain of Change.

Meanwhile, E. Timber Bram, figuring out obscure dates and events, compiled the History of Xanth, a digested portion of which is included in this volume. The complete edition contains a list of the dates for all the novels, spot biographies of the known kings of Xanth, a chart of the eras and ages of Xanth, a table of the Mundane Waves of colonization, and genealogies of significant characters, as well as the main history with authoritative footnotes. He sent it to me via his Mundane alias, who is too undistinguished to mention here.

There were a few other suggestions which I meant to use but which got squeezed out. I'm sorry to disappoint the folk who sent them in, but they will surely appear in a later novel.

Michael Stasco was one of a number of readers who sent complicated lists of questions. I hate it when readers prove they are smarter than I am. So I'm getting even by running the main part of my response to him. If any of you have similar questions, stifle them; I might not manage to figure out the answers next time.

Dear Michael,

Sigh; you have excellent questions. Okay, I will answer them here, and maybe run these answers in the Author's Note to *Question Quest*, which I am now writing.

Why didn't Electra awaken during the Time of No Magic? She did, but realized that there was no prince handy to kiss her, so she went back to sleep, and in a few hours the spell resumed.

When Electra went to Mundania she aged physically, but she should have remained childlike, because maturity comes with experience. No, not necessarily; some grown folk are immature, and some children are mature in outlook. But it is the nature of humorous magic that age does bring maturity; this may be unscientific, but we're not talking science here, but magic.

If sex is just a natural function for centaurs, why do they take part in the Adult Conspiracy? Because they honor the foibles of those with whom they associate; centaur tutors, for example, must set good examples for the human children they tutor.

Since Grey Murphy was raised in Mundania's sexual realities, is it possible that he may begin a slow corruption of the Adult Conspiracy? *Possible, but unlikely, because Ivy is bound to Enhance his Xanth morality.*

Why can't centaurs assume the three forms of their crossbreed? Probably because they never thought to try it, and believe it to be uncentaurly to assume any other form. (Three forms? Only for the winged centaurs!)

Why didn't Millie the Ghost change from book to human form during the Time of No Magic? *Because she had been restored to living form before then.*

Why didn't zombies cease to exist during the Time of No Magic? They did; who saw a zombie then? But they resumed when the magic returned, just as did tangle trees and such.

Why didn't Murphy and Vadne age rapidly when they went to Mundania? Because the Brain Coral's pool had kept them in suspended animation, in contrast to Electra's magic sleep.

If wiggle swarms aren't as bad as they are thought to be, then why did the Simurgh panic? I don't recall the Simurgh ever panicking; are you sure this isn't someone's slanderous story?

Could Xavier use reverse-wood to fill the holes made by wiggles? Why should he want to? Few folk would care to be patched together with reverse-wood slivers!

If Ivy touches reverse-wood, would her reversed talent then lessen the effect of the wood? *Yes—so she has little to fear.*

Would a combination of Ivy, Arnolde Centaur, and reverse-wood in Mundania make a Mundane magical? No. The reverse-wood would make Arnolde's magic aisle into a Mundane aisle, and nothing would change.

Would trace amounts of Xanthian magic in Mundania account for people like Uri Getter, whose power is to bend spoons, and the Amazing Randi, whose power is to prove that Uri Geller cannot bend spoons with magic? *No; fakery and the exposure of it require no magic.*

If Hitler had released a couple on the condition that their son come and run Auschwitz, would it be dishonorable and unethical for the son to tell Hitler to go to hell and not run Auschwitz? Technically the answer may be yes, but the reality of the situation says that dishonor is okay if honor causes more evil to occur. So why couldn't Grey just tell Com-Pewter to go to Hell? Because Grey Murphy has a better sense of honor than you do. Just as an honorable son will pay off his father's debts left when the father dies, he will honor his father's other lingering commitments. The idea that an existing commitment can be renounced just because you decide you don't want to do it is sheer mischief. Try telling the IRS that you won't pay your income tax, because the income tax law was passed before you were born. Try telling the government that you refuse to obey its laws, because you don't like the way it spends money on missiles designed to kill people. The fact is, it is not your province to decide what prior deals you will honor unless you are prepared to pay the consequence of breaking the law. That is a decision that some folk do make, and they do pay the price. The ends do not justify the means; the end of making your own life better does not justify the violation of solemn prior commitments. If you run for president and win, then maybe you can see about changing things.

As I was completing the novel, came a fan letter—actually I answered several hundred letters in the course of the novel, but this was one of the last—from the West Indies. What I noticed was the stationery: hand-pasted pictures of roses on each sheet. Rose of Roogna had sent me a fen letter! Well, almost; it was a nice Xanth fan letter from an exotic place, but the lady's name was Sharmila Ramsingh. Still, she may be related, because of those roses.

And of course we have a Jenny update. Jenny Elf appeared in *Isle of View* and has only a bit part in the present novel, but she will play a larger role in *The Color of Her Panties*. No, they aren't *her* panties in question; what kind of a series do you think this is? But it's Jenny of Mundania I'm concerned with at the moment, and her life is not as pleasant as that of Jenny Elf. For those who did not see the Note in the last novel, Jenny was struck by a reckless driver when she was twelve and almost killed. She was three months in a coma, until my first letter to her brought her out of it. I have written to her regularly since, and met her and her family in NoRemember 1989 at Sci-Con 11, a convention in Virginia, when she was thirteen. Richard Pini of Elfquest who attended, and his graphic (that is, in comic form) edition of *Isle of View* was made and published. Jenny looks like Jenny Elf, only with more fingers and less pointed ears.

Jenny is slowly making progress. She is now home after about a year in the hospital, and going to a special school that caters to those with disabilities such as hers. There was a newspaper article about her, and that resulted in many calls and offers of help. A clown came to entertain Jenny and her friends, and she was given tickets and an ambulance ride to see a program by The New Kids on the Block. She is working to move both arms instead of just one, and to move her legs when she is held upright. She is learning to speak words, one by one. She understands words, you see, but the connections between her brain and her mouth are scrambled so she can't just *say* them. In short, Jenny has not given up on the recovery of the use of her body, and intends somehow, someday, to walk again. She will be a young lady of fifteen when this novel is published.

Also, during the course of this novel, I attended my one convention of the year 1990—I don't like to travel—which was PhoenixCon in Atlanta, Georgia, Mundania. I went only because of friendship with Bill Ritch, who was one of the convention organizers. He had helped me get computerized in 1984. I was on several panels, read a selection from my mainstream historical novel, *Tatham Mound*, and met with business associates, deciding how to handle the Xanth calendars. By the time this novel is published, you may have seen me on TV, hawking calendars. Thus the convention was both business and fun. Then disaster: I had to attend two more conventions that year.

Back in Florida, my elder daughter, Penny, graduated from college, achieving her BA in Human Resources (social work). No honors, no awards; she takes after me, being scholastically indifferent. The educational establishment has yet to recognize whatever special talents folk like Penny and me possess. (I once applied for a position as a college teacher of writing; I had my teaching certificate and a teacher's test score in the ninety-ninth percentile, but I learned that they weren't interested in having a real writer teach that subject. They wanted a Ph.D. So I am now the subject of papers on writing, not a teacher of the subject.) But Penny did seem to have the longest hair in her class, which made her easy to spot across the crowded auditorium.

Meanwhile a problem that developed as I wrote the prior novel may have carried through to its conclusion in this one. My tongue hurt. I thought it was getting scratched on a tooth, so I saw the dentist, and sure enough, two of my onlays—those are like inlays, but more so—were wearing thin and developing edges that my tongue touched. The dentist tried smoothing them down, but the problem continued, so reluctantly he replaced the two onlays with two gold crowns. And—my tongue was still sore. I had to use bubblegum to protect my tongue. (Regular gum falls apart too readily.) Could it be that roughness on the lower teeth was responsible? He made me an appliance to cover the lower teeth—and still my tongue hurt. But we were catching on to the pattern of it. My tongue gets most abraded when I'm talking—and when I'm editing novels, such as this one, because I read them aloud to myself, getting the sonic feel of them. Maybe my tongue was hitting a rough spot when I talked, then settling back to an innocent spot when I relaxed—and so I felt it in the innocent position. That could account for a lot. So the dentist made an appliance to cover my upper jaw, trying to nail down the problem once and for all. And as this novel finished, my tongue was on the way to recovery—we hope. And yes, I hear those muttered remarks from readers about how I should tone down the temper of my remarks so that I won't melt any more onlays and burn my tongue. I would answer you—if my answer weren't apt to prove your point.

That was about it for excitement. Mundania, as you know, isn't much.

Piers Anthony, Mayhem 1990

PS: Yes, my troll-free number remains in operation. We have the Xanth Calendar, Ogre video interview, Xanth T-shirts, an ongoing newsletter, and a stock of every Anthony novel in print, including this one. Call 1-800 HI PIERS to be possessed by our mailing list.

ABOUT THE AUTHOR

Piers Anthony is one of the world's most popular fantasy writers, and a *New York Times*–bestselling author twenty-one times over. His Xanth novels have been read and loved by millions of readers around the world, and he daily receives letters from his devoted fans. In addition to the Xanth series, Anthony is the author of many other bestselling works. He lives in Inverness, Florida.

THE XANTH NOVELS

FROM OPEN ROAD MEDIA

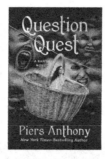
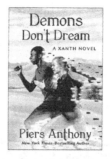

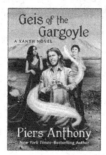

OPEN ROAD

INTEGRATED MEDIA

Find a full list of our authors and
titles at www.openroadmedia.com

FOLLOW US
@OpenRoadMedia